A MAN FROM NOWHERE

ELSPETH HUXLEY

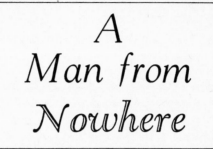

A
Man from
Nowhere

WILLIAM MORROW & CO.
New York, 1965

A MAN FROM NOWHERE

chapter I

If anyone had asked him, he might have said that he'd come down for the hunting—although, he believed, you didn't hunt in August. A sleek month: stoats, foxes and the few rabbits fat on the young of other species, or on sappy grass; the shiny summer coats of cattle, corn heavy in ear and pale and bleached-looking, or else red-gold like polished bronze, against skies that filled suddenly with proud and angry clouds of deep, dramatic indigo. Along the margins of the lanes red poppies, yellow ladies' bedstraw and the creamy meadowsweet formed an ornate tapestry.

On a fine evening, after tea, Dick Heron walked the lanes briskly, swinging a hazel stick, flicking as he went at dry grass heads and wondering at the weight and numbers of the pigeons that rose with so great a clatter and took off heavily, like overloaded aircraft. The profusion of this northern growth, the richness of crops, the density of the tree leafage, astonished him.

He smiled a little to himself as he walked, and hummed a snatch of tune. All beginnings were exhilarating. Then came the weakening of impulse, the boredom and routine, the despondencies. Then your purpose faltered, like a rock-borne spring that slows to a trickle among reeds and papyrus and may peter out in thirsty shale and sand.

But some rivers flow on. It was a question of will, and Dick Heron didn't doubt his own. This river would gather force and reach its end. Meanwhile would come all the pleasure, skill and daring, the patience and strategy and endurance, of the hunt.

He'd not yet seen the quarry. But he was collecting scraps of information and storing them up, like the pigeons pecking grain and bits of leaf to fill their crops. All he'd known when he first came to Larkinglass was the quarry's name, the name of his house and what could be read in Who's Who. Now Dick had seen the house, walked round it, watched a gardener sitting on a mower chugging over the lawns to shave carefully round the boles of big oaks and ashes and wych-elms as a man guides a razor round his lips and nostrils.

The house was called Chaffins and was neither grand nor insignificant, a mansion nor a hut, pompous nor humble— a compromise, like everything else in England: the weather, houses, town and country, the people who were seldom warm or cold, fierce or meek, honest or dishonest, elated or despondent, but vacillated somewhere between the two.

Chaffins had started life as a manor, been rebuilt after a fire in the time of William and Mary and later deteriorated into a farm; Jacobean panelling that had survived the fire had been preserved by grease in the wool clip stored in the big hall. It was built in a stone neither grey nor brown, but of a halfway colour that looked, in winter, as if a residue of northern sunshine, pale as lime honey, had been stored in the old mortar. Its face was kind, decorous and symmetrical, neither self-assertive nor self-effacing, its body decently clothed in friendly and respectable trees, like a squire's lady in her brogues and satisfying tweeds.

Between the wars a Midland industrialist had restored

both the structure and the status of Chaffins, and modernized it very well. It was now neither too large for modern life, so long as it had a rich owner, nor too small for one whose duties obliged him to entertain. It was just right—a compromise. Within seven miles there was a station with a fast service to London whose first-class patrons arrived, as a rule, either in Rolls-Bentleys or Land Rovers, nothing in between, and were met on Friday evenings by slim, astringent wives or daughters in slacks, duffle coats and diamond rings, talking of Spanish servants, foreign travel and the hunt or specie roses according to season, and accompanied by dachshunds or boxers on leads.

In a few days Dick Heron had found out more about Chaffins than about its owner, which was natural enough; the place, after all, had been there for three or four centuries, the Buckles for less than twenty-five years—a lot less, if you were to count only the time they'd actually spent there. They used the place almost as a week-end cottage. Peter Buckle farmed about two hundred acres, but of course the bailiff did it all.

Dick had supposed the Red Lion would be the best gleaning ground for information, but in fact the villagers hadn't seemed to take much interest in their distinguished man. Or perhaps they were just being cagey. Mrs. Harris was more forthcoming. Dick had managed to persuade her, with difficulty, to take him in as lodger just for a week or two, while he looked round. She and her husband kept the village shop and sub-post office, but there wasn't enough in it for a living and Ted Harris worked in a factory that had sprung up in a field along the Horsington road. When Dick asked what the factory made the reply had been components, but no one seemed to know what the components were for. Presumably Ted Harris did, but he was always out or else busy in the garden, tinkering with the car, doing some odd job or other.

Ted was a useful man, dependable—a retired policeman. For years he'd been a sergeant in Horsington, well respected—no teds in those days, people said; if any of the local lads got up to that sort of nonsense, Ted Harris hauled them out behind the King's Head, made them take off their jackets and gave them a good hiding, and then a glass of cider afterwards. Now he did a lot for the Youth Club and didn't like to be reminded of his old authority. Although he was proud of his service and had loved his job, he'd spent his working years like a beast standing just apart from the herd, a little distrusted, never quite a part of things, and now he wanted to forget all that, to merge and blend and be entirely one with the rest.

"These wasps," Mrs. Harris complained, flapping at one. Dick was helping her to tie up dahlias after tea, and pluck out groundsel. "Do you have wasps where you come from?"

"No, not wasps. Bees."

"I used to keep a hive or two but Ted wouldn't have it. He was afraid of them, though he wouldn't admit it. For all his talk and uniform, afraid of bees. There's men for you."

Mrs. Harris was a small, trim, bustling woman, a little like a bee herself, a great talker and down on people sometimes, but not spiteful—she couldn't stand slackness, indifference and people who gave themselves airs. Ted thought her too free with her tongue and pulled her up for it sometimes and then they had words.

"I suppose that's a fine garden at Chaffins," Dick suggested. "I'd like to have a look round."

"They open it two or three times for the nursing, in the spring and then in June when they try to hit off the roses. But roses have a mind of their own, haven't they? This year they were late. You get hold of Walter, he'll show you round."

"He's the head gardener?"

"Not much head about it these days, he's only got a lad that isn't quite right, you know what I mean. And then the

Spaniard is supposed to help but Walter don't reckon a lot of him. It's too much for one man."

"Can't they afford to take on another?"

"It's not so much the money; getting one, that's the thing. They've pots of money—hers, they say, they reckon he started with nothing but a suit of clothes and a quick tongue. Mind, he's worked for it in his way. I've got nothing against him, nothing at all. They give us the weekly order and pay regular—always paid their way. More than can be said for some."

They had finished the dahlias and were cleaning up among rows of peas and beans, and among cabbages whose stiff leaves amazed Dick with their weight and sappiness. It was a thick, heavy evening without sun but with a kind of mist that was not quite mist, soft and enervating, a greyness, filling the air. It went with the cabbages, Dick thought. Already he was beginning to recognize the climate as an enemy. The Harris garden was on a slope with a ditch at the bottom which sometimes turned into a rather stagnant brook. You could hear cars going along the road, a clatter of tractors, children's shouts, twittering sparrows.

"This withwind," Mrs. Harris complained, tugging at a long whippy tendril. "They say it goes down twenty feet in the ground. This place was shamefully neglected, you should of seen it when we came."

"How long have you been here?"

"Five years come Michaelmas. Seems a lifetime sometimes. There's a lot of work, you know. Often as not it's ten o'clock on Saturdays before we finishes. All the bookwork. And not much profit in it nowadays."

"The Buckles have been here longer, I suppose," Dick remarked. He enjoyed the weeding, doing something practical.

"Them? Goodness me, yes. Since before the war. Their kids was born here."

"He's older than he looks from his photographs."

Mrs. Harris laughed—a sort of giggle, youthful for her middle age. "Never gone short of anything, has he? Keeps you young. She's been a good wife to him, that I will say. If he has grey hairs they won't be on account of trouble at home, not unless it's that eldest boy, Martin, he don't seem to have settled down to make his way, not like he should. Too much money."

"It softens people."

"They're all the same, these days, too much money when they're no more'n kids, they grow up thinking it's their right and they don't need to work for it. Not like when I was young, we married on two pound a week and thought we was lucky to have it, a steady job was everything then, and the hours—"

Dick moved away towards the marrows. Although he'd not been long in England he knew this gambit already, the complaining note, the sense of injustice felt by older people who'd worked so much harder than the young, for so much less. They were the ones who'd said: "I don't want my John to go through what I did," and now that John was doing nicely, and took it all for granted, they were eaten up with resentment.

He'd also learnt the answering gambit—"Look how far the money went. Beer threepence a pint and tobacco ninepence. And people were happier then." It was almost like a game of chess, with set openings and ripostes. Dick was surprised at the formality that still underlay English life, the pattern which continued to shape the response of people to each other even though it had become faint, almost vestigial. After an interval he moved back to the runner beans and tried again.

"I suppose you're all proud of him, now he's famous."

"Who, Mr. Buckle?"

"Yes. A Cabinet Minister. He could be Prime Minister one day."

"Well, I don't know about that. Always gallivanting about, one country or another, giving the blacks their freedom or whatever it is. And giving them our money. Who pays? That's what I always say. It's us who pay in the end."

"Someone's got to pay."

"I don't know why *I* should, I and Ted and everyone in Larkinglass. It's all right for Mr. Buckle, they say he gets paid five thousand a year."

"I suppose he works for it."

"Well, every Wednesday, when he's not off on one of these jaunts, or away in London, he goes to the Feathers in Horsington and anyone can go and tell the tale, and he'll write letters about it. Sometimes he'll get things put right. That's his job, and he knows he won't get himself elected next time unless he does it. Still, he does it, that's something, I suppose."

Dick smiled. "You sound as if you're in a mood to be thankful for small mercies." Again Mrs. Harris giggled— she came down the scale like a quiet peal of bells, rather engaging.

"I don't take much notice one way or the other. I've got my work to do. When he first started they say he dressed up in breeches and gaiters and walked about on Wednesdays, that's market day, talking about the price of lambs and that. Always got it right, too. He's clever. But then someone must of told him farmers don't wear gaiters any more, only gentry pretending to be farmers, and now he wears a proper suit with a buttonhole. Carnations. Walter has to find him a carnation every Wednesday, winter and summer. Of course they've got heat. And lovely grapes, you should see them. Mrs. Buckle takes some every year to the hospital. Quiet, she is, but nicely spoken. We could do worse, I daresay."

It was like developing a bromide print. The whole image

was there, previously implanted, but you saw nothing—a blank sheet of paper. Then, as you rocked it in a tray, bit by bit a pattern formed, a line here, a smudge there. At first the bits were separate but gradually they coalesced to form a picture. In photography that took perhaps two minutes, but when your image was a man, your tray a county, your solution all the fragments of opinion, fact, impression, prejudice collected from neighbours, friends and enemies, the process would take a long time, months perhaps. But he had all the time in the world. No need to hurry, he was going to make the image complete. Complete. And then he was going to take it in his two hands and tear it up.

Mrs. Harris was inspecting marrows which had hidden themselves under a green canopy as if trying to escape notice until they had swollen into great, striped monsters. Long yellow petals and baby fruit the size of cigars lay joined together on the same stem.

"There's some as say you should eat them when they're little," she remarked. "Nip them off when they're no bigger than a bean pod and then you don't have to peel them. I tried that once and it was right, they were good, but I didn't dare tell Ted. He'd think it wasteful—murder, almost, you might say. He does like his first girt big marrow, as he says. They used to stack them in the aisle here at harvest festival. And make little sheaves, like miniatures, and bake thanksgiving loaves. They don't do it now."

"A pity," Dick remarked.

"Well, it's the work, and people not interested." She watched him pulling out weeds, snapping some of them off instead of drawing out whole roots, and laughed, but not derisively.

"I can see you're not a gardener, Mr. Heron. Not born to it anyway."

Dick was put out. He'd enjoyed the feel of roots coming

out of soft, sweet-smelling soil and had thought he was efficient.

"There, you're helping and I have to say something like that! I only meant it didn't seem to come quite natural to you, that's all. I suppose where you come from the blacks do all this sort of thing."

Dick paused before he answered because the remark riled him. "There's a lot they can't do. Or don't anyway."

"I daresay you'll be going back there, after your holiday?"

Dick stood up and looked intently at the cottage up the slope, gripping the handle of the Dutch hoe. He had made a mistake in letting slip even the few crumbs of information he'd yielded up to Mrs. Harris's curiosity—few enough certainly, the mere mention of a continent, a calling and a short visit, but sufficient to make him vulnerable.

For a mere brush against a nerve tip could send a shock of pain, like a jet of flame along a hollow tunnel, through his damaged mind. The sickening, overwhelming panic flared up without warning; he could feel it now even in this temperate garden, with a grey sky blackening as if the arched wings of a monstrous vulture were blotting out the light. He felt it now: unthinkable, unseeable, the blade of terror slitting him from crotch to throat to leave his naked organs palpitating but alive; or like a huge cold, green, obliterating wave rolling closer, roaring and rushing and thundering towards him.

The wave swept over him and roared away into silence and he was still standing in the garden among the beans, hoe in hand, scarcely able to keep upright, his ears singing, sick, devitalized. Panic died away like the wave's echo but then visions always followed, flickering across his mind like moving pictures. A sheep on its back, kicking, its stomach tight as a drum; sunlight striking down a red crinkled tree trunk; a mangled mass of feathers, blood and bits of blown-up bird spattered over rock, still warm and fluttering; the look in a bullock's eye as it dragged itself along in blazing sunlight with legs severed at the hock; a pair of arms jerking upwards in water as a head sank with a cry; a river of black ants writhing across a floor.

His mind must be stocked with far more scenes of beauty than of fear, but after the green-black wave they never came. And, at the end, one always lay in wait. A face, a woman's face, mottled and purple with lips like slugs and glazed, bloody eyes starting out to show the blood vessels behind like threads, and flies buzzing and the mouth askew and the neck swollen and the cord buried in the swollen, purplish flesh.

"You do look queer! Are you all right?"

Dick couldn't answer but the voice came through a wall faintly; the pictures faded and a lot of fireworks shot across his field of vision, red and orange, in all sorts of bursting shapes, and then enormous flowers began to unfold, to swell and grow. And then they faded too and there was nothing, nothing at all. Cautiously he opened his eyes. The world was there: grey, strange and familiar, solid and about to float away.

"Are you all right, Mr. Heron?" Mrs. Harris repeated. She had walked a few steps towards him, and looked concerned.

"I'm all right." In his own ears his voice sounded dry and brittle as a piece of dead skin.

"Better go in and sit down, I should, rest a little. I hope you haven't eaten anything."

"Just a giddy turn." The phrase came back to him from childhood, as if someone had laid it on his tongue.

His strength was returning but all the same he walked back into the cottage and went up the narrow, steep stairs, dipping his head automatically to dodge a beam, and lay down on the bed without even stripping off the patchwork bedspread. It was a work of art, handmade, and he respected it, but not now. His closed eyes saw only blankness, a grey void; with thankfulness he allowed a mist of lassitude to seep into the crevices of a mind only vaguely conscious of a tractor clattering along the road, the swirl of a car, children's voices, the distant ping of Mrs. Harris's shop bell. Then these sounds, reassuring as bandages to a hurt limb, also faded, his muscles loosened and he slept.

chapter 2

"Reckon the fellow's a bit queer in the head," Ted Harris remarked, spearing a pickled onion. They were his own and full of flavour, sharp and firm.

"He's quiet enough, Ted. No trouble. It's something come over him."

"Epileptic, most likely."

Mrs. Harris looked concerned. "Do you really think so?"

"He didn't stagger about or fall down or anything, go all rigid?"

"Well, he sort of froze like a rabbit, if you know what I mean, and looked as if he'd seen a ghost. Gave me quite a turn. You remember that Mrs. Cottle down at Fosse Dyke? The time she . . ."

"It can take several forms, epilepsy," Ted said judicially. "If it's bad you slip a bit of cork between their teeth. I don't say that's what's wrong with this fellow, though. He seems quiet enough, pleasant-spoken. All the same—"

Ted paused to munch his bread and jam. It was always black-currant jam because he had a theory that this prevented colds, and certainly he kept remarkably free from them, winter and summer. He was a thin, bony, energetic-looking man with sandy hair and a close-clipped moustache and deep-set blue eyes that had a curiously innocent, uncomplicated look, as if he was still able to accept the world at its face value after thirty years in the police. Although he'd seen his share of human stupidity, greed and deceit, he went on believing these to be departures from a norm of law-abiding decency which comprised the natural state of man.

Perhaps he didn't believe this consciously, it formed a part of the fabric of his mind and could not be changed without boiling him down, as it were, and reconstituting his nature. He had never been boiled down, but had gone on as he'd started, respecting himself and his fellows. Now, watching the television, he never ceased to wonder at the things which went on in great cities among modern men. It hadn't been like that when he had joined the Force in Horsington at the age of nineteen.

"It's only temporary." Mrs. Harris referred to the sojourn of their lodger. She knew Ted didn't want lodgers, so she had a guilty conscience. This Mr. Heron had seemed so lost, he was a total stranger to the district and she'd felt sorry for him. And he looked clean and quiet. Or so she told herself. The truth was that her curiosity had been aroused. His was a new face and you got tired of the old ones. Ted never went away, said he'd done enough moving.

She thought it was a good face, the lodger's. Once, as a child, Nancy Harris had been taken to the seaside in Suffolk and on the beach she had picked up cornelians. Somehow, goodness knows why, the first time she'd seen Mr. Heron he'd reminded her of those hard, reddish-coloured pebbles. Perhaps because he was reddish too, more amber-coloured really—his hair, even his skin, with a little reddish down growing below the temples; and under the skin his bones, she thought, would be smooth and hard and rounded like cornelians that had been pounded on a stony beach by furious breakers, and yet kept themselves whole.

The lodger had something like that about him, hard and

indestructible; he'd go on, if he had a purpose, till he reached the end. And what was his purpose? Why had he come down here without knowing a soul in the district, so he said, to lodge in the village shop and work as an ordinary farm labourer?

An ordinary farm labourer he wasn't, you'd only to look at his hands and hear him speak; and yet he wasn't quite a gentleman either. She didn't mean he wasn't a gentleman in the sense that he was something else, a non-gentleman so to speak; just that he wasn't the same as Mr. Buckle or Colonel Crozier or Lord Hemperstone, all of whom belonged to that special breed that set them apart, however much they might look like tramps or scoundrels, or indeed be scoundrels for that matter; it wasn't a question of right or wrong.

It was just that Mr. Heron didn't quite fit into any of the niches, he didn't belong and yet he must belong to something, somewhere—no man was by himself in the world, he must have a family, an origin, a position, however obscure. To be without a position was not to exist, to crumble or perish like a lone brick without a wall, a bee that had lost the hive.

A notion of the same sort evidently came into Ted's mind.

"What does he want down here anyway?"

"Mr. Heron? He's on holiday."

"Queer place to spend a holiday, without he knows anyone. And no family or anything."

"If you ask me, there's something happened there." Mrs. Harris sounded oracular.

"Something happened?"

"Well, something gone wrong. You can tell he's not a bachelor."

Ted Harris smiled; this crinkled up his face and made it look bonier than ever. "How?"

"Oh, I don't know. You can always tell. But no photographs or anything, that's queer, isn't it? And all his things new."

"You've been prying!" Ted's tone was accusing. Built in to his idea of proper conduct was a residue of the belief that you needed a warrant to look into anyone's belongings. His wife's disregard of proper conduct always bothered him.

"I've not!" She was indignant. "What do you expect? Me to leave his room till the dust's a foot deep? I've got eyes in my head, haven't I?"

"No doubt of that."

"You'd expect to find at least a snapshot or two."

Ted stretched his legs and filled his pipe. The ceiling was low and not quite even, the room full of furniture and cavelike in its feeling of recess, its darkness and assertion of privacy. Ted seemed almost to overflow. A heavy old-fashioned black stove, let into one wall, glowed quietly all day and kept the room warm and even-temperatured. A ginger cat lay curled up on one easy chair and Ted Harris lounged in the other, sucking at his pipe, which always seemed to give trouble.

"You say everything's new. You mean his clothes and that?"

"Well, it's natural, isn't it? He's been living abroad."

Ted looked at his wife in mild surprise. "What d'you mean, natural? They wear clothes abroad, don't they?"

She giggled. "What about those hula-hula skirts in the South Seas?"

"You think he's been going about in skins, now's his introduction to trousers?"

"No call for that sarky tone, Ted."

"I tell you this straight, Nance, you're too gullible. Here you are, a bloke you've never laid eyes on comes along and straight away you take him in. You know what I've said, we don't want lodgers. And you say he's got all new things, and has these queer turns. I don't like it."

Mrs. Harris's eyes got rounder and she stopped clearing away the tea and stood suspended, one hand on a plate. "Ted, you don't think . . ."

"I think you've been hasty," Ted said, weighing his words—his wife could fly off the handle. After a pause he added: "All new things," and shook his head.

"You can't forget all those copper's notions, can you?"

"Don't have to forget the ABC when you leave school."

Ted wrapped up his tobacco pouch and took a box of matches off the mantel shelf and made his simple preparations to go out. In summer he was out every evening at his odd jobs, and once a week he had the Youth Club in Horsington and taught the lads boxing, though there wasn't much enthusiasm these days, not like when he was a kid. He kissed his wife on the cheek before leaving and made his stock remark: "Back in an hour or two."

"You want me to turn him out into the street, I suppose." She spoke accusingly, but he didn't answer. He reckoned he'd sown a seed that would germinate on its own.

Now he'd made her uneasy. She climbed the stairs and knocked on the lodger's door. No answer. More uneasy than ever, she turned the handle and looked in. Empty. There on the bed was the mark of his body, right on the patchwork too. She clucked, thinking of dirty shoes and slovenly habits, and then stared as if mesmerized at the slight depression where his weight had rested, reminding her of places you came to in the fields, the grass all flattened where a cow had lain. She tried to see him there, what he looked like, but that wouldn't help—all that mattered was what went on inside. Even when you lay with a man in bed, naked, you didn't really know that, because they changed, they were half a dozen people rolled into one.

On the chest of drawers, its top protected by a cross-stitch runner, lay a pair of new hairbrushes with wooden backs, the cheapest kind, and a comb, nail file, a folding shaving mirror. Handkerchiefs—plain white ones without marks—in one top drawer, socks in the other with a few ties and a pair of plain navy braces. Below that the under-wear, then shirts and pullovers; very little really and, as she'd said, all new, plain, inexpensive. Even the suitcase on top of the wardrobe was a new one. And all so tidy—unlike a normal man. As if he wasn't giving anything away about himself. A quiet man—quiet, and deep, and queer.

Of course he'd have his wallet with him, and everything personal in that. But her sharp eyes spotted a piece of paper under the hankerchiefs. She hesitated, not for long, and drew out a letter. It was typed, and from a bank she'd never heard of called National and Grindlay's, addressed to him at an hotel in Cromwell Road, London. It said he had a credit balance of £218 13s. 9d. after the transfer, and the bank held a life insurance policy for £10,000 of which the beneficiary was Mrs. Emma Stanhope Young, with an address in South Africa; that a sealed package marked "three rings" had been placed in the safe deposit and arrangements made for him to draw cheques at the Horsington branch of Lloyd's bank.

He had a bit put away, then—not much, but enough to pay his board for longer than she'd be able to keep him. That was something. But again nothing personal, nothing to give a hint where he came from or why. He'd let it out that this was the first time he'd been in England. Seemed funny, never to have been in England when you *were* English, spoke it and looked it and acted it, by and large.

Colonial. Colonials were English and yet they weren't.

They were loyal to the Queen and fought for England when needed, for which they got little thanks. She'd only once been to a meeting of Mr. Buckle's and she remembered that he'd said we should never forget the debt we owed to them but they were not colonials now, they had turned into something else—the Commonwealth. But the Commonwealth had mainly black men, black and brown, who didn't feel the same way, naturally. It was all too confusing.

She put the letter carefully back, not knowing whether to be reassured or the opposite. Something in the bank, but had it been honestly come by? And those rings? And this Mrs. Emma Stanhope Young? She sighed, knowing what Ted would say, that she was nosey. But what else was there in Larkinglass?

From right at the back of the drawer she unearthed a small cardboard box with a foreign name on it, Sutterjee Ranji. Her fingers closed on it with a pleasurably mixed sensation of eagerness and apprehension. Would she find something outlandish, queer, indecent? She imagined a wizened flake of flesh perhaps, part of an organ or some heathen charm, a baby monkey's skull, a dried frog—she'd heard of such things. Even a deadly spider? Ought she to open it with Ted out of the house?

With a resolute jerk, she pulled off the lid. Inside lay something shiny and mottled—nothing but an empty shell. Not the kind she'd brought back from Suffolk with the cornelians, more like tortoise shell, dark brown and cream, handsome, almost barbaric.

But just a shell, sitting in a wodge of cotton wool. Queer! And disappointing. Like a child. She put it away, shut the drawer and retreated downstairs in a bad humour. That was all her nosiness had got her: serve her right, Ted would say. They called his judgment common sense.

chapter 3

ONLY about half a dozen men were in the bar of the Red Lion and no women save for Mrs. Peabody, the landlady. Her husband had died a few years before and she'd carried on, but without much heart; she didn't go out for trade, for skittles matches, farmers' dinners, Young Conservatives and the like. She was a wispy, faded woman with bleached hair and restless hands, always patting and smoothing and rubbing, and a lopsided smile that was sweet and rather pathetic. Dick sat by himself and no one spoke to him; he knew they were eying him surreptitiously and would talk of him behind his back. They spoke in hushed tones, almost as if in church: doughlike, solemn, each guarding his own notions.

A man with a bit more life about him came in and said good evening to everyone—he even nodded at the stranger. Tall, thin, slightly pop-eyed and with a long, weather-beaten face, clean-shaven; you could tell at once his job was in the open air. When he spoke he craned forward a little so as to give greater weight to his words and displayed a wrinkled, reddish neck. With him was a plump and dark-eyed woman who might have been a beauty once but had let herself go. She was smiling a bit inanely, but with good will.

"Evening, Mrs. Peabody. Evening, Walter. Evening, Bill."

"Evening, Ray." The one called Bill stood next to the newcomer at the bar: a man with bushy eyebrows and red, rotund, good-natured face. "How's everything?"

"Mustn't grumble. Busy, mind."

"Corn coming off well?"

"Bet you never seen it better, not this twenty years. Never would have thought it, not after that dry spell at the start. Over three hundred sacks off Drover's Common and nearly five hundred off the Gleve, true as I'm standing here."

Ray spoke as if he expected no one to believe him; the others nodded. They were used to Ray. Every season, the harvest was the best for twenty years so long as it was Ray who was getting it in. Other peoples' harvests were never so heavy.

"All right for the boss, then," Bill remarked. "Any bonus?"

"He treats us fair. I'm not complaining."

Several people smiled. The one called Walter swirled the beer round in his glass and drained it, exuding disagreement, but saying nothing.

"Wish I had a ha'penny for every quid he's got," Bill commented.

"Well, you didn't pick the right horse, Bill."

Bill snorted. "Politics! Tell the tale like one of them carpet-selling fellows, that's all there is to it."

Ray laughed. "I'd like to see you up there on a platform shouting the odds. Ladies and gents, vote for I and there'll be twenty quid a week and a labour-saving bungalow and free beer for everyone, and a month at Butlins' for the wife and kids. And no more Russian bombs."

The man called Walter said gloomily: "It's the women's votes counts these days."

"That'll be right for Bill, then."

Everyone laughed. They started to pull Bill's leg about someone called Doris. Dick Heron moved across and stood up at the bar next to Walter, a small, dark man in steel-rimmed glasses, younger than the others. Dick wanted to start a conversation but didn't know how to begin. All these men knew each other, probably from childhood, and spoke a cryptic language of allusion and suggestion he couldn't follow.

"Evening," he said.

"Evening."

A pause. Ray and one or two others were still enjoying jokes about Bill's triumph with Doris. Two newcomers, young men with long, shaggy hair and leather jackets, carried their beers across to a table and switched on two transistor radios, each tuned to a different station. Pop music and wailing voices, one in French, filled the room. The group at the bar stirred as when stout flies begin to disturb dozing cattle.

"That bloody din again," Bill muttered.

"Every night the same," Ray agreed.

"Drive anyone daft."

"Least they could take the bloody things in the kitchen." About seventy years ago, the Red Lion had been a farmhouse, and the saloon bar was still called the kitchen. The youths, sardonically enjoying their elders' disapproval, finished their beers, sloped across to get the other half and did, in fact, move on, transistors at full throttle, to the next room; at the bar you could still hear a cacophony, but muted.

"Bloody shame," Bill commented. Things were spoilt these days at the Red Lion, no wonder people stayed away, leave aside the television. Dick addressed himself again to Walter.

"A good harvest round here, from the sound of it."

"Fair to middling."

"The crops look pretty heavy. But some of the corn's flat."

"Real storm we had, three weeks back. Come down like a ton a bricks and spoilt my borders."

"Your borders?"

"Gardening's my trade."

"For Mr. Buckle?"

Walter nodded, and sipped his half-pint. Dick had no clear picture of what a gardener ought to look like, but felt that Walter didn't conform to any of the stereotypes. Too small, perhaps, too wiry, nervous like a race horse, and even though he didn't speak much you felt energy there, like an electric current. Dick looked down at Walter's hands. They were more like it: grime-encrusted in the pores and wrinkles, with soil-blackened nails.

"I've heard there's a fine garden at Chaffins. Hothouse fruit and so on. And the lawns."

"It isn't what it used to be nor what it should be, neither. I don't get the help I ought. There's limits to what a man can do. In Colonel Milton's day there was five or six in the garden. They kept it up together then."

"That's right. Five or six it was." Ray had overheard, and moved across to join in. "I mind the time when they used to win all the shows round about. Sweet peas, they was Colonel Milton's favourite. Thought a terrible lot of his sweet peas. I recollect . . ."

Ray was an older man and remembered Colonel Milton, the Buckles' predecessor, from his youth. The Colonel, he said, had worn a grey bowler and gone about in a trap drawn by a fat grey pony, and entertained at Chaffins, in his heyday, houseparties of elegantly dressed women and well-fed men for shooting, tennis and cricket. He'd bred Short-horn bulls and never married—too comfortable as he was.

Then the gardens had been tended and prolific, fed on horse dung from the stables; every morning barrow loads of vegetables had gone into the house and piles of plants and flowers: banks of cinerarias and begonias brightened the hall, lilies and delphiniums and gladioli grew taller than a man, dahlias much bigger than dinner plates. There'd been a couple of men doing little else but bedding out all through the summer.

Colonel Milton had never allowed a joint to be served twice. Off it went, perhaps scarcely dented, to the servants' hall and sometimes to Walter's father, one of the grooms and the begetter of fifteen children. Chaffins had shone with glory then, and even though the gardeners had drawn no more than fifteen shillings, why in those days for fifteen bob . . . They were off on the cost of living.

It was the past that really brought these people to life, Dick decided. To the future they seemed indifferent, to the present apathetic, but touch upon the past and you touched a nerve that brought animation to their voices, passion to their opinions and a glow to their hearts. The past in Larkinglass had been significant and they had all drawn from it some trace of splendour. Even Walter, who was probably not much over thirty, seemed unenthusiastic about a present that provided him with twelve pounds a week and a free house but obliged him to skimp and make do in the gardens, and to dwell nostalgically on the five or six gardeners he'd never known in the days of a father who'd thought nothing of a sixty- or seventy-hour week.

But Dick didn't want to hear about the past, it was the present that concerned him.

"Have the other half?"

Walter nodded and said "Thanks." Dick glanced round and saw that Ray's glass was empty and caught his eye.

"Same for you?"

It was a slow game but he was inching forward. A false

move, just a grain of overeagerness, could put him right back behind the starting post.

"You can't do much to mechanize a garden," he suggested. "I suppose it's not exactly Buckle's fault."

"Away three parts of his time buggering up the bloody government," Walter said sourly.

"Someone has to run the country, Walt." Ray sounded magnanimous.

"And a fair mess they're making."

"I reckon a lot of it's they Americans. They—"

Now they were off on politics. Ray liked the sound of his own voice. Dick learnt that he was Peter Buckle's tractor driver; also that he picked up a bit on the side cutting pigs and cats. Anything male, Walter said, Ray wouldn't rest till he'd castrated it. He loved the job.

"Could I see the garden sometime?"

"Friend of Mr. Buckle's?" Walter inquired.

"No. I'm a stranger. But I'd be interested."

"Daresay there'd be no objection. Mrs. Buckle's the one for the garden. Does a main bit herself when they're here."

"They're here now?"

"Up to teatime they was, any road."

"They been out harvesting," Ray said.

"Harvesting!" Walter's contempt was withering. "Bloody play acting."

"Simon can work when he wants to."

"Ah, an hour a day, when it suits him."

"You'd do the same, Walt."

"Not much bloody chance of that. Scort me guts out till I'm due for me pension and then what? Shoved on the bloody scrap heap like an old bus."

Ray exchanged glances with Bill and they both smiled. Walter was close with his money, very tight, and was known to be putting away a tidy bit. He spoke sometimes of going to Australia.

Dick offered him a cigarette. "You have one of mine," Walter responded, and felt in his pockets: first his jacket, next the trousers, then he slapped his waistcoat, a surprised expression deepening on his thin, terrier face.

"Would you believe it?" he exclaimed. "Must of come out without any. Left 'em behind." He accepted one of Dick's and there was a shout of laughter. This appeared to be a well-known routine. Walter looked savage for a moment, then grinned sheepishly. When the laughter subsided Ray added:

"Extra hand on today. The boss's daughter."

"What, Julia?" Walter gave a cross between a grunt and a whistle. "Who's she after, then? Sweet on you, Ray?"

It was Ray's turn to look displeased. "She can manage the Fergie. Glad of it today, we was shorthanded. George is off, hurt his back."

Dick offered a cigarette to Ray and said:

"D'you want extra help for the harvest?"

"We can always use an extra man."

"I can do a bit. Drive a combine, for instance."

Ray looked at him properly for the first time. "Any experience?"

Dick nodded. "A bit."

"There's plenty of work. You'd better see Mr. Tompkins in the morning."

"Mr. Tompkins?"

"The bailiff."

"Oh, so there's a bailiff."

Ray laughed. "You don't reckon Pete Buckle buys and sells for himself, do you? He's got the government to see to. You talk to Jim Tompkins—big, heavyish fellow with a Jimmy Edwards moustache and a toff's accent. He'll put you on if he likes the looks of you and the weather stays fine."

"Thanks. I'll see him first thing tomorrow."

Dick finished his half-pint and ordered a last round for Ray and Walter. They didn't seem to mind his paying for the round, perhaps that was a stranger's privilege. He was struck by their lack of curiosity; they'd asked him nothing —where he came from, what he was doing, who he was; for them, he might not have existed. A dog will sniff, stiff-legged, round a strange dog; perhaps they'd been doing this secretly, looking and getting the feel of him, but they'd asked nothing. Indifference or a form of tact? He couldn't make out.

In fact, he could make out very little; the English people moved like shapes gesturing in a mist of ambiguity. There was nothing clear-cut about them, they were afraid to be sharp and definite, afraid to commit themselves. Afraid? Or just not caring? Even that he didn't know.

The door opened and a boy came in: tall, fair and lean, in blue jeans and pointed shoes; he looked about nineteen or twenty. A girl followed. She was small and slight, seven stone (Dick thought) at most, with light hair rather straight but ruffled now by wind; she wore jeans too, tight black ones. There was a resemblance between them—their eyes, perhaps, and a wide, handsome brow. Both were good-looking and walked with a sort of lope. The girl said:

"Hello, everyone. We're out of beer. Can we have two dozen Mackesons, Mrs. Peabody? Actually the harvesters drank us dry."

"I'll carry it out," said the boy. His pale hair fell half over his face, which was peeling from sunburn. Dick wondered where he'd got that: not here, for sure, in this sunless land.

"What shall I have?" the girl inquired. "I must have something, it's been quite a day."

The men had moved quietly along to make way for her at the bar. The arrival of these two struck the others silent, they suddenly became an audience and the boy and the girl actors on a stage. The atmosphere changed completely but it was hard to say how. Dick didn't think the feeling was exactly resentment or hostility but it had a trace of that, a withdrawal. Mostly it was perhaps just strangeness. A new animal had walked into the cage, or a new chemical been dropped into the beaker and the solution had changed colour and suddenly produced crystals.

The girl ordered a gin and tonic. "Here's luck, all." She drank it quickly and turned to Ray. "I hope we gave satisfaction. We both worked like blacks. Only apparently they don't work hard at all, it's the other way round. What time shall we start tomorrow?"

"It's all according to the weather. If it doesn't rain we'll be able to do a bit before dinner."

"Well, Simon and I'll help out, but that idiot Jim Tompkins won't trust either of us with a combine. He keeps telling us they cost two thousand pounds."

"We've got a new recruit," Ray informed her. "This gentleman here. Says he drives a combine. I've told him to see Mr. Tompkins in the morning."

The girl glanced at Dick as impersonally as if he'd been a clock, or an undistinguished picture. Her eyes passed over him without engaging, as a hand may pass over smooth metal: and then, checked by something, they moved back and held his own. Suddenly in them there was recognition of him as a man, not as a piece of furniture. To Dick this was all extraordinary and rather horrible. She'd seen that he was not quite like the others, not working class—quite unconsciously, and that made it worse.

"Dropped from heaven, obviously," she remarked, "to replace George. Are you an expert?"

"No, but I can manage. At least I hope so."

"I'm allowed to run a sort of shuttle service with a tanker between the combine and the drier. It's all rather like a military operation when everything goes well, but usually the rain stops play."

"Some of the corn's pretty flat."

"The reel picks it up and we don't lose much, or so they say. On the other hand, I think we do because of pigeons. The place is lousy with pigeons, carrying off my poor father's substance in their bulging crops. Can you shoot pigeons?"

Dick answered evenly: "I can shoot." He could feel her interest and awareness flicking him very gently, like a switch. Her desire to learn who he was and why he was here kindled in him a spark of power and enjoyment. The advantage, for the moment, was his.

Her brother came round from behind the counter carrying a case of bottles. "I'll dump these in the Land Rover," he said. "Buy me a beer, Julie. I'll pay you back."

"That's the worst of having a rich family," she remarked. "You never have any money. They won't give you any because they're leaning over backwards not to let a silver spoon get within a mile of your mouth. But if you're a teenage worker you have about ten quid a week to spend."

No one commented on this. A second gin and tonic had appeared in front of her. She looked surprised, and asked: "Did I order that?"

Mrs. Peabody nodded at Dick. "The gentleman did."

"Well, that's very handsome, I must say. I can't keep calling you the gentleman, what's your name?"

"Heron. Dick Heron."

"Well, thank you, Dick. Here's luck. Do you live round here somewhere?"

"No, I'm staying in the village for a week or two."

"I shall look out for you tomorrow. And if you smash a gate post I shall laugh like hell, they always think men drive all this machinery better but I don't see why. Look at Russia. Not that I model myself on a female Russian, and the only good-looking men they've got are shut up in capsules. Drink up, Simon, we must get home to Mother."

They went out as they had come, half loping, Julia first this time. The others moved back into the gap they'd left at the bar and the conversation that had, as it were, taken cover, came out into the open again.

Several of the men had smiled faintly when Simon and Julia left—a touch of condescension. The professional deriding the amateur. Something vestigial, Dick thought: like cattle still distrusting dogs, remembering the fanged wolf atavistically. Now fangs were drawn and Julia stood at the bar with the tractor driver and the gardener and men from the components factory but there remained a memory. And there was top and bottom still, power and impotence, master and man.

"Mr. Tompkins." Ray wiped the back of his hand across his mouth, addressing Dick. "You'll have to satisfy him."

"Will that be hard?"

"Mr. Big-mouth," came from Walter.

"She's grown up real pretty," Ray's wife remarked—her first utterance. She had put on a sentimental smile. "Plain little kid too."

"All that talk about no money." Walter was scornful. "Buckle could spend my wages for the year on toilet paper and not notice. Makes me tired."

"Take up politics, Walt," Ray advised. "Regular gold mine."

"Lot of boloney."

They were off again, an hour to closing time. Dick walked back through a soft, half-luminous darkness that was neither night nor day. The village lights looked warm and friendly, like those of ships at sea. Luck had been with him that evening. An omen? But then he was overcome by a desire for solitude so acute that he almost ran down the hill to reach the shelter of his small, clean, monastic room.

chapter 4

At ten o'clock every Sunday morning Peter Buckle met his bailiff at the farm. Then they went up to the house together and talked business until about half-past eleven, when Tompkins had a glass of sherry and left. A weekend conference at Chaffins, or a Cabinet crisis now and then, would vary the routine; and sometimes Buckle strolled down to the farm of an evening, or looked in at the milking or the drier or the piggery or whatever caught his fancy. Jim Tompkins said he kept a closer eye on things than you'd expect, and on the business side he was as shrewd as they come, but of course there was a lot he didn't know and never would.

Dick had volunteered as a relief milker while George's back was bad, and Tompkins had jumped at the offer. To persuade anyone to milk at weekends grew harder every year. They all wanted their Sundays. A man who didn't mind—who actually offered—seemed almost too good to be true. Tompkins made inquiries of Ted Harris who said the lodger was a quiet, decent-spoken fellow, gave no trouble and didn't drink, and then hoped for the best.

Sunday was a gusty, grey August morning after a wet

night with boughs thrashing about and doors flapping if you didn't shut or wedge them. Peter Buckle wore a heavy, shiny belted raincoat and a cloth cap and carried a stick flattened on each side and painted white, with the name of a patent feed printed on it in black letters, handy for driving pigs about. Dick was in a white coat and cap, hosing down the milking parlour, when they came in.

"This is the fellow I was telling you about." Tompkins was a florid man in his early forties with small eyes. He wore loud checks and was almost a stage version of the wizard ex-R.A.F. officer; the men thought he talked a lot of nonsense but that he wasn't such a fool as he made out, and sometimes people who wrote him off as a nitwit got their fingers burnt. Buckle wouldn't have kept him five minutes if he'd really been incompetent, but no one entirely trusted him.

Peter Buckle walked up to Dick and shook hands. He made a point of knowing personally anyone who worked on the place, even the casuals, and speaking to them at least once a week—the old master-and-man relationship. That was one of our most intractable questions, he was fond of saying; all labour relations depended on the personal touch. And while this was still possible on farms and in small businesses and little factories, in the monster industries like cars and engineering it was out: hence all these crippling strikes, go-slows and unrest.

"Glad to have you with us for a while," he said, smiling. "I understand you're more or less on holiday. Don't think I'd call it much of a holiday myself getting up at five to milk on a Sunday, but I'm glad *you* do. Helps us over an awkward patch. What part of the country are you from?"

Dick's arms hung loosely at his sides. His right palm was tingling from the touch of Peter Buckle's flesh, he could feel his own flesh curling up as if he had forced himself to grip a hot iron.

"I've been abroad, mostly."

"Oh, really? What part?"

Dick smiled. He had his answer pat. "Where there's more sun and less democracy."

Buckle raised his eyebrows slightly and regarded his relief milker. The clean smell of cows and fresh dung and oilseeds and washed-down cement enveloped them and water trickled from a plastic pipe Dick held in one hand. The parlour, all cement and aluminium piping, would be clean as a model kitchen by the time the milkers went to breakfast.

"Come to think of it, they don't seem to marry, do they?" Peter Buckle observed. "Sun and democracy—I must work that up for some speech or other. Tompkins tells me you know your way about a dairy."

"I've handled cows."

"What do you think of this lot?"

"They're magnificent."

Dick meant this. It was true, and quality a thing he cared about. The devil's cattle could be good cattle still. Buckle was delighted. "I'm awfully glad you think so. It's uphill work, you know, establishing a herd and we've had some ugly setbacks. But Rodney King, now he's a genius. I'd back him against any herdsman in the country. The lynchpin of our whole show. Well, I hope you'll enjoy your spell here, Heron. For our part we're very glad."

"I'm glad of the money."

Buckle laughed. "Aren't we all? Still, farming's one of those jobs where it *really* isn't everything. If it was, every one of our blokes would be off to the factories. Up to thirty pounds a week at Pressed Steel. We'll never be able to pay those wages. But farming's a way of life."

"I shouldn't trade on that too much, sir, if I was a politician," Tompkins said.

"I'll pass that on to my colleagues," Buckle said lightly,

"but I don't think we do. Anyway, we don't fix the wages, thank God. Well, good luck, Heron, I'll be seeing you around. I don't get out on the farm half as often as I'd like to, worse luck. Politicians, cowmen, policemen and doctors, we're all alike, always on call. A whole-time job. But I suppose none of us would change it, though we often say we would. We must have another talk sometime."

He nodded and walked off, followed by Tompkins a step or two behind like a bodyguard. Dick stood motionless, staring after him and fixing the image in his mind. Buckle was a good-looking man, in a way that was indefinably a bit flashy and yet at the same time, if this were possible, based on a certain heaviness and stodginess. As if he might wear vivid-coloured nylon socks with thick, square-toed shoes. Somewhere a split, a dichotomy.

Dick fixed him in his mind. Thickset, medium height, could have been a middleweight boxer once. Dark hair brushed straight back, thickish and greying at the temples; thick dark eyebrows, hazel eyes, a squarish face with a good mouth and chin. When he smiled white, even teeth showed up and the flesh round the eyes crinkled attractively. Dick knew the face from photographs in newspapers but Buckle was more impressive than he'd expected; he would carry people with him by his charm and his air of sincerity. Even the smugness exuded by his speeches and interviews wasn't obvious.

Buckle was one of his party's television assets, though his personality didn't come over quite as well as his looks and ready tongue might have warranted: perhaps just a shade too glib, lacking in that touch of self-deprecation and avuncular coziness so endearing to British audiences. He was good on panels but, as a Minister, had become too exalted to exchange platitudes with back benchers, journalists and junior dons.

"Enjoy the boss's pep talk?" It was the herdsman's Sunday off, George was sick and so the milking had been entrusted, with misgivings, to Dick and to a lad called Bert who helped with odd jobs. Bert was seventeen and had a mop of curly hair worn in a coif; he was filling in time before going to a technical college. He added: "Doles it out like sweets to the kids, regular every Sunday."

Dick laughed, directing a stream of water from the hose along the concrete standings. The cows had to jump on to a two-foot platform to be milked but they very quickly learnt to do this with agility, and were rewarded by a delicious meal of dairy nuts released from a hopper.

"It should be a privilege to work for a Minister of the Crown," Dick suggested.

"Privilege, my arse. I'd like to see him out here in winter when the yard's a sheet of ice and the pipes is froze and a load of cowflop hits your face and that bloody Duchess lands you a crack on the kneecap fit to split a log. Then he can talk about his affluent society and way of life and all that crap."

Dick was surprised at his vehemence. "You don't seem to love the boss."

"They're all the same. Sweat the guts out of you and tell you how bloody lucky you are to afford a pint when they're swilling champagne on the expense account. Mean lot of buggers, the lot of them."

Dick felt inclined to agree. Absurd how manual work made you self-righteous; you felt superior to the brain worker, and for no good reason. But it wasn't reason that mattered, it was how you felt—a form of snobbishness. Brain workers knew it and felt apologetic, they'd accepted defeat. Hence all the antics and postures, indeed betrayals, of the liberal left: simply a form of apology, of grovelling almost, because they worked with brain instead of hand— and in the past, though not always now by any means, had got more money for it. Dick could feel himself sharing the emotion while he recognized its absurdity.

So he and Bert agreed, they despised Buckle—not as a man but as a symbol. He'd become, as it were, a man in uniform, a servant of the state. Probably he was an ideal husband and father, a good employer, an astute, hard-working politician, a model citizen. None of that mattered. Once a man put on a uniform he ceased to matter as an individual, he became a symbol and must win or lose, kill or be killed. Buckle had killed and now his turn had come to be killed. It was as simple as that.

Simpler still, Dick went on to reflect, if you were religious, because then you'd leave it all to God. Religion was a handy way to pass the buck, to shelve responsibility. But if, like Dick, you had no God, you had to face a problem. "Vengeance is mine, saith the Lord: I will repay." No Lord meant no vengeance in the next world: someone had to arrange it in this one. The law was not merely useless, it was perverse. The law didn't crush people like Buckle, it rewarded them with honours, position, public acclaim, private satisfaction. So if someone didn't step in, you were faced with a situation where a murderer thrived and fattened, the wicked triumphed, the dead and ruined went unavenged. You were faced with the question of responsibility: where it lay, who should exercise it. Beyond threatened a prospect of chaos. For without justice there must be chaos, nothing made sense.

While Dick rejected God, he did believe in pattern and order because he had observed it in his own life, and in the lives of others. There was cause and effect. Now and then he'd felt the touch of an exterior direction: a choice that had seemed free hadn't really been so, since each course open to him could have led, like a move in chess, to the same end. No divine chess player moved the pawns, it was merely that the whole universe observed a certain order; man was a part of that universe; therefore each man, like each particle within the structure of an atom, could not be free, but must follow a predestined course, determined in the last resort by natural laws.

The conviction that it was he, and no one else, who must act as an instrument of vengeance had come to Dick suddenly. He could recall the moment, but it was a moment he had buried in his mind. The intimation had been brutal, unquestionable and final. His line of destiny had crossed and fused with Peter Buckle's and now no man, and no god, could put them asunder. Buckle had acted as a symbol and as a symbol he must pay with his life for the lives he had destroyed. Neither could evade responsibility: Buckle for his acts, Dick for his destiny. Dick was ready, and he was glad. He was shaped for his task like a well-made tool, a wrench fitted to the nut, tempered by a controlled but indestructible anger stronger than his own desire to live. An executioner who thought about his own safety was undone before he started, three parts of his effort must go to plan his own retreat. But once life had ceased to be a factor, everything was simplified. Nothing could be done without planning and life lost its savour if you hadn't something to plan.

So far everything had gone better than he could possibly have expected and this had convinced him beyond doubt of the truth of his belief. Things were falling into shape, he was tracing out the pattern and nothing could go wrong.

Against his thigh, hard and reassuring, he could feel the automatic pistol that never left his pocket except to go under his pillow at night. This was the easiest and cleanest method of killing, the one he best understood. It was merciful, too. Dick wasn't a cruel man.

And yet Buckle had to know what was coming. It wouldn't be enough just to blot him out like a beetle; he was a man, entitled to know and understand what was being done. He must know, and understand the justice of retribution. He who'd broken other peoples' lives must know why his own life had to be broken. That there were two sides to everything but death.

Buckle must be told; and this meant that Dick must speak to him alone. But Buckle seemed always to have a bodyguard, whether it was Tompkins on the farm, in the house some member of his family, and on Wednesdays at the Feathers in Horsington his agent, Colonel Watts. In England solitude was extraordinarily rare. Perhaps, now he was on the payroll, Dick's simplest plan would be to ask for a private interview. He mightn't get it, but he could ask.

Even that wasn't straightforward. The explanation would have to be followed by the act immediately, there'd be no time for everything to sink in. Buckle had a quick mind but not, Dick thought, a deep one, certainly not a mind open to doubt. It was hard and enclosed, like a nut. Dick had to crack the nut, to open it to doubt, and then fill it with a comprehension of ideas naturally repugnant to it: of truth, honour, loyalty—of the concepts behind these faded, derided and unfashionable words.

This would take time but Dick would not have time: he must be practical. You couldn't say to a man "I'm an agent of justice and I've come to execute you" and then walk off for a couple of days to let the meaning sink in. Sentence must be pronounced and carried out in a single operation. Yet he must be fair to Buckle, who had at least the right to know why his life was forfeit.

It was difficult, but nothing could be done without planning and Dick was almost glad there were obstacles to overcome. Otherwise it would all seem too easy, the hunt too tame. And he had plenty of time.

chapter 5

================

WHEN the milking parlour was sluiced down you could
have eaten your dinner off the concrete, enjoying meanwhile a fresh smell of cow and cattle cake and the late
summer morning. Outside, the yards glistened greyly; it
had rained in the night and everything looked washed and
clean. The round cowpats held brown pools on their con-
cave tops, like crater lakes in miniature. Dented silvery
churns stood with their tops askew, like hats at rakish
angles, waiting to be shut and labelled. The dairy smelt of
fresh milk and of the sharp, antiseptic chemical that sterilized the rubber parts of the machine.

Outside it was windy, boughs lashed and soughed, but
the sun emerged for a few minutes from bright-edged cloud
gravid with moisture to make everything golden, and its
warmth rested benignly on Dick's shoulders. He was having
difficulty rolling out the churns; it was an art, you had to
spin them on their rims at just the right angle. Although
each churn weighed about a hundred and fifty pounds, Bert
spun them as easily as if they'd been wooden hoops and
with a great clatter, whistling as he trundled them out.

"Getting on all right down at Harrises'?" he inquired.

"I'm very comfortable."

"Ah, grub's all right, I daresay."

"First rate."

"I reckon once you been a copper you got that number branded on for life. Not that I've anything against Ted Harris, mind. But when you see him coming down the street you think Christ, did I get that L-plate fixed and wonder if he heard them shots over Frogmere way last Friday night. You know, sort of automatic."

"He seems to mind his own business, pretty much."

"It's his missus, she's the one. What she doesn't know hasn't happened, and what hasn't happened she invents. Said she saw Jack Kirby lock the door behind him when he went into Gwen Sillery's place, courting. Well, I ask you. To start with it's fifty yards down the road and round a corner, and then you'd need eyes that sees through doors, wouldn't you? You watch your step, mate, or she'll have you up against a wall with the parson's wife or taking one of the school kids down Bagley wood or something. Dangerous, she is."

Dick laughed. "My life's an open book."

"You'll be surprised the dirt Ted's missus'll find in it if she tries. You a married man, Dick?"

"No."

"Well, you got some sense. They get you in the end, like you're a bloody fat cock pheasant roosting up a tree and some dark night a fellow comes along and slips a wire over your head."

"That must take a bit of doing."

"Comes with practice. Fellow called Gordy used to be about here when I was little, he used to go off nights with a long bean stick and a loop of wire and pull the birds right out of the branches; clever bugger he was. They never caught him at it, not for want of trying—Ted Harris'd tell you a bit about that. Real tasty pheasants are, too. Ever tried one?"

"Never. We don't—" He checked himself just in time. Yellow-necks, guinea fowl, sand grouse, yes: but not pheasants.

"The boss rears six or seven hundred all under hens. They're some girt big birds down Bagley wood, fat as mud. The foxes and stoats gets a tidy few. Got some pretty clever foxes down Bagley wood. Some of 'em uses guns."

Evidently Bert was an enthusiastic poacher. Dick brooded on the vastly different meanings that can be attached to a single word. Where he'd come from, poaching was a bloody business done for profit, inflicting extremities of cruelty on harmless beasts who, searching for water in a dry land, would be held in wire snares until hyenas had gnawed away the living flesh; or, hamstrung, they'd drag their limbs after them, eyes desperate with unimaginable pain, until the eyes themselves were pecked out by vultures, and then their anuses and guts.

Here, at Larkinglass, poaching was a matter of village lads trapping a few hand-reared pheasants, or shooting them after dark in trees, quickly and cleanly, with a blind eye turned by an avuncular policeman—so long as no one went too far. Always that nebulous, uncharted but unforgiving line—the line you must detect by instinct and never cross, come what may—never go too far. Here everything had been attenuated, even emasculated: fangs drawn, stings removed, savagery domesticated. People buried life deep under civility, its crassness and cruelty decently hidden—yet, like graveyard bones, the withwind roots, never extinguished. Quietly, secretively, the pain went on below.

A day or two before he'd walked round Bagley wood and seen willow herb glowing in the undergrowth like a reddish-purple fire, white seed fluff already forming, and tightly clenched berries still green on the brambles, and hazelnuts like small green fists. On the far edge was an empty cottage: broken windows, no curtains, a flapping coal-shed door. He'd asked Ted why no one lived there.

"Too isolated."

"It's quite close to the road. There must be buses."

"It's two mile from the village. The women won't put up with it these days."

It had been a keeper's cottage, Ted had added. Dick had thought what a cozy little place it could be made into, tucked into the trees, a robust little cottage with thick walls and everything you wanted: sheds, outhouses, a garden run to waste but once gay with flowers and symmetrical with vegetables. But Ted had said it was unlucky. A man had lived there with an illness the doctors couldn't cure, very painful they said; one day his wife, who couldn't bear to see him suffer, bought a tin of the poison used to put down vermin and gave some first to him, then to herself.

"And what a day that was, the day they was buried," Ted had added, leaning on his fork. "Thunder and lightning right overhead and rain, whew, you should of seen it, and a gale fetched down a grit big ash and blocked the road so the hearse had to go round by Chaldecot. Never knowed a day like it." The weather seemed to have impressed him more than the disaster; perhaps he felt that God had spoken through the storm.

"Then a woman came to live there with a crippled daughter," Ted had gone on. "This daughter, she had a head too big for her body that stayed bent over to the one side, always nodding. I don't know if you saw a pond up there just outside the wood?"

"Yes, with a lot of reeds."

"Ah, the wild duck get about there in the spring time. Well, this woman, one day she waded out into the pond and drowned herself and her daughter. I had to help fetch them out. Both of them. It was February and Christ, wasn't it cold. Ice crunching underfoot and a wicked wind blowing. Must of been a cold job, that woman." Ted shook his head. "T'aint a lucky place."

Yet there it stood, solid as an oak, innocent as a February lamb. Life went on underneath somewhere in this queer country, like a river flowing underground.

Now everything was done, hoppers filled with cake ready for the afternoon milking, the bleats of shiny-coated calves in their separate pens quietened by gruel fed warm from buckets, the pinbones of a down-calver prodded to gauge whether she'd calve before milking time. They could go home to breakfast. Bert gave Dick a lift in the dark blue van that did the milk-round. Through the trees, they caught a glimpse of Chaffins, its honey-brown façade glowing softly in the mild morning light of this season midway between summer and autumn, neither warm nor sharp, growing nor dying.

A spotted dog ran across the lawn, a Dalmatian, princely and exotic, putting Dick in mind of a picture he'd once seen of a carriage with cockaded footmen on the box and prancing horses, and another of a bewigged beau served with chocolate out of splendid porcelain by a turbaned Negro boy. Lumbering in the Dalmatian's wake came a portly liver-and-white spaniel, like a hedgehog in pursuit of a hare; then a human figure, running lightly, overtook them both. It was a girl in black jeans.

The Dalmatian skidded to a halt with its forepaws together, turned, and bounded back towards her. She threw a ball, and the dogs charged or lumbered off in a new direction. For some reason Julia Buckle lifted her arms in a gesture that might have been a supplication, the sun shone on her hair and she stood for a moment as if she were a favourite of the gods endowed with grace and immortality. Then she moved on, walking quickly, and the sound of a voice clear as a blackbird's came faintly across the lawn, calling to the dogs.

Such a daughter, Dick thought, would make you proud, and pride was brittle; you could crack the shell of pride to reach a vulnerable pulp inside.

chapter 6

THE gardens at Chaffins were opened twice a year, once in spring and again in late summer when dahlias and gloxinias blazed so intently they seemed to be distillations of the pure colours themselves, the reds and purples, yellows and bronzes. But Walter was a perfectionist who resented the smallest deviation from some imagined ideal attained in Colonel Milton's day. Mrs. Buckle did a lot herself and took on any casual labour she could find, but everyone was busy with the harvest.

This year there was to be something quite new: dancing in the evening in a marquee, with a proper floor, then fireworks over the lake and a procession of boats with torches and lanterns—like Venice. That was, weather permitting. And an actress down from London to present the prizes. It was all very ambitious for a church fête which had never before aimed higher than side shows like bowling for a pig, sticking pegs into the lawn for buried treasure, guessing the weight of a cake and letting off balloons. Older villagers reluctantly supposed that you must move with the times and attract townspeople if the church roof was to be repaired at a cost, these days, not far short of a thousand pounds.

Directly after milking, Dick changed into a suit and went up to Chaffins on a borrowed cycle. His suit felt tight. He must have put on weight since he'd been working—muscle, not fat. It was good to feel again so fit and well, fitter than he'd felt for a couple of years. Single-mindedness; it was fretting that destroyed a man, being pulled in several directions.

The evening managed to be at once oppressive and cold. A spatter of rain led to a great unfurling of plastic raincoats and a mushrooming of umbrellas; it passed, and people started to congregate in the marquee, remarking how the days were drawing in. The house was open as well as the garden, and older people got the weight off their feet on comfortable sofas and Regency chairs, admired the flowers and gazed with mute respect at pictures and china. The curtains and loose covers had narrow stripes, Regency again, and the general theme was simplicity, a country feeling. The rooms were high and light and not cluttered: just one or two oriental vases, two Crown Derby vases over an Adam fireplace, some late eighteenth-century English water colours, a chandelier. Bowls of potpourri gave the drawing room a faint musky flavour.

Mrs. Buckle's money, everyone said, had paid for all this, and certainly her taste had created it. Peter Buckle might have learnt his way about this world in which anything that had happened after 1820, like electricity and plumbing, was ignored or concealed, but it was not his native element; he was coarser-grained and the brandy bottle, cigars, the racecourse paddock, the golf club, the leather-chaired board room with a big mahogany table and heavy glass ash trays and smoked salmon in the directors' room overlooking the river—these were his natural element: or so they had become.

The pale beams of an early autumn sun nudged a way between cloud and horizon to gild moist lawns and gnarled tree trunks: and when these faded, an indeterminate dusk imperceptibly possessed the atmosphere. There was nothing you could grip on, no real "night" or "day," the two blended and failed to decide which was which. At such times the English scene appeared to Dick unreal and immaterial, as if he were immersed in a slow-motion dream, or moving about under water. This was a world of margins, nuances, suggestions, where to shout might set to flight ghosts that were part of the family, to be sure of anything would be presumptuous. All this irritated him. How could you penetrate an armour made of jelly?

As daylight faded, Japanese lanterns of crinkly coloured paper sprang to life among the branches and bushes, deepening the unreality and summoning notions of fairy palaces and castles in the air. Lights came on in the marquee, a man in shapeless trousers and a darned pull-over tested loud-speakers wired to a van parked alongside. Hundreds of dressed chickens waited in rows on trestle tables under an awning, and a young man in a white coat and chef's cap presided over a charcoal fire smouldering under a grid. A girl was helping him. A crisp, appetizing smell and a sound of sizzling drew people towards the barbecue like insects drawn to a lamp. Recognizing the girl, Dick drew back, but as he did so Julia Buckle turned and saw him. She waved a long fork.

"Hullo, Dick. Studying how the natives relax?"

He was surprised that she remembered him. "How did you know my name?"

She laughed, clearing a lock of hair from her eyes with a jerk of the head.

"What do you expect to be known as, a number, like the army? Anyway, we were properly introduced. Have you got a date tonight?"

"Not really."

"Then how about lending me a hand? It's always a

hideous rush and you could ferry bits of bird across from over there."

Dick hesitated, and Julia added:

"All right, I don't want to spoil your fun. Run along and play." Immediately he felt guilty.

"No, I'd like to help. These smell awfully good."

"Are you hungry?"

"I didn't think so, but now I think I am."

"That's the idea of a barbecue. I'll do you a wing and that'll be your rate for the job. Hold on a minute."

The wing sizzled, browned, steamed and was quickly done. She speared it with a toothpick and held it out to him and their hands touched as he took it; he knew she had intended this. She let her hand rest on his a moment and then turned back to the brazier. People were putting half crowns in a bowl on the table and queuing up for their portion. Dick wiped his hands and started to carry trays of dismembered chicken across.

Dance music was pummelling out its rhythm, and figures jerked and gyrated under the canvas with its strong, fibrous smell. Soon people converged on the marquee and, for the moment, the run on the barbecue was over. The young man in the chef's cap and apron threw down his long fork, stretched and strolled over to Julia. He was tall and lanky, narrow-chested, with a thin face Dick thought weak—he wasn't sure why; perhaps he was merely reacting, as men of action and physical strength so often did, to those of, as they suspected, superior intellect: an instinctive, if unacknowledged, contempt summoned to redress a feeling of inferiority.

The young man wore horn-rimmed glasses and didn't look more than three or four and twenty. He pulled off his cap and wiped the sweat from his face with his apron.

"I don't see why I have to wear this fancy dress," he

complained. "It's too damned hot. How much longer have I got to keep this up, Julia?" He sounded querulous.

"Think of all the money we're pulling in."

"Yes, and what for, a church roof of all things. Frankly I don't give a damn about your church roof. There's enough churches in this country to sink the bloody island. Pull the whole lot down and sell the stuff and spend the money on a few decent housing schemes and you've got something."

"I'll book one of the pulpits for you, Evan. Cut it out now, will you? I'm going to see the fireworks."

"It's not time for them yet. Considering that you pushed me into this—"

"Oh, come on, Dick." Julia seized Dick's wrist and pulled him after her, then dropped it and ran into a darkness less than half dispelled by Japanese lanterns, leaping over the ropes securing the marquee. Dick caught her up as she slowed down halfway across the slope to the lake.

"Never happy when he's away from Trafalgar Square," she said irritably. "Protest marches and bomb demonstrations and things. It's all very well but—I mean I agree with most of it but sometimes he does go on so. I shouldn't say this really, I'm fond of Evan and he's got his worries. Martin's horrible to him sometimes."

"That's your brother?"

"Yes. Brother Martin."

"Not the one I saw at the pub. That's Simon."

"Simon's all right, he's no problem. Not all that bright so he's gone into the army, just his cup of tea. Martin's bright but it doesn't seem to get him anywhere, except into trouble. At least not into trouble actually, sort of on the edge. He likes thin ice. I suppose it all comes from having a dominant father, famous in a way, and having to assert himself. We all seem to spend our lives bouncing off each other, don't we, like a lot of billiard balls. But I don't suppose my family interests you. What about yours, Dick? Married?"

"Not now."

"Intending?"

"No. You must be fond of Chaffins. It looks marvellous."

Floodlights had been switched on and its shapely face glowed magically among the trees, more unreal than ever.

Julia laughed. "Heading me off. You go round with 'Keep Out' signs hung all over you, Dick."

"Do I?" He didn't want to sound unfriendly. "You wouldn't find much if you got in. Ghosts on an empty stair."

"Why do you say that?"

"I don't know. Some old quotation I've forgotten, I suppose."

They were standing by the lake and heard water lapping faintly near their feet like people kissing very softly, persistently and without passion. In a faint, reflected light Dick could see dark blobs of birds riding the water with their wings close-folded, motionless. From the marquee came a glimpse of limbs jerking like the branches of wind-riven trees to the thump and wail of music.

"All right," Julia said. "It's not my business. There's an old jetty here, and a boat house. Fallen, as my father says, into desuetude. He picked that up from Winston. We can get a good view of the fireworks from there if you like."

"Oughtn't we to go back? They'll be missing you."

She was standing very close and he could feel her warmth, as if a bird hovered there and he could touch it merely by stretching out a hand. He wanted to move away but something stopped him—her will, his own fear of hurting her, the stirring of rebellion in his blood, he couldn't say.

"You're pretty good at snubbing people, aren't you?"

"It's not that. Your father—"

Julia laughed; her shoulder brushed his chest and then she took his hand.

"My father—" She mimicked him. "What are those things that bury themselves in the mud for years on end—lungfish, aren't they?"

"Yes, and terrapin. Lots of things."

"I think you're like a lungfish, Dick. Of course I'm only guessing but sometimes one picks the right draws. I think you've got ideas that people had fifty years ago. That's a bore as a rule but—"

He started to draw back his hand, and she said quickly, "Sorry, I didn't mean to hurt your feelings. I meant with you somehow it isn't a bore, it's odd and rather sad."

He disengaged his hand from hers, moved by a prick of the sort of anger he'd once felt when he saw trespassers walking over his land.

"You're perfectly right. I'm a kind of leftover fossil. But fossils have to go on being fossils, I'm afraid. You can't bring them back to life. All the more reason to leave them alone."

"Instead of throwing myself at your head."

"It's not that—"

"It *is* that," Julia said. "But I don't mind."

Her arm moved up his shoulder and she spread an open palm against the nape of his neck and pulled down his head, and her body flattened against his. He stood rigidly with his hands on her waist and the intention of pushing her gently away. But he didn't. She was like some warm, quick, sweet-smelling animal. Instead he slid his hands round her waist, feeling the softness of her flesh, pressed her against him and felt her lips opening before his own.

For eight years Dick had made love to no one but his wife and known no other end to love but its fulfillment; he hadn't played it as a parlour game or drawn back halfway. So now that he had in his arms a warm and living woman not merely responsive but inviting, there could be only one end; but all round was only mud, reeds, wet bushes, soggy lawns full of moss and worm casts—not even a rug. And beyond that, people.

In England it seemed that desperate couples made love standing up, in doorways and against walls. This was something he couldn't imagine—not depraved but insulting, flippant. Meanwhile she'd asked for it and now she got it; she was pushing herself against him and jerking out little moans, and then while he kissed her shoulders and felt her nipples she slewed his head round and explored his ear with her tongue. Nothing for it but the moss and worm casts; and just as he bore her down a low, swishing noise like linen being torn shocked his ears.

The first rocket arched across the sky. Its head burst like an exploding diamond hurling brilliant fragments, so much brighter than the stars, into the arch of heaven, to flutter down to earth in a dazzling cascade. Others followed, hissing softly, spitting and swishing, and filling the overcast night sky with parabolas of light as if great waves were breaking in glittering foam and then drifting down, slowly, in wide curving arcs, dying as they fell. And a reflection of these bursting, expanding and down-drifting stars sparkled back at them from the lake's black surface.

Dick and Julia stood mutely face to face, their heads thrown back, their eyes dazzled and their passion slowly draining like sea water from a sand pool. To Dick, the scene took on a symbolic meaning he couldn't fully understand. Soaring into the sky towards infinity, towards some ungrasped ideal, rose a great fountain of human endeavour, aspiration, hope and fervour: up it all went, golden and magnificent to the very walls of heaven, then down it all came, fading as it fell, to expire as black, spent squibs on a disregarding earth, into mud and reeds: sparks which rose in glory, burst in pride, fell in futility and ended in ignominy, forgotten and expunged.

"I'm all for rocketry," Julia said at last, "but that was the wrong moment so far as I was concerned."

Dick felt thirsty, and at once cheated and relieved.

"I'm sorry I lost my head just then. I'm afraid I—"

"For Christ's sake, don't apologize. Haven't you any sense?" In her voice was a suspicion of hysteria. "Or too much sense, I don't know. Come on."

They walked back towards the people who were standing in clusters on the lawns with upturned faces, like a field of fungi, their greyish skin whitened by bursts that now, as the bombardment thickened, made the whole sky blaze. The band in the marquee had stopped playing and everything was silent save for the swishing of the rockets, almost as if people were waiting for the end of the world.

chapter 7

THE procession of boats started late because one of the Roman soldiers fell into the lake—in fact Walter, who accused Bert of pushing him. Bert denied this hotly and they had a blazing row on the jetty and Jim Tompkins, disguised as a centurion, had to separate them. The fancy dress had come down from London and while they all laughed at the effect they were secretly delighted with their bronze breastplates, scarlet cloaks and tin swords. Only it was a funny sort of dress, they agreed, in which to go boating, and much too cold to shed their underwear. They had little pleated skirts that left the knees and legs bare, and there was a lot of backchat about pants, kilts, and the virility of Roman soldiers.

Their legs, normally so sheltered, showed up white and knobbly and queerly shaped in the light of torches. For they had to assemble on the old jetty, climb into leaky, half-rotten boats and paddle out to the reed-fringed island, all in the dark. On the island, where a little Greek temple stood among nettles, brambles and a tangle of weeds, a helmeted Aeneas and the Queen of Carthage, dressed all in white, awaited them. As soon as they reached the island, flood-

lights were to fasten on the Greek temple and Aeneas was
to enact his lover's parting, clamber into a boat and sail
away with his attendants, leaving the white-clad Dido to
sing her tragic farewell. Then silence and darkness, a
pause, and a final burst of fireworks, a set piece re-creating
in the heavens, in coloured rockets, Dido's funeral pyre.

It had all been planned and organized by Lavinia
Buckle, with help from Tompkins who had drafted Romans
from the farm and garden, from Simon who played
Aeneas, and from Simon's regiment who did the lighting. A
singer known, if not too well known, on television, had
come down from London to fill Dido's part. (The others
were to keep silent.) The boats leaked, the lake needed
dredging, the island was extremely brambly and the Greek
temple crumbling away; harvesting had stopped rehearsals,
in fact there'd been only one to speak of and that hadn't
gone well; everyone feared the singer might take umbrage
at the lack of professional expertise.

Still, it made a change, as people said; and the audience,
fortified by beer, hamburgers and barbecued chicken, and
in any case indifferently acquainted with Dido's legend,
would be in no critical mood. Extra fireworks, a TV singer
in the flesh and the sight of old friends like Jim Tompkins,
Walter and Ray dressed up in skirts and breastplates was
all anyone could ask for. And then more beer, jiving and
twisting in the marquee.

At last the boats got under way—only three of them—
rocking and bumping into each other. A smell of mud,
bilge and rotten timber enveloped the Romans, whose oars
creaked and splashed about in the darkness and provoked a
good deal of cussing and swearing.

"There's adders on that island," Walter muttered to the
oarsman behind him, the lad Bert. "Plain daft, barging in
there in the nighttime when a fellow can't see the nose in
front of his face."

"Sea serpents, too, in the mere," Bert agreed. "The Loch Ness monster's come south, haven't you heard?"

"You laugh, but you wait till them adders catches you, no trousers either. Suicide. What's the idea, anyway, sticking this woman on the flipping island? All among the nettles and brambles? Catch her death of cold."

"She's saying good-bye to her lover," Bert explained.

"No wonder, if that's his idea of a good place for a snoggle. What's she supposed to be?"

"A queen or something. In love with this fellow, see, he buzzes off, she lights a bloody great bonfire and hops into it."

"Silly bugger, roasting herself for a soldier," Walter remarked. Bert gave a half-laugh which he suppressed. "Well, it's Simon Buckle."

"Him. Get like his sister if he goes on."

"Ah, Julia." Bert's tone was heavy with meaning but the meaning was obscure. "I reckon she's—"

"Pipe down, can't you?" a voice hissed from the stern. "Might as well of brought the bloody band."

"Bloody rot," Walter muttered. First chopping nettles round that old hut on the island and now this. He'd been a fool to volunteer and he'd pay for it, rheumatism most likely with bare legs and the damp. He'd have to keep on at the beer all night to get what he'd earned. Bert was thinking that the song she'd come out with at rehearsal was pretty ropey, no rhythm, she ought to sing something they could join in—"Moon River" would be just right.

Their oars pushed against mud, the boat swished among bent reeds and nudged a low bank smelling of rotten tree trunks and watery decay. Someone grabbed for a root, hung on to it and pulled the boat in. Whispers, curses, low instructions: a whistle blew to show they were ready. Powerful searchlights blazed up and the white temple sprang to life. Dido stood with arms stretched out towards the young soldier, whose bent head was golden like a newly minted coin.

"Got her flipping nightie on," Bert whispered. "Christ, she must be cold."

"Warm her up, if he's got any sense," Walter commented. Dido started to sing. Her voice drifted with a strange, pallid purity across the water, like a bird calling, or the spirit of the lake.

A damsel with a dulcimer, Dick thought, standing on the shore. What was a dulcimer? It was all a bit absurd. Julia had vanished and he was disgusted with himself: not because he'd given in to Julia but because he'd allowed himself to lose his thread of purpose in the labyrinth. He'd let it slip out of his hand. A few more moments and it might have gone for good. In the nick of time—again that sign of destiny working out behind it all, the pattern—he'd found the thread and picked it up, and from now on he wouldn't let go.

Directly Aeneas set foot in his vessel, fairy lights that had been festooned all over the boats blazed up and the oarsmen pushed off to proceed slowly round the island. Now the boats were slung with necklaces of coloured gems reflected in the water, a sight that drew a little flurry of oohs and aahs from the onlookers. Light glinted on bronze armour, on sunburnt forearms, on the hafts of property swords, on the centurion's helmet. Dido's lament was dying softly, as if its liquid notes held the last essence of sorrow. Then came silence broken only by a gentle splash of oars; and the swirling colours of a mighty funeral pyre burst overhead.

"Too much like the old flak for my liking," Jim Tompkins objected as the boats drew alongside the jetty, where Peter Buckle waited with fulsomely delivered praise. "Quieter, though. Quite a bird, isn't she? Regular nightingale."

"She was marvellous," Simon said. He was standing up

in the boat looking back at the island, now half lit by leaping rockets, still feeling himself to be that very hero for whom a queen had died aeons ago.

"You'd better fetch her off before she catches cold," his father reminded him. "She's got a good thick sweater and my duffle coat, but she won't thank you if you hang about. Besides, we'd better not start supper till she comes."

Dick moved up close to Peter Buckle. The feeling possessed him that now, tonight, the chance he'd travelled half across the world to find was going to spring out, complete and ready like one of the centurions, sword in hand. His part was to keep close to Peter Buckle and be ready when the moment came, almost of its own choice, presenting itself to him as the chosen instrument.

The Romans had removed their cloaks and armour, replaced their trousers and made for the marquee. Aeneas and Tompkins had gone back to fetch Dido, the jetty was abandoned, the show over, pop music blared out and shouts and laughter came across the lawn.

Peter Buckle saw Dick as he turned to go.

"Heron, isn't it?" Dick assented. "I've been wanting a word with you. This seems as good a chance as any. Have you got a few moments to spare?"

"My time's my own now."

"I'm going back to the house, if you'll come as far as . . . It won't take long. Tompkins tells me you're one of the best workers we've had here for a long time."

"I like to earn my keep."

"You're doing more. So don't think we're not satisfied, not glad to have you. All the same . . ."

Buckle hesitated. He was finding this difficult and Dick did nothing to help.

"Well, you're a bit of an enigma. A newcomer, aren't you, lived abroad, this is all strange to you. I suppose we haven't met anywhere before?"

"Not that I know of."

"I didn't think so, but you know how it is, one meets so many people on these tours. Whistle-stop meetings with the upcountry farmers, that sort of thing."

"I never took an interest in politics."

"So you didn't find your way down here to this particular place, my particular farm, just to—well, shall we say, make my acquaintance?"

They had reached the foot of a grass bank; above it a terrace ran the length of the house. Through uncurtained, lighted windows Dick could see tables, movement, people walking about. A shortish man sprouting a shock of hair was standing back to the window, gesticulating with a glass in his hand; it was like a scene from a play. Music from the marquee came tinnily across the lawn.

Dick's hands were clammy, his throat dry, his breathing had quickened. Now his quarry was standing in full sight, unsuspecting, exposed. Dick's right hand was in his pocket, his fingers on the butt of the loaded gun. There'd never be a better opportunity, there couldn't be. Suddenly, without planning, here it was in front of him, the moment for the debt to be paid. The pattern was complete. His life and Buckle's, and the lives of those revolving round them, had reached their predestined moment of fusion, their point of no return.

But, now the hunt was all but over, a reluctance to finish it came over him. So short a hunt, and so unskilled. Always it was the hunt you relished, the stalk, the pitting of wits; the kill itself was nothing, just mechanical—the snapping of a thread, the arrest of a wheel. Once that thread had snapped what would you hang on to? The moment was here and yet he doubted his own readiness.

"So you didn't come all the way to Chaffins," Peter Buckle repeated, "just to talk to me?"

"That might be part of the reason," Dick said.

"Then now's your chance."

"Yes, now's my chance."

Buckle felt in his pocket for his case, pulled out a ciga-rette, returned the case and flicked on his lighter, a little thing no bigger than the first joint of his thumb. His eyes kept moving and Dick knew him to be nervous and uncer-tain. "Then I take it you've nothing to say," Buckle added.

"There's a lot I could say."

"Well, you've had your chance. Now see here, Heron. If you want to go on working here you're welcome, only you must keep away from the house. I suppose this sounds old-fashioned but I don't want you hanging round my daugh-ter. She's at an impressionable age and it's—well, I should think you're a sensible sort of fellow and know what I mean."

Dick rubbed the rough butt of his gun, his thumb on the safety catch. "Women don't interest me, not any more."

"You can spare me the details of your private life. I just want to warn you not to interfere in mine."

"It's too late now," Dick said.

"I don't know what the hell you're talking about, Heron, but this has gone far enough. I've warned you and you'd better pay attention. The party's over. Good night."

Buckle half turned to go and Dick moved the gun in his hand. Two shots and the hunt would be ended, justice done. But this man must give up more, he thought, before he dies, be forced to yield some of his secrets, his inner essence, feel the squeeze.

"You know, we've got a lot in common," he said conver-sationally. "Take our families, for instance. Yours, two sons and a daughter. I've got three sons. A lot younger, of course."

Buckle paused, held perhaps by bewilderment, or perhaps by the onset of a sneeze; he pulled out a handkerchief and blew his nose.

"Seven, five and three," Dick added. "Well spaced. The eldest one, that's Andrew, he's got quite a lot of imagination. Makes up all sorts of stories—there was a man called Rollo, I remember, lived in a cave and had a magic bird called Pug who took him all over the place, especially to Peru, where people ate diamonds and rubies and kept flocks of stars instead of sheep. Of course, he'd never seen diamonds and rubies but I suppose they came into stories his mother told him. That's what I mean—imagination. I daresay yours were the same."

"The best thing you can do, Heron, is to push off home." There was no mistaking Buckle's uneasiness now—even his voice had lost some of its plumminess. He was uncertain whether it was safe to turn his back on Dick, so as to climb the bank behind them.

"People used to say it comes from their mother, but I think that's a silly thing to say. Every child's born with its own character all there, I think, waiting, not yours or mine —like a seed. The whole tree, it's there already in the seed which mayn't be bigger than a peanut."

"You must be out of your mind," Buckle said. "Go home and get a good night's sleep." He turned and scrambled up the bank, but Dick sprang up behind and circled round to block the way. He didn't touch Buckle but he stood squarely in front of him, a black shape against the lighted windows, and Buckle seemed to shrink a little, to withdraw.

"But of course, that's what they are, children, a mixture. You keep seeing traces of the mother in them as if someone had taken her to bits and stuck in the pieces, and I suppose she sees that too. I think that's why a man loves his children, not because they're helpless and dependent and all that. Not even through vanity, because they flatter us by thinking we're like God, at least when they're little. There's something else. A child's the result of loving the mother and you keep seeing bits and pieces of her broken up, each little piece reminds you of something and there's the mother sort of trapped in the child, embedded there you might say, and that's what you love. I'm expressing this very badly but I daresay you see what I mean."

"For God's sake, Heron, stop this nonsense and go home." Buckle attempted to walk away but Dick kept between him and the house and there was nothing Buckle could do except use force. He raised an arm to push Dick out of the way but then changed his mind.

"Of course, all this presupposes that you love your wife. I don't mean just find her a good housekeeper and lie with her regular as clockwork every night. I mean you make a unity, two separate people and yet you blend into one, you don't really exist on your own any more. You can talk and be silent and laugh and argue and quarrel if you like but that doesn't matter, in a way it's all an illusion because you don't really exist on your own. There's something new been created, as the egg and the sperm grow into a fruit or a calf or a child. You can't unscramble again, ever. Of course I can't express all this, poets and philosophers have been trying to ever since the human race began, so naturally I can't. Speech is only a kind of shorthand anyway, but I think you know what I mean."

Buckle didn't answer, nor even try to get round Dick who still squarely blocked the way. All he could do was to stand quite still and pray for help.

"I think you know what I mean because you love your children, and it's your wife you're loving in them really, the bits and pieces you see. The unity they're part of, too. But of course this unity can come to an end. It can die, or be killed."

Buckle pulled himself together and took a step towards

Dick and said in a tone unexpectedly harsh and loud:
"Heron, get out of my way, I'm warning you that if you
don't I'll call for help and have you chucked out of here."

"You could simply say that people stop loving each
other and leave it at that; but then you're using another
piece of shorthand. Why do people stop loving each other?
You can say because they start loving someone else. So
they do, but they don't do that until the unity's already
damaged. Till they're really maimed and bruised, though
they mayn't know it. Take fruit, for instance, on the tree
that's attacked by insects—you say the insects attack the
fruit, but that's only half true. They don't attack the fruit
unless it's damaged already by a fungus or something like
that. It's the same with people. When you fall in love with
someone else it's because the unity's already been damaged. It's a tender thing, that unity, a sort of magic, it can
be destroyed so very easily and yet stand up to anything.
Queer, isn't it? Like a little thread of fungus that can force
a way through eight inches of concrete. When there's unity,
life's bound to win. It's all so simple, really."

Buckle took a deep breath ready to let out a shout. But
would a shout be heard in the house with so much talk and
all the windows closed? Even if they heard, would they do
anything? And with the Lord Lieutenant there. . . . It all
seemed too absurd, shouting for help in one's own garden,
confronted by a lunatic, and yet a lunatic who wasn't actually threatening or molesting you: simply talking, talking,
all moonshine, yet with such hypnotic intensity you
couldn't stop listening, you even didn't want it to end.

"What keeps the unity strong and healthy is simply
mutual respect. In some ways that's another term for love.
If respect goes, then so does the unity. I don't say it's killed
stone-dead, it sort of withers and rots. I've seen that happen, but this is only secondhand because it never happened
to us, never. I daresay there wasn't time, in eight years. It

was growing steadily, this unity, like a fruit that's slowly swelling on a tree. Every little bit of experience you share gets absorbed, thickens and strengthens it. But all good marriages are like that. I expect yours is too."

Down below, in the distance towards the lights of the marquee, Buckle thought he saw something white moving towards the terrace. It could be Dido with her white dress showing under the duffle coat. A soft drizzle had started.

"That's why I'm telling you all this, because I think you understand. And now I'll tell you my discovery. It'll astonish you, I think. Suppose you kill one of the partners. Naturally, you'd expect that to kill the unity. It stands to reason, you can't have one dead and one alive and still have the unity. But, you know, you can."

Dick paused, as if still taken aback by the force and strangeness of his own discovery. In his pocket, he had his gun in his hand. Over his shoulder, Buckle saw that the white had vanished but a blur, a knot of darkness, was moving towards him. People were approaching the terrace. There wouldn't be any need to call out. Heron hadn't seen them, he started off again.

"You can still have the unity. Not if it rots away inside you, decays like gangrene, then it's finished. Dies of its own accord. But if it doesn't want to die, if someone comes along and kills it, then that's different. You know, that's a wonderful discovery. It makes you go on living, but only for the time being. Only till you can see justice done. For of course there has to justice, doesn't there? If there's a murder, someone's got to pay. You understand that. And I expect you understand by now what I'm driving at. You're the one who has to pay, Buckle. You killed my wife."

Dick pulled his hand out of his pocket. Buckle stood stock-still. The blur of figures was close now and voices could be heard, growing louder.

A woman said, "Isn't that Peter?"

"Weren't we lucky? It's just starting to rain."

As Buckle moved towards his deliverers, Dick raised his arm and aimed the gun and tightened the muscles of his hand all in one smooth, easy, practiced motion. He didn't need to sight the pistol. Buckle wasn't more than three yards away, moving, but not too swiftly, a core of density in a night not wholly opaque.

Dick braced himself for the crash, for the kick of the gun in his hand like a living animal, and the bitter explosive smell. He spoke his wife's name and squeezed the trigger. There was a soft hollow click, silence, then Buckle's voice, pitched unusually high.

"Mind the bank, Marianne. The rain's making it slippery. My God, that was a magnificent performance. I've never heard that better sung, never. I cried like a child."

A woman's laugh. In Dick's ears the click had sounded like a thunderclap. But no one else had heard it: the pistol had misfired. There was a cartridge in the breech all right but the striking pin had failed to detonate it: a dud perhaps, or damp, something wrong. Buckle didn't even know the danger he'd been in.

Lavinia Buckle's cool, quiet, courteous voice came out of the night. "Who's with you, Peter?"

Dick turned without a word, jumped down the bank and walked towards the marquee. No one followed him.

chapter 8

WHEN Mrs. Harris got back from the fête she saw a light under the lodger's door. She knocked and, getting no answer, looked in. There were his feet with muddy shoes on her clean coverlet. She clucked angrily.

"And him so careful as a rule," she said aloud. "They're all the same, men, can't trust them in a house, like pigs." An alarming thought came to her. She leant over him to smell his breath and got quite a shock, he looked so stiff and queer. But he was breathing all right, and his breath didn't smell of alcohol—faintly perhaps of something sour or queer like aniseed. Even when she undid and pulled off his shoes he didn't wake. That was queer too.

"Poor fellow, he's worn out," she said to Ted. "I thought at first he might have been at the scrumpy, some of the lads did, got quite rowdy. And all that rock and rolling they do, indecent I call it."

"Lets off steam," Ted said. "He's a deep one, Dick is."

"Gives no trouble."

"We don't want him through the winter, though."

"I'll make a cup of tea."

She wasn't going to put it into words but Mrs. Harris

wanted Dick to stay. He was civil-spoken, no trouble, and he ate well. And then, he added the dimension of mystery to her life. Why had he dropped down in Larkinglass like a swallow from abroad to nest here? What had happened to his wife, his kids if he had any? Why didn't he talk about them as normal men did? Was he a spy perhaps? A criminal hiding out—she'd read of such things. Why didn't he get letters? She could hardly believe he was wicked, yet what did anyone know of people these days? Would he turn round and murder them in their beds?

Ted was right, they shouldn't keep him. Yet she'd got to feel responsible, to make him change his wet socks when he got in and his trousers, find out his tastes—he liked her pastry and blackberry and apple, but not parsnips nor Bath chaps; too fat he said. Wherever he'd come from, he'd been properly looked after and lived well, you could tell that.

Dick slept through the night and woke, as he always did, at half-past five, to watch the night's blackness turn deep violet, fade and lighten into a washed, pure, silvery blue. Then came an apricot glow above the horizon, and a silvery mist over fields and hedges, like some enormous, unstirred spider's web, lightly tinted orange by outriders of the sun.

Mist the colour of oyster shell lay deep over everything, and, like a shell, it glistened, almost translucently. From this flocculent ocean black trees stuck up like masts, their trunks invisible, their tops reddened very slightly; and pylons thrust delicate, spidery spokes into a sky streaked by blue and violet clouds with pink edges.

They had a rolled look, those clouds, Dick thought, like long swathes of grass halfway to hay rolled up behind a side rake across the pastures of the sky. The sun came briskly, orange red; the silver mist turned red as if a stain had spread across it, the trees stood up black as ever and sun filled the sky. Just below Dick's window, in an apple tree with boughs laden down with green fruit, he watched a speckle-breasted thrush giving long, high whistles—not a tune, as in the spring, but probably a young one testing its voice.

Dick had seen mists like this before, many times. A sun ten times fiercer, gold not red, a sun too bright to look at, would suck up the mist and there would lie the landscape's bare, hard bones: tawny hills rising to a blue infinity, a plain speckled by bush as by vast herds of grazing cattle, singing with crickets, scoured by a hot wind, pounded by heat. Shadows sharp and clear, thorn spikes hard against a sky of piercing blue. All doubt, there, was burnt away, all fuzziness dispelled, beasts and men were lean and predatory, nothing wasted. Cruelty was in the soil like iron, under the grass roots; in the air, indifference; beauty in clouds and mountains and in the hard, metallic glitter of a starling's wings, a scarlet aloe in a dry gulley like a clot of blood among rocks.

At Larkinglass the mist didn't exactly clear, it slowly and imperceptibly retreated into hedges and fields and lay about in shreds, untidily, revealing wet grass and the roots of cottages and an orchard with apple trees and henhouses and wire netting and telegraph poles, and a barbed-wire fence and washing lines and a mongrel dog hunting across a field. Everywhere signs of human beings who couldn't make up their minds—they didn't want to, they preferred fuzz, mist, obscurity.

Dick felt this half life spreading within him, little threads of mucous into every interstice, in between the cell walls. Before he came, he'd taken the clear-cut, irreversible decision to exact a kind of wild justice—he knew the quotation. All doubts had been settled and buried. Like all wild things, this wild justice was true and honest as nature, uncorrupted by men. It was a part of the natural law—life for life, tooth for tooth, balance and order which were sweet things, harmony and reciprocity.

So wild justice was the best and Dick had never been troubled by the least doubt that when he exacted it, as he would, his little strand would be knotted into the web of nature, of harmony. It was true that Peter Buckle hadn't murdered with his own hands. But the hireling with the knife wasn't the true murderer. Not the Scots thugs but Macbeth had murdered Banquo, not Exton but Bolingbroke had killed Richard. Responsibility must first be settled: and the rudest convulsion that ever cracked the earth's crust couldn't dislodge that load from Peter Buckle's shoulders.

All Dick had worried about was the difficulty of carrying out his mission. To find the man, track him down, get close to him, speak to him, all in a strange unvisited country—that had seemed to present such enormous obstacles that he'd made no advance plan. And everything had turned out the reverse of what he'd expected. He'd simply looked up Buckle's home address in Who's Who in a public library, and taken a single ticket, found lodgings, walked into a job on Buckle's doorstep and, last night, he'd cut the quarry out of the herd and said his piece and pulled the trigger.

It wasn't the failure of his gun that worried Dick, or even the cautioning of Buckle. A quarry that had seen or smelt its hunter could still be cornered. That only made the hunt more interesting, giving scope to ingenuity and endurance. In one way, Dick was glad the shot had failed; success at the first attempt would have made it all too easy.

If the task itself had proved much simpler than he'd expected, an obstacle he couldn't name had risen out of English mists and flocculence. Was it climate, atmosphere, an aerial charge like the reverse of electricity? He thought of marsh gas, created in minute quantities by innumerable aquatic plants, by roots and tentacles, by moist vegetation;

millions of these little gaseous molecules forming a blanket to stifle living lungs and deprive you of the power to reason, the impulse to protest and the will to struggle. And so you'd fall down, inert, done for, to rot away and putrify and create more marsh gas in your turn. Larkinglass was thick with marsh gas and Dick had felt it seeping in. But if you had enough warning you could either dodge it or wear a gas mask—the mask of awareness. You had a chance then.

By now the mist had gone, leaving a world dripping and tender, lit by a slanting sun. But heavy clouds were forming already, soon it would be overcast again. Dick dressed quickly, refreshed by sleep. His first job must be to get the gun working. Buckle would sack him, of course, and then, most likely, have inquiries made. To find out who he was, where he'd come from and his past history, would be plain sailing. So much the better. Dick smiled as he shaved; they'd go to endless trouble, people disguised as commercial travellers would draw out Mrs. Harris, top secret telegrams would be coded and despatched and decoded and passed round in sealed envelopes or locked boxes, the police would be consulted, dossiers compiled; after days or even weeks of effort a sealed report would come to Buckle and all the time, if anyone had come and asked Dick, he'd have written all the information down on a half sheet of paper. In fact he thought of writing it now, and posting it to Chaffins. But that would spoil the game, and no doubt all those inquiring people needed exercise and employment.

Now the quarry was alerted, Dick wanted him to feel the uncertainty, the unease and finally the fear of the hunted. In fact, Dick was beginning to think he'd been mistaken in his resolution not to make the victim suffer. Nothing physical, that never; but mental pain, why not?

Awareness was everything. If Buckle thought Dick to be

a lunatic with a grievance, every time he saw Dick he'd feel uneasy. In that case, the more he saw of Dick the better. Buckle could sack him, of course, but not get him thrown out of his lodgings. Dick was on the right side of Mrs. Harris and resolved to remain there. He went down to breakfast with a good appetite.

The only problem that he hadn't solved was Julia. So after breakfast—his Sunday off—he faced the question while he walked the lanes briskly in a raincoat, ready for the drizzle that didn't quite come. The startling, blatant greenness of the fields still amazed him, their vivid quality under grey skies, speckled with white by gulls, and sometimes black by crows or distant flights of starlings. Shafts of sunshine now and then made everything gleam like enamel, then they faded as a fat, full cloud drifted across a watery sun. Telegraph wires sang, pigeons flapped heavily off the blue tarmac into heavy-foliaged trees, the pale, greenish-yellow flowers of travellers' joy, reminding him of passion flowers in miniature, wreathed round branches of hawthorn. Hazelnuts in their green, fringed capsules dangled above. Wherever you looked were roofs or sheds or barns or something built by humans, no solitude.

Three ways to deal with Julia lay open to him: flight, surrender or guile. Flight was the safest, but then he'd have to lose sight of the quarry. Surrender he dismissed. There remained guile.

He had seen once, in Ceylon, a great rock fortress into which a parricide king had retreated with his army to escape a brother's vengeance, and so long as he'd remained there he'd been impregnable. But the brother, by taunts and stratagems, had tempted the king down to the plain and there slain him and routed his army. The moral was not to be tempted by taunts and stratagems, and that was just what Julia was doing. Could he incapsulate himself, safe from her attack? Or was this just vanity, would she leave him alone and forget him, a casual encounter?

Julia was Buckle's daughter and now Buckle, who'd been an abstraction, was turning into a man. Men created doubts about them as a wasp creates unease, or a spider its web; doubts and questions in the mind of others. There is nothing precise and certain about a man. Here was this man perplexed by his children and wanting, like other men, to love and be loved. If Buckle was to feel pain, to suffer as he'd made others suffer, if wild justice was to be done, then Julia might be the instrument placed in Dick's hand.

Dick could use Julia, in fact, while Julia thought that she was using him. Buckle could be made to feel uneasy by Dick's presence here—a lunatic with a grievance—and angry by knowing, or suspecting, that his daughter and the lunatic, a casual labourer at that, were (as Mrs. Harris would say) carrying on. It was a dangerous game, but what did that matter? He had the gun and nothing to lose. He that is down need fear no fall.

A young cock pheasant broke from a tall, untrimmed hedge, ran along the verge and stood still, eying him, half tame and half wild. Reared under a hen, and then turned out and left to grow wild enough to be shot at—another piece of English make-believe. All English life had this self-deceiving quality. The cows were half cows and half factories by turning compounds into milk, the villages half towns and half country, the houses half villas and half cottages, the people half men and half automatons, citizens of some future state only half formed. This pheasant was such a handsome bird with its gold and russet colouring, so bold and flamboyant, that to see it here on this quiet verge was startling. Then he remembered it wasn't English but Asian. In its plumage shone the colours of the sun. He would like Andrew to see it. Andrew was fascinated by birds.

Andrew, Patrick and Duncan—all good, strong, possibly Celtic names chosen by the Mother. That was the term he used, the Mother—an abstraction, as Buckle had been; the Minister and the Mother. Now the Minister was turning into a man while the Mother had become an abstraction once called Rose who could be admitted sometimes into the circle of memory in connection with the boys. The Mother's sister had the boys; they were safe and he was paying forty pounds a month towards their keep and when he died they would get the insurance. So Andrew wouldn't see a pheasant, unless there were some in a South African zoo.

chapter 9

"MORNING, Mr. Hedger."

"Morning. Nice day."

"Cold wind." Dick took the empty bottle off the doorstep and nodded to Harry Hedger, a pensioner, who lived by himself in one of the old cottages. It was not a nice day at all in Dick's opinion; chilly gusts crept under his jacket and up the small of his back. Still, it wasn't actually raining.

"Ah. The wireless says there'll be storms later. More winds this year than I can remember, not since the time a gale lifted the roof clean off the hall."

The milk round was one of Tompkins's worst headaches. He'd put Dick on as driver while Bert was off sick and the boss away on one of his African jaunts, shaking another independent country out of the blanket or handing out more taxpayers' money to keep sweet the fat black politicians with their posh fin-tailed cars and golden beds and armed bodyguards.

The boss's parting instructions had been to give Dick his cards immediately and no fooling. "He's got it in for Dick and no mistake," he'd remarked to Rodney King, the herdsman—it was almost as if the great Peter was afraid of the man. Of course Dick ought to have gone by now, but they'd never been so shorthanded at harvest time and the boss wouldn't be showing his face at Chaffins for a fortnight and Jim Tompkins had decided to chance his arm. In a fortnight Bert might be back and things easier. So Dick drove the van.

The hazard of the milk round was the thwarted desire for conversation nurtured by everyone in Larkinglass. Dick had been brought up to believe that the English never spoke to anyone they hadn't known for at least ten years. In fact, the difficulty was to stop them. He walked back along a path lined with antirrhinums now all but over, straggly and tangled but still with a few blooms. Old Hedger followed him down.

"They say it's going to be a hard winter."

"Let's hope not."

"Good job, mind, for the ground. Drives out pests. Like a slice of cake before you go? I made a good 'un yesterday. Plenty of raisins."

"No, thanks, Mr. Hedger. I must get on."

"I'll have a piece wrapped up tomorrow. You can eat it in the van."

Old Hedger's cakes were another hazard. Since his wife had died he'd taken to cooking with such enthusiasm that he had put on at least a stone. His cakes were like lumps of rock, or else had soft middles. He paid regularly every Saturday without fail—all the pensioners did. Those who could best afford it were the worst payers.

"Morning, Dick."

"Morning, Mrs. Ryan. Nice day."

Dick was picking up the drill—it didn't need much learning, you slipped into it naturally and found yourself exchanging the same remarks every day with the same people. Mrs. Ryan lived in one of the council houses. There were two Larkinglasses, an old one of small, low-ceilinged, steep-staired, inconvenient cottages built at odd angles to the street and every one different; and the new Larkinglass of up-to-date, much larger, identical and ugly semidetached council houses on either side of a service road. Each had a strip of garden at the back bounded by a split-stake fence and a front patch behind a privet hedge. While no newcomers lived in the old houses, some of the old Larkinglass families had been rehoused in the new ones; on the whole they liked the houses but disliked their neighbours—newcomers, strangers, Welsh or Irish even, all sorts.

"Nasty cold wind, though," Mrs. Ryan replied. "Sneaks through the kitchen like a serpent when the back door's open. The draughts in these houses, you wouldn't believe."

Mrs. Ryan nearly always had a grouse. She was English, her husband a big Irishman fond of drink and quarrelling, who never thought twice about muddy boots or cigarette stubs in the kitchen or lifted a finger in the house, but earned good money. He was a shop steward at the components factory. The Ryans had six children; four earning, one at school and an afterthought called Stella. The neighbours reckoned there must be seventy or eighty pounds a week coming into the house at least and the rent was thirty-five shillings. All the Ryans were spenders and, as a rule, short of ready cash. Between them they had two cars and a motorcycle to keep up, and so many things on the hire purchase, people wondered how they got them all into a three-bedroomed house.

On Saturday the milk round took longer because Dick had to collect the weekly payments. Most of the customers left the cash with their little books propped up against empties. Only four had fallen behind with the money and, on the Saturday, one settled and one paid something on account.

Then came the Ryans. None of them worked on Saturdays—except Mrs. Ryan, of course—but only one was about, a lad tinkering with his motorcycle; the others, Dick supposed, were still in bed. It was said that Mrs. Ryan took breakfast up on trays at the weekends. Dick knocked at the back door till she came.

"Now look here, Dick," she said. "I know we owes the money and you'll get it, you don't think we're going to flit, do you? It's just this week there's been the cars to licence and the electric to pay and Dave's been on short time and I don't know which way to turn, that's a fact. Things go up while your back's turned. You'll get it next week sure as I'm standing here."

"I'm only following instructions, Mrs. Ryan. If it isn't settled at the end of next week my orders are to stop supplies."

"Stop supplies now, is it, the sods. How do they think I'm going to manage with eight in the house and two of them kids?"

"I expect your husband will find the money, Mrs. Ryan."

"Him find the money like that all together, twelve quid, where do they think it's coming from? Anyway I'd like to see *them* getting twelve quid out of Ryan. Bash my head in more likely, you never seen him, he's a terror when he's roused."

"I'm sorry. I'm only passing on instructions."

"Dennis reckons there ought to be free milk same as there is the water, on the rates. It's a necessity and there's the rich making fortunes selling necessities to the poor, it isn't right he says and I agree with him. They ought to make the milk free."

Dick smiled. "Tell that to Mr. Buckle."

"Ah, him! Spend twelve quid on one of his snacks, I shouldn't wonder, while the working class goes short to get a drop of milk for the kids. And then they say—"

"Quite right, Mrs. Ryan, only don't blame me. I've got my job to do like everyone else."

"Bring half a pint of cream tomorrow, will you? I got my sister coming with her kids, they do like a cake with a nice cream filling. The shop stuff's not the same."

Dick made a note of it, disconcerted to find his sympathies on the side of his employer. The Buckles, it was true, were rich, but it was stretching things a bit to say the Ryans were poor. Tompkins said the milk round wasn't paying and soon they'd have to get a new van which would cost the best part of £1500. You'd have to sell three times the milk they did, he said, to take that in your stride.

The Croziers lived about two miles out of the village, off the road and down in a hollow: a middle-sized house smothered in wisteria but in need of repair, and a bit too close to the railway. Mrs. Crozier was crippled by arthritis and deaf into the bargain. She really needed a nurse, but they couldn't afford one and the Colonel looked after her himself and did the cooking, such as it was. That left him with little time for the garden, which had got out of hand.

They only had a pint a day as a rule, but a married daughter with two children had been staying; she had ordered extravagantly by Crozier standards and evidently left without settling up. The Colonel came to the door: a thin, stringy man with a heavy white moustache and tired eyes, and hands stained from gardening and washing up. After his military career he'd done a lot of public work, County Council and the Bench, but had no time for it now and believed in getting younger men, if you could find them. When Dick said his piece, Colonel Crozier scratched the back of a scrawny neck and looked puzzled.

"Fallen behind, eh? Sorry about that. Fact is, I thought my daughter had been leaving the money. Daresay she forgot. What do I owe?"

Dick told him and he frowned. "Sure there's no mistake?"

"That's what the book says."

"Well, books can be wrong. Still, hold on a minute, will you, while I fetch it." The Colonel's back managed to express resentment, as if he was being cheated but considered it against his dignity to argue the point.

Dick looked round the kitchen. It had an old-fashioned iron stove, the kind that needed blacking and cleaning out every day. Beside it was an armchair with a very worn loose cover, and a basket nearby for a dog. The walls, streaked and stained by damp, hadn't had a coat of paint for years, and paper was peeling off a ceiling kippered by smoke. The pans were old and battered, the plates cracked, but things were clean, even the porcelain sink, chipped and stained and much too big, flanked by wooden draining boards. Stuffed birds in glass cases lined one wall. Fly-dirt speckled the glass, the birds' plumage was tatty and one had sagged at the knees, giving it a drunken look. This was a big, brown-speckled, tall bird with very long legs that Dick thought he recognized.

The Colonel caught him looking at it. "Know what that is?"

"It looks like a bustard."

"Just what it is. Not many people recognize it. The last bustard in England was shot in 1869."

"Then that can't be the one I remember."

Colonel Crozier smiled. "You're new, aren't you? Been down here long?"

"No, only a few weeks."

"I haven't enough cash to settle this account till I go to the bank. But you shall have it next Saturday.'"

"You understand I'm just passing on a message. Mr. Tompkins said—"

Dick hesitated, all this went so much against the grain. Colonel Crozier reminded him of his father, when he'd been an old man. The Colonel stiffened.

"What did Tompkins say?"

Dick had to get it out. "Only that if it isn't paid next week he'd have to stop the milk."

"I've told you it will be paid next week, haven't I?"

The icy tone of voice angered and distressed Dick. He turned without a word, carrying an empty bottle, and went back to the van. If he'd known what was coming he'd never have agreed to take on the round and he'd tell Tompkins he wouldn't come next Saturday.

On the way home the road curved round a wood that clothed a hill—what they called a hill in England, just as a narrow ditch was called a river—and he stopped the van to calm down and look at the view. The fields meandered away, rolled up like a sleeping child in a green and gold blanket: gold where the straw had been baled and the stubbles glistened, not a rich gold like his own stubbles with dry, hard earth below, but a half-gold, half-silver with green already showing from the sprouting grass. If you didn't plough these stubbles they'd be green fields by Christmas. Always life was coming through, strongly but quietly, in a gentlemanly fashion, so that you didn't notice what was happening until it *had* happened, till the stubbles had become a green field.

There was a kind of pact here between man and nature never to push anything too far, to give way to each other, let matters take their course, see both sides. But in cities, where the country had been killed, the pact was broken and men reverted sometimes to forms of savagery. Men could be savage in the raw jungle of nature and in the human jungle of the cities, but where the two met, savagery was bled away and tamed.

He should have killed Buckle when he'd had the chance —thrown away the gun and done it with his hands. Even the gun had been castrated, its fangs drawn. It was working all right now, he'd taken it into an old quarry and tested it, but Buckle had gone. A fortnight to wait. Well, he'd wait, months if necessary, keeping his mind clear and his purpose constant. Buckle might be absent in the flesh but his image was imprisoned in Dick's mind. He'd hold on tightly to that image and feed it with the hatred that, he now realized, was needed to keep it alive.

That was it—hatred. Hitherto he hadn't hated Buckle personally, only what he stood for, but Dick saw now that a wish for justice wasn't enough. Matters must be put on a personal basis, Buckle must be hated—Buckle and his family.

chapter 10

At Chaffins the back door was open but the kitchen empty. Dick put down the pint of cream he'd been told to take up to the house and called "hello." Through an open doorway, he caught the gleam of stainless steel but he could hear no movement, only the hiss of an electric kettle nearing the boil. The kitchen had been modernized regardless of cost and a long, planned unit ran the length of one wall with steel cabinets, a dishwasher, a built-in eye-level oven, everything you wanted to hand, electric mixer waiting on the Formica-topped bench and other gadgets handy, all in cream and pale blue. He noted signs of occupation: not only the kettle ejecting steam but a board with half-chopped eggs and a mixing bowl, utensils awaiting their washing up, a crumbled tea cloth thrown over the back of a chair, a tea tray with milk in the jug and cut bread and butter.

He called again and no one answered. Like most of the rich houses round about, Chaffins had passed through the Italian stage and got on to Spaniards, who were still, for the most part, acquiring the language, while their employers were in turn learning Spanish from them. A famine of domestic workers had at last accomplished what the demands of travel, curiosity, war, diplomacy and culture had failed to accomplish since the Norman invasion: taught richer English families foreign tongues. When the Spaniards in their turn took to factories, Dick supposed it would be something else—Portuguese, Maltese, some Eastern language?

He heard a telephone ringing in the distance, movement, a door opening, then footsteps and Lavinia Buckle came into the kitchen, the fat spaniel Pompey waddling at her heels. She wasn't beautiful but she was pleasing; about her was something restful, detached; in her presence you felt things slow down to an even pace and arrange themselves sensibly, in proportion. Dick could imagine that her hands, which were neat and small, could hold the power of healing, and yet she was withdrawn; her face, heart-shaped and gentle, wore an habitual expression of mild surprise, almost of drollery, as if constantly amused at the strangeness of the world. She moved lightly and with an air of control, like a girl despite her greying hair and the creases coming round her neck with middle age.

She smiled at Dick and said good afternoon.

"I've brought the cream. I thought perhaps . . ."

"I'm sorry you couldn't make anyone hear. It's the Spaniards' afternoon off, they leave me with the kitchen to play with and that's my weekly treat. I think I saw you at the fête."

"That's right, Mrs. Buckle. I hear it was a great success."

"It raised nearly five hundred pounds, a record. That's a lot for a small village. It's given us all very grand ideas for the future: pageants, almost searchlight tatooes. But next time it's sure to rain."

The Dalmatian came bounding in—an unlikely and exotic beast Dick thought—possibly Asian, like the pheasant? The dog jumped up, lashing his tail, grinning and sniffing at Dick's clothes, demanding praise.

"Don't let him bother you," Lavinia Buckle said in her cool, light voice that made Dick think of dry hock, a good cast with a fly on a clear pool or a light breeze just ruffling the sweet-smelling, crisp eucalyptus leaves. "Down, Sebastian. It never occurs to him people won't be overjoyed to see him. He means well."

She pulled at his collar, while Dick patted him; and then looked up to see Julia in her tight jeans and a striped red and white seaman's sweater.

"I want my tea, isn't it—" She saw Dick and stopped. "Oh, hello, I thought you'd gone."

"I've been kept on while Bert's in hospital."

"Oh, I see." She seemed at a loss and Dick, too, felt awkward and hostile, despite her attraction, despite the peach-skin smoothness of her complexion, the slightly puzzled lines in her youthful forehead, the curve of her breasts under the sweater.

"I've been in London all the week," she added, and then frowned, perhaps thinking herself clumsy for having appeared to owe him an explanation, to owe him anything.

The young man who'd barbecued the chickens came in through the back door. Tall, stooping a bit, he shambled slightly in his sandals, slopping along with his head thrust forward and lank, dark hair half over his eyes. He had a big nose and a big Adam's apple and deep-set eyes and could not be called good-looking, but gave an impression of intelligence and of a barbed defensiveness. He wore an open shirt of Turkish towelling, pinkish rust in colour, a pair of black trousers that laced up at the sides and no sweater, despite the chilly wind, and remarked offhandedly:

"No one really *wants* tea, but if we've got to have it, it might as well not be cold."

"That's my fault." Lavinia was apologetic. "I was gossiping in the kitchen. People always do somehow, there must be something in the air of kitchens."

"Garlic," Julia suggested, picking up the tray.

The young man's name was Evan. He looked at Dick without enthusiasm, and spoke astringently.

"If it isn't the mystery man. I thought he'd vanished in a puff of smoke or gone to Baghdad on a carpet."

"No, I deliver the milk."

They looked at each other with an unexpected spurt of hostility that took Dick by surprise. The arrogant bastard, he thought. Sebastian jumped up again—dogs always liked Dick, something (he supposed) in his smell—and he patted the smooth spotted head and said to Julia:

"Is he yours? I had one once, he was a great hunter but not very bright in the head."

"All dogs are stupid," Evan ruled. "That's why we like them, they're so damned stupid they even slobber over *us*. Come on, Julia, for God's sake, with that tea." He ran his hand up the back of her neck and ruffled her hair, and she shook her head and frowned.

"Look out, I'll drop the tray."

"Give it to me." He took it from her, raised it above his head and then lowered it again and bowed in an exaggerated way, an affected piece of play acting that infuriated Dick.

"Now give me my reward, sweetheart," Evan said.

"Reward for what?"

"Carrying the tray. Light me a cigarette, there's one in that top pocket."

"Can't you wait?"

"Now don't be bloody-minded, do as I say."

"Has anyone been brave enough to swim?" Lavinia inquired.

"Only Simon," Julia replied. "He's the only hearty one. You can't see Evan or Martin horsing about in cold water, can you?" With a bad grace she took a packet of cigarettes from Evan's shirt pocket, pulled one out, lit it and put it in his mouth. Dick said:

"Will you be wanting cream tomorrow, Mrs. Buckle?"

"Thank you, I think we'd better have a pint."

As he reached the door Julia looked round and said sharply: "Don't go yet, Dick. Have you seen the swimming pool?"

"No, but I—"

"Come and have a look. Of course it's too cold for swimming, but a nice place to sit."

"I'm going to have my tea if no one else is." Evan's tone was petulant. "Come on, Julia, for God's sake, if you're coming. Unless you want to take to the bushes." He walked out with the tray.

Dick's immediate reaction was to hit Evan, he even took a step after him with tight fists before he remembered not only that milkmen didn't hit guests at the manor but that Julia was no concern of his one way or the other, nor Evan's insolence, nor any of these marginal people. But Julia had flushed and her eyes grew moist with rage.

"Come on, Dick, you've got to see the swimming pool now whether you like it or not. Bloody little tick, swollen up with his father's money and thinking he's God. Well, he'll see. This way."

She seized his hand and pulled him forward as she'd done before and he was in the same predicament, being used like any handy implement or weapon. Despite his anger he couldn't do as he supposed one of her contemporaries would have, pushed her hand away and told her to bugger off or something of the kind. He looked round for help from Lavinia but she had retreated into the pantry, sensibly washing her hands of the whole business.

Julia was like an obstinate beast, the more you pushed in one direction the more it would dig in its toes or move backwards in another. So he let himself be led across the back drive and through a door into an enclosure sheltered by a high stone wall. At one end lay a covered patio, then an open paved court and then steps leading down into a pool with very blue water, surrounded on the other three sides by shaven lawn.

The patio faced south and formed a sun trap full of long chairs with brightly coloured mattresses and smaller wicker chairs with round seats, like miniature coracles, on little aluminium sticks for legs. Tables bore bottles and tumblers, books and sunglasses and long-playing records. Plants in tubs stood at the corners of the pool and a couple of weather-worn statues, brought home on some long-forgotten Grand Tour and picked up at a local sale, appeared to be gazing with an air of surprise at a spotted red and yellow rubber horse lying on its side.

"Do-it-yourself Costa Brava," Julia said, still sharp and angry. "Just about as bogus as the real one. No one likes swimming except Simon, but it's an excuse to bare the torso and look manly and drink gin and orange to the swelling tones of the latest on the hi-fi. We're having a plaque put up, the President of the Board of Trade bathed here."

"Have some tea and stop bitching," Evan said. He had put the tray down beside a young man in bathing trunks who lay with outstretched legs on one of the mattresses. Dick's first impression was of brownness and the smoothness of a hazelnut. The young man contracted his muscles and pulled himself into a sitting position with his fingers intertwined behind a head which was going bald. This heightened the impression of nuttiness, of being polished and sleek, and his eyes were brown also, bright and quick under a high forehead. He had a neat, well-formed, small nose and chin.

"This is Martin," Julia said. "My brother. My elder brother, the artistic one with queer friends."

Martin smiled pleasantly and spoke with precision, and the barest hint of formality.

"Good evening. Are you staying here?"

"No, I deliver the milk."

Martin either concealed his surprise perfectly or didn't feel any. "Do you deliver yogurt? I've got a passion for yogurt but it's always being frustrated. With pickles and gherkins and red peppers finely chopped is the best way."

The tone was entirely friendly and yet Dick felt obscurely that they were getting at him, the lot of them, and his anger grew.

"It's your father's milk," he said. "You'd better suggest it to him."

"My father's got a mind above intestinal flora, he only thinks of the Commonwealth's appointment with destiny in the dawn of a new golden age. That was last week's happy phrase. If he only knew it, the golden age depends entirely on harmony among the intestinal flora. But you can't teach new men old tricks."

"It's better with brown sugar," Evan said.

Martin shook his head. "Sugar ruins it. Astringency is all."

"It's sour to start with, the whole point of sugar is the contrast. Piquancy."

"You couldn't be more wrong. But then you've got a sweet tooth."

"You make that sound as if I had a persecution mania or venereal disease or something." Evan was getting angry again; he had never really calmed down and Dick knew his own presence was a mounting irritant. "What's wrong with a sweet tooth?"

"Oh, for God's sake, lay off, will you, Evan?" Julia protested. "What's biting you anyway? Where's Simon?"

"Gone to change, he's going out," Martin replied. "Simon has a very active social life locally."

"Simon has a sweet tooth," Evan persisted. "I noticed it at lunch, two lumps with black coffee. Obviously it goes with being an extrovert. I bet Dick has a sweet tooth. Is that right, Dick?"

"Oh, for Christ's sake, Evan," Julia said.

Dick had been standing on the pool's edge looking into the clear blue water, not really listening. He was fascinated by the purity and cleanness of the chemically treated water; it had a sharp, vinegarish smell and there was absolutely no life in it, not a tadpole or a wisp of green algae or even a filament of waterweed. Complete sterility. So as not to contaminate the bathers whose bodies were stuffed with impurities of every kind, the intestinal flora, secretions from the pores, flesh that went on flaking off, decayed membrane, bacteria under fingernails. But in the water, man-induced sterility. He looked back at Evan and Martin side by side in wicker chairs; Evan sour, Martin sleek, both sharing with the blue, clear water this hard sterility. He replied indifferently:

"I've never thought about it."

"The point is, do you take sugar with black coffee and eat cakes? If you do, you've got a sweet tooth and you're an extrovert."

"I don't take sugar in black coffee but I do like cakes."

"There, you see," Martin remarked with an air of triumph. "That's what comes of trying to be clever."

"Do leave the wretched man alone," Julia snapped.

"He looks as if he can defend himself," Martin said, smiling. He was very friendly. But Evan wouldn't change the tune. He observed:

"Just Dick's line, I should think. Biceps and beefsteaks and skipping ropes, good clean living and bad dirty jokes in the bar."

"If he wasn't an exceptionally good-natured man he'd throw you into the pool for that." Martin's tone was light but barbed. "I apologize for our guest, he can be quite sweet sometimes only you wouldn't think so now."

"It comes from associating with intellectuals," Julia said, kicking at the base of a statue. Martin corrected her.

"It comes from jealousy."

"What balls you do talk," Evan said. "Who am I supposed to be jealous of?"

"Everyone in sight, in your present frame of mind."

"I'm sorry, Dick," Julia said, "I wanted to show you the swimming pool, not a disgusting exhibition of filthy manners by the spoilt rich."

"Bad manners are a luxury, naturally to be enjoyed by the rich," Evan pointed out. "The poor, if any, can't afford them."

"Do stop trying to coin epigrams," Julia said. "It doesn't suit you. Why are you trying to pick a quarrel with Dick?"

Evan gathered himself up with an unexpected agility, jumped from his chair and bounded, more or less, to the edge of the pool beside Julia. He grinned, his sulky expression wiped out, and suddenly looked younger and rather attractive.

"Just bloody-mindedness and something to do, like a nasty little boy tying a tin can to the tail of a poor pussy. Not that Dick's at all like a poor pussy, if anything a ravening tom I'd say, or something with a thick shell like a tortoise. Sheathed claws too, I daresay, he could tear me to shreds if he wasn't so patient, really I've been very brave." He put one hand on Dick's arm, partly circled it with long fingers curved like the beak of an ibis and squeezed. "I was right too about the biceps."

Dick pulled back his arm and Evan laughed. "It's all right, I'm not making advances, I'm practically engaged to Julia for one thing, only she won't admit it, but she will eventually because like all women she wants someone to reform. Not that I look at it as reformation but progression, broadening out, moving along life's great assembly belt."

"Will you for God's sake stop, Evan!" Julia had gone pink with anger and even stamped her foot and looked like a child. "I've had enough."

"You shouldn't interrupt me, I was about to make a striking parallel between the human condition and a broiler factory. Thousands of us strung up like chickens, with anonymous white-coated Furies tearing out our guts and then more anonymous white-coated Fates drawing our tendons and God the Factory Manager also in a white coat and possibly invisible. Just the job for one of our new wave dramatists, or someone newer still perhaps, the next wave."

"Sounds more like old, very bogus Ibsen to me," Martin remarked, extracting himself sedately from his wicker chair.

"Thank you for showing me the swimming pool." Dick spoke to Julia in a tone without expression. "I must get back to my tea."

"Now I've frightened him to death," Evan said, laughing. "It's all right, you're not in any danger."

"I'm out of my depth."

"Very shallow depths really, Dick. Just about do for a shoal of unambitious goldfish. An honest milkman should regard us with contempt, absolutely unalloyed by humility."

"It's getting cold, I'm going in," Martin said. "I should think Dick's had enough of us by now but if he can take it, Julia, why not give the wretched man a drink?"

Martin and Evan were standing one on each side of him and Dick had a sudden conviction that they meant to throw him into the pool. It was quite irrational, he knew it was absurd and yet it submerged him like a wave, this feeling: they were in league together, Julia had led him into a trap, the two young men had been talking to bewilder and disarm him and now they had cornered him. Buckle had put them up to it. They would knock him on the head perhaps with one of the stone statues and drown him in the pond.

A sick gripe of panic seized him and he felt clammy with cold sweat. He walked stiffly away from the pool. No one else moved. It was like a dream, everyone suspended, his own limbs felt heavy as lead. As he felt the distance widen between himself and the water a great surge of relief came over him, he was getting safer, but he wouldn't be really safe until he was out of the door and away from the pool with its high walls, its seclusion, the menace of its cold, sterile, blue water and the two young men who were indefinably menacing.

chapter II

THEY were standing beside the battered dark blue van with white letters printed on it saying P. Buckle, Chaffins Farm, Daily Deliveries of Fresh Farm Bottled Milk.

"I'm sorry about that," Julia said.

"There's nothing to be sorry about."

"Yes, there is. Evan's behaviour. Thank you for keeping your temper."

Dick laughed. "Water off a duck's back."

"No, I saw you nearly lose it and I don't wonder. You could have flattened him out." Then she added: "I wish you'd tell me what you're doing here."

"I have told you. And I shan't be here much longer."

"Where will you go?"

"I haven't decided."

"You're about as forthcoming as a clam."

Dick smiled and climbed into the van. He settled himself at the wheel and remarked: "You're very like your brother sometimes."

"Looks, or temperament?"

"Both, I daresay, I don't know."

"How old are you, Dick?"

"I'm thirty-five."

"Fifteen years older than me."

"Yes, you could have been my daughter in Elizabethan times."

"Why Elizabethan?"

"Didn't they marry about fifteen?"

"You've been married, haven't you, Dick?"

"Yes."

"You don't want to talk about it?"

"Not much." Dick examined the backs of his hands that rested on the wheel. He felt calm, he could speak about it now quite calmly just as if he were to talk about a trouble that had come to someone else a long time ago, and in another country. Everything would stay calm behind the barricade he had erected in his mind so long as he didn't move quickly, so long as nothing unexpected happened, no outflanking of the recognized routine of words.

"That's all quite ordinary too," he added. "My wife died. I only—" He paused. Far away came that warning sound of rising, rushing waters, the vision of the wave, the rough feel of a rope in his hands.

"I've got three boys," he said quickly. "So you see I have to work to support them. They're in South Africa with my sister-in-law."

Julia was silent for a few moments. "You can't be a cowman for the rest of your life."

"No. Only for about another ten days."

One of Julia's hands was resting on the open window frame of the van. She reached across and put it over his, and touched a gold signet ring on his little finger.

"Is this . . . No, I've asked enough questions. Come to mop tonight, Dick."

"To mop?"

"The fair in Horsington. It's a corny sort of job and clutters up the streets for days and people don't go like they used to, but it's all right for an hour or two. The local kids get high on scrumpy and win ghastly butter dishes at the hoopla stands. But I love the dodgems and the canned music. Come on, say yes."

"Thanks, but—" He looked down at her hand on his, warm and light, and thought that this was a test, like the temptations of St. Antony. His temptation wasn't lust or greed, power or riches, but simply pity and compunction, which could rot away a sense of purpose, not with acid cruelty, but with a syrupy sweetness. For sweetness, he thought, can rot as well as acid can. But a man's family was an extension of the man, they must suffer for his sins, as branches of a tree suffered if you ringed the trunk. He asked:

"What about the others?"

"You mean Evan? If he's really jealous he must pay up with it. I'm not engaged to him, you know."

"No?"

"No. He's maddening, but in a way I *am* fond of him I suppose; I mean, it's a bit of an act, all that smartness and flippancy, he's had his troubles and . . . Well, anyway, he and Martin can entertain each other, which they're only too well able to do as you probably saw, only Martin's a whole lot cleverer than Evan is and deeper. You never really know what Martin's up to and what he's thinking except that you suspect it's faintly sinister, a bit offbeat somehow. Well, then, that's a date, is it, Dick, nine o'clock, say?"

"Your mother won't like it."

"She's got enough sense not to try to stop me doing what I want to. We settled that years ago."

"I thought she was rather a marvellous person," Dick said. Julia pushed her hair out of her eyes.

"We're all bloody marvels here. Don't come if you don't want to."

"All right, I'll come." Looking down at her standing by the van with a flushed face, Dick thought he'd been a fool, these people could look after themselves all right, they were using him: the father as a cowman, the young men as a butt, the daughter as a stallion more or less. The only one who didn't try to use him was Lavinia, she was the only whole, untwisted one.

"Well, all right then." Julia's voice was now rather grudging. "I'll pick you up at nine o'clock, will that do?"

Through his mirror, as he drove off, Dick watched her go in through the back door, swinging a dog lead which she still held in her hand. Her mother had just finished washing up the tea things in the kitchen. In her soft, self-effacing voice she observed:

"He's a rum'un, you know."

"Yes, I suppose he is in a way. His wife died and I think it's knocked him endways or something. I suppose he's trying to get it out of his mind."

Lavinia glanced at her daughter with a twinge of pity and returned her attention to the cake she was restoring to a plastic container. She plucked out and ate a cherry, at once enjoying it and despising her own weakness. Pulling cherries out of cakes was a childish, untidy habit and a failure in self-discipline, but she did it sometimes when she was worried. She put the airtight container away in a cupboard and wiped her hands on a roller towel.

"He looks as if he's got a good digestion," she said.

"Who, Dick? What's that got to do with it?"

"More than you might think. An awful lot of lame ducks have poor digestions. They're not so much lame as windy, or in trouble with fats."

Julia, sitting at one of the blue-topped stools fiddling with the dog lead, glanced at her mother half with irritation, half amusement. In the end she smiled.

"I wish you wouldn't keep warning me off people, even in a roundabout way. I'm not a newborn infant."

Lavinia suppressed all the things she wanted to say. It was no good talking to the young and, in a way, Julia was right. What Lavinia was in fact trying to warn her against was a tendency to feel compassion for her fellows. If there was one thing sure to lead you into trouble in this world, it was a sense of compassion. Such a sense was strong in Julia and it was dangerous, an Achilles' heel.

It lay at the root, Lavinia reflected as she spread the tea cloth over a rail to dry, of this involvement with Evan. If you saw your daughter pursuing a course that couldn't lead to anything but failure all round, oughtn't you to intervene? Probably you'd fail, but you could try. Or hadn't you that right? Only by failures, through mistakes, could people mature. A search for maturity was the point of life, in so far as there was one—ripeness is all. Should you hinder your child's search for maturity any more than you should bind the feet of baby girls like the prerevolutionary Chinese?

But Evan, he stuck in the gullet, that she must admit. He might seem like a lame duck to Julia because he was unhappy and trying, possibly, to strike out on a new line; but his lameness was scarcely apparent to anyone else. His father was not merely rich but powerful, an owner of television companies and publications with vast circulations, with interests in innumerable businesses and firms.

Evan was trying to rebel, and his protest had taken the natural shape of rejecting the tough, commercial, money-making world of his father and taking up with intellectuals and left-wing despisers of the market place and money power. He was in fact, working on a monthly journal with a policy of disgruntled fury towards politics, *avant-grade* impatience towards the recognized arts, contempt for royalty, romantic idealism towards the coloured races, hatred for authority, indifference towards everything else and a small, dwindling circulation. And it was typical, Lavinia thought, of the times that this magazine, called *Megaton*, had been cheated even of the meagre glory of going down with flags flying and popguns blazing before the superior forces of the philistines by some international fund or other which was giving it just enough money to keep it afloat, and not enough to enable it to get anywhere.

To Lavinia, Evan was a problem, not, of course, because of *Megaton* and his father, but because of his relation with Martin. One learned to live with everything but it had been hard at first to live with the suspicions, then the certainties, aroused by Martin's friendships with young men and his tolerant, good-natured relations with women from which the sting of sex was missing. By calling it a phase she gave all this an ephemeral quality; she remembered the Greeks, and the frequent connection with creative genius; maturity, she told herself, sought its flowers in the whole garden of human experience, didn't narrow down its interest to a single species.

But even to admit all that didn't console her. Evan was among the most presentable of Martin's friends. Others were a great deal less congenial and there'd been rumours of involvement in a half-world of shady clubs, of pending prosecutions that so far hadn't quite materialized for reasons that could be in themselves discreditable, of unexplained trips abroad and peculiar telephone calls at odd times of night; a whole world of which she knew nothing save the particles, by no means all of them genuine, that had drifted into her orbit through an occasional film or television feature, a very infrequent remark Martin let drop and, of course, all those ripples Mr. Profumo's lethal brick had sent on their corrosive way.

The tea things were washed and put away, the supper table laid and it was not yet time to get from the fridge the cold food left ready by the Spaniards.

"It's quiet without Peter and his whisky-swilling chums,"

Julia remarked. "You'd think he'd get tired of all these conferences."

"I think they're rather like love affairs. You start each one full of hope, it's going to be a brilliant success. Then it gets tedious; but by that time you're too deeply involved to give up. In the end it turns out to be just like all the others, a partial success at the very best, but after it's all over you begin to think of it again as a triumph, and wouldn't have missed it for anything."

"You sound as if you had nonstop love affairs."

Lavinia observed mildly: "I read about them."

"I think Peter's love affairs are all with politics. What made him take it up originally?"

"He's a gambler."

Julia nodded. "Like Martin. It's funny, Martin seems to have picked out all Peter's worst qualities, or the ones he hasn't actually got but might have, and exaggerated them. Of course it's all Peter's fault really for spoiling Martin, he could never do wrong."

Lavinia got up and filled the electric kettle for something to do. There were some things she couldn't discuss with Julia, however hard she tried.

"I don't think I'm a gambler." Julia was making rabbit faces out of a pocket handkerchief and seemed to want to linger, though as a rule she was as restless as a hungry cat.

"Julia! You take risks the whole time."

She shook her head. "Only because I don't think they're risks. I think they're sure to be all right. If I think it's a risk I shy away. I can't stand failure."

Lavinia laughed. "You've just described the essence of the born gambler."

"They all think it's sure to come off?"

"Of course."

Julia frowned. "What am I supposed to do? Turn my back on everything?"

"No, but ... People can't be changed."

Lavinia picked up a small pink plastic jug and poured water into a saucer in which an African violet was standing on the window sill. She said these things so glibly but were they true? Couldn't people be changed? If they couldn't, what a lot of wasted effort there had been—all the religions, all the movements to improve and civilize, everything from the Sermon on the Mount to *Megaton*, from Socrates to Gandhi. Of course societies *did* change people in communities over the generations; but what about each single individual in his own lifetime? Had she changed, had Peter? People unfolded like acorns, grew like seeds—that was her belief, it was all there to start with. Or did she merely mean that she couldn't change Martin or Peter, that Julia couldn't change Evan? Perhaps Julia *could* change Evan, if the will was there on both sides; she had no right to judge.

Julia got up and unwound the dog's lead from her wrist. "However did you and Peter come to produce anyone like Martin? We've got Italian blood somewhere, haven't we?"

"A little bit I think, some way back. But I don't think we can blame it all on the Ities."

"He was on his best behaviour just now with Dick. I wonder why."

Lavinia felt suddenly an overpowering weariness, a failure of support, as a bean plant might feel, she thought, if someone plucked away the stick it was climbing up. So often had she hoped for Martin, been warmed by his smile, his sincerity, his genuine remorse, thought the worst over and a new course set. And then a few months later, it would all begin again; and now, whenever he was pleasant and generous, one asked instinctively: I wonder why. . . .

"I'm going to get some herbs for the salad," she said. They were both lingering, reluctant to snuff out this little unexpected flame of intimacy. "You know Peter left instructions with Tompkins about your friend Dick."

"To sack him?"

"I'm afraid so."

"What's Dick supposed to have done?"

"Hasn't it struck you as a bit odd his being here?"

"Well, he has to be somewhere, hasn't he?" She lit herself another cigarette and said: "Nothing like jumping on a man with both feet and hobnailed boots when he's down."

Lavinia sighed. "That's not quite fair. Sometimes Peter can't avoid damaging people indirectly. Every policy's got to hurt someone."

"He doesn't think Dick's a thwarted nationalist or something, does he?"

"It isn't nationalists who are thwarted these days. They're on top, but that means others have to go under. It can't be helped."

"Like everything else that suits the bosses," Julia said angrily.

"I just thought you'd better know. I gather this Dick got overexcited at the fête and made a lot of incoherent threats. Peter thought he was either drunk or a lunatic and in either case not a very desirable under-cowman."

Julia drew fiercely on her cigarette and said: "I bet it was Evan."

"Evan?"

"Oh, never mind. Is this an awful warning about going to mop with the under-cowman?"

"I suppose if fireworks excite him, so might dodgems and hooplas. I know it's a very obvious remark but he has dropped rather mysteriously out of the blue. It may be just that fireworks are bad for him," Lavinia added, "and I don't think there'll be any in Horsington tonight. But if he's under notice I suppose he could have some sort of grudge, anyway Peter thought he had something on his mind."

"Well, thanks for telling me," Julia said.

Her mother's mildness had drawn the fangs of the argument, and that only increased her frustration. She felt as if she were groping about in a fog for something she could hear and smell but couldn't touch or see. If her mother had come out in the open and said she didn't approve of her daughter going out with an under-cowman, it would have been a lot easier.

chapter 12

DICK didn't think much of mop. Like the pony you very occasionally came upon drawing a dilapidated cart along a byroad, like a branch railway line or an open car and now perhaps the cinema, country fairs had had their day. Now almost the only things that hadn't changed were the blaring, strident music, the merry-go-round with its bobbing horses, covered with sprawling children like flies on lumps of sugar, and some of the side shows. Julia wanted to win an alarm clock as a present for Evan on the hoopla stand. It couldn't have been worth ten shillings and she spent more than that in sixpences before she gave up, having won a bowl containing two goldfish.

"Would you like them, Dick?"

He looked at them swimming perkily in their cheap bowl, their tails flapping, round and round, round and round. "Me? No, thanks."

"They'd be company. You could take them with you when you move on to wherever you're going. Two faithful companions, sharing your privations and triumphs, asking nothing but a few crumbs of bread, never answering back like humans. Then you could write a book about them and make a fortune. No one's done goldfish yet."

A long time ago he'd tried to keep fish in a bowl like this one and they had died. But they'd been angel fish, not goldfish, captured in a pocket in a coral reef where an undiminished sun had subdued the firmament—one thought naturally in larger words to fit greater elements: "firmament" instead of "sky," for "sea" the "ocean"; for "light" there should be some fat, heavy word like "coruscation" or "transplendency." But no word existed to match the intensity, the concentration, the vast power of the light which created life but could also kill it by sheer force.

And the sea: warm, silky, blue as gentians, quiet as a drowsy cat and yet alive, as if gently breathing, rocking almost imperceptibly the hot bright boat made from an aircraft's float by Dick's father, and sheltering a whole piscine and vegetable universe. For just below the shimmering surface lay a geography of bays and peaks and indentations in the coral where forests of seaweed, in the muted colouring of fungi and bruises, waved their branches with the grace and subtlety of Indian dancers, and between their pliant stems the fishes darted or reposed; fishes of every imaginable shape and pattern, fishes of electric blue and hibiscus red and blood orange, fishes striped and stippled and spotted and barred, fishes that looked like gliding butterflies and birds of paradise and fragments of mosaic from some ancient tomb. Encased in a snorkel mask, you could float and dive all day to watch this moving panorama, your eye entranced by its brilliance and variety, your limbs massaged by the warm, sleepy waves, your mind soothed by a sense of detachment and eternity.

It had been Hughie's idea to capture the fish—a pair for breeding. Hughie was always the one to canvass ideas, Dick more content to take things as they came, to accept and enjoy them, where as Hughie wanted to improve, alter and experiment.

"*You can't tell which are males and which are females*," Dick objected. *It nearly always fell to him to point out the snags in Hughie's propositions. He was three years older.*

"*If we get six, there's bound to be some of each.*"

"*No, there aren't. There could be six of one kind. It's the law of probability.*"

"*Oh, you and your laws, you're always against everything.*"

"*I'm not,*" Dick protested, *stung by the injustice.* "*Come on then, we'll get your blasted fish.*"

Once the hunt was on, it was Dick who was the leader, not only because of his age but because he was a natural athlete and the very exercise of motion sharpened his wits. They netted the fish and put them in an old oil drum full of sea water and Dick, with an effort, forebore to point out the unlikelihood of keeping them alive later at an altitude of over six thousand feet.

That year they had been sharing a white, palm-thatched bungalow with a family called Johnston, farmers like the Herons, with two daughters. Rose Johnston was a year older than Hughie, and Emma matched up with Dick's young sister Margery. Rose was freckled with a fuzz of pale brown hair, the wiry kind, pulled back and tied behind her neck, and wore a dental plate. Dick depised her for her sex and for her floundering, inexperienced way of swimming, and thought her bossy. She was collecting shells which fascinated him by their enormous range of shapes and colours, some as small as gnats yet perfectly whorled, others big and shiny like the large cowries, speckled like guinea fowl.

"*I want a clam,*" *she said to him that day when they were picnicking in the shade of an overhanging rock.*

"*What for?*"

"*They're the biggest kind of shell.*"

"*They're not.*"

"Yes, they are."

"Bet you they're not."

"All right then. Of course, a big clam."

"I'll bet all your cowries against my hunting knife."

Rose thought it over, frowning a little at the world of brilliant light by which their little pool of shadow was surrounded. She was a bit like Dick in that way, she liked to reflect properly before reaching a decision.

"You'll have to give it to me," she said.

"Give you what?"

"The shell that's larger than a clam."

"I never said that! All I said was, clams haven't got the biggest shells."

"How can I tell there's something bigger unless you give it to me?"

"Oh, come on, Rose, use your nut. It's obvious."

"If it's so obvious why don't you tell me?"

"We saw some yesterday. On their backs, waving their feet . . ."

Turtles! They had indeed seen some, helpless and protesting with waving flippers at the fury of the sun which was torturing their exposed bellies as they lay on their backs in an open lorry. They were being taken to the fish market in torment, dying in pain and indignity. Dick's mother had rushed up to the lorry and argued with the native driver who'd stared at her blankly as if she'd been a lunatic; it was no use, Bob Heron had told her, there was no law about it. Dick had felt rather sick, looking at the turtles, but realized that he'd never have thought about their sufferings if his mother hadn't kicked up a fuss and that his father was right, really; it was something that had always gone on.

Rose flushed to a lobster pink under her freckles; her light brown eyes, sherry-coloured, filled with tears.

"That's cheating! Turtles aren't fish."

"Who said anything about fish?"

"It doesn't count! It doesn't count! It's not fair."

Dick grinned with a great feeling of superiority. Girls not only tried to shift and jink and break their bargains but they couldn't even lose decently. He held out his hand.

"It's not a bad little collection of cowries. I'll let you keep one. Just to show there's no ill-feeling." This was a phrase his father often used.

Rose burst into tears and made off across the sand, calling him all sorts of names. Dick followed reluctantly, half contemptuous and half uneasy. He found her splashing in a shallow pool among the rocks. Her hair was tumbled round her shoulders in a mop and for some reason this increased Dick's discomfiture. It made her look wild and yet defenseless. Her legs were long and slender and dappled as a gull's egg. He stood there awkwardly supposing that he ought to apologize but fiercely resenting the injustice. After all, he was in the right. She splashed about without looking at him. He said at last:

"I was only joking. I don't want your cowries."

"You won them." Rose spoke in a stifled voice. *"You'll have to take them, they're yours."*

"I tell you I don't want them. It was only a joke."

"I shall sell them and buy you a knife."

"Oh, for Christ's sake!" Dick exploded. *"Leave it alone, can't you, Rose?"*

"Now you're swearing."

"It's not swearing. It's blaspheming actually, only I don't believe you can blaspheme unless you mean to insult God, and you can't think that unless you believe in Him."

"Don't you believe in God?"

"Not like that."

But Rose appeared indifferent to theology, which at the

*time—he was sixteen—had suddenly become of interest to
Dick. She said gruffly:*

*"As you won the bet, it's cheating if you don't take the
shells."*

"Oh, forget it, will you, Rose?"

*A fishing boat was edging a way along the reef to find a
gap; it rocked jumpily when it approached the coral bar-
rier. Two men were standing up, one looking intently
ahead to spot the passage, the other with a hand on the
tiller—brown or black, he couldn't see. Seaweed lay across
the rocks like long, coarse strands of hair, the combings of
some unimaginably great sea monster; when they had
dried, and were hard and brittle, Dick enjoyed pressing his
thumb into the raised pustules that covered each filament,
to hear the little pops they gave as they burst.*

*The boat had found the opening, the gate the fisherman
called it, and was nothing now but a black speck out towards the horizon. Dick suddenly felt himself to be one
with the fishermen in that boat, with the questing gulls,
with the hidden kingfish that ranged out far beyond the reef
towards India, and the clouds that would be drawn towards
the sun when it reddened for the setting, and the wind that
would awake later to lash the palm fronds and whiten the
crests of the waves. It was an extraordinary feeling of freedom and happiness that he'd never before experienced, and
he looked across at Rose wanting to share it yet knowing it
quite beyond words.*

*She was sitting on a rock staring down into the pool, her
face shielded by fuzzy hair falling over her cheeks, motionless as a carved figure. An emotion for which he was quite
unprepared and could not possibly have identified shook
Dick like a wave smacking against the sand. It was her look
of being vulnerable that shook him, though he was ignorant
of the word, and thought only that he wanted somehow to
catch and hold her attention, to explain to her this surge of*

feeling, this sense of power and freedom, but knew it was impossible, there weren't any words. And all this, the sun striking at a particular angle over low hills inland, the burnished sea, the swooping gulls, the pool and the sea-weed ropes and the warm, soupy water nibbling at his toes, and the girl on a rock staring into the pool—all this would vanish and disintegrate and be totally expunged; he'd leave this place, and so would she, and no one would remember them; this moment that held so much within it, like a seed, would have no existence, no reality. And he wanted with all his heart to hold this moment as it was and keep it for-ever, perfect, eternal, intense; somehow to preserve it as one could a butterfly or bird's egg, somehow to embalm its beauty and to hold off change and disruption and the ob-livion which lay all about them, threatening, advancing, edged with despair.

He called out to her in a voice that sounded in his own ears dry and brittle:

"Rose!"

She looked up and with a brown hand pushed the hair back from her eyes: the sun fell on her face and made her half-close her eyelids and seem almost to flinch from the rays.

He could think of nothing to say. They looked at each other for a moment across the pool and he felt a tightness in all his muscles as if he were being wound up like a watch, and a dryness in his throat, and an impossible mixture of happiness and despair, confidence and baffle-ment.

Whether Rose understood this or knew nothing of it all, whether she had an inkling of the urgency and desperation of his need to preserve the moment, whether she had even seen the fishing boat or heard the gulls or cared a cent for any of it—all this was a mystery. And it disturbed, tor-mented and infuriated him, this mystery that he couldn't *even define; he felt as if he had been swept out far beyond the reef into an ocean with no land, no rocks, nothing to cling to, only the unknown and terrible waters of infinity.*

Something made Rose look round; three figures were scurrying towards them over the white sand.

"I expect they're coming to fetch us," she said.

The moment was disintegrating, vanishing like a soap-bubble that was there and then was not, and in a last effort to hold it he jumped up and ran round to stand beside Rose, and stretch out a hand to touch her shoulder. Her skin was smooth and warm as a mango fruit twisted off a twig on the tree. He felt the slight abrasion of sand sticking to his palm, and the swell of a great compassion engulfed him, a wish to stand between her and all the coming threats to her innocence, as if she were one of those soft, creamy-coloured, curled-up mollusks that lay snugly in the whorled armour of its shell and writhed helplessly when, with un-thinking brutality, someone yanked it out with a penknife.

She jumped up without a word, throwing off his arm, and ran to meet the children, who had come with a message about tea.

Later, in the bungalow, Rose brought him a single, shiny cowrie shell and said brusquely: "If you won't take the whole collection you'd better have one. A sort of token."

Dick saw that she had absolutely made up her mind— she was bossy. So he said: "Well, all right, thanks, Rose," and put it in his pocket. "It's the best one," she added. "There's Emma calling." She smelt of sea and sand and coconut oil. That evening, he put the cowrie on the table by his camp bed and made a silent promise. He knew it was corny while he made it, sloppy, the sort of silly promise he'd made when he'd been an enthusiastic boy scout.

"I'll keep it till I die."

When he had married Rose twelve years later he still had the cowrie and now it was in his drawer at Mrs. Harris's, in a little cardboard box. But Hughie's angel fish had died one by one, and of course they'd never bred. By that time Hughie had lost interest and it was Dick who had fed them, watched them die and thrown into the river their limp bodies whose brilliant colours had faded to a drab, mottled kind of grey.

chapter 13

THREE QUARTERS of a moon spread over the outskirts of Horsington a mazy light drained of colour, and gave to the detached bungalows and houses, which thinned as Dick and Julia ran out of the town, a look of broody hens squatting watchfully, even defiantly, each in its own little plot, each keeping a proper distance from its neighbour. On the brow of the rise a gate led into Bagley wood and here Julia stopped the car and said:

"There's a flask in that pocket. Let's have a drink."

Dick opened the glove compartment and found a hunting flask with a pigskin cover, the kind of thing advertised for men's Christmas presents in glossy magazines and elaborate catalogues issued by expensive stores.

"I don't know that I want anything," he said.

"You've gone a million miles away."

A curious lethargy had come over him. In Buckle's absence, and despite all his resolutions, his sense of urgency had slackened. Between the sighting of the quarry and the sighting of the gun you always struck this dull, dead patch, you had to plod forward with nothing to focus on and no danger, trusting to your instinct and experience to pick the right path.

And now there was Julia, a disconcerting complication. He ought to hate her because she was a part of Buckle, part corrupt. He ought to use her because she was a weapon put into his hands. But he found his mind wandering, his purpose wavering, debilitating hopes and fears creeping like threads of fungus into his resolve. To brace himself he drank from the flask and handed it over. Julia said:

"I don't like whisky much."

"Why drink it, then?"

"That's a silly question. The effect, of course."

"That's a silly answer, isn't it?"

She tilted her head back against the seat to drink from the flash. The faint outline of her neck, pale against the darkness, at once excited Dick and touched a nerve of pity. Her gesture struck him as one of absolute confidence. He'd only to reach out and, with his two hands, extinguish her life as easily as he had once popped seaweed nodules, or could obliterate a gnat. He'd come for revenge: here was the means, offering itself without reserve: a deeper, a more lasting, satisfactory revenge than a simple bullet through her father's head.

He felt Julia's leg touching his, then the light of an approaching car shone on her neck, the chin upturned and on the narrow nose with its slightly flared nostrils, the smooth young brow and swept-back hair. She looked a child only. He moved his hands on his lap. To use them would be merciful: life held more pain than joy, to die young was a privilege.

The car went by and Julia said:

"You've got something against Peter, haven't you?"

Dick took back the flask and drank to give himself time. Now he was prickly with suspicion, her nearness was an irritant to his taut nerves. She was trying to pump him, probably the whole evening had been designed to lead up to this. She went on without waiting for an answer:

"Of course, he's pompous at times, I expect all politicians are, but funnily enough I think he really does believe in what he's doing. Not that I know what that is most of the time, but he does, I suppose. I daresay it isn't always what he'd like to do, it's what he has to."

The neat whisky had stung its way down Dick's throat, making his nose prickle, and was lying warmly on his stomach, generating comfort and a pleasurable feeling of recklessness. He put his hand on her thigh and her leg was still touching his.

"He made his own way, you know." There was even a note of pride in her voice. "He wasn't born into the so-called Establishment. Not working class either, which he could have used politically—lower middle, the worst of both worlds. His father was a salesman or something, who more or less deserted his mother and he left school I think at fourteen. In the Midlands somewhere. I can't remember what happened next, a clerk or something, but anyway he worked like mad and got himself called to the bar, like one of those success stories in magazines where you start delivering newspapers. That's why he's spoiled Martin so."

"Do you really want to marry Evan?"

"I don't know."

"It wouldn't work."

"We might make it."

Dick laughed. "We all think we can change people but we can't. All one can do is get used to them and that means changing oneself."

"You might change me, Dick."

"You're nice enough as you are."

Did that sound as trite and shallow to her as to him? Machine-turned. Even while he felt for her hardening nipples and pressed her lips open he was reserving the one thing that mattered, his true surrender. Hatred's shadow fell across the motions of love: she was to be a means to

an end and the end was not love but power. Here was his
revenge, or a part of it, in the warm embrace of this girl
Buckle had created, now defenseless in his arms. For on
her side she laid herself open to his passion as the thirsty
earth invites the rain and revelled in her sensual enjoyment.

And so, after the climax, he couldn't hold back a cleans-
ing wave of tenderness and gratitude that swept towards
those secret places of his heart where the sores festered. He
drew back, rattled by the headlights of a car which suddenly lit up their dishevelled forms as if in a crude black-
and-white negative.

"A car's a hell of a place for this," he said harshly. She
didn't answer, burying her face in his chest.

He was still fighting the wave. "Give me a bed any time.
And another thing. Look, Julia, I'm sorry but I wasn't ex-
pecting—I didn't come prepared—"

Julia disentangled and reorganized herself, fumbling for
a cigarette. "Don't worry, I did, and was."

If she had wanted to shock him, she'd at last almost
succeeded. At the same time he knew this was silly; to girls
like Julia sex was little more than a routine, like a good
bottle of wine or an enjoyable party. And she was right,
what more should it be? Yet he was shocked all the same.
Out-of-date morals and square-toed shoes. He was also
grateful: she'd helped him to fight the wave, hold back the
tenderness. She was using him just as much as he was using
her, if for a different purpose: fifty-fifty. Just as he'd
worked this out, she disconcerted him by saying:

"Don't be shocked, Dick. It isn't everyone. There's been
this between us from the start, hasn't there?"

"I don't know."

"Well, don't sound so mournful. It's supposed to be fun.
It is, too. Only rather exhausting. Give me another go at
the whisky and then we'll go home to bed. Separately."

The Harris cottage stood back a little distance from the village street. Slits of light emerged from the curtained windows of the kitchen. Dick explained:

"If they leave the door unlocked for me, they keep the light on to discourage burglars. Mrs. Harris locks the door even when she goes round to the butcher's. Larkinglass might be a nest of criminals."

"It makes life seem more exciting."

"Do you think Mrs. Harris wants an exciting life?"

"Of course, everyone does. That's why she makes up such tremendous dramas."

Julia stopped the car but not the engine and he got out, thinking how all that had happened had left no trace and perhaps it hadn't happened at all; perhaps he'd dreamt it. Could everything have been an illusion? One of those erotic daydreams he'd read of, all over in a flash, an hallucination? Threads of unease, almost of panic, plucked at his mind. The boundary between reality and imagination had been growing more and more blurred. He lived in two worlds and now and again, round the edges, the worlds met and exchanged experiences—a sort of osmosis.

"Good night. And thank you, if that's the right thing to say."

"Thank *you*." Her voice was ironic.

"Shall I see you again?"

"Do you want to?"

"Of course. Do you think that now . . ."

"You make it very hard for people to know what to think."

"I just don't believe my private life, such as it is, is of any interest to others."

"Look, Dick, I didn't drag you out tonight to probe into your private life, but you know you can't just perch in a village like this without exciting a certain amount of curiosity."

"There isn't any mystery."

"If there is, Pendlebury will dig it out."

"Pendlebury?" Dick tried to keep his voice level but it was a tone higher, he felt a mounting alarm.

"Peter's security officer."

"You mean a sort of bodyguard?"

"No, we don't go in for that here. Bodyguards are strictly for foreigners. But since Peter had his present job he's got various threatening letters and things. He doesn't take them seriously himself but Pendlebury's supposed to look into them."

"Fair enough."

"Most of the letter writers turn out to be sex maniacs or else dusky students who've failed their O levels and blame it on Peter. I'm telling you this because I expect Pendlebury's been checking on you."

"Well, I passed my O levels." Dick slammed the car door and kept his hand for a moment on the half-open window, his eyes on the glow of her cigarette and the paleness where her face was.

"When shall I see you?"

"I expect I'll be around. Good night."

She let in the clutch and the car moved forward. He watched its retreating rear lamps winking in the dark, quickly getting smaller.

When he went upstairs to his room, he switched off the light and stood for a while at his window looking out at silvery fields, glinting telegraph wires, the dark shapes of trees and henhouses and the white hump of a neighbour's car wrapped in a silver plastic sheet. A bird flapped in a tree and a cat slunk across the paddock with its tail down. Everything combined to make him uneasy.

He was putting away his suit when he noticed that the coat hangers had been shifted along the piece of cord from which they were suspended. And he thought his shoes had been moved. Probably Mrs. Harris had been tidying round. Or could the unseen Pendlebury . . .

He groped in the back of a top drawer under his handkerchiefs. The single cowrie shell was there, in its cardboard box. Had the box been disturbed? He rather thought so, but couldn't be sure.

He took the cowrie out and it gleamed in his hand, speckled and shiny, magically retaining the ghostly whisper of a lost sea.

A muttering at the back of his head, a thrumming like the jostling waves, was gathering strength and moving slowly towards the conscious part of his brain. He clenched his teeth and dug his nails into his palms to reinforce his struggle against the familiar rising feeling of panic. Disconnected, senseless pictures started to flicker behind his eyes.

The sea muttering gradually changed into the whine of a circular saw. Dick threw the cowrie as hard as he could out of the window, aiming at the pond. He thought he saw a silver flash in the moonlight before he screwed up his eyes and threw himself face downwards on the bed. The sickness and terror passed and in the end he slept, but then he had his worst dream of all. He dreamt that he was taken to pieces, bit by bit. Everything was unscrewed and unwound and lay there, like dismantled machinery, only red and raw: eyes, teeth, kidneys, lungs, testicles, everything, all separate, lying on a sort of bench or table with a speckled surface like a shell. Vultures hunched in corners stretched out turkey-red, filthy necks and somewhere his mother was standing, he couldn't see her, but she kept repeating "Hughie has the key."

Rose was calling out for help but he couldn't reach her.

chapter 14

It was dark now when Dick went to fetch the cows, dark and wet, either because of actual rain coming down gently, almost with apologies, or because of mist that smothered everything in a soft, indefinite, clammy kind of cotton wool.

In this mist the cows vanished like ships lost at sea and Dick had to search through a dripping darkness that yet wasn't wholly dark. When he came upon them, guided by faint sounds of grasses being cropped by rough tongues and the sucking of hoofs extracted from mud, they loomed out of the mist like black hulks, legless it seemed, immobile, as if he had encountered a fleet of abandoned vessels drifting upon an ocean unruffled by the smallest wave.

Darkness was fading that particular morning as Dick escorted the cows into the yard. Each day he breathed with pleasure their fresh, clean, sweet aroma, resting one hand on the flank of the rear guard beast to feel the quiver of her soft, supple skin. The smell of earth, of air, of trees, of everything here, was different from the smells that he was used to, but the cow was the same.

Rodney King's milking parlour was like a hospital with

its rows of gauges and indicators, its antiseptic smell, its swilled-down cleanliness, its multiplicity of rubber tubes. And his punctuality was almost fanatical. At five-thirty precisely he would press a button, the machine's pulsators would start to throb and the first cows in the milking order, lined up on raised platforms with their udders already washed, would feel the cups grip their teats and the squeeze of the rubber linings.

Rodney never hurried and never raised his voice or made a sudden motion—unless a cow with a sore udder lashed out at him, when he would move with a ballet dancer's speed. He knew at once if a cow had a sluggish appetite or an uncomfortable udder, or if she was coming on to bull, or if the rhythm of one of the pulsators was not quite true. A network of awareness below the threshold of the ordinary senses seemed to unite Rodney with the cows, so that he felt their discomforts in his own nerves, shared their feelings, registered their mute protests.

He was putting the machine together in the dairy in his white coat, a clean one every morning, when Dick ushered in the first six cows, who jumped with agility on to their respective raised stalls in search of a breakfast of dairy nuts released into the crib by a lever from the hoppers.

Rodney came in with a milking bucket in each hand, and Dick squatted down to fix the cups to the cow's udders, feeling a little tug as the suction caught hold and pressing his forehead into the cow's soft, sweet-smelling flank to hear a gentle rumble from coiled guts inside as she digested her night's meal, and the soft plop of moist dung, neither too hard nor too loose, as it fell steaming into the gutter— sweet-smelling, too, nothing but grass in another form. Milking was a peaceful time, well organized, combining the comfort of routine with the unexpectedness of all living creatures—you never knew what each cow would be up to next.

Rodney nodded, his eyes on his charges. "Nice morning." It was always a nice morning if it wasn't actually pelting or blowing a force nine gale.

"Bit of a drizzle."

"Won't do any harm."

"Petronella's bulling."

"Always makes a song and dance, Petronella."

"She's a good milker."

"Nearly lost her last time. She came down with magnesium deficiency."

"One gets a lot of trouble," Dick said.

"Females. What do you expect?" Rodney grinned, massaging the rear of a big, stiff udder so full and heavy it looked like bursting.

"A bit light on one quarter?"

"Nature's not out of it yet."

Dick pressed his hand on a cluster of milking cups to strip the udder, removed the cups and released the first cow, who advanced in a stately and decorous fashion to another yard to make way for the next.

"How's Bert getting on?"

"Not too bad. Back in ten days, most likely."

Now it was Rodney's turn to release a cow, install another, wash her mud-stained udder with steaming disinfected water and slip on the throbbing cups. He added:

"You'll be pushing off next."

"That's right."

"You ought to stay."

It was foolish, Dick supposed, to feel pleased, but he did. Rodney's standards were so high that very few men or women measured up to them. At least he could handle cows, that was something, and the fact that they were Buckle's cows provided a sardonic amusement. But neither he nor Rodney thought much about their ownership. So far as Rodney was concerned, they were *his* cows, and no one dreamed of interfering.

Buckle would be back in just over a week and Dick knew that he would be getting his cards. So when Jim Tompkins invited him in for a spot of breakfast before starting the milk round he knew what to expect. Mrs. Tompkins was as tidy and fastidious in her home as Rodney in his dairy and Dick felt as clumsy as a bear when he entered, and conscious that he smelt of cow. In the front parlour plastic daffodils and tulips, regularly washed, stood on a polished table, there was a menagerie of elongated and distorted glass animals on the mantel shelf and many little mats about the place; a veneered cocktail cabinet, Impressionist prints and china ducks on the walls.

After they'd eaten and Mrs. Tompkins had withdrawn to do the washing up, Tompkins lit a cigarette and began:

"Well, Dick, there's just a couple of things. First of all this milk round. I've got to get it sorted out before the boss returns."

"You mean the bad debts."

"That's right. After tomorrow, no one gets delivery unless they've paid. You'll have to shove mud in your ears if they try any hard-luck stories."

"It's no concern of mine. Although old Colonel Crozier . . ."

"Well, there you are. Worst of a place like this is, it's too personal."

"Aside from the Colonel, there's only the Belchers and the Ryans who've got right behind."

"That's another thing," Tompkins said, none too happily. "The Ryans are to run on for a bit."

"You mean owing money? But they're the only ones who can afford to pay up on their heads."

"They've got a couple of small kids," Tompkins spoke defensively.

"And Mrs. Crozier's an invalid."

"Well, theirs not to reason why, old man. Boss's orders."

"Ryan's a shop steward or something at the factory, isn't he?"

"Look, Dick, what Ryan does for a living isn't our affair. You're not to stop deliveries but try to collect what you can tomorrow on account, see? You and I are paid to do as we're told."

"That's not a fashionable point of view."

"You're bloody right there," Tompkins agreed, bending down to rub a foot that had a touch of cramp. He belched slightly and said: "I oughtn't to have had chips *and* sausages. Now the other thing is, you know the boss doesn't want to see your ugly mug around when he gets back from his palm beaches and cannibals and things. It's a bloody shame, I wish you hadn't got the gaffer's back up, I must say."

"The summer's over." Dick looked down at his hands. "I'm a casual anyway."

Tompkins grinned and prodded Dick's arm.

"Trouble is, my lad, you've been a bit too much of a hit. Roving eye of boss's daughter alights on handsome farm hand, that sort of thing. Not that anyone'd blame you, old man. Still, there it is—I'm sorry."

Dick was touched by Jim Tompkins's embarrassment.

"Don't worry, I'm moving on. It suits me, anyway."

"It doesn't suit me but that doesn't count, naturally. Got to do as I'm told. So long as you know it's not my idea."

"I know that."

"Got any plans?"

"I thought I'd stay on at Mrs. Harris's for a week or so."

Tompkins pulled at his moustache and looked cagey. "The boss won't like that."

"He can sack me but I don't think he can turn me out of the village."

"That's true enough. Well, it's your business, Dick, but if you don't mind a word from a well-wisher, I don't think you'll be doing any good here either to yourself or anyone else. I mean, that sort of thing never leads to anything but complications, does it? No offense, I hope."

"I'm not after Julia Buckle, if that's what you mean."

Tompkins laughed rather too noisily. "She might be after you, eh, old man? That's about the size of it."

"Don't turn my head." Dick forced a smile. "I'll move on."

"I think you'll be doing the right thing." Tompkins got up. "Matter of fact, there's a fellow the other side of Horsington been inquiring after you. Wants a good man and your fame's spread. Bloke by the name of Tyndall, farms a couple of thousand acres and has the best shooting round about. That's what the boss is hurrying back for, between ourselves, doesn't want to miss the opening shoot on Saturday. I daresay Tyndall would fix you up with some decent lodgings."

"Thanks." Dick got up too, and folded his napkin. "I'll think it over."

chapter 15

Buckle looked pleased with himself as he climbed out of his Land Rover that Saturday of the opening shoot; apparently the conference had gone well. Or so, at any rate, the newspapers had decided, and a television interview the night before. It was not quite clear what had been settled, except another interest-free loan, but there'd been an agreed communiqué and despite a lot of sabre rattling, no one had left the Commonwealth.

Martin was with him, dressed for the part in a tweed jacket and breeches and a green porkpie hat with salmon flies stuck in the ribbon. Dick could scarcely imagine Martin as a proficient shot, but then this scarcely ranked as sport in his opinion. The pheasants had been bred like chickens under hens and then in coops, the beaters often had a job to make them rise. The guns stood in rows like people in a spaced-out bus queue, while the birds were driven over them and dogs and beaters did all the work—about as invigorating as a game of dominoes.

They had gathered at one of Tyndall's farms up on the downs in a fine drizzle—a good day, the beaters said, not too much wind. In the yard, dogs sniffed at trousers and

were called to heel. Dick kept his back to the Minister and
his raincoat collar turned up. He was a grey-brown figure
like the rest of the beaters, colourless, damp, with a stick in
his hand, ready to move off when Tyndall gave the word.
Tyndall was talking now to his important guest and Buckle
was apologizing with a gay smile.

". . . Cabinet papers at the last moment," Dick heard as
he slouched by with an old man called Herby. "No nonsense about a five-day week for farmers and politicians but
I wasn't going to miss . . ."

Tyndall was a big man, heavy and slow-moving but
clothed in a quiet authority. Under shaggy brows his quick
blue eyes took in everything—a gatepost dislodged by an
implement, a leaking ball cock, a heifer bulling out in a
field. His little empire he had built up gradually over a
lifetime, starting at thirteen as a carter's boy and then rent-
ing a five-acre field. Now he was the biggest farmer round
about and had the best shooting; he sat on committees and
people deferred to him and came to ask his views from
newspapers and television studios.

" 'Mazing old bugger," Dick's companion commented.
"Past seventy. Brings down them birds like he was knock-
ing apples out of trees. 'Mazing old bugger."

Herby himself couldn't have been much younger than
Tyndall—older perhaps, there was no way of knowing with
these countrymen, they looked the same from about forty
on with their lined, roughened faces, complexions pasty
from a diet of bread and margarine, their slow deliberate
movements.

"You come from these parts?"

"I've been working for Mr. Buckle but I finished yesterday."

"Buckle, eh. Plenty of money spent down there from
what they say."

"Doesn't throw it around," Dick said with a smile.

"Rich folks never do. Wouldn't be rich if they did, would they? Stands to reason. Buckle, at election times he comes round full of promises as a churchyard's full of worms. Don't see no more of him arter that, not till 'lections comes round again. Got no lunch, mate? You can have a bit of mine and welcome."

Dick declined. Mrs. Harris had put him up some sandwiches but he wasn't hungry. He felt as if someone had tied a tight knot in his insides and he was afraid his bowels might play him up. This was how he always felt at the start of a hunt.

"What about his politics?" Talking was like a curtain drawn across a stage while someone out in front held the audience with his patter, allowing the scene to be set for the real performance.

"Politics?" Herby was munching bread and cheese and spoke indistinctly. "Don't set much store by politics. My father voted Liberal. Reared nine of us, our mother did; and the wages wasn't never above fifteen shillings. We was glad to get a penny opening the gate on the common I can tell you, or sixpence from the drover taking beasts to market. But for all them big wages they get these days, I don't reckon these youngsters is better off. Twopence a loaf in them days, beer a penny and baccy threepence, now it's five shilling near enough, and the coal's gone to 'leven shilling. . . ."

"I mean, say, about Africa." Dick got in. The old man's views didn't really interest him but he knew now from experience that anyone who got started on the cost of living must be headed off, or he wouldn't draw breath for twenty minutes.

Herby carefully folded his paper bag, returned it to his pocket and wiped his fingers on a crumpled handkerchief. "Africa? They'm a lot of savages out there, that's what it is. Savages."

"Not now they're being educated."

"Ah. Educated." Herby pushed back his greasy hat: underneath he was bald as an egg. "My father, he bred canaries. Dozens of 'em there was, us couldn't move but knock up against cages. Used to sell 'em to a man came round with a shop over Bristol way."

The dogs were whining and wagging their tails, the beaters starting to move towards the gate, sticks in hand.

"There was fellows in the trade, used to catch gold-finches and smart 'em up a bit and pass the buggers off as canaries. The real canaries, they'd fetch half a sovereign. These goldfinches, they was worth a shilling. Came off nicely, the dealers did."

"But the goldfinches couldn't sing," Dick objected.

"That's it, a'nt it? That's what I'm saying. Buggers couldn't sing." He left it at that.

They moved out of the yard and up a lane, slithering in and out of muddy ruts. The grass bent under the weight of moisture, everything was still and heavy.

Dick felt the gun's hardness against his thigh. His feet were cold and he was sweating under the armpits; in some extraordinary way it managed to be hot and cold at the same time. His boots became immensely heavy, clogged with great lumps of thick yellow clay. Through a gap he saw sheep staring with long, blank faces. Hawthorn berries in the high hedges glistened like drops of blood, ash pods hung down in limp, yellowish-green clusters.

"Bloody wet in them roots," a fellow beater remarked as they trudged along.

They fanned out across a stubble field that sloped down to a dip. More stubble rose the other side and prickled up a gentle slope towards a blurred horizon. Here the downland lay in fine, open sweeps but Dick was amazed by the scale to which he couldn't grow accustomed—the smallness of everything. What people called a valley was just a fold in the landscape, hills were mounds that rose fifty feet, at most a hundred.

"Cock up, m'lord! Cock up, m'lord!" The cry rang across the stubbles, sharp and raucous. All the beaters took up this hollering cry, traditional as the "rhubarb" of actors. Dick couldn't help laughing as he joined in—even the beaters' call had ambiguous undertones, you could give it several meanings or none, as you pleased.

A covey of partridges whirred away to the left where the guns were stationed along the edge of a wood. A fusillade brought some down, others zoomed up and skimmed safely over the wood. Voices called to dogs while the beaters moved on steadily, swinging round to encompass the dip. The stubble was at once soggy and stiff, and a lot of dwarf daisies were growing amongst it, white against the brown earth.

"Cock up, m'lord! Cock up, m'lord!" With a whirring clatter a brace of pheasants took off cumbrously from under Dick's feet; they flew right-handed, down the line of beaters and away from the guns.

"They'll have them buggers," old Herby promised.

Dick was trying to keep Buckle in view, though it was hard to see which gun was which, they were all dressed alike. Buckle's hat looked a bit darker than the others and his dog was liver-coloured with white patches. He was somewhere in the middle of the line of guns, next to Tyndall. Dick had no worked-out plan. For one thing, the birds directed the movements of the guns; for another, his belief that he was working to a pattern, that events were moving him, not he them, had possessed him as strongly as ever since Buckle had returned. This damp air, he believed, that seeped into his lungs would be the last he would breathe. His body would lie limp and crumpled, like the pheasants, on these dank and slippery stubbles before the light faded and the others went back to their spitting fires, their dry clothes, their hot tea.

"Me feet's bloody cold," Herby complained. "You're a bit far over, mate. Dunno where the bloody birds is got to. Gives anyone a thirst, this hollering do."

Dick moved out to keep the spacing even, feeling his gun against his thigh, and allowing his thoughts to slip back into the sunlight, giving them a little freedom since this would be their last chance. It was a risk, but this was a day when all risks might be taken. Half-remembered words throbbed in his mind: to everything there is a season and a time to every purpose under the heaven; a time to be born and time to die; a time to plant and time to pluck up that which is planted; a time to kill and a time to heal. A time also to remember, if memories could be kept out in the open in the sunshine, which now, in his mind's eye, poured down on an almost shadeless park.

The trees were still only about fifteen feet high; in another ten years the showground would be pleasantly shaded by the grouped plantations and avenues.

Dick had fixed a red rosette in the halter of the heifer Kestrel's Marigold and was heading the procession round the ring. There was a ragged burst of clapping as he passed the stand, like a flower bed with all the women in bright, printed flowery frocks. Someone shouted: "Well done, Dick," and he glowed with pleasure; dust and the sharp, clean smell of cow tickled his nostrils, his white coat was clean and starched; the sun was on his bare head and filled his body like wine poured into a glass.

Marigold was back in her stall, swishing her tail and refusing hay or water, she was too worked up. He stood scratching her ears and there was Rose at his side. Rose had been south for training and now she was teaching in the little town thirty miles away. She was the same but different: the adolescent awkwardness had gone, her hair —still fuzzy—was shaped into a kind of halo with the sun shining through it, a reddish gold. Her face was freckled still, but it was the face of a woman, not a child. For the second time in his life he felt awkward with Rose.

"You've taken over the farm, I hear," *she said.*

"More or less."

"I'm terribly sorry your father . . ."

"It's pretty awful for him, you know how he's always done everything himself. And now stuck in that chair."

His father was virtually paralyzed and getting worse: a kind of arthritis had seized him suddenly, a long-delayed result (the doctors said) of war injuries, and they knew no cure.

"I suppose one could say it's lucky, in a way, you were able to take things over."

Dick wanted to tell her about the feeling that was fretting at his peace of mind. All his life the farm had been his passion; to own animals, to care for land. It wasn't enough to work on someone else's farm, he needed to possess the land and shape it as he wished, to breed his own herd according to ideas he'd worked out, clear and definite. But there was no money, barely enough to develop the farm his father had bought very cheap thirty years before, although they'd ploughed back into it everything they'd ever earned.

People said that if you wanted something badly enough you always got it in the end. He'd wanted a farm very badly and now he had it, and his father was stuck for the rest of his life in a wheel chair, companioned by pain. Fate was perverse and had granted his wish at the cost of his father. He was to blame. Dick knew this was absurd, yet he couldn't extirpate a sense of guilt. Would Rose understand? While he hesitated, she asked:

"What's Hughie doing now?"

"Hughie." *Dick grinned. People often smiled when Hughie's name was mentioned.* "You heard he got himself into a whaling fleet last year? Now he's back, learning to fly. He wants to be a pilot."

"He's rather at that stage, I suppose."

"Yes, he's only twenty. I expect he'll settle down."

Rose laughed. "You sound very elder-brotherly."

"Oh, I'm the steady one."

Dick looked at Rose and felt almost dazzled—the sun at her back, the red-gold halo and a blue dress.

Can one ever say of a pinprick of time—this was when such and such a decision was made? Passing time blurred everything; but this, Dick believed, was the moment when his mind and body, acting together, had decided not only that he loved Rose but that no love had ever been like this before, of this magnitude and certainly a surrender as total as the earth's when the morning sun flooded the sky: a love that could never change. For him all time, all the planet's revolutions, the slow emergence of life and the spinning aeons had led to this moment, and nothing could alter it. His hand kneaded his heifer's silky shoulder and he smelt the sweetness of her hay-laden breath. He wanted to say to Rose—take Marigold, she's yours, she's the best I've got and she's yours. Instead he said in a dry voice:

"What about this dance tonight, are you going?"

"I said I'd baby-sit for the Cronjes."

"You're the one who ought to go, not the Cronjes. There'll be lots of old friends."

"I've more or less promised now."

"Couldn't you find someone else?"

He looked at her so intently that she flushed a little and laughed to hide her nervousness. "I don't know. I'll see."

"Well, do. Or let the Cronjes mind their own kids."

"They hardly ever go out, Dick. Anyway I've promised."

"But you'll try."

"All right, I'll try."

She laughed at him a little, he supposed because he looked as if it were a matter of life and death. After a drought, you could almost hear the earth singing, smell its *rapture as it bared itself to rain. He had the same feeling when he looked at Rose. Animals, birds, creatures of all kinds, Dick believed, and also the non-creatures, trees and crops and even earth and stones, all shared a single current of feeling. One force circulated and charged them with unity. When he shot a buck and heard it squeal and saw its tortured eyes, he knew that he had torn a small rent in this unity; yet it would heal over, it couldn't be destroyed. Now when he put out a hand to touch Rose's brown arm, warm from the sun, he felt with every nerve the strong compulsive force of this power that charged them both, and knew that he was following the path of the inevitable.*

"I'll stand you a Pepsi-Cola," was all he actually said.

chapter 16

At dinner time, around twelve-thirty, guns and beaters gathered in a cluster of farm buildings on top of a ridge. The sun was trying to shine behind a misty blanket, the drizzle having stopped, more or less. There was an empty house—one of Tyndall's, the farm it had served was run in with another and the disused, isolated building had begun to crumble away. The guns were to eat their lunch under its roof. Dick watched for his moment and, seeing Buckle pause to collect his dog and check over his cartridges, walked up to him, halted for a moment, but didn't speak.

Peter Buckle glanced up, recognized him and frowned, his face suddenly heavy, one hand checked in the cartridge bag. He stood immobile as a stubborn bullock while Dick turned away without speaking or glancing back. He'd felt a shock pass through Buckle, a shock of alarm, as clearly as you could feel the kick of an electric fence. It was just the effect he'd wanted. He doubted whether Buckle would enjoy his sandwiches.

Dick circled back to join the other beaters in an old barn and glanced round to see Buckle speaking to Tyndall. There was an air of urgency in Buckle's posture. Tyndall was looking over his shoulder at the beaters, most of whom had gone into the barn. When Dick had volunteered as a beater he'd applied to the keeper and Tyndall wouldn't know him by sight.

Dick didn't touch his sandwiches. The knot was getting tighter in his insides. Not much time left now—perhaps two hours. Two hours to oblivion. After dinner the beaters were to drive the wood and the guns would be standing in the open on the far side. That would bring the opportunity. Buckle was alerted but he couldn't take the measure of his own peril—he didn't even know his executioner was armed.

The wood was full of brambles which clung to raincoats with an animosity that seemed personal, they were spiteful brambles and tried to spring back into your face. There was a tangle of dead, tall-stemmed willow herb whose white down, like cotton lint, clung here and there to little semi-circular fibres, the skeletons of perished flowers, jutting out from the stalk. They looked metallic—like clusters of pig rings made of very fine wire. The green of the braken, wet and heavy, was just beginning to fade into a dull brown. These coarse fronds, matted with long black brambles, dead willow herb and whippy undergrowth, all soaked in moisture, created an effect of a profound, silent and time-less melancholy. Hard, half-wizened blackberries shone wetly among the leaves. On sapling oaks, green acorns were securely embedded in neat, smooth little cups.

It was hard going, in places Dick had to bash his way through a high wall of brambles. But they soon came out of it. Wildness, in England, was confined to little patches that only imitated jungles and forests, almost caricatured them —play acting again. The guns were ranged along the edge of the wood, pheasants came out like rockets and some plopped heavily on to sodden pasture, shedding a comet's tails of scattered feathers.

By now Dick could scarcely breathe, yet he was bashing through the brambles with extra vigour. Now and again he touched the gun lying snugly in his pocket. There'd be no mistake this time.

On the margin of the wood, the men were standing back a little in relaxed positions, smoking, patting dogs, swapping episodes and opinions. About forty yards away, Buckle stood talking to Martin who held a limp cock bird in his hand. His back was to the wood and he was lighting a cigarette.

The knot in Dick's insides hardened and tightened. Forty yards. He was going right up to the quarry, taking no risks. Sailing in: a ship of the line ramming another with her prow. But his step faltered as he took a deep breath to savour a valedictory smell of leaf mould, of moist earth, grass, air, spiced with a suggestion of the pungent scent of burning leaves. A good smell to have in your nostrils when you died. He walked briskly forward out from the trees.

Buckle still had his back turned but Martin began walking towards Dick with his gun over his arm, swinging the cock pheasant, whistling. Dick went on steadily, looking at the ground. Martin passed close to him and stopped.

"Hello, it's Dick, isn't it? Still watching the rich at play?"

Dick looked at him but saw only blurred features. His senses and his mind were solidified like cement and all outside sensations were bouncing off him.

"Rich-watching," Martin added. "We've had birds and fish, that might be the new sport. Are you all right? You look a bit green."

"I'm all right."

"Well, rather my job than yours." Martin nodded and walked on and then turned to look back at Dick, a little puzzled.

Dick put his hand in his pocket and gripped the gun and walked on quickly. Get it over.

Peter Buckle had the collar of his jacket turned up and a whiff of cigarette smoke drifted across—Turkish. His tweed cap was tilted at a bit of an angle, he stood with his legs a little apart in a self-confident posture, negligent, at ease. He put one hand up and gently, reflectively, scratched the back of his neck.

Dick pulled out the gun. Now it didn't matter whether anyone saw him. He'd call out Buckle's name and when the quarry turned he'd see the face of justice as the bullet hit him between the eyes. Now Dick was only four paces behind Buckle. On this green slope there would be an end to a long story, a rest from anguish, relief from loneliness, the circle would be joined.

Dick pulled out the gun and moved the safety catch and aimed at Buckle's head. The head would swing round as he called out. Then Buckle started to move away. Dick took another step, kept the gun steady and began to form the word, Buckle's name.

A blow caught him under the elbow, his arm jerked up and the gun went spinning out of his hand. Pain shot up his arm like a bee sting, the arm went numb, the gun lay there on the grass blackly; he lunged towards it but was barged aside, a figure bent towards the gun and whisked it up and turned and he was looking straight at Martin, who gave the gun a little toss and slipped it into his pocket. Dick's muscles felt as if they'd been knotted up with cramp. A red haze blurred everything.

"Are you mad or what?" Martin said.

Dick stood tense, awaiting the grip of hands he felt stretching out towards him from behind, from everywhere. He was encircled and they'd seize him and drag him apart.

"You'd better go home," Martin said.

A shiver went all through Dick's body and he felt icy cold. Now he couldn't stop shaking all over helplessly like a leaf in a storm. Summoning all his strength, he looked slowly round. Buckle was twenty or thirty paces away walking in the opposite direction. The beaters were moving off up the hill. Buckle's dog was bounding along after his master, sheep had lifted their heads to stare halfway up the slope, their soft bleats hung on the air. No one had seen: no one but Martin.

Dick took a step forward. He was still shaking and when he spoke his voice sounded high and thin like an old man's.

"My gun."

Martin was grinning. "Show me your licence, then." His voice was taunting: Dick said nothing, his hands hanging empty at his sides.

"I don't know what the game is," Martin added, "but anyway you've buggered it up and if I were you I'd go home." He was still grinning and looked excited, anticipatory, as if some new pleasure had been revealed, or a variant on an old theme. He wasn't big or muscular but he was wiry and had a kind of toughness that couldn't be ignored. Also he had the gun.

Nausea overwhelmed Dick, who turned and put his head down and walked away unsteadily, as if drunk, indifferent to his direction. Martin's voice came after him:

"We'll have a talk later on."

Saliva salted Dick's mouth, he felt like vomiting and everything was moving round, but he stumbled on, sweating. The wood brought him up short and he looked back. Martin had almost joined the others who were moving away downhill, brown blobs now on the silvery green. There was no stir, Dick was out of the picture like a satellite revolving endlessly round and round its parent, never making contact, neither getting closer nor drawing away. Martin had given no alarm and Buckle still didn't know he was being hunted.

chapter 17

"OBVIOUSLY the man's a lunatic," Peter Buckle said. He was sitting at his leather-topped pedestal writing desk, Chippendale with the original handles and one of the best pieces at Chaffins. It stood under the sash window and from it he could see over the terrace and sloping lawn, silvered now with late dew, towards the lake and the woods beyond, just beginning to turn.

"He seems a harmless one," Lavinia suggested. She visited his study by invitation only; they'd agreed to separate, so far as possible, his public from his private life. But this was Sunday morning when he liked to talk over family and household matters between breakfast and Tompkins's visit.

Buckle frowned. "The trouble is, according to Pendlebury's researches, his wife's death, coming on top of these other things, seems to have unhinged him."

"She committed suicide?"

Buckle prodded the papers on his desk as if they were in some way responsible. Hairs showed dark against a white hand, square nails were carefully trimmed, he smelt pleasantly of shaving lotion.

"He found her and cut the body down and all that. Hanged herself. They appear to have been very devoted. Before that, there was some business about a brother, a rather gruesome business, and then he got rather knocked about during the troubles out there. He—" Buckle paused, rubbed his neck and felt a cheek as if he suspected a faulty bit of shaving. Then he resumed:

"Heron was left with three small boys. He sold up everything for what he could get, not much I imagine, the kids went to a sister-in-law in South Africa and now here he is. The point is, why *here?*" Buckle lit a cigarette and watched a mallard land on the pond, braking with its wings. Beyond the pond, in the park, white gulls sat like lumps of chalk on a green pasture. "It's not a coincidence."

"I suppose not."

"It's inconceivable that he could blame me for his various troubles but of course that's just what these maniacs do, get crazy ideas into their heads, obsessions. That is, if he's really round the bend."

"He seemed quite a sane milkman, but of course why he's a milkman at all does seem a mystery. He hasn't threatened you, has he, Peter?"

"That's the part I can't make out. If he really came all this way to get his own back for some imaginary grievance, why does he just hang about and do nothing? In fact, the opposite, sign on in my employment and, according to Tompkins, work remarkably well?"

"It looks more as if he was grateful to you than angry."

Buckle inhaled the smoke and smiled. He had a selection of smiles, some suggesting good-fellowship and the sharing of manly jokes, others a more sardonic aspect of his nature. This one was wry and unrepentant.

"One has to do things that are bound to make one unpopular. One carries out government policy and if people get hurt, as of course they do sometimes, the Minister has to carry the can. It's part of the game, we all know that. In Heron's country my name stinks among a small minority."

"One can't make an omelette without breaking eggs."

"You have the *mot juste* as always, my dear."

"His eyes look odd sometimes."

"I thought he was drunk that evening after the fireworks, but I'm not sure now. He does odd things. For instance, he won a George Medal out there in one of those guerilla jobs, the lone wolf kind of thing that comes natural to that type of fellow. During the process he got his skull split open and a homemade bullet through the shoulder, and I daresay a bash on the head like that may have done some permanent damage the doctors didn't spot—they passed him fit afterwards. Mrs. Harris says he has dizzy spells sometimes, according to Pendlebury—whatever they are."

"It might be a good plan to interest Dr. Smith, rather than just move him on."

"Good God, he's perfectly hale and hearty!" Peter flared up like a turkey cock, Lavinia thought, gobbling, raising his red wattles, rattling an assertive tail. "I'm not his nursemaid, Vin, be reasonable. Tompkins says there's nothing wrong with him at all and as for dizzy spells, well, if every casual farm worker . . . Anyway, as I was saying, Heron duly got his gong and then, when at long last we'd signed the agreement ending the futile bloodshed and putting responsibility squarely on the nationalists to get down to governing the country—well then, he sent it back to the Queen, the gong I mean. Damned cheek, for one thing—showing off, a form of exhibitionism."

"Like T. E. Lawrence."

"There the resemblance ends. Not that I've much time for the Lawrence legend but at least he was a good archaeologist."

They sat in silence for a few moments, Lavinia perched on the arm of a leather-covered chair. She knew he wanted something from her or he wouldn't have asked her here: advice possibly, if he was unusually at sea, but more likely information of some kind, a bit of evidence. It was many years since they had talked things over companionably, without some other motive; he didn't value her opinion much now.

"You don't think he's come over as a sort of delegate, like David, to take you on in single combat on behalf of the friends he thinks you've let down?"

"That'd be too far-fetched even for Pendlebury, who enjoys thinking up all sorts of cloak-and-dagger plots to account for perfectly straightforward things. No, I think the most likely explanation is that he *is* a bit unhinged, he's got a bee in his bonnet about my being to blame, and came over with some half-baked notion of getting his own back. But when he got here his nerve failed, or else he just can't organize himself enough to *do* anything, it's all in his mind —I believe some of these psychopathic cases are like that. Or psychotic, which do I mean? Perhaps neither—off his rocker, anyway, we used to say."

Lavinia was gazing thoughtfully out of the window. "Walter's been burning the bean and pea haulms. It's a sad moment, isn't it? Although only symbolically now I suppose, a sort of hangover from the past, like superstitions and morris dancing. Nowadays it makes no gastronomic difference with the deep freeze."

Peter Buckle frowned and got up and stretched. That was just like Lavinia, he thought: she never concentrated very long, her mind darted about like a dragonfly, superficially attractive, but irresponsible. She wasn't taking seriously the possibility that his life was in danger—or, rather, she took too literally his own resolve to make light of the whole thing. But if he'd underlined the risk she'd have thought him pompous—he knew the signs, a little half-smile, and the way she pulled at her finger joints with the other hand. It was years since she'd been uncritical, even though she very seldom put her feelings into words. But now he could ignore all this and retain his self-confidence, he didn't really care. So, in an offhand way, he remarked:

"At any rate he doesn't seem to have any homemade plastic bombs tucked away among his underwear. Even a gun."

"I expect Mrs. Harris had a good look."

"So did Pendlebury. Anyway, he'll have to move on."

"Can you make him?"

"Not directly, I suppose, not from the village. It's a free country, still. But Tompkins has sacked him, rather reluctantly—he's a man after Rodney's heart, apparently—and I've had a word with Tyndall. He turned up yesterday with the beaters, this fellow Heron I mean. That was rather odd, too."

"What about the Harrises?"

"What about them?"

"You can't get him turned out, can you? A form of *droit de seigneur?*"

"Not if they want to keep him. But I rather doubt whether they do. And if Tompkins has a word with them in the light of Pendlebury's researches, they'll be even less keen."

"Pillar to post. Poor Dick."

"Poor Dick be damned!" Buckle swung round to glare at his wife, his arms at his side and his mouth a hard, bitter line. "You don't seem to realize he may be a dangerous schizophrenic. And my God, I should have thought *you* ought to be the one imploring me to get him moved on, not going sloppy over him as if he was a stray dog."

"Why should I want him moved on?"

She spoke very calmly and without raising her voice, looking down and smoothing her skirt over her knee.

"He's been messing about with Julia, hasn't he? Or trying to. His bloody cheek—"

Lavinia looked steadily over Peter's shoulders at a wisp of smoke curling up from the kitchen garden, where the bean and pea haulms were smouldering. After a short pause she said quietly:

"To be fair, I think it was Julia who made the running."

"All the more reason for getting him out of the way. I don't know what the hell's the matter with that child. Some times, though she is my own daughter, she seems to behave like a bitch on heat. Haven't you any control over her, Vin?"

"It's a sort of instinct, isn't it, to fly the nest at that age. The merest chirp out of mother and they flap their wings. I don't think any child really ought to live with its parents after it's eighteen."

"If you think that, you ought to want to see her married. But you seem against that too."

"I think Julia must decide."

"I thought she had decided, and quite frankly, Vin, I think you've done everything you can to put her against it. And I think that's a bloody selfish thing to do."

Lavinia raised her eyes to her husband's face and saw that it was slightly flushed and that he was breathing faster; his temper was like a kettle faintly singing before it came to the boil. She looked at him objectively, as one might watch a horse jumping fences, interested but not really minding terribly. At what point, she wondered, had she ceased to mind? To stop growing hot and fierce and miserable, or working out ways to soothe him, or distracting his attention, and crying afterwards alone? And then the flood of pleasure and relief when they spoke quietly again, even of gratitude for his occasional mumbled apologies?

The point of not caring, she supposed, had been reached when she'd stopped loving him; but lately she'd begun to wonder whether she had ever loved him at all. You couldn't sort out feelings into "love" and "not-love" like socks of different shades. She'd respected him, believed in him, admired him, and perhaps all that added up to love; or perhaps it was a by-product—an important question she still hadn't solved.

The respect and the belief, though, she knew what had blighted them: her discovery that Peter lacked qualities she had assumed him to have without ever taking the trouble to find out, qualities to which perhaps he'd never laid claim; like honesty, for instance. Not the legal honesty but the moral kind which was now so out of fashion, which made people all of one piece and unprepared to compromise.

How could you be a politician and not compromise? And, in any case, why shouldn't you? Not to compromise could be foolish, selfish, narrow, tiresome and obtuse. So she'd looked in Peter for qualities he didn't even want and couldn't have exercised. It was horribly unfair on him and, admitting this, with enormous effort she'd rebuilt the foundations on her patience, her forebearance and at least a semblance of trust.

Peter was not a sensitive man but of course he knew that something had gone wrong. But he didn't try to probe and diagnose and analyze for fear of what he might discover and, on the surface, they agreed well enough. Only Peter lost his temper more.

And the worst of it was that Julia had this quality her father lacked and didn't want, and that Lavinia had unjustly condemned him for lacking. Moral honesty carried almost to the point of masochism: not at all a good quality for a girl of twenty. And in some inner, hidden way her possession of this quality angered and disturbed her father and had perhaps damaged his love, just as Lavinia's love—if she'd ever had it—for Peter had been damaged for the opposite reason. It was all too complicated to be dealt with on a Sunday morning, and in any case there was nothing to be done.

"She's very young," Lavinia said.

"Good lord, I'm not trying to push her into anything. Of course if she doesn't want Evan she's only got to say. But she said she did, and now she keeps him dangling on a string. And messes about with a lunatic who turns up out of the blue and pretends to be a cowman for some obscure reason. It's not good enough."

"Do you think Evan is, Peter?"

"Do I think Evan's what?"

"Good enough."

"For Julia? Why not? His father's extremely rich, titled if it comes to that. Evan's picked up some silly immature ideas but he'll get over them, and one day the whole outfit will fall into his hands. He's intelligent and apparently in love with Julia. I don't know what more more you want."

"He's in love with Martin," Lavinia said.

"My God, you bitch, what right have you got to say that?" Peter Buckle was dark in the face and shouting. "You've got a mind like a sewer, just because it's in the fashion you've got to label him a homo. I don't know how the hell you can bring yourself—" He broke off breathing hard and hunching his shoulders, his eyes black with rage. She sat absolutely still. Buckle thrust his hands into his trouser pockets and walked across to the window.

"It always ends like this," he said.

"What does, Peter?"

"Any discussions we attempt to have about our children."

"About Martin."

"You're unnatural, that's what it is."

Lavinia said nothing.

"Most women love their sons. They'll put up with anything for them, stick by them through thick and thin. But you—you've always had your knife into Martin. You say the most atrocious things about him. I can't understand it. Are you jealous, or something?"

Lavinia got to her feet and smoothed her skirt. Her hands

were trembling. This was one of the occasions when she wished she smoked, it would have occupied her fingers, created a little flurry of activity. She looked at the picture over the fireplace and tried to draw from it a sense of repose. It was a Dutch landscape by van Goyen, not too brown, with wonderfully smooth, gentle water reflecting a luminous open sky, sleeping trees and the outline of a distant village. If anything could calm you, that could.

"Don't let's forget we've got guests," she said.

"Of course I haven't forgotten. Aren't those children ever going to get up? I should think they could entertain them for half an hour." He turned back from the window and she saw that he was all right, the flush had faded and his hand was steady as he took out another cigarette. He was smoking heavily.

"I'm sorry, Vin," he added with a bit of a smile. "I shouted like a sergeant-major. It was silly, gets one nowhere. I suppose we're both after the same thing in different ways. Who the hell'd have children, anyway?"

"I thought you were quite satisfied with Martin." A moment after she'd spoken, Lavinia cursed herself for a fool. She couldn't keep the bitterness from her voice when she spoke of Martin, and of course it was bitchy, she'd start him off again. But now he had himself well in hand. He perched on a corner of the desk and rubbed a hand through his thick hair. Peter was a better-looking man at fifty than he'd been at twenty-five. Confidence had rubbed away the unevenness, the gaucheries, leaving a polished surface. The heaviness of jowl, the depth of chest, the tightness of mouth, these suited him.

"As a matter of fact I'm worried," he confided, snapping the top of his lighter.

"About Martin?"

"About that business of his."

"The art gallery? I thought it was doing well."

"I think it is. At any rate he hasn't had to come to me—
to us—for money lately. My guess is he's doing better than
most."

"That's all right, then."

"I'm not sure it is. I've been hearing some rather disturb-
ing rumours."

"You're very mysterious, Peter."

"It's hard to put one's finger on these things. People
won't come out into the open. You know, this art world is a
jungle and I daresay it has some pretty crooked paths. I'm
sure Martin wouldn't do anything that was, well, that
wasn't straight, deliberately. All I'm afraid of is, he might
get taken for a ride. He doesn't know his way about half as
well as he thinks he does, and some of his friends . . ."

Lavinia said nothing. This picture of Martin as an innocent amongst the wise boys silenced her. It was typical of
Peter to assume immediately that someone else was to
blame, never Martin. Martin's virtues were all his own, his
vices always the fault of other people.

"Do you mean something illegal?" she asked.

"I shouldn't think so for a minute. Martin would never
be such a fool as that. No, I think he's just got mixed up
with some rather bogus people who probably use him as a
kind of front. It may not even be as serious as that—just a
lot of rumours."

"You better speak to him," Lavinia suggested. Peter
smiled.

"Remember what you said about Julia just now? But I'll
try. At least Martin trusts me. For a father and son, each
with pretty definite views of his own, I think we get on
remarkably well."

His complacency filled Lavinia with despair but, suppressing all she wanted to say, she merely remarked: "I'm
sure he'll listen to you. Meanwhile I'd better deal with the
guests. Can you manage a walk before lunch?"

"I hope so. The dogs need it. Pompey's getting fat."

"He's getting old."

At the door she paused. Peter was all right now and she could bring up a triviality. After twenty-seven years she still didn't know which was genuine, the anger and abuse or the confidence and good humour. Both, perhaps, fizzing like an acid and an alkali mixed in a test tube. She said:

"There's one little thing, Peter—Colonel Crozier was up here last night."

"Who? Oh, old Crozier."

"He was in rather a taking. Apparently Tompkins has cut off his milk."

"Has he?" Buckle sounded offhand and started to move papers on his desk. "Presumably hasn't paid."

"That's the trouble. I'm afraid the Croziers are rather up against it but he swears he *will* pay, and in the meantime his wife's worse, I gather, and milk really does seem to be a necessity."

Buckle tore the date off the pad of an old-fashioned day-by-day calendar and studied the motto. It was difficult to get these calendars nowadays, he had to order them specially. "Ask yourself whether you are happy, and you cease to be so—John Stuart Mill." Peter frowned.

"The farm's a business, you know, Vin. We can't provide free milk for all our broke neighbours or we'd soon be broke ourselves."

"He only seems to get about ninepence worth a day. I'm sure he'll pay in the end."

"I believe he owes money all over the place, a poor show for a man in his position. If he's really on his uppers he can go to the National Assistance like anyone else."

"You know he—" Lavinia broke off, looking fixedly at the back of Peter's neck; he was settling in his chair and sorting out papers.

"It's just a question of tiding over," Crozier had said.

"That's it, tiding over. If you—if your husband—of course affairs of state . . ." He'd looked at the floor, at her feet, but never at her eyes. They had both been terribly embarrassed.

"Anyway, Peter, if you could give him another month's grace . . ."

Peter gave an impatient grunt. "He's had more than that already. I can't keep interfering with Tompkins in matters of detail. It's up to him." The telephone rang and Peter picked up the receiver. "The which? Oh, yes. No. I've nothing to add to what I said yesterday, no, Friday night. Has he? No, I haven't. I can't make any comment till I've seen . . ." Lavinia went out and closed the door.

chapter 18

"IT's for you, Mr. Heron." An extension from the shop had been installed in the front parlour and Mrs. Harris took the call in there. The parlour was seldom used and always damp. Dick knew at once who it was. The police would have come in the flesh, in uniform.

He had been waiting for this. He had waited all the previous day, the day after the shoot—waited and waited but no one had come. Time had stretched out like a piece of elastic and he'd begun to wonder whether it hadn't all been part of a dream. But he had no gun. He'd gone on feeling in his pockets, turning them out a dozen times or more, each time with a heightened desperation. There was no gun. Martin had the gun. He must get it back. On those three points, fixed bearings, he concentrated, like a lost traveller trying to navigate without charts across an unfamiliar sea.

"I wondered if you'd come up to Chaffins and have a cup of tea," the voice said. It was gentle, smooth and pleasing, and Dick blinked. It might have been the vicar inviting a distinguished bigwig to open a church fête.

"Tea?" Dick's voice was thick and stupid in his own ears.

"Something stronger if you like, Dick," Martin offered. "But there *is* tea, and a rather good cherry cake."

"I can't come to Chaffins."

"You mean you've no transport? I can run down and fetch you in a jiffy."

"You know I don't mean that. Your father—"

"Oh, that's all right. Everyone's out. I thought we'd have a little chat, just you and I. Besides, the cake wants eating. And I'm all on my own. Do come."

Martin really was pleading. Dick didn't know what to say.

"That's fine, then," Martin added. "Tell you what, Tony can pick you up, he's got to run down to the post office anyway with some letters. He'll be along in a quarter of an hour. Seeing you." He rang off.

It was probably lack of sleep that made Dick so heavy and bewildered. Mrs. Harris put her head round the door to say she had the kettle on and found him sitting with his head in his hands.

"I don't believe you slept a wink last night. I heard you walking up and down. I said to my husband, 'Ted,' I said, 'there's Mr. Heron walking up and down like he was in trouble, I'm going to knock on his door.' But Ted said, 'Leave him be, if he wants anything he'll holler, it's worry most likely and there's nothing good for that but only time,' so I said, 'Well, I don't like it but all right I'll leave him be.' Then I must have dropped off and next thing I knew it was morning. Now I've just got the kettle on and a good—"

"I shan't want tea, thanks, Mrs. Harris. I'm going out."

"That's the best thing you can do. I said to Ted, 'He ought to go out more, a young fellow like that,' if you'll excuse me, Mr. Heron, 'it's not right to spend so much time cooped up by himself, he ought to get about more and make some friends, though of course—' "

She broke off, hardly liking to finish the sentence. If he was to move on there was no use in making friends. She'd had to give him notice, though she hadn't wanted to—Ted had insisted; and when she'd spoken up, Ted had said there was more in this than met the eye. In fact, he'd hinted that Mr. Heron was a bit queer, dangerous even. He *was* queer, that she'd admit, but nothing harmful so far as she could see, more solitary. And he'd had trouble, you could tell.

It was all to do with Pendlebury's visit. Pendlebury was on the lookout for spies and Russians and communists and the like and it was to be supposed Mr. Heron was mixed up somehow in all that. If this was really so, of course he might be dangerous: there was logic in it, she agreed: but somehow she couldn't really believe in his badness. Men made mistakes often enough and probably they'd made one over Dick Heron.

"There's no call to leave tomorrow or the next day," she said. "If you'd rather stay on a day or two till you find something suitable. Was you thinking of stopping in the neighbourhood?"

"Yes, for a while."

At first, everything had seemed perfectly simple—go to Horsington and buy another gun. He had the money. Full of confidence, he'd planned to catch the first bus, but when he'd sounded Ted Harris at breakfast on the procedure his hopes had crashed like one of Tyndall's fat birds.

In England, you couldn't just go and buy a revolver. You had to get a licence first from the police, and the police didn't issue licences these days.

"Never? But surely . . . ?"

"Very exceptional circumstances." Ted spoke with a weighty, judicial air. "In fact, you might say, so exceptional they don't exist, not for any ordinary person, not these days. It's all these gunmen about, all this lawlessness—

stands to reason, don't it? Got to stamp it out. That's one thing the courts won't stand for, carrying arms. Get anyone fifteen years."

"But if someone just wants to protect himself . . ."

"With a gun?" Ted shook his head sorrowfully, dismayed at his lodger's ignorance. Funny ideas people had about England, even if things had changed, and all for the worse, since he was a lad. "We're still a civilized country, Dick, even if we got teds and that, like the States almost, and all these foreigners. Television, that's a lot of it, these gangster pictures, giving all the kids ideas. But protection —that's still the coppers' job, you know, life and limb. It'll be a bad day for England when you or I can pay our money down and walk out with a pistol and drill a hole in anyone we don't like the look of, or the first harmless old lady we come across behind a till. Far too much of that as it is." He shook his head again. "A licence? Win the treble chance more likely these days."

And why was Dick asking, anyway? He didn't like it. No harm in him, maybe, but time he was gone.

The parlour looked on to the village street. Mrs. Harris saw a movement outside. "There's the Chaffins car stopping."

Dick got to his feet. "I'm going up there for tea."

"Well I never!" Mrs. Harris bustled out fit to burst. There was the Chaffins people hounding her lodger out of the village and then asking him up there for tea.

Martin said: "I thought we'd have tea in the library." It was a splendid room: square, a fine moulded ceiling, the walls white where they weren't lined with books. Over an Adam fireplace, with carved stone fruit above it and an old iron fireback, hung a picture of dead birds and live prancing dogs and the hanging head of a dead stag with blood issuing from its mouth, and a lolling red tongue. A fire reflected light off polished mahogany. The carpet looked much too good to be trodden on; the Arabs had more sense, they hung them on the walls, and Dick had done the same with the only reasonably good rug he'd owned, one his father had bought off the dhows that came down from the Persian Gulf on the northeast monsoon.

He looked at Martin carefully, trying to fathom his game. A clever face: dark, almost swarthy; rounded; lips curved in a persistent half-smile; deep-set eyes. A mobile face, attractive, quick. Cruelty somewhere—in the lines under the nostrils possibly, the set of the mouth. Martin smiled a lot, a friendly interest was the predominant impression. His hair grew in fuzzy sideburns and petered out on top. He was dressed in a pair of dark, tight trousers and a heavy sweater with a polo neck, Italian probably, and pointed shoes, and wore a gold signet ring.

"They've all deserted me," he said. "Evan and Julia off billing and cooing, I suppose; the rest gone out to tea with the nobility and gentry. Come and sit near the fire. Strong or weak?"

"Why have you asked me here?"

"The pleasure of your company. Milk and sugar?"

"Why did you take my gun?"

Martin smiled, and proffered a tea cup. "We were shooting birds, Dick. It's still the closed season for politicians."

"Have you handed it to the police?"

Martin, still smiling, raised his eyebrows. "They've got enough work already, poor dears. I don't want to add to it at the moment, anyway. Now this cherry cake really *is* good."

Dick tried to gulp his tea but it was too hot and his hand was shaking, so he put the cup down and stared at the fire. He thought of himself surrounded by a mob of angry buffaloes with tossing horns and lashing tails, all about to charge down on him, and he had his hand on the rough bark of a tree, a refuge. He thought of the tree: he'd passed it on the way up with Tony; it had looked like a mimosa coming into yellow flower but with all the colours faded like a badly fixed photograph; he knew it for an ash really, but its clusters of yellowish seed pods were like young wattle flowers at a distance: he'd read a warning in this tree, a message. And suddenly he felt immensely tired, as if he'd lived a hundred years and couldn't die, like some old magician. Martin was saying:

"You're eating nothing and you don't look well. I'm worried about you, Dick. Not sleeping? I've got some excellent pills I can strongly recommend. I expect you've been overdoing things."

Dick went on looking at the fire and said nothing.

"Or better still, how about a trip abroad? It's late in the year, I know, but there's a lot to be said for October. Much less crowded, and still quite warm. Yes, I think a short trip abroad might be the answer. Set you up for the winter."

With an effort, Dick took his eyes off the fire and looked at Martin, who appeared quite benign.

"You're wasting time," he said, "this beating about the bush."

Martin leant back in his chair, his hands knitted behind his head, one leg cocked over the other.

"You're a period piece, you know, Dick. Pure Edwardian, straight from a novel by A. E. W. Mason, or even A. C. Benson. Neglected, still—the Edwardian period's yet to find its Betjeman. Well, that'll be the next thing—we'll have to do for Pryde and De Laszlo what's already been done for, say, Frith and Egg. Only I'm afraid they weren't nearly such accomplished painters. Still, what does that matter? It's the presentation nowadays, isn't it, that counts

—the image, so-called. Dick, why did you try to kill my father?"

Dick in his imagination gripped on harder to the tree. He wasn't being prized away, but gently sucked off, as it were: beguiled, as if a net were being floated down to entangle and immobilize his limbs. Leaning forward, he gripped his hands together between his knees and demanded:

"What are you going to do with the gun?"

"My goodness, Dick, you've got a one-track mind." Martin left his chair and stood with his back to the fire, looking down and laughing, crinkling his eyes in a way which recalled his father. "That gun is really an obsession. You're all of a piece, aren't you? No loose ends. In a way, that makes you more attractive. You *are* attractive, you know."

Dick got up too, feeling a weakness in his knees. He stood opposite Martin and looked down on him; he was about six inches taller.

"You haven't touched your tea," Martin added in a tone of reproach.

"If you're not going to discuss it there's not much point in my staying. Time's getting on. . . ."

"What's more, you attract my sister," Martin said. "She's a dear girl, Dick, and I don't blame you; anyway she's fairly hurled herself at your head, but don't forget she's supposed to marry Evan. They were made for each other. Whom God hath joined, or certainly will join . . . Perhaps, in this case, not actually God but some unworthy substitute, such as my father. Still, it comes to much the same thing."

"What are you driving at?"

"Evan'll make her a wonderful husband—too good almost. Money, influence, devotion—she's a very fortunate girl. And, being a devoted brother, I'd hate to see the tiniest little spanner lobbed into the works."

"You're barking up the wrong tree."

Martin tilted back his head and laughed. "I love the way you talk, Dick—full of wise saws, if not of modern instances. You must come and stay with me in my flat, you'd like it, I think. Meanwhile, I've got a suggestion."

Dick sat down again and put his hands to his temples. He was hopelessly at sea. Was Martin trying to strike a bargain —keep away from Julia and he'd return the gun? Was he trying to make advances? Dick had no experience to go on. The only thing of which he could be certain, the fixed point, was that he wanted the gun.

"Listen," he said, "that gun is my property. I want it back. If you give it to me I'll go right away from Chaffins, from the village. I'll even clear out of the country. I'll give you my word."

Martin chuckled with delight. "The word of an English gentleman, Dick? Or colonial gentleman, rather. Much more reliable, I grant you that. Leaving, of course, one dead Cabinet Minister in your wake."

Dick made a defeated gesture with his hands.

"What do you want me to do?"

Martin touched his arm, smiling. "Well done, Dick. You're learning. What I have in mind is pure pleasure, nothing but a holiday. No, no, not what you think. This combines business with pleasure. Would you like a trip to Italy?"

Dick gave his head a little shake as if to get water out of his eyes, screwed up his face and then relaxed. Martin watched with interest.

"Why do you want me to go to Italy?"

"A little errand. Come to my flat and I'll explain."

"Are you offering me the gun if I go?"

"Certainly."

"Why?"

"Why? Because you want it, Dick. It's only fair you

should do something to earn it, and only fair you should be paid if you do. You see, like you, I believe in justice. We share a common passion. Is it a bargain?"

"I'll have to know more about it. And the gun—"

"Oh dear, how you do go on about the gun! If you come and stay with me, Dick, you must make a solemn promise not to mention firearms once the whole time. They've never been a hobby of mine. But I promise you, you'll get your gun. Like Annie. She got her gun, didn't she? I seem to remember—"

There was a sound outside the door and Dick, his spirits quickly rising, began to panic. He couldn't face Buckle now, or Julia—any of them. But Julia, with Evan behind her, was standing in the open doorway, her hands on her ruffled, shining hair. She walked forward calmly and nodded to Dick and looked at her brother.

"I hope we're not interrupting a seduction scene? Just right in here with comfy sofas and a nice cozy fire. Is there any tea left or is it cold?"

"There's some hot water. Dick likes his strong."

"With three lumps, I expect. Evan likes his with lemon, there must be some significance in that, I expect. Why does sweet tea make me think of damp socks? Poor Evan, he's got a blister on his toe." She stretched out a hand and took Evan's to pull him towards the fire. "I must give him a poultice. What is a poultice? It sounds like a pudding made with suet."

"I don't know what came over Julia, she walked and walked," Evan complained. "I never knew she could do it before. It's a great mistake, anyway."

"Much better Julia should reveal her vices before you marry her than leave you to find them out afterwards," Martin suggested.

"The vice department's all yours, Martin," Julia said.

"You'll shock Dick."

"Oh, the hell with Dick, what's he want to come and haunt us for? You dragged him here, Martin. I don't know what your game is but why can't you leave him alone?" She turned to glare at Dick, who saw a resemblance to her brother, but simplified and unsubtle, the bee without the sting. "You'd better get the hell out of here, Dick, the party's over."

"I'm just going."

"He's such a monosyllabic man," Evan remarked. "Don't you ever waste words, Dick? You're like one of those thrifty housewives who save bits of fat. They go mad in the end."

Dick smiled. Now he saw the way ahead again he felt lighthearted. So long as Martin still had the gun, and the police hadn't, and Martin was prepared to bargain, he'd get it back. He could almost feel it now against his thigh.

"I talk a lot sometimes," he volunteered.

Evan remarked gloomily: "But only, I expect, when you've something to say. The great thing is to talk when you haven't."

"I'm going now," Dick announced, standing awkwardly by the door and not quite knowing how to say good-bye.

"For God's sake, go, then." Julia had kicked off her shoes and was sitting on the floor wriggling her toes as near as she could get them to the fire without burning them. Martin commented:

"You're not in your most gracious frame of mind."

"I'm sick and tired of the lot of you." She jumped to her feet and kicked a shoe to one side. "We're all too much alike, that's our trouble. Then Dick comes along looking like a cross between a father figure and the hero of a bad western and everyone thinks he's round the bend. Either he is or we are. Oh, get out, Dick, for God's sake." She turned to face him and shouted. "You've been standing there for half an hour like a bloody great bullock, what are you waiting for? Get out, can't you! Go, go, *go*."

Dick shut the door behind him. With a sense of panic he realized that he'd minded—not the words Julia had shouted at him, but the desperation that lay behind her need to wound him: that he was beginning to understand and feel responsible.

chapter 19

MARTIN answered the bell. The tufts of hair below his temples were fuzzy like a baby's, he smiled and took Dick's arm and drew him in with an eager, childlike pleasure.

His flat was light and sunny; it was perched high up in the tower with a view over roofs and trees and, in the distance, a gleam of river. Everything was light—furniture, walls, curtains, covers, a few vivid modern pictures. It was a cell in one of those new, high boxes. Thick, expensive carpets extracted even the human quality of noise—life here was pasteurized. Martin said:

"Evan's terribly sorry to miss you, he's got some stupid business thing he couldn't avoid. He sent his love. You've made a great hit with Evan, he finds you *simpatico*. As indeed we all do. Gin or sherry?"

Dick chose sherry.

"He and Julia will be very happy," Martin added. "Plenty in common but different temperaments. Evan's a nice, solid suburban stockbroker at heart, the safe kind that deals in gilt-edged. One day his *Megaton* will fizzle out, not with a bang certainly and probably not even a whimper, and he'll go back, or forward rather, to seats on half a dozen of his father's boards. It's Julia who's the gambler. There's a lot of my father in Julia, though he'd never admit to gambling; he'd call it a calculated risk, which sounds so much more respectable but is, of course, double-talk for the same thing. Here's to them, anyway." He raised his glass.

"What do you want me to do?"

Martin laughed. "I do adore your bluntness, Dick. No bush-beating—all that waiting for the coffee stage so as not to upset the digestion." He glanced at the hand in which Dick held a small, fluted, trumpet-shaped goblet of considerable beauty. "You know, you've got remarkably slim wrists and ankles for your size."

Dick put his glass on a table as if it had stung him. "Shall we stick to the point? It's kind of you to ask me to lunch but I don't want your hospitality, I simply want your instructions."

"And your weapon."

"And my weapon, as you say."

"It's all quite simple and straightforward. Shall we have lunch first? It's cold, I'm afraid. For a hot meal we have to use the restaurant and I always find—"

"I haven't much time," Dick said.

Martin raised his eyebrows, leading the way to a table by the window. Sunlight fell on to the mahogany and on to a Georgian silver rose bowl full of chrysanthemums which glowed as if they were throwing out flames of red and yellow and a purply bronze.

"Time's merely something we've invented in order to make ourselves into slaves. If there's one thing on which the members of the human race are absolutely determined, it's to become enslaved to something or somebody. We've done away with human masters so we've had to invent time instead. I don't believe slave societies ever bothered about time, they didn't need to. It's just a substitute. So forget it, Dick, and eat up your melon. I think this one is just right."

Then came cold duck and salad and a fluffy orange soufflé, and all the while Martin chatted away. Afterwards, Dick knew, he wouldn't remember a word and yet the interest lived at the time. Martin's talk was light, entertaining and subtle—like a woman's when she lays herself out to please. That Martin should set out, quite ostentatiously, to please the man he held in his power was a kind of self-mockery, perverse. As they sat over the food and wine an easy and, indeed, a pleasing intimacy did seem to germinate between them. Although Dick was on his guard, he felt his defenses softening, nearly giving way.

Out of the window, down below in the street, he watched foreshortened people, propelled by secret purposes, scurrying about just like the termites again. He thought of a trick the natives of his own country sometimes played: they tapped with sticks very lightly and quickly, to imitate the fall of rain; then, at the right season, out would come flying ants, millions and millions of them, to be caught and eaten. If some joker were to play that trick here—imitate the fall of bombs, perhaps?—Dick felt sure that all these people would come surging forth from their cells in factory and shop and office, from these buildings like great termite castles, without reason or question, to acquiesce in their own destruction.

It seemed to him that all these people had sacrificed their separate individual identities in order to indulge themselves in the pleasures of gregarious existence (whatever these were) and were now forever seeking the lost kingdom, but it had gone and they would never find it again. They jostled, sweated, swayed, muttered, pushed together in this great river of humans, walking always on concrete, dominated always by brick or stone, wrapped always in clothing, as insulated from the current of life as surely as a pylon was insulated from the current that flowed along the wires it supported.

One day the earth would shake and topple over all these conglomerations of mutilated humans who had lost their humanity but were fiercely living out an illusion, the dream that they were real human beings and mattered twopence to anyone. They didn't know they were all expendable.

"Now for coffee," Martin said, "and our bit of business which won't detain us long. I'm glad you enjoyed your meal, Dick. Your little *contretemps* hasn't ruined your appetite."

It was impossible to explain that everything like that, the fretting and the turmoil, lay in the past: that what sustained him now was the prospect of action.

"But of course it's been balanced, the *contretemps* I mean," Martin added, "by a triumph in the affairs of the heart. It's quite untrue, don't you find, that love destroys the appetite? I've always found it stimulates mine. One pleasure heightens another, I think."

"Shall we stick to the point?"

"This *is* the point, you know, and I'm surprised a man of your perception hasn't seen it."

"Let's talk in plain English." Dick spoke impatiently. Martin looked at his guest and laughed, his head a little on one side, and for an instant there was Julia—perhaps in the sharp, quick sound, the crinkles under the eyes, the curve of the lips.

"Poor Dick, you *are* in trouble. You came over here, didn't you, with a purpose? A nice, clear, simple, if perhaps by our bourgeois standards, rather bizarre one. Once you lose that, you're sunk."

"I'm a strong swimmer."

Martin shook his head. "On the contrary, I think you'll sink at once. You're not one to enjoy splashing about in shallow water having a lovely time but getting nowhere. That purpose, it's like a lifeline you've got to hang on to with your manly grip. And now it's been cut."

"I don't understand you."

"Then you're regrettably obtuse. The knife has been wielded by my sister. The knife of love. Dear me, how involved one gets with these metaphors. But I'm sure you take my point."

"I don't know what you're talking about. I came here to get my gun. If you won't discuss it, there's no object in my staying any longer." Dick put down his crumpled red linen napkin and got to his feet.

"That gun again! Oh, dear, I thought we'd got away from it for a few moments. You never let go, do you, Dick? You're too proud. That's your humour, in the seventeenth-century sense—pride. You're soaked in pride like an onion pickled in vinegar. Do sit down."

He uncorked a thermos jug and poured them both some black coffee. Dick hesitated, feeling towards his host intense irritation and the kind of fascination certain people find in snakes, a mixture of admiration and repugnance. Then he sat down.

"Admittedly my sister threw herself at your head. But you fielded her very neatly. She'll give you a reason for living and that'll destroy your plan."

Dick stared at the chrysanthemums which, in a shaft of pale sunlight, seemed to sing with colour, to burst with it, hurting his eyes. His mouth was dry and anyway he had nothing to say.

"Julia and I don't like each other very much but we understand each other. The same people attract us or don't. Sometimes we even fall in love with a common object, as it were, and you can imagine how complicated that can become. But so far we've managed to sort things out in a reasonably sensible way. Sometimes Julia even listens to my advice—quite a concession, don't you think? She kicks against the pricks but in the end she generally comes round

to my point of view. You still want your gun, Dick, but you
won't use it."

"You saw me trying to shoot your father."

"And saved his life. That's something I never thought I'd
do. And he's no idea I've done it, either. I wonder what
he'd think his life was worth? Quite a lot, I daresay. The
trouble is, Dick, you're no good at the game. He'll slip
through your fingers again."

"You're prepared to give the gun back because you
think I'll be afraid to use it? Isn't that a bit of a gamble with
your father's life?"

"Frankly, my father can look after his own life—a thing
he's always been remarkably good at. And if by any chance
he should fail for once, it wouldn't break my heart. No use
pretending, is there? Between us I think we can be quite
frank." He put a hand lightly on his guest's sleeve and Dick
stared at it as if entranced by the thin white fingers.

"People like you, Dick, are apt to be all manly bluster on
the surface but soft as kittens when it comes to taking independent action, deciding things on your own. You're a man
who has to serve under orders. Admittedly the orders may
come from yourself, but they've got to be there. There's got
to be orders of some kind, or you just crumple. And now
Julia . . . Well, never mind. I can see you'll throw me out of
this window soon if we don't get down to business so I'll be
thoroughly unselfish—because I really am enjoying your
company so much—and come to the point. Or what you
think's the point, because of your obsession with this gun.
You really want it back, I suppose."

Dick was fiddling with his coffee spoon, turning it round
and round in his fingers. "You know what I want."

Martin laughed. "I wish I knew what anyone wanted,
myself included. One's cake and eat it, I suppose. I'm letting you off extremely lightly, Dick, because I've really got
very fond of you. All you've got to do is to fly to Milan

tomorrow, first class, too, go and see a friend of mine and come back when you want to—next day, spend the week-end or a week if you like, go on to Rome. That'll be up to you entirely. My only concern is that you go and see this friend of mine and give him a little present I'll entrust to you."

"Drugs?" Dick inquired.

Martin looked really hurt. "My dear Dick! What an unpleasant suggestion. I don't deal in anything like that and never have."

"You deal in pictures."

"Exactly."

"I'm to take a picture?"

"Two, actually. Rolled up, I thought, and strapped on to the inside of your leg. They're very light."

"Are they stolen?"

"You do make the most insulting suggestions, and if I wasn't both a good-natured man and mellowed by claret . . . It's a matter of the Customs, that's all. I'm sure you'll agree, with your philosophic bent, there's no moral difference between slipping through a pair of nylons and a picture or two. The Italian laws are most unreasonable. However, Dick, the ins and outs are really no concern of yours. And there's virtually no risk. The only stipulation is that if, by any freakish mischance, you *should* get searched, a million to one at least against, you'll keep my name out of it. Do you agree?"

Dick got up again to look out of the window and down at the tops of the trees. Some were green as in full summer, in others patches of gold and yellow showed up here and there.

"I've no choice," he said.

"That's a very sensible point of view. Of course, if anything went wrong and you gave the game away then naturally there'd be no gun. There'd also be a lot of trouble for you. If, on the other hand, you did your stuff, I think I could guarantee to pull your chestnuts out of the fire. The worst would be a fine, and that'd be paid for you of course. But I'm quite sure it won't come to that. You'll sail through the Customs with your little packages, have a marvelous holiday, come back and collect your property. Can't imagine anything nicer myself. You're a lucky chap."

"How do I know I'll get the gun?"

"You mean you don't trust me?"

Dick laughed. "Would you? Considering . . ."

"You say such wounding things, Dick. And as you've pointed out, you've no choice."

"Where is it? The gun?"

Martin slipped a hand into the pocket of his tight black trousers, pulled out the pistol and tossed it in his hand. Dick took a step forward and found its muzzle looking at him like a cold little eye.

"Naturally I didn't like to meddle with your property. So far as I know it's still loaded."

Martin looked perfectly at home with the gun, relaxed and confident. He moved with a springy motion like an athlete and Dick now recognized him as the sort of slight, flimsy-looking man apt to come out on top in irregular, guerilla warfare, a fighter without squeamishness or scruple —the sort he himself had learnt to value, if never to trust, in the bitter, individualist war he'd taken part in against a savage enemy who'd fought back with knives and home-made guns, man-pits and poisoned arrows.

"I'll tell you what," Martin said agreeably. "We'll stroll round to my bank together, there's just time"—he glanced at a perfectly proportioned bracket clock on a bookcase— "and we'll hand it over to them and they'll sign for it. Then you'll know it's absolutely safe. And when you come back we'll go back together and collect it. That's fair enough, don't you think?"

Dick agreed.

"I've got your ticket. Your plane goes tomorrow afternoon. The best plan will be for you to come round to the gallery at two o'clock. Then I'll give you your ticket and the little canvases and off you'll go. Honestly, Dick, I'm quite sure you won't have the least bit of trouble. The great thing is not to panic and I'd say you're totally unflappable. It just can't go wrong."

Martin put the gun back in his pocket and Dick abandoned an impulse to finish off the whole business by using a trick or two he'd learnt during his single-combat training. He was much the stronger of the two but Martin, he now understood, the more ruthless; and Martin had the loaded gun.

"I like your pictures," he remarked, strolling over to the fireplace to inspect a long, narrow painting of a stream or lake surrounded by reeds and foliage; he seemed to peer into a green tunnel, and bold brush strokes of subtle colour, blues and browns and reds and yellows, crisscrossed among the greens, suggested other elements—sky perhaps, birds, space, light, unsullied air. Martin came and stood beside him, so close that Dick could smell the freshness of shaving lotion, the homeliness of the thick woollen sweater, and Martin's arm brushed his own.

"An early Ivon Hitchins. I'm glad you like it, Dick. Such a romantic painter in those days. . . ."

Knowing he wouldn't get a straight answer, Dick nevertheless asked:

"Why do you do all this when you don't have to? I mean the smuggling, or whatever it is? You've got all the money you need. There are plenty of honest art dealers, at least I suppose there are. Is it like motor racing, ski jumping, that sort of thing—a way to get a kick, a new thrill?"

Martin smiled. He smiled a great deal. "A sort of substitute for Outward Bound courses with the Duke of Edinburgh? You may be right, but there could be other reasons. In fact there are. And then, of course, reasons—they're terribly dull. These paintings here, what are their reasons? Everything that's worth doing is irrational. You know that as well as I do." Dick thought before he said:

"No, I like reasons."

"You pull them over your head like a child with a blanket when it hears a loud bang: they're something to hide behind because you're a moral coward, Dick. You won't face the truth, and the truth is you're afloat on a glorious and dangerous ocean of the totally irrational. Well, good luck to you, my dear. Reasons can safely be left to the computers, people have got better things to do. And that reminds me, so have we; we'll miss the bank if we don't hurry. You'll excuse me, won't you, while I wrap up the gun."

Dick nodded. Underneath his feet the ground was crumbling away. The floor quivered and his mind swelled with a vision of a great bank of earth heeling over. An enormous chasm opened in front of him, and a thundering of distant waters roared up, as from a flooded river far below in the blackness of a seething earth.

chapter 20

Then the rumble of the river changed into a hollow thud of feet, hoofed feet, and he was back among the heaving shapes of buffaloes, their black-bossed sweeping horns, their whipping tails, dust and trampled grass and a jumbled smell of bull and bruised undergrowth and cedar forest.

Everyone agreed that buffaloes were treacherous except Rose. Traitors betrayed their own cause, she'd said, and how could buffaloes do that when men were not their cause, but their enemy? No animals would hurt a man until some man had first either hurt or frightened them. Mistakes could be made, animals might lose their tempers, elephants have abscesses below their tusks, but all the hunters and tough guys who boasted of their courage, the hairy-chested Hemingway characters, had deliberately provoked the animals in order to show off what big, strong he-men they were. That was Rose's belief.

Even when it came to Hughie she had not been proved wrong because Hughie had, undoubtedly, provoked the buffalo. He'd intended to kill it—had killed it, for that matter. Hughie was a first-rate shot but a poor hunter: he wanted the thrill, not the hard work that led up to it. Every *thing about Hughie was quick—decisions, pleasures and sorrows, the comeback. You always felt he needed looking after, that one day he'd run into trouble and fail to extricate himself with his wits and speed and charm.*

He'd come up for Andrew's christening and a good party the day before. He'd landed in the paddock below the dip in one of his company's Cesnas and taken a girl for a flip and hedge-hopped all over the place, bringing her back a nervous wreck. Rose had been really angry then.

Next morning, the headman came with a long face, very early, to say a herd of buffaloes had broken through a double fence and destroyed the best part of forty acres of wheat.

"There's nothing for it," Dick said. He didn't in the least want to shoot the buffaloes, but what else could you do?

"It's Sunday," Rose objected. "Wouldn't tomorrow do?" Her objections weren't Sabbatarian but partly because she thought he needed a rest, mainly because she hated the shooting. And she added: "Besides, Hughie's sure to join in, and you know what he's like. He's going back this evening."

"They'll be miles away by tomorrow."

"If they're miles away, they won't do any more damage."

"Perfect logic!" Dick laughed, despite the damaged wheat. He still hadn't got over the extraordinary existence of Andrew, who lay asleep on the veranda with a tuft of pale hair on a skull tender as a bud, his skin like wax. Dick had half expected to be jealous but found he wasn't, Andrew could be shared.

There was a cow calving awkwardly so in any case he couldn't start off at once in pursuit of the buffaloes. By the time the calf had been extracted and he came in to breakfast, the Land Rover had gone. Hughie had taken it along a rough track into the forest. Buckle was not to blame for what happened to Hughie, at least not then. It was Hughie's own impetuosity.

"Damn Hughie," Dick said. "He's no right to go off like that on his own. Which rifle did he take?"

It was the light one.

"Damn Hughie. I'd better chase him."

"How? He's got the Land Rover."

"He's no right . . ."

"Well, you know Hughie."

Dick smiled. "Might as well try to keep the weather under control."

"Your mother spoilt him."

"I suppose she did. He's all right, though. Only I hope . . . The trouble with Hughie is, he makes one feel responsible."

"That's because you're like that, Dick. The kind of man who is."

"It sounds awful."

"I don't think so. Come and have breakfast. It's a wonderful morning."

He laughed. "One or the other of us says that every morning."

"I wonder sometimes if we're not too lucky," Rose agreed.

He'd never imagined anything like it, this easy-flowing intimacy on a sun-flooded veranda, a morning glory wrapped round one of the posts, its trumpet blooms so blue as almost to hurt, and clusters of golden shower hanging down from the roof, sunlight on Rose's fuzz of hair and her bare arms the colour of ripe apricots, the feeling of repose and confidence and satisfaction—in fact of happiness. Only he scouted round the word—names were dangerous. Tempting providence. The peace of that morning was broken by a shout in that high note of crisis: they stopped to listen, Rose had a slice of toast in her hand.

A rainbird called, its notes falling down the scale as if poured from a bottle. Then shouts came again from the direction of the forest. Dick jumped up and went out into the sunshine and heard there'd been an accident, that was all.

Hughie was conscious and grunting ferociously, his legs a mass of blood and pulp. He had the same look in his eyes as a wounded buck imploring to be put out of its agony. He was lying in blood-stained grass and screamed when they moved him, and asked Dick again and again to finish him off. There was a great gash up one thigh and groin and into his side, and bits of trouser had got mixed with the raw flesh. How anyone could lose so much blood and live Dick couldn't imagine, and he wondered whether he ought to do as Hughie implored, put a bullet through his brother's head. Then came the awful jolting in the Land Rover and Rose trying to dress the wounds, but they were beyond an amateur and the only thing was to drive hard for the hospital, thirty miles, and hope for the best. Luckily Hughie became unconscious, therefore silent, after a while.

That was the end of Hughie, Dick thought, at twenty-one. But it wasn't so. The surgeon himself was surprised. Blood transfusions, grafts, more transfusions—and four months later he was out with one leg off at the hip. It was a miracle; but Hughie was bitter, he hadn't wanted to live. His face was pinched and hollow, as if the pain and mutilation had wrung out all the juice and sparkle of his youth.

That was the word he harped on—mutilation. "You put a mutilated beast out of its misery. Quite right, too."

"Lots of people have artificial legs," Rose said, "you'll even be able to go on flying. Look at Douglas Bader."

"Oh, yes. I know. I'll be a crashing bore if I go on belly-aching. I really won't, Rose. Only . . ."

"Of course, Hughie." Rose kissed him. "When you get

the leg you'll feel quite different." He was on crutches then.

"It's not only that. I don't know if I'm going to be any use to women any more."

Dick was startled. "The surgeon never said . . ."

"To begin with no normal girl would look at me."

"That's nonsense, Hughie," Rose answered. "You don't really think a woman would be put off by an artificial leg? Things like that don't count if . . ."

"And other things. The buff made a proper mess of all that region. It counts, presumably, if you're impotent."

"There's no reason to suppose you are," Rose cried out almost violently, refusing, denying, the possibility, the horror.

Hughie's face went white and then he smiled, and to Dick the smile was like a knife jab. When he looked at Rose, tears were running down her face.

All that was in the past; and it was one thing, Dick repeated to himself, you couldn't blame Buckle for. But for what happened afterwards, you could.

chapter 21

By two-thirty the next afternoon, his business with Martin was over. A thin roll of canvas wrapped in linen pressed against the inside of his thigh and sticking plaster gripped his skin. The awkward part was when he bent his knee.

"Quite a surprise," Julia said. She was perched on a corner of her brother's desk, hunting a cigarette in an expensive crocodile bag. "What's the idea, Martin—are you teaching Dick the secrets of the art world in six easy lessons? I shouldn't have thought he was cut out to be a sort of modern Duveen."

"Just a social call," Martin answered shortly. He wasn't attempting to conceal his displeasure. "I thought you were supposed to be at work."

"We're allowed out to eat."

Martin glanced at the small French clock on his desk and raised his eyebrows. "The conscience of the rich."

"This is a new line for you, Martin, the stern unbending clocker-in, time and motion studies in the studio. Peter gave me lunch and I looked in with a message."

"He could use the telephone."

Julia slid off the desk looking angry. "You've got the

most atrocious manners sometimes. You won't win Dick's affections that way." There was spite in her voice.

"I hope they're based on something more solid. Come on, Julie, I'm busy. What's Peter want?"

Julia wore a red suit and looked different out of jeans and a sweater: not more feminine, Dick thought, but more impersonal, as if in a kind of uniform that invited a certain response. He felt he ought to comb his hair and clean his nails. At the same time she gave him, in a curious way, a feeling of pride and contentment.

"He wants your advice."

Martin raised his eyebrows.

"About a little writing desk he's seen at Sotheby's. He's thinking of getting it for Mother."

"Furniture—just because I deal in pictures he thinks . . ."

"I know. I told him it was a mistaken idea. But, as usual, he thinks you know everything. If you want to please him you might have a look at it."

"Why should I want to please him?"

"Generous soul, my brother," Julia remarked, looking at Dick. "As a matter of fact it's for her fiftieth birthday and there's to be a party at Chaffins. If you can come down they'd—"

A white telephone rang and Martin answered it. Dick was standing awkwardly by the door waiting to go, but in no hurry; he had nearly an hour before he was due at the air terminus and everything was organized. In a few hours he'd get rid of his encumbrance and then have a good dinner in Milan. Julia asked:

"What are you really doing here?"

"Your brother borrowed something from me and I came to get it back."

"And did you?"

Now she was close to him Dick was on the point of trembling, and wanted to put out a hand to touch her, as one might want to touch a squirrel to feel the warmth and softness of its fur. Her eyes were bright like her brother's but, unlike his, they held interest, concern, desire for understanding—and, at the moment, doubt. Or did he imagine these things?

"I'll get it the day after tomorrow," he said.

"It's no business of mine, only—" She looked round the little office, made by portioning off a section of the gallery, with an expression he thought apprehensive.

"Only it's time you got back, my dear Julie, to your work and left me to mine," Martin said, putting down the receiver. "I'll see what I can do about the desk. Only it seems ridiculous to give Mama presents with her own money, because that's what it comes to."

"That's their business, isn't it? Martin—"

She looked at him and hesitated, and it occurred to Dick that she was afraid of her brother, or, if not quite afraid, then dubious, uncertain. "I don't know what sort of a racket you're dragging Dick into, but why don't you leave it all alone?"

"Why not mind your own business, Julie dear?"

"It might become my business."

"What the hell do you mean?"

"I wasn't going to mention this but I think Peter's worried. He's been hearing rumours about you and he tried to pump me."

"Then I'm afraid he found the well dry."

"I just thought you might like to know. Apart from anything else, you could bitch up his career."

"Poor helpless suffering bastard, you'll have me in tears in a minute, starting a fund to send him away for a seaside holiday." Martin's voice was ferocious. "Look, Dick, I don't suppose you find all this edifying and anyway it's time you were on your way. See you in a few days."

Julia said angrily:

"All right, all right, I'm going. An appeal to your better feelings is about as much of a dead-end job as one could find, and I suppose that was what I was doing. Come on, Dick, he wants to get rid of you too. I'll take you wherever you're going."

"That's all right, thanks, I'm in no hurry. I—"

"Where *are* you going, actually?"

"The air terminus," Martin told her. "Dick's fond of foreign travel."

Julia turned without a word and went through the little gallery with the loping stride Dick remembered from the time he'd first seen her, in the Red Lion. He followed, feeling the roll of linen and the plaster against his thigh. It wasn't exactly uncomfortable, but it made him want to rub his leg as if there was a bite, and he imagined that people must notice an awkwardness in his gait. He crossed the gallery, his feet silent on a thick carpet, passing a heavy, fat man with his hands behind his back and his head on one side communing with a canvas of sombre black and yellow shapes. Out in the street it was fine and sunny and there was a smell of leaves coming from a nearby square ringed by shiny cars in all colours, like a border of enormous artificial flowers.

"Are you really going to the air terminus?"

"Yes, but I've plenty of time. I don't want—"

"Is that all your luggage?"

Dick had a rucksack over his shoulder—it didn't go with his first-class ticket but it held all he needed. In any case he hadn't yet made up his mind whether or not to go to Milan. He wanted his gun, but then so did Martin want his pictures out of the country, and now each held the other by the short hairs. What he needed most, now, was time to think. He asked:

"Won't you have a drink or something?"

"I ought to go back to the office."

"I don't suppose we'll see each other again.'

Julia's car, a red Simca, stood beside a parking meter; he followed her across to it and opened the door.

"It's a pretty hopeless occupation, anyway. Seeing each other, I mean."

"There are too many people in the world," Dick exclaimed as they drove amid a stream of countless vehicles, wing to wing, bumper to bumper.

"I daresay the bomb will take care of that."

"I suppose that's what it's for."

"This doesn't seem a very cheerful farewell conversation," Julia remarked, fishing in her bag for a coin for the next meter. "If you like I'll have a cup of tea at the air station. I don't think quite so badly of the human race as you seem to."

"It's just so damned pleased with itself and with so very little reason. Let's have that tea."

Next to them at the buffet was a fat Asian woman in a sari with a small, brown, grave-eyed boy and a pasty-faced baby whose mouth was smeared with sticky food. The baby wailed and the woman's earrings clinked as she moved in a slow, statuesque manner and the husband, a dapper and bespectacled little man, came and went restlessly, reminding Dick of the kind of male spider that gets eaten by its mate. On the other side were two dark, sallow men volubly talking in an unknown tongue which didn't seem European —Turkish perhaps, Persian, Hebrew? One had a fringe of beard, yellow teeth and rimless glasses, and might have been some kind of student or professor; the other, small and pudgy and continually smiling, carried a paperback by Ian Fleming. The weak, milky tea was served in plastic cups, pop music emerged without a break from a hidden loud-speaker and a careful, sexless voice emerged at frequent intervals from some oracular cave, announcing a flight's arrival or departure.

"It's like some ghastly modern purgatory thought up by Sartre or someone," Julia said, blowing on her tea. "I feel at least a hundred and ten years old. It's because I feel *responsible*. Like some awful matriarch or organization woman or headmistress or something. Why should I feel like that? Do you, ever?"

"I used to. It was like having a grindstone tied round one's neck. Then the whole thing collapsed and since then I've ceased to feel responsible for anyone or anything. It's a wonderful feeling. As if one were floating about in the air."

"I suppose that's what makes you so odd. I even feel responsible for you, because of Martin. He's using you for something, isn't he?"

"He thinks he is."

"Don't imagine for one moment you can stand up to him, Dick. He's not only much cleverer than you are but he's the only person I know literally without a scruple in the world. You haven't a hope."

"All the same there's one thing that makes me even stronger."

"You mean not caring what happens?"

"I mean having a time limit."

"I wish you wouldn't talk like a crossword puzzle," Julia said impatiently. Where are you going to, Dick?"

"Milan."

She blew smoke through her nose and nodded. "Yes, I might have guessed that. More or less the capital of modern crookendom. If there's one person in the world who . . . Well, I suppose it doesn't matter. I must go." But she made no move to do so; and, holding a little book of matches, started to strip it like a child pulling petals off a dandelion.

"The trouble is I'm bloody fool enough to mind. For instance, Peter—I suppose he's a crook too in the way that all politicians are because they have to be. The way a boat is when it tacks into the wind. But you see he does care about things—himself of course like everyone else, and I've no doubt it's only an illusion, but he really does believe in what he's doing, he thinks it's right. And then Mother believes in him, or at least I think she does, it's a chain, and then Simon. And then there's Evan. Basically he's a tremendous believer. Martin's a sort of unexploded bomb."

"I can explode him for you if you like."

"Yes, I expect you can." Julia put out her hand and touched the back of his, and all his senses sprang to life as if they'd been awakened, but without any shock. "What are you going to do, Dick? I mean, after Milan?"

He shook his head as if to clear it of dust or cobwebs. "It's time I was going," he said. Her fingers tightened on his hand.

"Don't go."

"I must."

"I know Martin's blackmailing you about something but you can blackmail him back. With this Milan caper, whatever it is."

"I'd thought of that."

"Well, then . . ." Julia laughed. "I'm not trying to save you from yourself, Dick, or even from Martin. Look, I've got the car outside. Let's get in and drive somewhere, it doesn't matter where. It's a glorious day. A sort of last gasp of summer. Milan can wait, my blasted office can take a running jump at itself, we can sort out all the bits tomorrow. Don't you feel now as if you'd sort of got halfway?"

All he could feel at the moment was her hand on his own, their flesh touching, the tingling under his skin and his blood warming and racing. She looked small as a bird, defenseless, innocent and unreal. He pushed aside the cup, picked his rucksack off the floor and stood up. "Then let's go."

The red Simca shone in the sunlight, looking eager and obedient. Julia asked:

"North, south, east or west?"

"Let's toss for it."

"We'd need a four-sided penny."

They laughed buoyantly as children while she tossed a florin on the pavement. "Heads for east, tails for west."

"Tails." They climbed in, still laughing, and headed into a declining sun.

chapter 22

THE red Simca came to rest in the yard of an inn they liked
the look of, on a road that wound among the mountains
and here descended to a valley between two humps of bare,
sweeping hill.

"It looks clean," Julia said. In fact the pub looked much
like any other, its flat white front set at an angle from the
main street, its tiled roof uneven and a swinging sign with a
portrait of a fat, red-faced, wigged man on which the paint
was cracking. The lounge had a bar at one end crowded
with people all talking at once. They got as close as they
could to an open fire surrounded by horse brasses and
warming pans, with two old muskets crossed above the
beam and, over that, a plaster fish in its glass case wearing
an expression of mingled protest, anger and scorn.

"I hope there's something good for dinner. I'm hungry,"
Julia said. "One's taking a bit of a chance in Wales, you
always are with nonconformists and it's too late in the year
for salmon, though I expect they poach it all the year
round. That woman behind the bar who I think's the landlady's fat, which is a good sign."

The plump landlady left the bar to come over and discuss their dinner: cooked to order, she said, with artistry and talent, succulent, fresh, nothing out of tins. Without false modesty she announced to them:

"I'm a good cook though I say it as shouldn't, at any rate I'm one who likes my food and that makes all the difference, doesn't it? These skinny types who aren't interested they get me down, something wrong with them I always say, after all if you do something three times a day you might as well enjoy it.

"Well, now, what is there you'd fancy? I've got a nice bit of steak, best fillet off the loin, what a price but worth it—done nice and rare. Or I tell you what if you don't mind waiting for it, there's a bit of tenderloin, tender it is as a baby's bottom, melt in the mouth like a soufflé. Talking of that I can do you a nice cheese soufflé after if you fancy it, I can guarantee you've never had a better, or if you'd prefer a pudding, what about a damson pie with a crust'll make your mouth water, or pancakes if you like 'em wouldn't take any time. Or I could do you a nice bit of roast bird if you like, with bread sauce and bacon rolls and chippolatas, very tasty. That is of course it's Friday, I suppose you're not Roman Catholics?"

"We're not Roman Catholics," Julia agreed. "How wonderful to have it all described like that, only it's going to be agony to wait. Let's have something that doesn't take long."

"Now you mustn't hurry things, dear, if you don't mind my saying, if there's one thing you can't do to good cooking it's bustle and skimp. Turn the gas full on, whip it all up, over it boils, or fries to a frazzle, nothing's good cooked that way, believe me. It's the gentle cooking counts, slow and steady. You wouldn't want to spoil an evening's fun rushing at a girl like a bull, knock her off her feet and all over and done with in a few minutes, would you?

"Now then we've settled on a nice piece of saddle

haven't we, with red currant jelly homemade and a good rich gravy and a fresh cauliflower. There won't be a better piece of saddle in the country I can promise you. I get it from Elwyn Evans and he's got a name for Welsh hill lamb all over England and in New York even I've been told. There's several customers get it by air, that's what they think of it, but Elwyn Evans saves me one or two a week from the very best he's killing, firm all over as a ripe plum, just the right amount of fat and not yellow fat either, clear as a bell, and you know the secret, dear, it's just what I was telling you, take your time and don't hurry, not the way they force their lambs in England these days so they're scarcely born before they're big as donkeys and off to the butcher, you'll never get the quality that way. Rank, that's what it is. Now Elwyn Evans . . ."

Half an hour later they were on their third gin and their saddle was presumably cooking at the right speed, while Mrs. Davies was about the place like a pullet—not that she was young but she half darted, half waddled as if after corn, now behind the bar, now bending over a customer telling him a dirty joke judging by the roars of laughter, now vanishing to the kitchen to reappear with something in her hand, a dishcloth or a wooden spoon, an egg-whisk on one occasion. The place was crowded and convivial and hummed like the generator of a ship throbbing its way across a calm sea.

"They all look so prosperous," Dick remarked.

"Well, they are. You sound surprised."

"I don't know why, I suppose I've never thought of Wales as prosperous somehow."

"Druids in caves and women in red petticoats and deserted lead mines and mists and mountains and the unemployed. You must catch up, Dick. And give a bit of credit, even, to poor old Peter. At least he's tried."

Dick frowned slightly and she thought it had been a mis-

take to bring that up, and yet it was necessary; between
them these mysteries and ambiguities must be resolved.
Julia hankered after the black-and-white, and she'd been
born into a time of greys. She knew it was her own impulse
to change and remake people that had drawn her to Evan
—what he'd called her ministering angel complex, Martin
her power-lust. And now Dick—it would break her heart
to see him broken, to watch the erosion of that sublime
confidence in his own purpose (whatever it was); yet, at
the same time, she wanted to see him enticed on to a level
where they could meet on equal terms.

Was it all really selfishness, at bottom—her desire to feel
superior? Once more, nothing was straightforward. She
looked at Dick and her heart moved; shorn of his certainty
he was childlike and in need of reassurance and she
couldn't help working on his doubts, widening the cracks.
Delilah, she thought, we are all that, we have got to punish
Samson for his overbearing pride. Had Dick been proud?
Yes, and still was, even with his pride damp and torn. It
had been the pride that had drawn her and excited her,
the pride that she both respected and wanted to destroy.

"Oh, damn and blast it all!" she suddenly exclaimed,
clenching her hands and drumming on the table like a
child. Dick was alarmed.

"Getting hungry? I must say the old trout's taking a hell
of a time, all that talk about her cooking, she might just as
well have given us some cold ham."

"You know it isn't that. I'm not hungry."

"What is it, then? I am."

"Oh, Dick, can't we ever straighten out things between
us? It's like groping through a fog for something and you
don't know what. I can't stand it."

Dick looked hard at the table, his fingers tight on his
glass. "There can't be anything between us, Julia."

"Why can't there?"

He didn't answer.

She repeated: "Why not? You had a wife, I know. She's dead. I'm sorry, but you can't keep up this sort of tight-lipped mourning act for the rest of your life. People's wives do die. They marry again. They have love affairs. You're just refusing to face facts. If your wife really loved you, she—"

"For Christ's sake, shut up, Julia. Don't you see it's something beyond discussion, right outside—"

"That's the whole point. You're trying to shove it out of sight because you can't face it and that's messing up your whole life. You're—" She broke off with a gesture, putting her face to her hands. "Oh, God, why do I always lecture people about what's best for their own good? I'm sorry, Dick, but you know it's true, if you'd only talk about the whole thing openly everything would be all right afterwards and there wouldn't be this sort of unspoken doom between us like a great unburied corpse stinking to high heaven. It's all so stupid and pompous and I—oh, hell, I'm sorry, I've had too much to drink again, it's always the same, but when I get as far as this I have to go on, get me another, there's a darling, will you?"

Dick didn't seem to have heard; his face was heavy and stiff and he was twisting a spoon in his fingers. He said:

"It isn't as simple as that."

"I'm tired of hearing that. Nothing's simple. So what? Like trying to swim through treacle. Even dying isn't final these days."

"Not the way Rose died."

"I'm sorry, Dick. I won't say any more."

"She committed suicide."

"Oh, God, I'm sorrier than ever now. God knows why I've been going on at you. Try to forget it, Dick. Try to stop blaming yourself."

"I don't blame myself. I never have because it wasn't my fault. It was someone else's."

"We'd better find something else to talk about."

"No, I want to explain." Dick's words were coming out in a rush. "Do you ever read about the Greeks, mythology I mean? For instance, about Achilles?"

"A heel," Julia said, trying a very feeble joke to distract him; now she thought he really must be mad, and felt nervous, there was such a wild look in his eye. But he wasn't to be checked.

"The handsomest and bravest of the Greeks, I believe. So when the Trojans killed his friend Patroclus, he decided on revenge. Quite simple, the revenge, he didn't argue about it like people do now. Hector it was who killed Patroclus so he was going to kill Hector and he did. You could say that Hector wasn't in the least to blame for killing Patroclus, it happened in a fair fight, anyway it was Hector's job to kill Patroclus because he was threatening the security of Troy. So there were lots of arguments against Achilles taking his revenge and probably no good ones in favour of it, not by modern standards, but that was what he felt like and he did it, and pretty brutally too. What's more he got killed himself later on and he expected that too, but it didn't put him off. Why should it, he'd had his revenge?"

"What's all this supposed to prove?"

"Nothing," Dick said, smiling. "I'm not proving anything, just telling you a little Greek mythology. I'm not a handsome Greek with spears and shields and plumes. But even a poor cow-keeping clod with straw in his hair can sometimes get the same sort of damn silly ideas into his head. So even if it wasn't—if she—"

There was something in his throat that stopped him bringing out Rose's name. "Hang on while I get that drink and then we'll find old mother Davies and get hold of something to eat even if it's only spam and sardines. . . ."

He walked away still talking and left Julia feeling cold all over and with a buzzing in the head. She'd never gone cold before when drinking and her throat was dry, her head swimmy, a kind of excitement gripped her stomach and tingled in her veins. This was it, then: this was what was eating him, making him tick. He had put it, in the end, so clearly and simply, the desire for personal revenge. You couldn't justify it and he hadn't tried to, and that gave him his strength; he didn't feel the need to justify himself like most people, to be right and everyone else wrong. He just made his own rules.

Mad, of course, she'd always known it; but then who could say what madness was, where it began? Another line you couldn't draw, another zone of grey. How sick she was of all the havering, the ambiguities, the well-on-the-other-hand; and here was Dick, he just went straight in like a plough cutting through turf and paying no attention to humps and molehills and turds and stones. She loved him for that, among other things: even though she knew who was the Hector to his Achilles, the man he didn't personally hate but held responsible and meant to kill.

All at once she found herself shaking with laughter. It was ridiculous, the whole thing; Dick was pulling her leg and she was the sucker. A warm wave of trust and affection swept over her; all a joke, she kept saying, as you said over and over to yourself when you came round from a nightmare, thank God it was only a dream. The smoke-filled bar, the dark oak, the shiny brasses, the worn chairs and the warming pans, all these were immensely funny, everything was glowing and flashing in a warm light and she was sweating, but gloriously happy, and there was mother Davies swaying like a sailing vessel in a fitful wind tacking towards her, a-glitter with bangles and things.

"Dinner's ready, dear, at last, dreadfully sorry it's been an age, but Christ are we busy, well you see for yourself a real rush on, good for trade of course but murder on my feet I tell you. Hope your stomach hasn't fallen through your feet, it's worth waiting though, that I promise, you won't be disappointed and I'm doing you some cheese croquettes to finish with after the pudding, juicy as a ripe melon, melt in the mouth, you'll see. Now where's that man of yours got to, it doesn't do to let things get cold and the saddle, a real treat. . . ."

Dick was back and put his hand under her elbow and half lifted her and she had to steady herself and move very carefully and slowly, one leg in front of the other put deliberately down, clinging to his arm.

"Don't you go and do that again, Dick," she said. "I mean leave me alone with all those people and mother Davies, her bangles are like claws, they frighten me." When they reached the dining room she doubled up with laughter because of an enormous dark oak sideboard, carved all over its front with elaborate, heavy, shiny figures, horses prancing and dogs and people and banners, a jousting scene with knights riding at each other on their armoured horses and heralds blowing trumpets and lots of pennants and flags.

When Dick said: "I don't see what's particularly funny about it," she laughed even more because he was like a large puzzled dog with a wrinkled forehead. Hector and Achilles and Patroclus were chasing each other across the sideboard with gallumphing great horses, pricking at each other with lances, and where was Peter in all this, a knight in armour too, brandishing a shining spear? Peter with his funny little speeches and his cigars and his eighteenth-century wine glasses and his well-cut dark suits and sweet-smelling after-shave lotion and black Anthony Eden hat and carnation buttonhole and his belief in progress through

collective bargaining and agreements on restrictive prac-
tices and self-determination for emergent nations and aid
for underdeveloped states and increased productivity. It
was too ridiculous, the wole thing. Dick was nothing but a
coelacanth, a very old fish with whiskers. She laughed
again.

"I'm glad that's sorted out," she said. "I'm glad we know
where we are."

chapter 23

"I MUST warn you I've got a jealous nature," Julia said. A light shining through the window from the road half illuminated a bedroom crowded with rickety furniture, and sounds came of people saying good night and starting cars. "I don't mean I go round throwing vitriol about or scratching out people's eyes, I merely make myself bad-tempered. It's a beastly thing to be. Were you ever jealous of Rose?"

"I never had any reason."

"The children. Fathers can be jealous of their sons."

"I don't remember being. I mean it was a sort of joint effort, wasn't it?"

"It all sounds too good to be true."

"It's past," Dick said shortly. "We've agreed to avoid it."

"Yes, I'm sorry. Only sometime she's got to be dug up and buried."

"Oh, for Christ's sake, leave it alone, will you? Who said you could tidy up my past life like a muddle in a drawer and throw out what you don't like?"

Dick walked angrily over to the window and stood looking out; mixed with her anger she felt admiration for his muscular body, the straight back and slim hips and power

and repose. Why did artists concentrate on the female
body, with its bulges and rolls and fat bottoms and pendu-
lant breasts, when the male was so much neater and better
balanced, the skin drawn over the muscles and tendons like
a glove?

"I'm too bossy," Julia said. "I try not to be but how can
one stop one's faults? I suppose I get it from Peter. He's
just the same only more so and Mother's marvellous with
him. She must ache to shut him up sometimes, and snap
like you did just now, but she doesn't. She just looks remote
and smiles and says something rather funny in that small
voice of hers and it sort of quietens him down. I'm sorry,
Dick."

"No, it's my fault, I didn't mean . . ." But he was still
standing at the window with his back to her, not even looking round.

"Let's not talk any more." Julia had got into bed and
drawn up the blankets, it was getting chilly and the sheets
weren't properly aired. He turned round, but still didn't
move from the window and his voice sounded stiff and
withdrawn.

"It's no good, all this."

"Oh, my God, you're not going to get an attack of puri-
tan conscience?"

"It's nothing to do with that. I can't help you, you'll only
get hurt. We shouldn't have met."

"Well, we have."

"There's still time . . ."

"Are you simply trying to say you don't want to sleep
with me? Because if so I wish you'd say it straight out, not
in riddles. I shall quite understand."

"Of course I want to sleep with you. But you want more
than that." She was silent, hiding her face. "I don't think I
really exist, not in the sense you want me to. I can't explain."

"Well, all right." Julia's voice was muffled by the sheet. "What shall we do, pretend we're brother and sister, unfashionable now with no incest, or do you want to knock up Mrs. what's-name and get a single room?"

Dick came over and sat on the bed beside a narrow worn mat, a dressing gown pulled over his shoulders. "You still don't understand. If you were just a tart or something it wouldn't matter, but you want something I haven't got. It just isn't there. You'll go on looking and that'll make you miserable because it's dead and nothing you can do can change that, even though . . ." He made a helpless gesture with his hands. "I'm making an awful hash trying to explain but do try and understand."

"You're thrashing about all over the place trying to say something absolutely simple. All you're saying is you don't love me. I never thought you did. You don't suggest you've got to be in love with everyone you sleep with, do you?"

"Good lord, you're impossible," Dick exclaimed. "You sound like a kid of sixteen when you say things like that."

"I'm over sixteen. So you're quite safe."

"That doesn't suit you, being flippant, Julia. You're too— Am I being very pompous?"

"Intolerably."

"Well, you've been warned."

He laughed and turned off the bedside light. "That's all right, then. Move over, will you?"

The street light went out at midnight and Julia lay for a while in darkness while he slept in her arms breathing as steadily as the beat of the sea. Lying there comfortably and happily, a hibernating shrew in its nest or a nut in the soft fur of its pericarp, she tried to remember how many men she had slept with. Not so many as it seemed, a number had got to the brink but not quite gone over. Four or five, perhaps, completely, and she'd always had to get a bit drunk, not to enjoy the act itself but to work up to it so as not to feel self-conscious and to find the whole performance merely absurd.

With Dick she didn't need anything like that, it was too natural and enjoyable to be absurd, and at the same time too serious. Real enjoyment was serious, she understood that now. Dick had known it already, he was wise because he'd once been happy. Had he been happy tonight? Or just oblivious? She couldn't tell. Perhaps there was no way of telling: opposites, like circles, met and joined.

A lorry humped by, growling, and casting as it went a momentary beam through the window, dim like sheet lightning. The sound died away sadly down the valley. Dick stirred and turned on to his back, she lay curled into his side.

"Dick?"

"You ought to be asleep."

"Let's go right away somewhere together."

"It's such a lovely name—Julia. I wish you could keep it only for me. That, and everything, and always be here."

"You're not listening."

"Let's talk tomorrow."

"Then tomorrow comes and it's the next day."

Dick laughed. "That's the way to live. The way animals do."

"Australia."

He murmured sleepily: "Blue gums, bush fires, boomerangs, koalas . . ."

"It's really all seaside bungalows, high teas and healthy young women with brown legs, I believe. You could get a job there. And we'd have one of the bungalows."

He turned and pulled her closer and kissed her, but didn't answer. Although she lay limp and relaxed in his arms she felt angry, then defeated, almost in despair.

"Oh, Dick . . ."

"I'll tell you a bedtime story. There was once a hunter

who decided to catch a buffalo and teach it to pull a plough. So he went after one of those lone bulls who've been kicked out of the herd because they're a failure. Sometimes they're bad-tempered and sometimes just rather lethargic and sad, they give up the struggle."

"Why do you treat me like a child?"

"The hunter got this bull at last shut in a pen and invited his friends to see it. They all came and looked in the pen but they couldn't see any buffalo. 'There's nothing there,' they said. 'But there is,' the hunter insisted. 'There's a very splendid buffalo bull.' 'Well, none of us can see it,' the friends replied. Then the hunter looked again and he couldn't see it either, just a shadow of a bush that looked like a buffalo. 'That's a queer thing,' he said. 'Well, it doesn't matter,' the friends replied, 'because what's the use of a buffalo anyway? It gives no milk and nobody has ever taught one to pull a plough.' The hunter was unhappy because he'd set his heart on taming this one, but after a while he went off into the bush and shot a very splendid elephant and felt better. Now, my darling, go to sleep."

"I hate riddles and parables and things. I wish you'd talk sense."

"I will in the morning."

Julia felt angry and defeated but increasingly drowsy; she'd had a lot to drink and it was doing its job, floating her gently along through the rapids and rocks and into a warm pool of sleep.

But her fears and doubts returned in the morning. Dick was a phenomenon lying right outside her experience, but there must be a way to deal with him if only she knew it. The trouble was she didn't, and you learnt only through failure. Would a French girl, she wondered, know at once how to handle Dick? Probably this was a myth, like most things; French girls, no doubt, were just as much at sea, they couldn't be *born* knowing about all the different kinds of men in the world and how they reacted; but the very fact they'd built up the myth must help, at least if they believed it themselves.

"Do you think the French are better than we are at coping with love affairs?"

"Good lord, I don't know. I don't think I've ever known a Frenchwoman. I was brought up in the ooh-la-la Fifi school."

"Let's go to France in the Simca," she suggested. "Next week. It's not quite too late in the year."

She was uneasy and on edge, a bit queasy, perhaps a mild hangover; she had a strong head for drink but not a strong stomach and sometimes felt awful in the mornings and cursed herself for her stupidity and lack of will. But if you *hadn't* a strong will, what could you do about it, any more than not having a talent for music or languages?

"You have marvellous ideas, Julia, but for one thing I've hardly any money."

"I can lend you some till you start earning it."

"I'd rather earn it first."

"That's hopelessly square. Besides, you may be in the nick before long."

"I don't think so."

" 'They'll never take me alive,' he said."

"I must admit I don't fancy an English jail. But there can't be any proof about the pictures. That's still needed, isn't it, for British justice?"

"You don't know Martin," Julia said.

chapter 24

Dick had stripped the roll of canvas from his leg and pushed it into the back of an ill-fitting drawer. But its presence there made Julia nervous; at any minute she expected a policeman to arrive and make inquiries and search their room.

Martin could accuse Dick of stealing his pictures. Or had he stolen them himself in the first place? Or were they forgeries? Whatever he'd done, you could be sure his tracks were covered. So it was decided they'd climb the bare hills which rose abruptly from the tree-lined valley and find a foolproof place to dump the roll of canvas—a deserted lead mine if there was one, a fox's earth, a rabbit's burrow. But when they got some way up, panting and puffing, they couldn't find a single lead mine, or even a hole.

"We'd better wedge them under a rock in one of these streams."

"It seems a shame." Dick hated to see anything spoiled or wasted.

"I don't think for a moment Martin would entrust genuine pictures to you, he'd naturally assume you'd make off with them if you saw half a chance. I should think he's got a blackmailed painter tucked away somewhere turning out Mondriaans and Picassos by the dozen for the tourists in Italy."

Dick rolled up his raincoat carefully and put it in the rucksack with a thermos and a paper bag containing sandwiches they hadn't eaten. Every now and then Julia observed, quite without warning, that something closed inside him like a shutter falling, his face hardened and he seemed to go a long way off. She'd read that certain savages bored a hole in the skulls of their dead for the spirits to emerge through. Like them, he had a sort of trap door through which he let out something, a kind of essence, whenever he encountered a situation he couldn't square with his intentions or needs.

"Let's move on, shall we? The wind's cold. But we ought to get a terrific view from the top." Dick smiled at her and she thought: he's opened the trap door again and called back that bit of himself that went away, the essential bit, the unapproachable.

There was a miniature waterfall in a dip just above the junction of two streams; under a rock, Dick found a peaty hollow. He took the thin tube stitched up in linen, doubled it and pushed it in as far as his arm would go, half drenching himself in the clear, swift-flowing water.

"It's bloody cold."

"That'll fox the keen-eyed coppers. They can't comb every inch of Welsh mountain."

"They might try. If Martin *does* report it."

"I don't think they're sufficiently art loving even to try."

He took her hand and pulled her forward and she couldn't help grinning, she felt so strong and healthy despite aching muscles and an incipient blister. Mountains were not her line but it was no good pretending, she was enjoying herself and felt invigorated, gulping lungfuls of air sharp as iced fruit juice, and touched with an upland smell of peat and grass and the dried pellets that sheep had left in neat little piles. A pair of hawks flew up towards the hill-crest, wheeling and sweeping and letting air currents carry them with little effort from their own black, outspread wings. Dick watched them for a while and said:

"They're part of it, like the streams and sheep and grasses. We ought to have a dog, a collie. Dogs are part of it too. Let's get to the top and see the view."

Julia's feet slipped on wiry, withered grasses and some-times she had to grasp the twigs of a brittle little shrub whose leaves were dropping and whose roots came out if she pulled. She went up crabwise, panting, the calves of her legs aching and blood pressing against the backs of her eyes. To make things worse Dick charged on ahead like a mountain goat, apparently forgetting her existence and going up without any sign of effort, rucksack on shoulder and a brown scarf flying out behind. She clambered to the brow of a crest and paused to recover, searching for his moving figure, trying to pierce through rocks and peat to where he must be standing—watching her?

Suddenly an unforeshadowed surge of panic rose like bile and made her ears drum and her throat dry. Here she was, alone, totally alone and solitary among these empty and solitary mountains, among rocks and bogs where she could perish and no one would know. She'd never been quite so completely alone before and the emptiness, the bareness, the coldness of the solitude overwhelmed her, they were like a strangler's hands. She wanted to scream, to turn and throw herself down the slope.

She was afraid of Dick. Why had he vanished, where was he now? Watching silently, with calculation, with love curdled into hatred? Or with that insane kind of love that made men want to kill a woman out of a perverted passion for complete possession?

Was Dick mad enough for that? What did she know of

him? That he'd turned up from nowhere with a crazy obsession about Peter, that he'd got involved with Martin in some shady deal, that a mind half unhinged by his wife's suicide was filled with half-baked notions of revenge. And in her stupendous folly she'd climbed this mountain alone with him, not even leaving word with Mrs. Davies at the pub. He could strangle her up here, hide her body in the peat and disappear. No one would know.

The hawks had come back, or perhaps another pair, and were gliding, wheeling, sideslipping down towards the valley. Nothing else moved but grasses bent by the wind. Wisps of mist or cloud were swirling down from the head of the valley and soon everything would be enveloped in the kind of thick, wet fog in which you quickly lost your sense of direction, went round in circles, panicked, until night came on coldly and you died.

Julia turned back and searched the hillside again but there was still no Dick. A sound came on the wind, whether a bird's call or a distant shout she couldn't say. Anything was better than the solitude, any human contact at all. Hunching her shoulders, she went on up the slippery hill, her hands clammy, her heart icy cold. If he kills me, she thought, at least I'll be out of this agony of panic. She'd never thought it mattered much, dying; it was just the going, the manner of death you feared.

She plodded on, cursing her own folly. Why did she never learn? If she'd minded her own business, left Dick alone that evening at the fireworks instead of trying to use him as a goad to provoke Evan, instead of giving in to curiosity, all this wouldn't have happened. What people said was true, you made you own fate; what happened to you sprang from what you were, from all the flaws and stupidities. But then those flaws in your own make-up, were you responsible for them? You didn't make your own character. That came partly from the kind of childhood you'd had, how your parents treated not only you but each other, and partly from your parents' genes, controlled by a chemical known by initials she always mixed up with Moral Rearmament.

Whatever else you could control, it wasn't all that. So you were back where you started from. Your mistakes were your own fault because they resulted from your own character, from which you spun your fate like a spider; but you weren't responsible for your character because it was formed by agencies quite outside your control, any more than the spider had designed its built-in mechanism for spinning webs. So you *weren't* responsible. . . .

Then what about Martin? He wasn't responsible, in that case, for a desire for power so degenerate that he tried to manipulate weaker men like Evan as if he had them on strings; for his utter egotism; for a diseased mind he tried to alleviate by perverting others, as men with syphilis had once believed they'd cure themselves by poking virgins. It was more Peter's fault, then, than Martin's.

And what about cruelty? Could you get away with torturing a small child or helpless animals by blaming it on your parents because they'd quarrelled, or your mother had been jealous, or even on your genes? That was just a bit too easy. Somewhere there must be a line beyond which you had the choice, and so must take the blame. That was the trouble with life—no rules, each person must draw his own line with invisible ink on a dark night, blindfolded.

And there was Dick: the line he'd drawn put almost everything on the side marked responsibility. And then he had his vague, mystical belief in the unity of everything from a speck of dust to a Nobel prize winner, a unity now disrupted by man's own inventions: by too much mind, or mind headed in the wrong direction, like cancer cells.

How much of it did he really believe? Perhaps his need to believe something, anything, was more important than the beliefs themselves. Ideas got into the minds of men like viruses in the blood and created fevers, and then nothing else counted. Men only pretended to love women; as soon as they smelt an idea in the distance they were off like a bullet out of a gun, saying over their shoulders I could not love thee dear so much loved I not honour more— honour being a synonym for killing people. . . . Believe in nothing, enjoy everything and life could be a paradise. It was all too difficult and she gave it up.

On their way down the day before in the Simca a late, lost bee had got into the car, tempted from its hive, no doubt, by the October warmth and sunshine. It had buzzed against the windscreen and she'd slowed down and Dick, instead of crushing it, had carefully picked it up in his handkerchief and released it through the window. She'd laughed at him and asked whether it would find its way back to its hive, carried, as it had been, so far from home. He'd taken her quite seriously and given her a little lecture on the intelligence of bees, on how they found their way about by taking bearings from the sun and performing little dances at the entrance of their hives to show their mates the direction in which to search for honey.

Surely if he'd spared the bee, he wouldn't strangle her? But then, the bee didn't clash with any theory; theories were the trouble, beliefs, principles, they were what caused the suffering and cruelty in the world. Suppose she clashed with an idea, as Peter had, Dick would think no more of crushing her than most men would think of squashing a bee.

chapter 25

At last he felt safe, protected from a hostile world by the silent, moisture-laden mist as by a thick layer of insulation —as a live cable is protected by its rubber sheathing, a sheltering mollusk by deep-sea waters, an embryo by the membranous womb. He drew the saturated, fungus-grey air into his lungs gratefully, no longer hunted, bewildered, tugged at, but mercifully alone.

Down there, invisible and therefore to be taken on trust, existing only in imagination, lay a wide valley from which the moisture-laden particles surged and swirled like cold steam rising from a cauldron. Dick saw a different valley, as full of sunshine as this of fog, as bright and pure as this was grey and dank.

The Cape chestnuts had been out at the time. You looked down onto a sea of mauvish-pink froth, as if a wave had broken there and all the creamy foam been held suspended. He had stopped the car on the hill.

"There can't be anything else like it in the world," Rose had said.

"No. But there can be other scenes."

"*They belong to other people.*"

"*One can adopt them.*"

"*It's not the same thing.*"

"*Not for us, no. It could be for the children.*"

"*The children. . . .*" Rose's hands were always restless nowadays, they were crumpling a handkerchief in her lap. She kept moving her legs, crossing and uncrossing her knees, and she worried too much about details, about everything. He needed all the patience he could call on, and sometimes that gave way and he snapped.

"*Andrew simply must see the dentist,*" she said. "*I know he's got decay in one of his molars. But now Gilchrist's gone and they say you have to wait three months to see the Indian, Gopal, he's so booked up. And in three months he'll probably have gone too. We must do something.*"

"*I'll see Gopal today and ask him if he can't fit Andrew in.*"

"*Then there's Duncan. He's made such an awfully good start, Mrs. Prest is such a good teacher and now she's closing down and going to Australia.*"

"*Things are bound to settle down eventually.*"

"*Eventually!*" Rose turned and looked at him savagely, unlike her usual self. "*Did you hear the Armstrongs' house has been broken into and everything looted? They even pulled up the floor boards.*"

"*Well, if you leave a place empty these days . . .*"

"*They may try one that isn't empty next time.*"

Dick looked down on the frothy blossom and the silent drift sleeping in the heat, and at a harrier hawk perched on a fence post by the side of the track. Sometimes there was a bird on every post along the road; and clumps of forget-me-nots on the verges, under a huge sky alight with moving clouds.

"*Time we moved on,*" he said.

Rose looked down at the drift also. Her face these days

was peaky, she allowed things to prey on her mind. "I don't want to move on."

"Beggars can't be choosers."

"Who made us into beggars?"

"I suppose something called the wind of change."

"It's not like you to give in so easily."

"You know it's not myself I'm giving in for, even you. It's the boys."

"They were born here."

"We've been into all this, Rose, scores of times."

He'd noticed that her skin was dry and her lips pale and flaking a little and her face had a sculpted, hollow look. She'd lost weight, and had ulcers on her legs. Worry, he supposed. Three boys, he with no skills but those of farming and no chance of that in future; they'd have no capital, they'd be lucky if they had enough to buy passages and tide them over for a few months while he searched for a job.

You couldn't get more than a fraction of their value for the cattle, the pedigree lines you'd worked so hard to establish would be broken and dispersed; farm machinery fetched a song and the land—if you were lucky someone would mine it for a few years, paying a nominal rent, otherwise squatters would move in with their hoes and scrub cattle and very quickly bleed it to death. All that you'd built up and worked for, your hopes for the future, your schemes and plans, your capital—the wind of change would scatter these like thistledown. It was worse for Rose, she was a tremendous home lover, dug in, the third generation of white farmers in this black land.

"We'll have to see," Dick said, and drove on, worried about her nervousness and fits of depression—not worried enough, all the same. Was it true he didn't blame himself? He should have noticed more, understood the strain, not only of the children and the hazards of the future but the insecurity of the present, the news of friends' going, of *empty houses, abandoned farms raided by gangs, the thefts and arguments and constant nagging of uncertainties, the sense of things running down, of futility and waste. "A short-term view," someone had said. But a long-term sentence. He ought to have seen and understood.*

When he'd emerged from his meeting he looked for Rose at the hotel but couldn't see her, so he walked down a main street lined by jacaranda trees. He'd always had a soft spot for the little cow-town; it was unpretentious and everyone was friendly, though lately it had begun to sprawl and there was even a five-storey building on the site of old Abdullah's warehouse, where people had put up their mules and ponies in his father's day.

He found Rose in a draper's store trying to make up her mind about a length of material. Always, before, she'd come to decisions of that kind very quickly, but now she havered, puckering her forehead, walking indecisively to and fro between counter and door, crumpling the material in her hands to test its crease-resisting properties. The narrow-chested little Indian was patient and quiet. The store smelt of clean cotton and plastic bags and, very faintly, of spices that touched the air in so many Indian places, a sort of oiliness deriving perhaps from saffron and cummin, coriander and betel.

He rested his bare forearms on the bolts of material and felt their cool smoothness on his skin. It was quiet and dark in the shop and no flies. Afternoon heat lay on the town and flattened it, and he was sweating on neck and forehead. At the back of his mind was the thought of getting home for the milking, although they didn't milk until it got cooler, after tea.

"Well, any news?" Rose asked.

"Colin's going."

Colin Blakeney had the biggest ranch for miles, he was more or less king of the district. At harvest time four or five

combines drove across his five-hundred-acre fields in eche-
lon and the wheat came off in thousands of tons. Combines, ploughs, discs and drills were sometimes in one field
together, planting at the bottom while the grain was coming off at the top. If the Blakeneys went, Dick and Rose
had often said, then they'd go too; for one thing, there'd be
too much empty land all round that would fill up in no time
with riffraff; for another, if Blakeney couldn't make a go of
it, with all his resources, then who could?

Rose carried a bolt of material to the doorway and
peered at it without replying. Then she said crossly:

"I do wish you'd help me decide! Everything nowadays
claims to be crease-resistant and it isn't when you get it
home, or else the colours run. It's no good getting something . . . And it's got to wear. . . ."

He picked out one and suggested: "I like that pattern."

"A lot of use a pattern is if the colours run!"

"Colours guaranteed," the Indian said.

Dick's mind was whirling like a dust-devil, he couldn't
concentrate on dress materials. "Look, Rose, we've got to
face this now. I think I ought to go to Australia to look
round on my own. Then send for you and the boys if I can
find an opening."

"And leave me alone?"

"Naturally we'll make some arrangements with a neighbour."

"There won't be any neighbours soon." Rose exaggerated nowadays.

"We can fix up something. Australia's a complete shot in
the dark. At least, here, you and the boys'll have a roof
over your heads till I can find another. That's what Colin's
going to do."

"No creases guaranteed," the Indian repeated.

"This one's the right colour but it's too thin." There was
a plaintive note in Rose's voice. "I want something heavier.

What about that one up there?" She pointed to another
pile.

"Let's go home," Dick suggested, "and have a cup of tea.
And talk this thing over."

"But I haven't got my dress length yet!"

"Oh, blast your dress length! They all look perfectly all
right to me."

"Can't you see they're all different? The prices too. It's
not as easy as you think. You oversimplify everything,
that's the trouble. Now this one here would do but then it's
the wrong shade of blue."

It was another twenty minutes before Rose was handed
over four yards of a cheap cotton print. Dick was itching
with irritation, Rose almost strident, only the quiet Indian
appeared unmoved, still courteous though aloof. He hadn't
got much future either, Dick thought. If youth-wing thugs
looted his store he'd get no redress, provided they belonged
to the right party; if the local political boss walked in and
ordered half a dozen of his best shirts he'd never get his
money. He had to make the same decision as Dick. One of
the family who owned the little local store and petrol pump
near the farm had gone to India to look round. But everything in India was overcrowded, no openings there and no
sale here for his little business.

That was the real trouble with the world—overcrowded.
People rubbed up against each other too much, trod on
each other's heels, generated friction, suspicion, hatred,
pressed each other down. Everyone needed space and
elbowroom and an individual relationship with the world of
plants and other living creatures and they were cheated of
it by their own self-indulgent fecundity. They were trapped.

The gale swept aside a swirl of mist, as wind would sometimes part the billowing smoke of bush fires, to reveal a
small, dark figure struggling towards him up the slope,

stumbling on slippery grass and peat holes. It looked so forlorn, defenseless, a hand seemed to pinch his heart. Through a mist closing in again he shouted:

"We've missed the view but it's splendid up here, superb!"

"We don't have to climb this bloody mountain, just to see a fog, do we?" Now Julia was cross from relief because, after all, he wasn't going to kill her.

"It's not just *a* fog, it's magnificent. Come on, there's a beacon over there, a triangulation point."

"You can't see a beacon or anything in this."

"We can cut across over there. Come on."

She supposed this was where the springs rose. Sometimes the mist rolled away for a moment to reveal wet, colourless grass tufts and black peat patches under their feet. Near the top, through a gap, she saw a pale grey object sticking up from the sodden grass.

"What's that?"

"A sheep's carcass, I expect."

"It's too big."

She moved forward and stubbed her toes on a twist of silvery metal. Strange shapes loomed all round, whitish, enormously menacing, ghosts trapped for all eternity in positions of agony. It was as if something spewed from the vent of the moon had solidified there: the monstrous, petrified excreta of a machine.

All over the crest of the mountain, bits of metal had been flung out from a great explosion. The mist clothed them with menace, now parting to reveal some bulky, nameless object, now closing in again. Some of these objects could be half identified: the close-lapped flanges of an aero engine, a chunk of fuselage, a buckled wheel.

"They hit the top."

"Another ten feet and they'd have made it," Dick calculated. "Probably a fog, like today."

"It must have been over quickly for them. Unless it burst into flames."

Dick looked round. "They must have gone smack into the hillside and blown everything to smithereens."

"I wonder what they thought of when they hit the hillside?"

"You don't think at times like that. You're all instinct or whatever it is. Non-thoughts, panic. . . . I wonder how long ago it was."

"Someone must remember. We'll ask."

All these mangled remains of a dead aircraft were terribly sinister—so silent, so enduring; mostly aluminium and that, Julia supposed, wouldn't rust or disintegrate. Would it last forever? A million years? A millennium almost certainly; in a thousand years' time anyone who climbed the hill would pick up bits of metal belonging to some crude, forgotten weapon, as today's archeologists found flint arrowheads or scrapers used by primitive, forgotten people.

Dick was poking about among the wreckage trying to make out what bit was what, stirred by a purely factual curiosity. Her fear had changed now to tenderness, she went up to him and pressed her face against his shoulder.

"Don't leave me, Dick."

He kissed her gently, stroking her hair. His face was wet and cold and she took it in her hands. He exclaimed:

"You're warm!"

"I'm alive."

"Let's go back and have tea and hot scones by the fire."

"I said please don't leave me."

"I'm not leaving you, am I?"

"Tomorrow . . ."

"There's plenty left of today. I want to make love to you but I can't in a howling gale on this soaking grass. Come on down."

"You always slide away from the subject."

"I thought that *was* the subject, more or less."

She pushed him gently away and they stood close together, not quite touching, hearing the wind's steady rush in their ears. Julia's nose was running and she took out a handkerchief and wiped it and said: "Oh, Dick, won't I do?"

He made a quick movement that might have been hope, panic or rejection, she didn't know. Then he said: "The mist's beginning to clear," and they turned and went down the hill, leaving the wreckage to stay a thousand years, or perhaps ten thousand. When they asked about it in the bar, no one remembered hearing of a crash on the mountain. It must have been a long time ago, they said: perhaps in the war.

chapter 26

Now they were back in England, among houses and bungalows and fat fields and fat big cattle and drive-in cafés
and petrol pumps and wide roads, though never wide
enough to take the traffic. England was all towns or half-
towns, neither town nor country: the raped fields were
house-speckled like a skin covered with pimples. People
were burning leaves and hedge trimmings in their gardens
and the sweet smell of bonfires, pungent and enchanting,
drifted across the road. Perhaps this autumn smoke woke
Julia. She sat up and yawned.

"How about tea?"

"Let's stop somewhere," Dick suggested. But they didn't.
Either the cafés looked too sordid or too pretentious, or
they didn't see the sign until they'd gone past and would
have to turn, or they'd just overtaken a line of five or six
heavy lorries and couldn't face having to do it again.

They'd missed out lunch, too. When, after a lazy Sunday
morning, they'd gone up to the bedroom to pack and tidy,
quite without premeditation they had made love more completely and successfully than before and lay quietly afterwards, the tensions gone, doubts appeased. Julia snoozed

like a grub, she thought, in a cocoon of happiness, silky and protecting; this was it, this was what she'd wanted and been searching for. Incredibly lucky to have found Dick, luckier still that he was kind. So, after they got under way, Dick at the wheel, she'd buried her head in his side and gone to sleep. He could feel her warmth against his ribs and was careful not to swing the car too much round corners, cutting them sometimes to avoid waking her.

Now they were missing tea and Julia said: "Never mind, we'll stop a little later for a drink and then change over. It's less than two hours now to Chaffins."

"Do they know you're coming?"

"When we stop I'll telephone. What about you?"

"I'll stay at the pub in Horsington."

"You may find a reception committee waiting for you." She was thinking of policemen, questions, complications; of Peter's anger and Martin tunnelling away in the dark like a deathwatch beetle. "We must stick to the same story."

"It's simple enough."

"We'd better make sure. I need that drink. The next decent-looking pub . . ."

The one they stopped at had been modernized. It had a cocktail bar with concealed strip lighting and shiny, Formica-topped tables and red Rexine-covered chairs and a Polyvinyl floor. A radio crooned subserviently from some hidden orifice, emitting harmonies like warm, sweetened soup. Plastic daffodils and tulips occupied plastic bowls in pastel colours.

"No oak beams," Julia commented. "Does that disappoint you?"

"No. It's just that they're what you think of when you think of English pubs. If you live overseas, I mean. Oak beams and inglenooks and darts and the honesty and the sturdy common sense of the British working man. The public image. A hundred years out of date I suppose."

"Instead of shop stewards, demarcation strikes and football pools. The reality."

"I'll tell you a funny thing about England," Dick volunteered. "You never hear a cock crow."

Julia looked at him warily, her first gin glowing inside an empty stomach. Was he serious? With Dick you never quite knew what was going on. "Did you expect to?"

"I suppose I took it for granted. It's the first sound I've heard every morning all my life. In the dark, just as the sky's beginning to get a little pale."

"Yes, I know about cock crow. Nowadays we have radio pips instead. But there must *be* cocks here all the same."

"Not with all these battery cages and broiler houses—efficient prisons. No sex life for hens."

"I never thought of that," Julia said. "All those sex-starved birds. We'd better have another drink on it."

"If you have another drink, I'd better go on driving."

"No, it's my turn. Anyway it's not far now. Dick?"

"Yes?"

"I don't want to butt in or anything but what comes next exactly? I take it you aren't settling in for the winter in the pub in Horsington."

"I couldn't afford to, for one thing."

"Well, you must have some sort of plan."

Dick hesitated, twirling the liquid in his glass and looking round the room, but not at Julia.

"You talk as if life was a kind of military operation. Must one always have a plan?"

"Perhaps not a plan exactly, but some sort of general idea. Otherwise one just drifts. That's all right for some people but not you, I should imagine. Not your line at all."

"One has to change one's line sometimes. Or it's changed for one."

Julia pushed her empty glass across the table with a spurt of irritation.

"Do, for God's sake, get me that other drink and then we'll go. Why do you always slide out of everything so?"

Dick got up calmly, saying: "I don't think I do."

"You won't *face* things, Dick."

"Face things! I—"

The shutter had come down again, that heavy, closed look—not anger exactly, not hurt feelings, but a kind of remoteness, a cold detachment; he'd gone a million miles away into a country where she could never follow. He looked as if he'd been chiselled out of stone. Julia's skin tightened, the goose walked over her grave; a twinge returned of the same fear she'd felt on the mountain.

"Oh, well, forget it. What does it matter anyway? Let's have that drink and get on."

She drank the gin and tonic almost without drawing breath, savagely. The calm and trust between them had been broken, the jagged edges grated together. Why did she have to keep on trying to drive him into a corner? But then, why did he keep sliding out from under her feet, dodging the issue? Surely there *was* an issue? He must have some idea?

"Eat, drink and be merry," she said, putting down the empty glass. "No thought for the morrow, lilies of the field, the birds of the air, neither do they gather into barns or something. No gathering into barns for our Dick. Let's have another drink on it."

"You've had enough, Julia."

"For Christ's sake, granny." She stook up with a jerk. "Anyway there's no reason you should go on paying, this one's on me."

"I don't want any more."

"Well, I do. If you were half as good at running your own life as you seem to be at telling other people . . ."

He stood stolidly by the table,, tracing a pattern on its shiny yellowish surface with a thumbnail, seeing beyond it shapes perhaps, scenes, memories, things she could never share. She came back miserably, almost in tears.

"I'm sorry, Dick. I'm such a bloody fool. It isn't true, God knows what's the matter. I bugger everything up, going on at you. It'll work out in the end."

"In the end." He smiled at her, back again from his private country. "Not long to wait. I tried to warn you, Julia. I'm sorry, it's not that I don't—"

"For God's sake, don't *you* start apologizing to me, we seem to get everything mixed up, don't we? Upside down, topsy-turvy. Ridiculous expression, topsy-turvy. Come on, let's go, mustn't keep all those policemen waiting. Chaffins will be packed with them I daresay."

"You'd better let me drive," Dick suggested again when they reached the car. Julia pulled open the door and slid in behind the wheel.

"Grandmother Dick. With a great big shawl on, sitting up in bed. Oh what big eyes you've got, Grandmama, not to mention all those motors, I mean molars, a nasty great big hungry wolf. You aren't nervous surely? I know this road inside out, come on."

She let in the clutch with a jolt and they shot away. She'd got Dick in a corner now, frightened; this relieved her feelings and she drove wildly, swinging about the road and passing cars too closely and cutting corners. He gripped the edge of his seat and sat there rigidly but she couldn't force a protest out of him and it was a protest she was after, a token of surrender.

After they'd narrowly missed an oncoming car which hooted furiously, she sobered down and drove more sensibly, though still fast. Three gins on an empty stomach had left her neither wholly drunk nor wholly sober. But they drew up safely at the Feathers in Horsington. He asked:

"Will I see you tomorrow?"

"I'll telephone later, when I've found out the lie of the land. Thank you for a nice week end."

"Now *you've* got things upside down. There's not much I can say, is there?"

"There's one thing, but you won't say it. It's very hackneyed anyway. Oh, Dick, I've remembered something."

"Yes?"

"I'm sure we've got a cock at Chaffins. I daresay several."

He laughed uncertainly, standing in the dark with his rucksack in his hand. "Perhaps you have."

"I'll get one sent down to the Feathers to wake you up. Like the young man of Khartoum."

"Julia, do you think you ought—"

"To drive home? Yes I do. He kept a black sheep in his room to remind him, he said, of a friend who was dead, but he couldn't remember of whom. Evan's favourite limerick."

"Oh, Evan."

"Yes, Evan. Good night."

She drove away feeling as if she were made of lead. A mist lay in the vale, patchy and treacherous; the lights of oncoming cars were bent upwards as if by thick wool. She took a pocket transistor radio from the glove compartment and plugged in the aerial, allowing the Simca to lurch across the road to the indignation of the driver of a following car who wanted to overtake. When the set was working she accelerated and soon left the angry car behind.

Up the rise, past the wood and down a slope into the village, its houses black and solid with lights shining from their windows as in Christmas cards. She passed two cyclists abreast, a courting couple with their arms tightly encircling each other's waists—difficult to walk, she always thought, in the clamped position—and then a knot of children on the corner by the council house turn. They should be in bed by now, but village kids never retired at hours considered reasonable by the middle class and gentry. Why should there be a class distinction in the hours of getting in or out of bed? There seemed to be.

Going slowly in the mist, not more than twenty-five, Julia swung out to pass a van parked on the corner. A small figure emerging from behind the stationary van showed up momentarily in her diffused headlights. As she braked there was a slight bump, no more.

Julia fumbled with the door handle and jumped out. A dark bundle lay by the curb. Running feet clacked on the tarmac. Someone pushed her aside to lift the silent bundle and a street light just down the road revealed a white face, a limp form in red trousers. One side of the face was black and squashed and messy.

She had run over a child.

chapter 27

At this time of year, towards the end of October, plenty of roses were always out at Chaffins but their buds were brownish at the bottom, from the damp. Hips in scarlet clusters loaded the branches among withering but still abundant leaves of specie roses and, here and there, small, pale flowers had unfolded, delicate as sea shells, to the damp autumn skies. The lawns were full of moss and worm casts; Walter had mown them for the last time that year. He was standing by a barrow in his shirt sleeves and waistcoat, a cigarette jumping between his lips as he talked. Walter's cigarettes seemed always to have reached the same stage, nearly down to the stub, damp and yellow.

"Ah, mild for the time of year. Touch of frost last week but not enough to cut the dahlias, they'm still in bloom but that'll be the next job, take up the dahlias." Walter made the task sound as formidable as building a cathedral. "The wireless speaks of frost later in the week," he added gloomily.

"It's always wrong," Julia said. The lawn and roses and yellowing trees, a blackbird whistling as if it were spring, the quiet lake silvered by mist with moor hens bathing in the reeds, the glowing dahlias, leathery leaves gathering on the gravel and Walter with his barrow and his grumbles —all this was normal and enduring, the true reality. Everything that had happened the night before was like a black smog, plugging the very pores of her skin. If she could only purge it from her system it would disperse and life would go on as life always had.

Now two worlds coexisted: the orderly, real world of Walter and Chaffins and falling leaves and frost-threatened dahlias, and then a nightmare, unrelenting world of policemen and questions and humiliation, of fear and remorse and disaster, and with worse to come—prosecution, publicity, even the death of the child. Who was Damocles? Whatever he'd done, Julia was sorry for him. There ought to be a chance to bargain—everything one possessed or ever would possess to reclaim from the past a single instant, a speck of time. But there was no one to listen, a blank.

". . . with my back," Walter was saying. "Plays me up something terrible. Shouldn't wonder if it weren't a disc. Got to be X-rayed, doctor says. What with that and me hernia I been proper put about this autumn, I can tell you."

"There's a lot of work at this time of year."

"Ah, that's a true saying, that is," Walter warmly agreed. "True as steel, that is. All the plants to lift and the digging done and the winter cabbages planted and on top of that there's all these leaves to be raked, I don't know how I . . ."

Julia wanted to throw her arms round him and kiss him, small and ugly as he was and committed to nervous ways and spectacles. With the natural tact of villagers he wouldn't say a word unless she spoke first, although of course he must be aflame with curiosity to hear her version. But he didn't show the least sign.

What made it ten times worse was that she knew the child. Stella Ryan. Julia could remember her, a few years back, strapped in her pram outside Mrs. Harris's, playing with a multicoloured ball; Julia had given her a couple of conkers—too big, she'd hoped, to be swallowed. The child had looked at her with round, wondering, puzzled blue eyes and then smiled and thumped with her small fists on the blanket, seemingly a gesture of approval. Mrs. Ryan had emerged from the shop and they'd had the usual conversation about teeth and digestion.

Julia would have liked to gratify Walter but she couldn't. She had to concentrate on the real, normal world and keep out the other. It wouldn't stay out, though; back it came to nag and question, chew and twist and torment.

And now Dick. She'd been right about Martin. Martin had produced a witness—bogus probably—willing to swear he'd seen the pictures handed over, and had heard Dick agree to take them to Milan. It was a wonder the police hadn't arrested Dick already. Under restraint, he might do anything: go berserk like a rogue elephant or shut up like a clam.

And now she couldn't help Dick at all, she needed help just as much as he did, and he couldn't help her either; they were of no use to each other. That was ghastly, too. They were in it together and they ought . . . Her voice agreed with Walter about the bone-idleness of boys these days; at Chaffins they'd taken on three school-leavers, one after the other, but none had stayed, they'd gone off to the factories and high pay and card games behind packing cases, except one who'd joined the army and probably, the way the army was these days, had breakfast brought to him in bed by the sergeant and settled down to television for the rest of the day.

"Oh, well," she said, "they might as well make hay while the sun shines."

She was dizzy too, weak at the knees, perhaps from so much black coffee. Lavinia had tried to make her eat lunch but she couldn't swallow more than a mouthful. Funny how all the clichés came to life: it stuck in my throat. Stuck in my throat. Stuck in my throat. The phrases rolled over and over in her head like a record stuck in a groove. Stuck in a groove, stuck in a groove, stuck in a groove.

Lavinia was advancing across the lawn.

"Come and have tea, Julia. It's ready."

"Them tomatoes," Walter was saying, "might as well throw 'em out as bring 'em in the house. They got the mildew something terrible, like they was bruised all over. Never got enough sun."

"They'd do for chutney," Lavinia suggested.

"Well, you could cut 'em up for that, I daresay," Walter admitted with reluctance. "Lot of wastage, though."

"And really we've got enough chutney, even if we lived entirely on cold meat. Still, it's very handy for bring-and-buys. Perhaps you'd bring some of them in, Walter; pick out the best."

As they walked across the lawn together, Lavinia said to her: "Peter telephoned. He's coming down."

"He can't do anything."

"He's very resourceful in times of crisis."

"He'd better be, with Martin and his crooked picture racket probably getting into the papers and all the sordid details of his daughter going off with the picture-stealer and now a prosecution, drunk in charge—squalid as a drain. Poor Peter, his splendid career will be lying about in shreds in the gutter when the shouting dies down."

"It's early days yet."

"I can scarcely wait for the later days, all the same as this."

"I rang up the hospital. There's no change."

Julia swallowed with difficulty; her stomach felt as if it had been tied in a knot and was going round and round. She wanted to bury her head in something soft, to pull it

round her ears and disappear. Regression, she recognized
—back to the womb, warm and dark and secret. But now,
hands like claws everywhere, outstretched to grip and tug
and pull apart, like a fly tortured by a sadistic boy.

"She's still on the danger list and in a sort of coma. I
should imagine that every day she lives improves her
chances. But it's no use pretending it isn't touch and go."

"I don't care who was driving, they couldn't have
avoided it. If I hadn't had a drink for a hundred years it
wouldn't have made any difference."

"It'll be all right," Lavinia said.

"My God, the way they went on last night, on and on.
Their own doctor was a stinking fat old sod, flabby, with
eyes like something on a fishmonger's slab. I should think
he's tight half his life, a hundred times more than I've ever
been. Spoke to me as if . . ."

She broke off in a trembling fit. Lavinia said: "He's
never been a favourite of mine," and led the way into
Peter's study, so much cozier than the big drawing room.

Julia had been forced to go with a policewoman and
produce a specimen of urine. They had made her keep on
getting up and sitting down, the fish-eyed doctor had
prodded and tapped her and leaned over her with bad
breath to stare into her pupils, pulling her face about with
his podgy fingers. The policewoman had been horrible too,
with blond curls showing all round under her cap and a big
bust and fat bottom, and her manner had the frigidity and
inhumanity Julia thought of as Teutonic: no slit anywhere
to emit the smallest drop of humour or sympathy or compassion. A cold, hard, *fat* woman was the most frightening
thing in the world.

"I suppose they'll come back."

"I should think it's probable. They're thorough in their
duty, the police."

"I've told them everything. There's nothing more I *can*

tell them. And really there's nothing much *to* tell. The way they went on about the weekend, which had absolutely nothing to do with it whatever, as if the fact that I'd been away with Dick made it certain I'd killed a child on the way home. 'Did you have intercourse?' one of them asked, as if that had got the slightest bearing on it, filthy-minded sods; and anyway it's such a bloody silly word."

"It's the official one," Lavinia pointed out. "I don't want to be tiresome, Julia, but do please try to eat some bread and butter. Starvation makes people lightheaded, I believe."

Though the day was muggy, Julia was thankful for the wood fire. The study looked enduringly secure and comforting with its big armchairs, Peter's leather-topped pedestal desk in the window embrasure, the mahogany-cased clock above the fireplace, a carved bear he'd bought in Austria on a lampstand, books lining two of the walls.

In her childhood there'd been sporting prints on the other walls—obviously sporting prints were right, with foxes' masks mounted on wooden shields with the dates of their demise inscribed on little metal plates. While she was a schoolgirl, the prints had given way first to minor English water colours, plus the genuine van Goyen in the place of honour, and then by vivid, clean-looking lithographs of paintings by Picasso, Dufy and Chagall. Peter's callers, whether of the grand, county variety like the Lord Lieutenant, or lesser fry from the local party headquarters, always made the same remark: "Can you *understand* these things, Peter?"—or Mr. Buckle or sir. Peter had the answer pat, supplied by Martin. "Can you understand an elephant?" It nearly always silenced them.

"I'd like to see Dick."

"These scones are good," Lavinia countered. "Maria really is improving, though she'll never have a light hand."

If Lavinia had learnt one lesson, it was the futility of

either trying to arrange other people's lives, or of reproaching them when their own arrangements broke down. It was, of course, one thing to grasp this and another to act on it, but she had tried, even with—or especially with—her own children. She had been commended in this, for her restraint, but put it down herself to indolence. While sadly conscious of failure, she remained unconvinced that direct intervention would have succeeded any better. People, however young, weren't puppets; you couldn't control them by jerking strings.

The result of all this was Martin, and now Julia: considerable failures from the point of view of any normal mother. But then the anti-puppet policy, as she sometimes thought of it, had been only half carried out. There was Peter, a manipulator if ever there was one, tugging at strings with insensitive vigour, and the wrong strings at that. Or so she believed.

Julia asked: "D'you mind about Dick?" Her hands were sticky and she had a little smear of butter on the side of her mouth and looked about fifteen. Nursery teas: an ancient rocking horse in one corner, a gramophone with a handle, bread and dripping with spring onions, while the nanny who had once been Lavinia's sang Irish songs in a cracked voice and thumped on an old piano. It was alarming how one had to pick a way across a bog of sentimentality which seemed to underlie all one's memories.

"Frankly, you can hardly expect me to be pleased. You know I'm not one to interfere but, if I was, this might well be an occasion."

"Sometimes I wish you'd interfered more."

"You wouldn't have paid any attention."

Julia smiled—a tired, not exactly joyous, smile, but a start. Tea and warmth were having an effect.

"I suppose not. But sometimes, you know, one *wants* something to kick against. If the door's wide open already, perhaps one feels flat, I don't know. I thought you rather liked Dick."

"I like quite a lot of people. That doesn't mean I think you'd be wise to go off for weekends with them."

Julia rubbed her hands on the seams of her jeans. "There doesn't seem to be an answer, does there? To anything."

"Well, don't let's despair." Lavinia glanced at the clock: it was almost time to fetch Peter. She hesitated, and added: "This Dick. He's a sort of lame duck, isn't he? Surrounded by stiles. You don't think perhaps that's at the bottom of it?"

Julia shifted her position by the fire so as to toast the other side, her back to her mother. "A ridiculous idea, isn't it? I mean, helping a lame duck over a stile. To begin with the duck would go under it, not over. More to the point to treat the leg."

Lavinia sighed, surrendering to a sense of failure too familiar to be devastating. One had the skill or hadn't, like golf or embroidery. "I must go and fetch Peter."

"One can't help wanting to try and help people sometimes, can one? I suppose the mistake is thinking one knows how."

"Of course you can help people. All I was driving at was, that isn't always the same thing as love. But I'm no authority." She got up, and added: "Will you take the tray through to the kitchen?"

"About Dick." Julia got up too, rubbing her legs, to press the heat of the half-scorched material against her skin. "He's in a hell of a mess about those pictures. It's all Martin. He's furious with Dick and means to get his own back, that's all. If Martin would drop the whole thing there'd be no trouble."

"Perhaps he will, now this other . . ."

"You might think so, but I doubt it. I don't believe it's any use my asking him, he'd only gloat. I was wondering whether you could say something to him. Or Peter."

"Obviously Peter." Lavinia was perhaps unconscious of the edge of harshness in her voice.

"Will you ask him?"

"If you like. But to be quite honest, I think it would be better if it came from you."

Julia rubbed a hand through her uncombed hair. "I suppose so. Only you know what Peter is, the least criticism of Martin and he flies clean off the handle. Perhaps Evan could help. Only Evan's such a rabbit."

"I'll see what I can do," Lavinia said.

She looked at her daughter sadly. It was always too late, she thought, one never saw things coming in time. By the time you grasped the necessity, the harm had been already done. If there was a time when everything was still malleable, you never spotted it, or at least she didn't.

"I must be off," she said. "Will you wash up the tea things?"

chapter 28

"As if there wasn't enough trouble," Peter Buckle said. "It looks as if we're going to lose East Kirkwood."

"Will that be a great blow?"

"It's always a blow when you lose a by-election and this is a particularly awkward one. Of course the press'll play it up just when it looks as if we might persuade the Americans—but I didn't come down to talk politics. Know anything about this?"

Peter held out an evening paper and tapped the folded-over page as if he were calling a meeting to order. He stood in front of the fire bracing himself with a stiff whisky and looking round his study, for once, without pleasure.

"It's about Martin," Lavinia said with surprise. She had expected to see Julia's name. Peter turned to kick at the fire with the toe of a well-polished shoe.

"I know it's about Martin. The whole perishing family seems to have got itself into the news."

The evening paper—one which belonged to Evan's father—carried a brief story of the theft of two Modigliani canvases, the property of Mr. Martin Buckle, the West End art dealer and Minister's son, on their way to the airport en route for Milan. There was a bit about Martin's gallery and the art boom, and a couple of sentences loaded with a hint of something just a little phony about the loss of the canvases: a friend of Mr. Buckle's had volunteered to take them to Milan and he was missing too. *The police have interviewed a man who they think will help them with their inquiries. I understand he was traced to a village near Chaffins, the West Country retreat of Mr. Martin Buckle's father, the Minister for . . .* The possibility of a connection with several recent art robberies was being explored, Interpol alerted; and the pictures were believed to be insured for a particularly large sum. Peter inquired:

"Any idea who this friend of Martin's is?"

"You should ask Martin that."

"I couldn't get hold of him. He's a young fool if he's trusted valuable pictures to anyone he isn't absolutely sure of. It's a good job they're fully insured. Now, what the hell's Julia been up to? It sounded pretty bad on the telephone."

"It is bad, Peter."

"Had she really been drinking?"

"The police say so. They're going to prosecute. I didn't see her till they brought her back more or less in a state of collapse."

"Bloody young idiot. Was she alone?"

"You'd better ask her yourself, Peter."

He took a quick prowl across the room and glared at the barometer on the opposite wall. "Whenever I look at it, that damned thing says change. You know, Vin, I've never interfered with the children, have I? We've always agreed they must make their own mistakes and their own friends, it's no good trying to run their lives for them. That's all very well but it can go too far, with girls especially. I daresay that's an old-fashioned point of view but I can't help it. I've always left Julia pretty much to you. That's a mother's job, isn't it? And now look what's happened. She takes up with every sort of man, the morals of a barnyard fowl to be quite blunt, even if she is our daughter, and without the elementary sense to keep off the drink when she's driving. All right, I *am* old-fashioned, but it's going too bloody far."

"I agree entirely."

"It's a bit late in the day just to agree, isn't it? If she'd been brought up short a bit sooner, subjected to *some* kind of discipline—I don't mean anything absurd, lock up your daughters and that sort of thing, but good heavens, there are limits and she's gone beyond them. A long way beyond. If you'd only—well, I suppose it's too late now. How about the kid?"

"The one she ran over? She's alive."

"What are her chances?"

"A badly fractured skull and lots of broken bones. She's survived one operation and there may be others. Julia says she darted out right in front of the van."

Peter frowned. "I suppose if she dies it'll be a charge of killing by driving, but the drunk in charge is quite bad enough. They won't show any leniency."

"Do you think you can do anything?"

"It's put me in a ghastly position. I shall speak to the Chief Constable of course, but even if he wants to help, his hands are tied. The least hint of interference and there'd be a most appalling row. You know what the papers are, it's the sort of thing that could even bring the government down if it leaked out. I'm worse off than any Tom, Dick or Harry when it comes to something like this."

"All the same you'll try?"

Peter finished his drink and looked at the clock. "I must be honest with you, Vin, I don't believe I can do any good at all. The thing's gone too far. The very fact that she's my daughter means they'll come down on Julia like a ton of bricks. The jury'll start with their minds made up to take the mickey out of this spoilt little rich girl with a father in the government, who do they think they are? The judge'll give her an exemplary prison sentence if he possibly can and everyone'll go home and say you see what British justice is, no favouritism *here* whatever foreigners may do. And of course it *is* favouritism really, only inside out. That's one of the penalties of public life."

"One can only hope it has its rewards," Lavinia said. "There's another thing that won't help, I'm afraid. The child is one of the Ryans."

"You mean these Ryans here, in the council houses?"

"Yes."

"My God, Julia's just about thought of *everything!*" Peter glared at his wife with a look reminding her of Sebastian the Dalmation when affronted by injustice, and poured himself another whisky. "Of all the kids in England she had to run down one of the Ryans! He's red-hot Labour, practically a communist, a hundred per cent disgruntled Irish, always raising hell in the factory, a real troublemaker. Always hated my guts, and all I stand for. He'll stop at nothing to make capital out of this."

"He may be genuinely upset," Lavinia suggested.

"Well, of course he is, I'm not saying that, it's a rotten thing to happen, but politically it's played right into his hands and believe me, he'll go to town on this."

"Despite all that free milk."

"Free milk?" Peter looked baffled for a moment. "Oh, that. Of course Ryan can perfectly well afford to pay for his milk but he knows that if I stop it, he can blow his top at politicians who preach higher living standards and then deprive the children of the working classes of their milk through ruthless profit-seeking. So I daren't stop the milk and he gets away with it, damn him."

"Unlike Colonel Crozier, who really can't afford to pay."

"What's old Crozier got to do with it?"

"He was the other bad debt in the village and his milk was stopped."

"I told you, Ryan's got away with it and no one's more annoyed than I am. But this is all beside the point, Vin. Where's Julia? I'd better get this over."

Lavinia looked into the fire, and got up to put on a log. "She's hardly eaten anything and I'm afraid she may collapse altogether if the police go on bullying her. And if the Ryan child doesn't pull round . . . I know how you feel, Peter, but just at the moment I think there's nothing to be gained by speaking your mind, if you don't mind the suggestion."

"Good lord, I'm not a monster, of course she's upset, but what about the rest of the family and whose fault is it anyway? To be honest I get a bit sick of all this kid glove stuff—not even kid gloves but pulpy fingers underneath, afraid of taking a grip. Nothing's anyone's fault these days, it's their age, or their health, or the state of society, or something wrong with their subconscious, or they're worrying about the H-bomb or what their father said to their mother when they were three or something. All these teenage delinquents, everyone makes excuses for them, has a sense of guilt or something, so they think they can get away with murder and they do."

"In this case I'm afraid that Julia—"

"It's just the same with her. What's Julia ever gone short of or put up with, I should like to know? Now she's knocked her stupid little head against realities and got a bloody nose we're all supposed to mop it up and sing her to sleep with lullabies and blame the wall she ran into. Don't worry, I'm not going to reach for the riding whip or anything, but she's got to face facts for once in her life. For one thing she's got to realize that what she does affects other people. God knows it's not been easy, Vin, to get where I am, it still isn't—like a greased pole, politics, one slip and you're down and out for keeps. If something goes wrong in your Ministry it may be nothing to do with you whatsoever, a nonsense by some junior civil servant you've never even heard of, but you've got to carry the can—look at Tommy Crathorne in the Crichel Down case, or Galbraith and Vassall. And then when one of your own family . . ."

"I'm very sorry, Peter, I'm sorry it all comes back on you and so I'm sure is Julia. But I'm afraid that just at present she's in rather an upset stage emotionally and she—"

"For Christ's sake, don't tell me she's a crazy mixed-up kid. I'd better go and find her, I suppose. If I send for her to come here it would be like the headmaster's study and I suppose *that* would be wrong."

"I'll find her for you." Lavinia was thankful for the excuse to leave Peter before some molten phrase erupted through her self-control.

She found her daughter's bedroom empty. It was not even as untidy as usual, as if Julia had lacked heart to strew quite so many things about. A collection of wooden animals was ranged along the top of a bookcase full of paperbacks, snapshots had been thrust between the glass and frame of the mirror, discs were stacked on a window sill, a pair of jeans and a sweater lay on the bed. Evidently she had changed and gone out.

Lavinia dug her finger tips into her palms and concentrated on the control of her facial muscles. Lately, she'd been unable to resist an impulse to grimace for no apparent reason, and was afraid that one day Peter or Julia, or worse still Simon, would come upon her with an open mouth stretched across her face, her nose screwed up and her teeth bared.

Julia. To disappear just when Peter had arrived from London, cutting an important dinner, in an attempt to mitigate the disaster: to leave no word and go straight back to that ghost who haunted them, a sort of poltergeist who brought nothing but disaster: back to drink with him at the Feathers, and then drive the car. . . . Lavinia stood uncertainly outside the door, hot with anger, wondering what to do and what to say to Peter.

Julia was in a small room off the bar. There was an electric fire fitted with a flicker, and imitation lumps of coal. Dick said:

"I told them you were sober but they didn't believe me. And I'm afraid one or two drivers may have complained."

"What drivers?"

"Don't you remember you cut in several times, and wouldn't let several cars pass?"

"We didn't hit anything."

"Not quite."

"Have you joined the police or something?" Julia demanded furiously. "Whose side are you on?"

Dick rubbed one of her hands between his own—it felt cold—and she pulled it away and sat back, polishing off her drink in a few gulps. "I wish you wouldn't be so bloody calm and reasonable. Oh, well, forget it. There's this huge great machine churning away in the dark, invisible, with everything behind it and then there's just you, or me rather, a single breadcrumb fed into a sausage machine. And these bloody doctors don't know or won't say about the kid. If I didn't *know* her it wouldn't be so bad. She had on red trousers. . . . Well, anyway, I suppose they've been grilling you too about the pictures, I can't think why they haven't pushed you inside."

"I don't think they're quite satisfied."

"In that case they must have doubts about my dear brother. Who's the witness supposed to be, the one who saw him give you the pictures?"

"They didn't say."

"They never do say a bloody thing. One feels like a sort of gnat pinging round a light and bumping one's head against it all the time but coming back, you can't leave it alone, can't go away sensibly and forget it in a nice dark nook or cranny. Get me another drink, will you?"

He looked at her awkwardly. "Not if you're driving back to Chaffins. It's just about—"

"Oh, for Christ's sake, here's my bloody grandmother back again. I'll pay for it, if that's what's bothering you."

"Cut it out, Julia, can't you?" She was like a wounded animal, he thought, lashing out in all directions, claws and teeth and tail, vainly, but using the only available form of protest. "You're not a child. You ought to get back and see your father."

"You're supposed to hate my father. Remember?"

"My feelings haven't anything to do with it."

"They're the whole point, Dick." She jumped up and moved across to him, just to touch him as if to be sure he existed, was alive. "When all this is over, if it ever is, let's clear the hell out of here, right out somewhere. Over the hills and far away. I don't see why we couldn't manage in Australia."

"Perhaps we could."

"Judging by some of the Australians, it can't be all that difficult. I'm quite practical really. The trouble is I've never had to stick to anything, but I would if there was a point."

"It wouldn't be enough for you," Dick said.

"What do you mean, enough?"

"I've told you, I'm not a whole man. There's only part of me. Besides . . ."

"Besides what?"

"I can't explain. Let's say, I've got a job to do."

"Can't I help you?"

He smiled and shook his head. "No one can."

"Surely you're not still . . . You will overdramatize things. People get knocked out by disasters but they come round, they have to. They start again."

"Sometimes with bits of them missing."

"Well, I know the most important bits of you are there."

"Now you're being coarse," Dick said, laughing. "You'd better listen to your father, he's full of ripe experience. He'll sort this out if anyone can."

"I hate your guts sometimes. . . . Oh, Dick." She was limp as a child in his arms and his tenderness a betrayal—Achilles' heel. He wanted her and yet he wanted her to go and leave him to his thoughts and calculations. There was so little time.

Did they or didn't they mean to arrest him? He might have only a few hours left. Tomorrow he might be rendered impotent. The time had come to bring the action to its climax. A time to plant, and a time to pluck up that which is planted; a time to kill, and a time to heal.

Something was bothering the detective-inspector who'd come down from London to put more questions—a bony man with sharp, mean eyes. He was waiting before he laid the charge, perhaps for some piece of information, to do with Martin probably. All three of them were playing blindman's-buff in the dark, probing with hands like tentacles. It couldn't be long before a tentacle touched and sank in and hooked on. It was all a matter of timing.

Dick was puzzled that Martin hadn't apparently, told the police about the gun deposited in the bank. If he had, surely the inspector would have asked questions about it? What was Martin's game? A double bluff behind it somewhere—blindman's buff.

He knew why next morning. A parcel came by the first post. Inside was a cardboard box and inside that, in cotton wool, the gun. There was no comment.

chapter 29

IT never rains but it pours," Lavinia mildly remarked. The government had lost the by-election, Tompkins had reported the sudden death of several heifers from a lethal and incurable infection and, on top of that, the Spanish couple was leaving in the morning.

"A hell of a time to choose," Peter grumbled, "with a shooting party at the weekend on top of everything."

"You'll have it just the same?"

"The shoot?" Peter frowned, walking about the drawing room drink in hand, waiting for dinner. The room with its decorated ceiling, its Persian rugs, the soft light thrown up from gilded wall brackets, the polished furniture and wood fire and the flower arrangements Lavinia did so well had always been a refuge from worry and tension; arguments had taken place, decisions been made, in the study or perhaps the dining room on occasion, never in the drawing room. But now worries permeated every room, every corner, like a fog.

"The only way to play this, Vin, is to carry on as if nothing had happened. After all, in law Julia's innocent until she's proved guilty."

"There's the child . . ."

"What's the latest news?"

Lavinia hadn't yet told him. She found it hard to get out the words. Everything else she'd managed to take calmly, indeed she'd appeared calm over this, but it had shocked her down to the very roots; it was something so appalling she didn't see how one could live with it for years and years. Julia had been numbed and then hysterical and Dr. Smith had come and put her to bed with sedatives.

"The child's alive," Lavinia said.

"Thank God for that." Peter swirled his drink in the glass. "That's one thing, anyway. Though I suppose we're not quite out of the wood."

"Alive," Lavinia repeated, "but not kicking. Very definitely not kicking."

Peter frowned. "Isn't that rather a callous way to put it? After all, you can hardly expect in a few days . . ."

"She's paralyzed for one thing. They say for life."

"Oh, my God."

"Everything. Hands and feet."

"I don't see how the doctors can be sure," Peter said angrily. "They do marvels nowadays in surgery, they keep on finding out new things."

"They say part of the brain has just been squashed."

Peter put down his drink and walked about with tensed muscles, curling up his toes in his shoes. "This is the worst thing that *could* have happened. The effect on the jury's sure to be . . . You said for one thing?"

"She'll also be an imbecile."

Peter gave a stricken sort of groan and went on prowling, looking at the carpet with a deep frown. "It oughtn't to be allowed. It isn't human, it's wicked. The child's five."

"I know."

"Fifty or sixty years perhaps—nursed hand and foot year after year, unless God's more merciful than man."

"One hopes so."

"Oh, God, Vin, I wish—" He wished many things: that it hadn't happened, of course; that Julia hadn't become such an irresponsible, immoral little bitch, that Lavinia . . . Many things too about Vin; but most, at the moment, that someone or something had power to shake her out of this frigid, glacial calm, this tightness, to make her flap, cry out, beg for mercy. It wasn't complacency, it wasn't even lack of feeling—the feeling was there but trodden down like compacted soil turned sterile. For years she'd been drawing away from him and now she'd gone too far to be pulled back, remote, receding—like stars, he'd read, all rushing away from each other, and from this planet, into space.

"But, as you say," she added, "the only thing is to go on as if everything was normal. There's nothing else we *can* do."

Peter took up his drink again and drained his glass. "I can't very well cancel this shoot. As you know, the Chancellor's coming and also Abdul Osmali. It's important they should meet down here informally, and anyway I can't let Abdul down; he's playing ball with us better than any of the other prime ministers, though that isn't saying much. Even he's dickering with the Russians over a dam, and they've signed a trade agreement swapping peanuts for transistor sets. You never know where you are, even with people like Abdul that one thought one could rely on. Of course they're under pressure all the time from their own left wing."

"It must be difficult," Lavinia agreed. Neither of them was really thinking about Abdul Osmali.

"Of course he's a devout Muslim; we mustn't have pork and he likes Ribena, I believe, instead of whisky; and we'll have to keep Pompey and Sebastian out of the way. But now there's this domestic crisis, d'you think you can cope? I suppose we *could* get them all put up at the Feathers."

"No, that won't be necessary. I'll manage."

"Couldn't you get a temporary from London, and blow the expense? No consideration whatever, these foreigners, and they've had everything they wanted, every whim gratified, not to mention fourteen quid a week and all found." Peter helped himself to more whisky and looked at the clock. He'd always meant to take up cooking as a hobby, a lot of men did nowadays and it would be soothing as well as useful—practical, down-to-earth, an art even, something right away from papers and reports and harassing decisions and endless talk. But he'd never had time. "Dinner's late, I suppose that's to be expected."

He kept piling sentences one on top of the other, like a man adding armfuls of sticks to build a barricade. "I don't so much blame Julia for the accident, I don't think it *was* her fault. What I can't get over is the way she went off like a common tart with this lunatic Heron, a casual labourer if you please, and literally a maniac; went off with him just like that for the weekend and then has the nerve to deposit him right on our doorstep. I can't think why on earth the police haven't arrested him."

"Perhaps they don't think he's guilty."

"Of stealing Martin's pictures? Of course he is. I told you, he's a lunatic. He's got a sort of vendetta against us all, some madman's delusion. It isn't safe, his wandering about like this. Whatever happens, Vin, don't let him hang round here. He's not to be allowed in the house, or the garden or farm for that matter. And you've simply got to stop Julia seeing him, or having anything to do with him whatever, I mean that. You can take my word for it, he's not safe. Julia mustn't see him; you do understand that, don't you?"

Halted in front of Lavinia, he looked at her intently, with an expression designed to be authoritarian but, in effect, one of pleading.

"I do understand, Peter, but I'm afraid dungeons and

chastity belts are out of fashion. You'd much better speak to her yourself."

"I have spoken to her, and I will again. You're right, of course; parental authority doesn't mean that much these days." He snapped his fingers and moved across to put another log on the fire.

"I suppose the doctors are *quite* sure?"

"They say so. Part of the brain . . ." Lavinia helped herself to another small glass of sherry.

"There'll be colossal damages, of course. The insurance company won't like it but they'll have to pay. There's no loophole, thank goodness."

"I'm glad there's a silver lining somewhere," Lavinia remarked. "I'll go and see about dinner. I'm sorry it's so late. You know Evan's here?"

"Evan? No, I didn't. You didn't tell me."

"He came down to see if he could comfort Julia."

"That was decent of him. Very. Considering Julia's behaviour, most men in his position would have simply walked out. I wouldn't blame him in the least if he did. I'm glad he's here, perhaps he can make Julia see sense."

Lavinia was looking at him with a half-smile, partly sad and partly something else: he couldn't make out whether it was tender or mocking. He went over to encircle her waist and kiss her lips. "Try not to worry." He drew away to look at her with a warm, intimate expression that once had never failed to stir her. But lately there'd been nothing, a hollowness, an alarming blankness, as if he'd heard, from behind a closed door, sounds of conversation and laughter, only to find an empty room. "We'll face this together," he said. "As we always have."

chapter 30

Evan had a bad cold and looked gummy-eyed, and kept blowing his nose.

"Vin and I appreciate your coming down," Peter said. "You'll be a real comfort to Julia."

"About all the comfort I'm likely to give to Julia will be my cold."

"Just being here is sure to be a comfort. Having someone to lean on."

"I'm not the one she wants to lean on," Evan said, putting down his spoon with his soup barely touched.

Peter blew unobtrusively on his spoonful, angry at the continual intrusion into his thoughts of this outsider, this enemy to his peace of mind, or what was left of it, in the last few days. Dick was like Banquo's ghost, popping up continually where he was least wanted, in the conversation, in people's thoughts, a spectre walking with an air of menace through what should have been the privacy of home.

"A good night's sleep is what she needs," Peter said. "Are you going back to London tomorrow, Evan?"

"Yes, I must."

"If you can stay till after lunch I'll give you a lift. I shall have to spend the morning here, there's some constituency business and I've promised Watts I'll see a deputation from the N.F.U. in the morning. It's potato prices again. Watts has arranged for me to meet them at the Feathers."

Peter frowned again, remembering that Heron was at the Feathers.

"Thank you," Evan said thickly. He seemed glum, and no wonder, with Julia playing him up; the idea that she could, for a single instant, prefer that roving maniac to a decent, intelligent chap like Evan (even if he'd had his left wing flirtations) made Peter hopping mad.

"Well, we've lost the battle at East Kirkwood," he said. "I was afraid we should. It's a bad moment with this trouble in the Middle East and the cost of living index up again and unemployment, and then the other side had an exceptionally strong candidate."

"The Liberals took a lot of votes," Evan suggested.

"From both sides. My own view, for what it's worth, is that the two sides about cancel each other out. But Iain I suppose will do one of his post mortems. In politics it's all guess-work, if you ask me."

"The pollsters don't think so."

"They can tell you how people voted yesterday, but not how they're going to vote tomorrow, whatever they claim. At least in this country if we can't change our climate, we can still change our minds."

"A happy breed."

"Assisted by people like your revered father. How's his arthritis, by the way?"

"I don't think it's much better. But it's no worse either, and I suppose that's something with arthritis."

"Beastly thing."

Lavinia wasn't helping in the least to keep the conversation going. After the soup there was a pause, then a cockerel Peter had practically to hack apart. Lavinia apologized.

"I'm afraid they didn't de-frost it properly."

"I hope Evan will forgive us," Peter said.

"I should think a tough chicken is the least of our worries," said Evan. Peter thought he sounded distrait and on edge.

"At any rate we'll have some burgundy."

After they'd eaten, Peter took the burgundy into the drawing room and he and Evan finished it with their coffee over the fire. Lavinia had gone up to bed with a headache, and he was glad, in a way, that she'd left them. He'd been itching all along to talk about Martin, but couldn't while she was there. By tacit consent, they had avoided the whole topic of Martin.

"I can't make out what's happened about Martin's pictures," Peter began. "They can't have just disappeared."

"For the moment they have."

"But he gave them to that fellow Heron, didn't he? I can't understand that to begin with. Why on earth did Martin entrust two valuable paintings to a lunatic like that?"

"You'd better ask Martin. I suppose he thought he *could* trust him."

"That's not a bit like Martin, you know. He's a pretty shrewd chap, by and large."

"He took them, anyway. Heron did, I mean."

"There's no doubt of that?"

"Not the slightest."

"Then why the hell don't the police arrest him? They're quick enough to put Julia through it but they leave this fellow hanging round the Feathers, free as air. I simply don't understand it."

"They're investigating, I expect." Evan was staring into the fire and cupping his hands round his glass of burgundy with a wrung-out, deflated appearance. Peter looked at him with a trace of impatience. A young fellow like that, nearly thirty years his junior, ought to have a bit more spunk. Of course he was upset about Heron, and no wonder; but he ought to show fight, not resignation.

"Investigating what?"

"Shall we say, the provenance of the pictures."

"What on earth does that matter? Heron's got to account for them or he's a self-proclaimed thief. I can't see there's anything else to be said. Evan, I think you know more than you're telling me. What's behind it all? You know you can trust me not to let things go any further. After all, Martin's my son."

Evan went on staring into the fire as if he hadn't heard, and Peter grew more and more uneasy. He looked round at the comfortable fire consuming logs sawn from the branches of a half-dead oak he'd had felled, the Meissen figures posturing for eternity on the mantel shelf, the revolving bookcase bright with the spines of clean volumes, the deep sofa with its velvet cushions, a bank of bright-hued cinerarias glowing in a corner, the rich pattern of the Persian rug. Secure, serene, civilized, a happy blend of simplicity and luxury—how could it be threatened from outside? Yet it was being threatened; he could sense the cold assault, smell the danger, as people in a laager might have sensed the prowling lion outside the circle, the slavering hyena.

"It's got nothing to do with the insurance, has it?"

"What insurance?"

"The insurance on the pictures. Probably I'm right off the beam but I just wondered . . ."

"If this was a put-up job, you mean?" Evan's voice was thick.

"I didn't mean it like that exactly. But Martin's very secretive, you know. I've no idea really what's going on. It did occur to me, I must admit, that possibly he'd got into temporary difficulties and was foolish enough to be trying to find a short cut out of them. Otherwise I can't see why the police don't act."

Evan leant back and crossed his legs and blew his nose on a damp, exhausted handkerchief. "You understand Martin better than I thought you did."

"I doubt if any us understands each other. We're all sealed up in our little capsules. I just wondered whether he'd got into difficulties, that's all."

"I always thought you believed him perfect."

"Of course I don't believe him perfect. Give me credit for a grain of sense. I just thought that if he'd got into difficulties I'd rather help him than let him flounder deeper into the mess."

"That's very handsome, I must say." A bit of animation was returning to Evan, as if the sluggish blood was flowing back into his arteries. He finished his burgundy and walked across the room to put his glass down on a table by the door.

"Do you really want to know the truth?"

"Of course I want to know the truth."

"You won't like it."

"D'you suppose I've been all these years in politics without learning to face unpleasant truths?"

"That's a rhetorical question."

"For God's sake, stop lecturing me," Peter snapped, "and tell me what you're driving at."

"To put it in a nutshell, Martin's a crook."

"That's sheer balls," Peter retorted hotly.

"He always has been, since he was at Eton I should think. He's been running a racket for years and so far no one's caught him out. Of course those so-called Modiglianis were forgeries."

"You're making all this up!"

"I told you that you wouldn't like it."

"You can't prove a word of it. It's a form of spite."

"I quite admit I haven't got a neat file of proofs locked up in a blackmailer's cabinet. That's Martin's line, not mine. In fact he's been blackmailing me for years."

"Do you expect me to believe all this?"

"I don't care a damn if you do or not. I've just got to pull it out of the cupboard, I suppose. I don't mean he's been bleeding me for money, or not much. It's more subtle than that—nastier, too. He simply makes me do what he wants me to. I've done a lot of things I've hated. He always knows just what the traffic will bear."

Peter was marching about the room with a prickling sensation in his limbs, breathing heavily, and his face had gone a dark, dangerous colour. If Lavinia had been there she'd have tried to restrain him. Ever since he'd had attacks of puffing when he hurried, and had a cardiograph taken, she'd insisted that he shouldn't get overexcited or make sudden, violent movements.

"You're flinging all these allegations about without a shred of proof. I know Martin a damn sight better than you do and he's not like that at all. Quite apart from the moral side, he'd never have been such a fool. If he'd really been dealing in forgeries, he wouldn't have entrusted them to a total stranger, a fellow like Heron especially."

"He'd been pushing out these forgeries for years," Evan said calmly. "In quite small quantities, naturally—as I've said, what the traffic would bear. It wasn't going to bear much more and so he was winding it up and Heron came in just right to feed to the wolves. I can't tell you all the details, Martin's plots are far too labyrinthine for me and anyway he never tells any one person more than a fraction. No one knows it all. I often wonder whether he does himself. I think he likes improvisation beyond a certain point. He's an artist in that way at least."

"You're making all this up," Peter repeated, but his

voice lacked conviction. "Obviously you're trying to work off some grudge against Martin." Evan paid no attention.

"He miscalculated this time. He thought Dick Heron *would* go to Milan, and take the pictures. So he tipped off the Italian Customs, or got his fellow crooks in Milan to. He'd got it in for Dick, hated his guts, and this was a good way to put him out of circulation. Less filial piety, I'm afraid, than incestuous jealousy—he couldn't take the way Julia flung herself at Dick's head."

"You've got a mind like a sewer. I'm not going to listen to—"

"But you are. It's time you did. The plan misfired. But Martin had a second string. That's where he's so clever, he always has something to fall back on. Like those ships they used to build with a series of watertight holds. They were supposed to be unsinkable, I believe. I don't think they were, but probably Martin is. Heron misfired and Martin had made one of his very rare slips—he couldn't prove that Heron had accepted the pictures. However, that was soon put right, he got me to swear I'd seen them handed over. Now he can claim the insurance, and they're insured for some fabulous sum. The only thing that's not quite right is that Dick Heron hasn't been arrested. You and Martin share an anxiety on that score. Of course, he took a risk in reporting the pictures as being stolen, seeing they're phonys, but not much of one really. For one thing it's practically impossible to *prove* a thing's a fake, for another I don't suppose he claimed them to be Modiglianis or whatever they're supposed to be. Probably he just called them valuable paintings, in which case the question of who painted them's irrelevant from a police point of view. I daresay the coppers know there's something fishy but I'll be very surprised if they're able to grab hold of any loose ends, even a little one. Very surprised indeed."

At first Peter had kept his anger under tight control but now the blood was throbbing in his temples in a threatening way. His palms were sweating, he was breathing fast and his skin was becoming contused. Evan looked at him with contempt. When it came to the point, no one ever would face facts they didn't like, a politician least of all.

"Don't believe me if you don't want to," he said. "I've just about had enough. I was fond of Martin once and in a way I still am; I've got a faithful nature I suppose. It was he who kept on pushing me at Julia, obviously a form of perversion—like a feudal prince marrying his mistress off to a gentleman of the bedchamber to keep her handy for use, and put her in the wrong at the same time. And then Julia, I think he's half in love with her. He's an ingenious chap, Martin, always turning over new ideas. If he—"

Something burst in Peter's head amid a shower of coloured sparks and the next thing he knew was a crash, a rattling sound and a yelp from Pompey. Without knowing what he was doing he'd seized a vase off the mantel shelf and hurled it straight at Evan; it had shattered against his shoulder and the bits scattered on the floor.

But Evan wasn't hurt, the vase was made of thin porcelain. All Peter had done was to break a fairly valuable ornament. Evan just stood there looking astonished, and Peter brought himself up like a wave against a breakwater feeling murder in his hands, a surge of primitive ferocity. He took a step towards Evan and stumbled over Pompey, who yelped again and looked up protestingly.

The surge receded and Peter felt sick. A middle-aged public figure who believed himself to be civilized going for a filthy-minded little sod thirty years younger, using violence like a teddy-boy—undignified to a degree, futile, absurd and also dangerous; the sort of thing Smith had warned him against.

"That was uncalled for." His voice was hoarse and thick.

"I'm not feeling very well. People don't realize the pace one lives, the strain one's under. I can't stand this. I'm going to bed, and for God's sake, don't let me see you in the morning."

Evan said accusingly: "That vase was one of a pair."

"Damn it, I know my own porcelain! Crown Derby, rather late—Bloor." Peter picked up one or two pieces and dropped them again; the vase was beyond repair. "And I'll thank you to keep away from Julia in future. I was wrong about you."

Evan gave his short barking laugh and then sneezed. "Unhand my daughter, sir. Julia makes up her own mind, you know, but there's no need to worry, she's not going to make it up in favour of me."

Peter blindly made for the door, his head throbbing.

"Sorry if I've shattered your illusions," Evan said, "but you asked for it, didn't you? I'll turn out the lights and pick up the bits."

chapter 3 I

LAVINIA was in bed but not asleep. She was reading, propped against pillows looking tired and, in the way he could never put his finger on, a little remote, as if she had an independent life apart from her body. She was like a bird that would always slip through his hands.

Tonight this quality that he'd once admired and envied filled him with a sickening despair. Something had died in him down there in his polished drawing room, killed horribly by Evan, forever shattered like the fragile painted vase. He could feel his strength, his confidence, his sap of manhood, bleeding away.

Only one thing could staunch the bleeding, only one: his wife's understanding, sympathy, compassion. He wanted to go up to her and lay his head in her lap as Pompey sometimes rested a warm chin on his foot, silently, inviting the caress of loving fingers behind the ears. Sloppy —the childish word formed itself uninvited in his mind. But wasn't it natural, human? Didn't every man need that sloppy kind of love—reserved, among the English middle classes, almost exclusively for cats and dogs?

In her quiet voice Lavinia asked:

"Have you put out Pompey?"

"Oh, yes, Pompey's all right, he's been out." Peter sat down on the bed and unlaced his shoes and kicked them off. "I suppose you realize that Martin's a crook, a picture forger, a blackmailer, a bugger and a few other things as well?"

Lavinia looked at him with a slight wrinkling of her forehead and was silent. Her book lay face upwards and open on the turned-over sheet.

"Didn't you hear what I said?"

"I heard you, Peter. Do you really want to talk about it at this time of night?"

"I don't see what the time of night's got to do with it. He won't have changed back into a decent citizen in the morning. Besides, d'you suppose I'm going to get a wink of sleep?"

"You've been talking to Evan."

"Bloody young bounder. I nearly—if he hadn't been a guest in the house—Vin, did you know all this was going on?"

"You mean about Martin." She said this as a statement, gently, and he could sense beneath her quiet reply a secret lake of silent anguish and resentment. His anger rose.

"What d'you suppose I mean? Of course I mean about Martin. He's a kind of monster apparently, if half of what Evan said is true. Not that I'd trust Evan a yard, he's a self-seeking little bastard like his father only without his father's guts and enterprise, but tonight . . . Oh, Christ, it can't be true." Rather histrionically, he buried his face in his hands and his greying hair, always brushed so sprucely off a wide forehead, became rumpled. But Lavinia didn't stretch out her hand.

"Surely you knew?"

"Knew what?"

"What Martin was up to."

"Of course I didn't know! I don't even know now how much truth there is in it. Apparently you're taking Evan's side. As Martin's mother I should have thought—"

"It's not a question of taking sides. It's a question of the truth."

"The truth! Who knows what's true and what isn't? It's all half measures these days. People used to know, my father knew, there was right and wrong but now . . . If you knew all this why didn't you tell me?"

"Because you wouldn't listen."

Peter took his hands away and looked at her with rage and astonishment.

"You think I ought to listen to every bit of malicious gossip about my children? I've been too loyal to my family, that's been my trouble. But if you'd told me sensibly—I can't understand . . ."

Lavinia was fiddling with the pages of her book and breathing deeply. "Don't you think you'd better go to bed, Peter?"

"No, I don't!" Now he was shouting, and with an effort he lowered his voice. "Every time I try to talk about something that really matters you change the conversation and tell me I ought to go to bed or take my pills or put the dog out or something. I know why; you're afraid—afraid of rows, of trouble, anything unpleasant. You want to lock yourself up in your ivory tower and stay there, above the noise and sweat and beastliness down below. And look what that's led to. Just look. While you were up there in your ivory tower looking at the beautiful clouds, your son was getting warped and twisted and you didn't lift a finger to help him, never even talked it over with me."

He paused, panting slightly; he'd never suspected the existence of such thoughts in his own mind. Now he'd said it all, he knew that it was true.

"Do you really think that?" She'd pulled herself up on

the pillows and the flush on her face made her look younger. He saw with satisfaction that he'd at last got through her defenses, some of them anyway. "You think I've kept things from you about Martin?"

"If you had any idea what was going on, of course you have."

"What's going on, as you call it, has been going on for at least twenty years. Time and time again I used to try and warn you. You wouldn't listen. I might as well have talked to a sewing machine."

"Are you trying to tell me that Martin's been more or less a criminal since he was seven years old?"

"It all started then. Or at least it wasn't stopped when it could have been, because every time Martin did anything wrong you made excuses; you wouldn't have him punished, you gave him the perfectly correct idea that he could go away and do it again."

"That's all utterly untrue. Because I tried to bring up Martin to respond to love and not fear, to feel secure, to regard me as a friend and not a kind of ogre, because I don't believe in corporal punishment, you put all the blame on me! If we're to blame, and I suppose to some extent we must be, it's because we didn't understand him enough, show enough patience. Something turned him sour and bitter. Affection doesn't do that. You did it with your self-righteous above-the-battle attitude, keeping calm, aloof. . . ."

Lavinia bit her lips to keep back the words—even now she wouldn't let them break through in a natural flood. Self-control, he supposed, became built-in, fossilized, and you couldn't break through it finally, ever.

"It's too late to talk about it now," she said.

"D'you think I'm going to get any sleep?"

"I didn't mean that. I meant it's twenty years too late. Don't you understand how completely you've ruined Martin?"

"*I've* ruined him? When it was I who . . . ? *Tu quoque*—the schoolboy's trick. That's not worthy of you, Vin."

"Do you remember giving Martin ten shillings once to buy some things at the village shop? Later on I found he hadn't paid Mrs. Harris, he'd put it all on the bill. You didn't want to say anything to Martin, and when I pushed you into it he told you he'd spent the money on a birthday present for Simon. So you laughed and said so long as he hadn't spent it on himself that showed a generous spirit, and he got away with it. Simon's present turned out to be a pocketknife he hadn't bought at all; he'd won it in a bet from one of the village boys. You said you were too busy to be bothered with domestic details and anyway you didn't think Martin had meant any harm."

"Fancy your remembering a little thing like that."

"A little thing! You don't see it even now. Anyway, the harm's all done, so this is waste of time. Martin can't be changed." She spoke with weariness.

"So you blame it all on me and wash your hands of it. Martin can get a long prison sentence and it won't matter twopence as it's all my fault."

Lavinia closed her eyes. Her hands were gripping the sheet in front of her, kneading and creasing the linen.

"It's still all Martin, Martin, Martin." She kept her voice level and low. "I thought fathers were supposed to think more about their daughters. Julia doesn't get a thought, does she?"

"Julia! I suppose that's my fault, too? I left you a free hand with Julia, didn't I? You brought her up as you pleased. And I suppose you're satisfied you did it splendidly. Look at the bloody mess *she's* made."

"She's been got at by Martin."

"So it's Martin's fault again! And mine, I suppose. Never yours."

"What's the use of blaming or not blaming people? They

do as they must, I suppose. But Martin won't leave Julia alone. It's he who pushed her into that disastrous affair with Evan. And you aided and abetted that."

"Well done, Vin." Peter got off the bed and stumped in his socks round the room. "You've brought it back to me again. D'you seriously think I've got time to work out all this psychology or whatever it is, and organize Julia's sex life for her, *and* play some part in public life? There's nineteen people in the Cabinet and we're supposed to run the government, and if we fail, at best the country goes under and at worst the world blows up. If you think that's pompous I can't help it, it's true. And if you think I ought to take time off to act as nursemaid to a more or less delinquent daughter, then you . . . Oh, well, what's the use. I've got a heavy day tomorrow, I shall feel like a piece of chewed string and be about as useful. By that time Martin may be under arrest and our private lives in headlines all over the world. I may even have to resign. So I hope you're satisfied. Now I *am* going to bed."

He walked towards the dressing room and came back to get his shoes. Leaning down he glanced at his wife and added: "Well, aren't you going to say anything?"

"I think we've said enough."

"Have you lost the power of speech?"

Lavinia shut her book with a snap and pulled herself up against the pillows and said: "No, Peter, but I've spent nearly thirty years suppressing it. When two people live together one's got to give way, and I made up my mind from the beginning it would be me. It's less trouble to hold one's tongue than to keep contesting every inch of the way. Also it makes for peace in the home and I've got a weakness for that sort of peace. Perhaps I ought to have argued and quarrelled and nagged at you and then you might not have spoilt Martin, and made Julia grow up with a sense of resentment because Martin always got all the attention. I don't know. Anyway I've bottled up my power of speech for years and years but I've had enough now."

Peter looked at her in amazement. It was as if Pompey had suddenly become a hungry tiger, or the rose garden turned into a tropical jungle full of serpents and orang-outangs.

"Not that I'm going to start nagging and criticizing, it's too late for that too. And of course I won't walk out and leave you stranded with no cook and Martin probably in jail. But when this ghastly case of Julia's is settled, that is, if they don't send her to prison, I shall take her away for quite a long time, round the world perhaps. And when I get back we shall see."

He stared at her speechlessly, tie in hand and made a helpless gesture.

"There won't be any scandal, Peter. Though with the ones already on us, a thing like a defecting wife would scarcely be noticed. But for thirty years I've put you first and now it's going to be the children. Julia and Simon, at least. Martin's beyond me."

"I think you've gone out of your mind," Peter said.

"Or come into it."

"But what have I done? You've never spoken like this before. You've never said anything. Now, when everything's gone wrong, you go and turn on me. Is that fair? Tell me what I've done, for God's sake, Vin!"

"You haven't done anything." Lavinia spoke wearily, feeling that all this had happened before.

"Well, then, what are you talking about? Of course it would be a good thing to take Julia off somewhere when the case is over. I'm all for that. But that's got nothing to do with you and me. With our happiness."

"Do you think we're happy?"

"Of course we are! Just at this moment one can't expect to be exactly hilarious with Julia and now Martin appar-

ently—Martin. I just can't get over it. I don't believe it.
Oh, God, it can't be true about Martin." He hunched his
shoulders and put his head down and this time his gesture
wasn't histrionic but stricken. "But anyway there's a basic
sort of happiness between us, isn't there? If we can hang on
to that everything else will pass, it'll still be there."

"Do you believe that?"

"Of course I believe it. Don't you?"

She looked at him in silence for a few moments and then
dropped her eyes. "The emperor's clothes."

"What do you mean?"

"Don't force me to hurt you, Peter."

"You're trying to tell me that you don't love me." He
sat down heavily on the bed again and sunk his head in his
hands. The histrionics had returned. The shock was genuine enough and yet he was acting the part at the same time,
the stricken husband, the rejected heart, the broken man.
Lavinia said impatiently:

"It's not so simple, love and not-love, black and white.
It's just that you will live in this world of illusion. Like with
Martin. You thought he was perfect, so he *was* perfect, and
nothing anyone could do or say would make you change
your mind, you wouldn't listen. So in the end, when the
illusion's shattered, you've got no defenses, you're like a
crab without a shell. It's the same with marriage."

"All right, go on. Love's just copulation, children a by-
product, a home somewhere to sleep in, everything else is
an illusion. All right, I'm facing facts now. I'm sorry you've
been plagued with such a fool for all these years."

Lavinia sighed. "You see, Peter, it was better to keep
silent, wasn't it? We might have been going on like this for
years."

"At least you'd have got rid of my illusions."

"You need them, I suppose. Keep them, Peter."

"But if I keep them, then I can't keep you?"

"I don't know," she said wearily. "Don't you think we've talked enough? The more one says, the less one understands. There's a dozen ways of looking at everything. Hadn't you better get to bed?"

"I want to get at the truth."

"Now do go to bed."

Peter pulled out a handkerchief, blew his nose, gulped and said: "Just as if nothing had happened. This has been the most ghastly evening of my life and you say go to bed as if it was a question of turning over and having a good healthy sleep till eight o'clock next morning. My whole life's shattered." He paused, but she made no reply. A thought struck him, and he added: "I'm afraid one of those Bloor vases in the drawing room got smashed tonight."

"I never liked them much, anyway."

chapter 32

A WAITER took their order: a young Italian in a striped jacket and crumpled trousers. He smiled at them conspiratorially, plumped out several cushions and moved back a standard lamp to keep the light out of Julia's eyes.

"He's new," Julia said. "They had an old man in that awful seedy waiter's uniform, he got thinner and thinner and the tail coat got looser and looser and dirtier and dirtier and he got older and older and I suppose he's died. The place was full of foxes' brushes and horns and things and people used to stay here for the hunting. Now it's all changed. The new man's put in lavatories and taken down the foxes and put up Dubonnet umbrellas in the garden and keeps a flock of caravans. I suppose it *is* progress. Only progress seems to mean more people doing the same thing at the same time, and building car parks and lavatories—toilets, rather. Are we really going to Australia, Dick, when we've both done time? Like the convicts, isn't it, and of course they may not let us in."

"You've got a good lawyer and I'm sure you'll get off. You've no need to worry."

"No one else seems to think that. You haven't answered my question."

The waiter came with their coffee and arranged it carefully; he was almost too attentive, especially to Julia, and took a long time. The pause gave Dick an opportunity to think but this didn't help him, his mind was a battleground between reason and fantasy, reality and a mass of inchoate, inarticulate emotions.

"I've got no money, no job and no future," he said. "One can't just ignore these things."

"One can change them. If you're thinking of what's going into the kitty I can contribute an unearned income of about six pounds a week, a lot of bloody-mindedness and now a criminal record."

Dick smiled, his eyes on the electric flicker that fascinated him, the way it seemed to go round like the spoke of a wheel: the simplest of illusions, yet it deceived him though he knew it was a trick. "That's a start, anyway. Though your father—"

"He doesn't come into it. The point's quite simple really. It's whether you love me or not."

Dick felt a cold shiver go right through him and die away in a tingling sensation like the faint echo of distant bells. After that his heart was racing and his palms clammy. The dodging, the evasion, the postponements, were almost over, he'd come back in a circle to the starting place. Taking his eyes off the flicker, he looked across at Julia and said: "You know I do." She squashed out her cigarette with a shaky hand. When she tried to speak her lips were dry and her voice uneven.

"Then that's all right, isn't it?"

"It's not so simple. I tried to explain that before."

"We both do better when we don't try to explain."

"There was an odd little story that Rose—" He broke off, confused and dumbfounded, an iron band seeming to contract round his chest. The name had sprung up like a magic tree and filled his whole mind and being, pushing shoots and rootlets into every crevice and fibre. Rose was there and couldn't be stifled, he couldn't lay an axe to the flowering tree. Julia saw his face stiffen with the look she didn't understand: the eyes seemed almost to solidify.

"I'm glad you've brought her name up, we've got to have it out in the open sooner or later. You've got to face the fact that Rose is dead and you can't stay in mourning forever, like Queen Victoria. It's the last thing Rose would have wanted if she loved you as I'm sure she did. You must see that."

"There's this story." Dick wasn't going to be deflected, his voice was hard as a frozen shirt on an icy washing day. "It was something Rose's grandmother had actually seen. This old girl, she lived to be about ninety, I think, in a village belonging to a dowager countess or something, a real old tartar who lived in the big house surrounded by footmen in livery and used to visit the poor in the cottages and literally, I think, take them soup. Beef tea."

"Have you got a photograph of Rose?"

Dick shook his head. "One day she came to visit Rose's grandmother—her father worked on the estate, the grandmother was a child then. I can't remember why they were to have beef tea, I expect someone was sick. Anyway one of the footmen in livery jumped off the back of the carriage and opened the door and leant down and put out his hand and this old dowager put her foot on to it, her boot right on to his hand, and stepped over the verge and on to the path. Then she walked up the path and the footman carried the beef tea or whatever it was. They had claret-coloured coats, she said, with yellow facings, very smart. It's always stuck in my mind."

"I expect she had button boots. It's a dear little story, Dick, but just what is it supposed to prove?"

"The point is I'd like to put my hand down and let you tread on it as hard and as long as you want, to avoid the awkward places. I'd like always to keep it between you and the ground. I know that's a completely corny idea, absolutely out of date. We've even lost the words to express ideas like that, they're not wanted now; even poets never write in that sort of way. I can't help it or express it but that's how I feel."

"You've put it very sweetly, Dick. Thank you." Julia was suddenly looking happy, more as she'd looked before the accident. "I'm all for corn myself, that kind of corn anyway; it doesn't last but it's sweet while it does. Rather intoxicating, like malting barley. Now will you do something for me?"

He smiled. "Anything."

"Come with me to the hospital."

"It won't help, will it?"

"Doctors keep on changing their minds. And I'd like to see the sister."

"Let's go now, then."

Julia hadn't been a patient since a childhood tonsillectomy, so the scrubbed and sterile look of hospitals, the disinfectant smell, the bare high beds and strong lights and stretcher cases being wheeled along corridors didn't terrify her with memories of pain and fear and indignity. Nevertheless all hospitals frightened her: the sisters were one cause of this. Not the bouncing, cubby little probationers and juniors, but the real sisters with their severity and toughness, their bossiness and authority. Why was it that these women, more compassionate than the average, more patient and unselfish, more anxious to help others and far less money-minded, should often be so much more forbidding than women who merely took what they could get from life?

This particular sister, sitting at her desk in a cubbyhole off the main women's ward, was Irish and had a large, flat chin like a purse, a hint of a moustache, spectacles and frizzy hair. "No change in the patient's condition." She rustled her papers to make it clear that she was being interrupted.

"The doctors still think she'll live?"

"When a patient's on the danger list we never make prognostications. But she stood up to the second operation remarkably well. I think we can say there's grounds for hope."

"Hope of what?" Julia inquired. "That she'll survive, or recover?"

"If she survives at all it'll be a miracle." The sister allowed some animation to inform her voice, which brought up the Irish in it. "Her skull was smashed like an eggshell; how Mr. Latham managed was a marvel to see. A real marvel. There's no one in the country could have done it better or taken more trouble. The best attention she's had, you can be sure."

"Can I see her?"

"That's out of the question, it's only her mother and father can come now. I must ask you not to be troubling us again at the busy times."

"I'm sorry, sister. You see, I was the one who knocked her down."

The sister clicked with her tongue. "Miss Buckle, is it? Well, that was a dreadful thing there's no denying it, a young life spoiled in a wink of an eye. The Lord gives and the Lord taketh away. Mr. Latham did all that skill can do but there's a part of the brain he had to amputate. There's only two or three men in the country can do that operation, so you see if she'd been the daughter of the highest in the land she couldn't have been better cared for."

"She'll be completely paralyzed for the rest of her life and she's five now." Julia said this as a statement, not a question, and the sister shrugged her shoulders slightly to express her inability to contradict.

Dick was standing by, watching the sister. She wanted to
get rid of Julia but he thought her feelings were engaged
under the armour, that she wanted to talk about the child
and perhaps felt an unacknowledged need to punish and
accuse. Julia added:

"Her brain's injured, too."

"There's a part taken away. It's a marvel, nowadays,
what the surgeons can do. The best of them, like Mr.
Latham."

"She's had the best attention, so she'll be an idiot as
well."

"Now that's an old-fashioned word," the sister objected.
"We don't use words like that any more. Stella won't have
the full use of her brain but it's wonderful what can be
done these days to teach the mentally handicapped, really
wonderful. There's some devoted women giving up their
whole lives to that."

Her look suggested that this was not a thing her visitor
was likely to do. Julia remarked: "It's lucky there's a regular supply of imbeciles and crippled children coming along
to keep the devoted women fully occupied."

"Miss Buckle, I must ask you not to take up any more of
my time."

"It's like the beef tea, isn't it? If there hadn't been any
deserving poor, the rich wouldn't have been able to take
round the beef tea and they'd have been stuck with all that
do-goodism, like market gardeners landed with a lot of
surplus cabbages. And if we don't keep alive the imbeciles
and deformities, all those devoted women will be stuck with
their devotion and patience and charity. So up with the
miracles of modern surgery that keep the imbeciles and
deformities going for the devoted women to practice their
devotion on."

"This is a hospital, Miss Buckle, not a public platform,"
the sister said. "Will you kindly leave us to get on with our

job? And that's saving life, not setting ourselves up in judgment as to who has the right to life and who has not."

"The right to life," Julia repeated. "You call that life, a body lying there for fifty years with half a brain? A hulk fed at one end and cleaned at the other day after day for years and years, rubbed I suppose twice a day to keep off bedsores, unable to move its hands even, taking up the time of the skilled nurses and doctors who might be helping people who really need the help? You call that *life*, do you?"

"It's life while the immortal soul is in the body, Miss Buckle. I'm not here to argue, I'm here to do my duty and leave those questions to people better able than I am to decide them, and I advise you to do the same. It's the will of God and that's all there is to be said."

The sister walked across to the door and opened it and stood aside for Julia to go. Dick put his hand on her arm. "Come on, Julia, this isn't doing any good." But Julia wouldn't hold her tongue.

"It's so very clever to know what the will of God *is*. Apparently it's the will of God for Stella Ryan to lie on her back for years and years drooling and paralyzed and idiotic. Apart from the fact that it seems odd to believe in an Almighty sadist and hypocrite and torturer, how d'you know God didn't mean the child to die in peace instead of becoming an object for the surgeon to practice his wonderful skill on, and the devoted women to lavish their devotion on? How d'you know the wonderful surgeon isn't simply frustrating God's will? *He's* the one who's decided the child's to live, not God, who obviously thought otherwise. He's the one, he and all you doctors and surgeons and nurses who use your skill and devotion to keep alive the deformities and monsters and thalidomide babies and paralyzed imbeciles God so obviously intended to get rid of. You don't see animals—"

"Come on, Julia, for Christ's sake!" Dick said.

"Clearly it's not sunk in, Miss Buckle, that we're busy people here." The sister was flushed, her eyes glittering with anger. "A great deal too busy to listen to the blasphemy and ignorant nonsense of visitors, even if they do happen to be related to Ministers in the government. Now will you go?"

"Frustrating God's will, that's what you're all doing." It was like vomiting, Dick thought: Julia couldn't stop, even if she wanted to, until it had all come out. He tightened his fingers on her arm. "All in a conspiracy to defeat God's mercy, when he wants to let someone die off naturally. And why? So that the wonderful surgeons can congratulate each other on their wonderful skill. Write papers about how they've kept alive monstrosities with flappers on their shoulders instead of arms, and idiots who can't speak and have to be fed and wiped and kept out of sight, and polio cases in iron lungs and people suffering agonies night and day from cancer. The doctors write their papers and get letters after their names and everyone says how wonderful they are, but all they're doing really is to contradict the will of God who wants anything that's suffering and deformed and unnatural to die."

The sister's chin was tilted back and looked more than ever like a purse, zipped up tightly, and her sallow cheeks had spots of colour. She beckoned to a passing nurse and said in clay-cold tones: "Nurse, will you show these visitors, out, please?"

The tension that had held Julia stiff relaxed, and she almost crumpled; Dick felt her sag and held on to her arm. She gave a feeble smile and added: "I'm very sorry, Dick. Standing in the middle of a hospital making soap-box speeches. You must—it's just that I—" She turned to address a last remark to the retreating sister's back. "Can't you let her die?"

The staff nurse touched Julia's other arm and said: "This way, please," in shocked tones. Julia proceeded almost like a prisoner between the two of them to the head of the stairs. "Straight down, you'll see the door." The nurse turned and left them. Two probationers with deep, high bosoms and short, fat legs came chattering up the stairs. ". . . never satisfied, I thought he was a smashing bit of work myself." "I've heard things, they say he's in with that mob from Torbury, well the other night . . ."

"Come on, Julia," Dick said again. "There's nothing you can do."

"I could go back and finish her off."

"Don't be a fool."

"If she was an animal that's what anyone would do."

"She isn't an animal. That's the point."

"She isn't as good as one, as happy. If she can't move and drools and has a bit of brain missing, you don't call her a human being, do you?"

"I don't myself, no. But I didn't make the law."

"The law." Julia started to giggle. "The law's a laugh. I'll tell you something—" Her giggles grew louder and she shook all over and clung to the post.

"For Christ's sake, Julia, shut up! Don't start hysterics here." He shook her. "If you do I'll call that sister. She's a bitch and she hates you. For God's sake, at least wait until we get to the car."

Julia couldn't stop laughing. In between spasms she gasped out: "This is funny. If that kid dies I'll be run in for manslaughter. But they won't let her die, so it'll only be drunk in charge. So I'm all right, Jack, keep her alive."

"Stop it, you fool," Dick said, and shook her again, until a fit of coughing started.

A stooping man with a yellowish-white moustache, bleary eyes that had been blue once and the sandpapery, sagging skin of age came hesitantly across the hall and halted beside them in a puzzled manner. He knew them; his mind was like a pin-table, the ball of recollection bounded about trying to find a resting place until it trickled slowly into a slot.

"Miss Buckle." He held a hat and a crumpled newspaper in one hand and his clothes were worn and stained. There was a tear in one knee of his grey flannel trousers.

"Colonel Crozier," Dick said. "You've probably forgotten me, I don't deliver milk any more." Then he remembered that Jim Tompkins had stopped the Croziers' milk so no one, presumably, delivered it.

"No more you do," the Colonel said vaguely. "We've left Larkinglass, you know. The house got too big for us. And now my wife—" he gestured towards the stairs. Dick said:

"I'm sorry. I hope she'll soon be out."

"Oh, yes." The Colonel waved his hat and newspaper in a large, circular gesture as if stirring a pudding. "Women's troubles, you know. Certain age . . ." Peering into Dick's face, focusing his eyes with care, recognition came. "Oh, yes, I know you. You're the young fellow who took an interest in my bustard."

"It was a fine bird."

"Last one to be shot on Salisbury Plain. They say the one at Trowbridge was the last but that's wrong. Got the date a year out. Mine's the one . . ."

Dick was afraid Julia's hysterics would return. She was trembling, but he wasn't sure whether this was an aftermath of the last fit or the start of the next. The Colonel added:

"Had to be sold. Smaller place, had to sell practically everything. Should have gone to a museum, a fine bird like that, but some dealer fellow got it for five bob." He shook his head. "Wicked price, what? I'll tell you a joke." He leant forward and a waft of alcohol reached Dick's nostrils. "A joke, eh? It went for a song!" He gave Dick a prod, and chuckled. "A song, you see? A bustard." He waited for a response with a fleeting look of anxiety and Dick achieved a kind of laugh. Colonel Crozier chuckled again. "The joke is, bustards don't sing!"

Still chuckling, he made for the stairs, but at their foot he halted, turned and came back. The alcohol smelled stronger, he had left a sort of trail. "I beg your pardon, Miss Buckle. Please give my respects to your father. Don't envy him his job. Some don't agree, but I say, got to give these natives their head, can't sit on them nowadays. Move with the times. Got to learn by experience, eh? That means they've got to *have* experience. Eh? I think he's on the right lines. Tell him with my compliments."

The Colonel looked at Dick. "You must come and see me one evening. I've got a room at the Crown, not a bad little place. Temporary, you know, while my wife . . ." He walked off but turned again and came back just as Dick and Julia reached the door. He took Dick's arm and leant across to breathe in his ear. "Just a matter of time." He shook his head. "They keep the pain under. In the liver now."

"I'm sorry," Dick said.

"Come and see me one evening, eh? Don't forget, the Crown. Not a bad little place."

"All right, Colonel. I will."

chapter 33

FROM his bedroom at the Feathers, Dick fetched his coat and pocketed a letter and then he tidied round, putting away a pair of socks he'd washed the day before, folding a shirt. He always liked to leave his room in a condition that would cause no trouble if he didn't return.

The Larkinglass road passed the entrance to the cattle market. Enormous lorries were manoeuvring in and out, racing their engines, reversing and letting down their backs to release bewildered animals, who stepped anxiously down the strawed ramps, snorting and quivering. Men in tattered, mud-stained clothes belaboured them with sticks. Flat-sided, shiny-coated calves were bleating with hunger or hanging their heads in fear and confusion and the sharp, penetrating smell of calf scour came from their pens. A man in a dirty white coat was going round with a sheaf of papers, checking their ear tags and pushing them roughly aside.

Smaller calves stood by mothers who were tied up in stalls, their dripping udders taut and heavy. The calves wore little string muzzles to prevent their sucking, and kept butting at the flanks of the cows; they were ravenous, having been kept milkless for twenty-four hours at least so that the mothers' udders would fill and swell to catch the buyers' eye, even though the cows suffered discomfort and sometimes injury and no one was deceived because the practice was general. The dealers in their old felt hats and gumboots, and stained coats or khaki drill overcoats, had flinty, rat-trap faces, tight mouths and quick, mean eyes. They had also the skill to judge instantly the weight of any beast to within a few pounds, to spot a short-backed pig or a cow's light quarter and to know as if by instinct, without consulting anyone, the trend of prices. They never despised a small sum and would haggle half the day over half-a-crown.

The houses began to thin out beyond the cattle market and Dick turned off along a lane leading to a couple of farms, then past woods and across the railway. Once off the main road he was able to breathe without smelling diesel oil or petrol, and to listen to the farmland sounds: the chirp of sparrows, a blackbird squawking as it flew out of a bramble, the sweet trill of a redbreast and the cawing of rooks as they wheeled like black leaves in the sky.

A cold wind was blowing from the southeast and, for the moment, the sky was clear of cloud and a late autumn sun shining thinly, threw long shadows across damp, close-cropped grass. Dick hadn't yet got used to its greenness, or to the fact that its greenness didn't change and in winter, with colours elsewhere muted and drained away, it looked greener than ever, as if lit by emerald fires.

Ploughland stood out rich and chocolate-coloured with a shine on the top of each furrow where the share had polished it by compacting crumbs of soil. This added to the tidy, manicured appearance of the land. That was a thing Dick had never seen before, that sheen on top of the furrows; you didn't get it in his country, where the land was torn up roughly by discs and turned over lumpily, not in these geometrically precise rows. A red tractor with a sack tied across its radiator against frost was chugging to and fro, discing the furrows for winter corn and followed by a flock of seagulls, white against the chocolate brown.

Dick walked past the ploughland and turned off again, this time along a track full of puddles that led past a wood and down to some worked-out gravel pits, flooded with water that reflected the washed-out, smoky blue of the sky. A jet aircraft had drawn a great wide arc of white from one horizon up to the very dome of heaven, where it had vanished; he couldn't see a speck, even one no bigger than a high summer lark. At the bottom of this arc the slash of vapour was dissolving into a string of flocculent puffs, but overhead it ended in a sharp point like a pencil's, hard and clean.

The surfaces of the gravel ponds were ruffled by wavelets brushed up by a steady wind. Black moor hens were swimming about. In the distance a pair of swans, proud and frowning, brooded on the water, and all round the pools' margins the pale reddish-brown, barren gravel lay in mounds and heaps, like a part of the moon. The contractors were supposed to put back topsoil, but they hadn't done so. On a hedge near the gravel the grey-white balls of old-man's-beard clung to blackthorn twigs as though a sheep had struggled through, leaving a little lump of wool on each thorn. Red hawthorn berries glowed among the twigs.

Dick found a sunken place strewn with heaps of gravel and wedged an envelope between two stones. It flapped in the wind, bending like a grass stalk, but the stones held it. Then he pulled his automatic pistol from his pocket and checked it over. It had come through the post with its six cartridges extracted, wrapped in cotton wool. He examined the pistol, loaded the magazine and looked round. Some young Friesian cattle were grazing in a field. In the distance a flock of lapwings rose like a cloud of black and white steam, circled, settled again. The tractor was out of sight. A train went by on a raised embankment but it was at least a mile away.

Stepping back a few paces, he fired two shots into the envelope. The pistol worked perfectly and the sound made a sharp, tearing noise, not loud, across the air. Some pigeons flapped their wings and took off from the wood, one or two of the beasts raised their heads, stared dreamily about them and went on grazing. The moor hens had dived headfirst. The envelope showed two blackened holes. Dick spread out the letter it had contained and sat down on the gravel by the water's edge, where he was more or less out of the wind. His hands were red and stiff with cold.

The letter was from his sister-in-law. Although he'd told her not to write, she couldn't believe he didn't want any news of the boys. Andrew had knocked a tooth out falling off a pony, Duncan had developed an artistic bent with coloured crayons, Patrick by now had cut all his teeth. It was as if he were reading about creatures in whom he had no special interest, inhabiting another planet. There'd be hot sunshine there, furious cascades of bougainvillias, pencil-sharp blue horizons, a smell of burning cow dung, a chattering of yellow weavers, liquid voices pouring out their warm communications, violet-blue jacarandas and a silvery-grey shimmer of blue gum leaves.

When he'd sent the boys to Emma and her husband, he'd promised a sum of ten thousand pounds to pay for their education and start them in life. She'd insisted that they didn't want it, but he'd told her it was all settled and so she'd grown to count on it, entered the boys for boarding schools, made the necessary arrangements. All she asked now was to know the position. No doubt, she supposed, he'd disposed of the farm, sold up everything and come away with capital in his pocket.

In fact, by now he had less than a hundred pounds.

That was one thing but there was another, more important. All hunts must end either in a kill, or by calling off the hounds. Twice he'd overhauled the quarry, got him cornered and botched the kill. Third time lucky: there'd be no mistake. He'd got it all worked out in his head.

A kill, or calling off the hounds. Since the hunt had started, his quarry had been transformed from an idea, an emblem or abstraction, into a human being, full of faults like all humans but also full of hopes not ignoble, frustrations not all deserved, affections not unreciprocated. A husband, a father, a master: in all these parts neither an unflawed success nor a total failure. A mixture, a muddle, a compromise, like the weather, the English character, the island skies.

He thought about Peter Buckle's family. About Martin: why had he returned the gun? Because he wanted his father shot? For money? The money was Lavinia's, but Martin might get something, inherit Chaffins perhaps. Or maybe he held against his father that overindulgence which might have twisted his nature at its roots. Or perhaps Peter stood between him and the full possession of his sister, who loved Peter but feared and despised Martin even when she was drawn to him. Or perhaps some deep, perverted jealousy had poisoned Martin's mind.

Or perhaps Martin hadn't believed the gun would do its work at all. Perhaps, summing it all up, he'd calculated that the attempt would fail again, or be abandoned. Perhaps he'd dismissed Dick's purpose as a grand illusion, like the dreams of men who enjoy a woman a dozen times a night in the imagination but their wives once a week in the flesh, or not at all. Or possibly he'd gambled on a failure of nerve, taking pleasure in the thought of Dick's humiliation.

Or perhaps he thought Dick would make the attempt, muff it, be taken in the act and so destroyed. Or had he simply tossed the ball against the wheel without much caring which slot it settled in, out of sheer curiosity? On balance, that seemed the most likely reason—a gamble. Martin liked to experiment and, whichever way things went, he couldn't lose. For him, fortune held no hostages. Indifference, a lack of love, a reservoir of hatred, these gave you a cast-iron, foolproof insurance cover against most of life's disasters.

Dick was throwing little pebbles into the water with his chilled fingers, watching them plop. The wind was cold about his ears. A black speck had emerged from the vastness of the pastel-blue sky and was drawing its white signature across the envelope of air that wrapped the earth. The cattle had grown restless and were gathering near a gate at the far end of their pasture. Probably they'd heard or seen a tractor and a man coming with hay; there was plenty of grass but not much goodness in it at this time of year. Dick wondered how Rodney was getting on, whether Maharajah's Lily had calved and if so whether she'd achieved her eight gallons; whether Rodney was still having trouble with solids-not-fat and the same feud with the milk recorder. Rodney, he thought, the salt of the earth.

Julia stood for calling off the hounds. The positive against the negative: life, contest, action, Australia—a symbol, here: you went down through the earth and emerged the other side into sunlight and freshness, where even animals and plants were strange and different, purged of yourself, remade; all that you were and had been you left behind in this hemisphere, the past cut away. The ghost of Rose and of his love and unity would dissolve forever in that bright air, as vapour made by the passage of the aircraft had now dispersed into the water-colour sky.

That was what Julia was set on. She had life on her side. Rose was over, Rose was dead. Already the unity that had sustained him, the wholeness, had dispersed like vapour in the sky. Australia waited for him on the other side of the world. He'd manage well enough there.

And Julia, who offered love: could she manage too? Was it love that she offered? Or an infatuation that blinded them both, a jack-o'-lantern light leaping from a bog of frustration, humiliation and jealousy—from Martin's cruelty, Evan's failure, Peter's ambition, Lavinia's withdrawal, from her own doubts and instability and need for love? For some reason, the image of a lily-trotter came into his mind. Those long-beaked, slender-legged birds hopped from one flat leaf to the next, pecking, dipping their heads, never still, their feet barely seeming to touch the floating foliage, resting no weight upon it: insubstantial, restless, not to be relied on; stretch out your hand and they would vanish. An illusion among birds.

Perhaps because there were birds all around him, moor hens and ducks and rooks, pigeons and lapwings and gulls and then the hedgebirds, the sparrows and chaffinches and finches, and the speckled chattering starlings—perhaps because of this his mind dwelt on birds and then he thought of nets. He'd never seen birds netted, only read about it; but he thought of it now, a man spreading a net over a blinded quail that called out in the dusk while the man secured the net's fringe to shrubs and brambles. When he looked closely he could see the man's face and it was dark and clever and was smiling, the smile as if carved on time-darkened ivory, tufts of hair below the temples and the head half bald.

The face was Martin's. He spread the net and smiled and Dick heard the quail calling. Then he saw the head of the sightless quail thrown back, twisting and turning, and it was Julia's.

Dick got to his feet and wrapped his coat closer round his body, impatient with these fancies that sprang uninvited into his head. They were something left over from childhood and while he'd been with Rose they'd left him, but now they bothered him again. Why should Martin have power to spread nets for anyone? Julia could break free if she wanted to. They were alike in so many ways. They couldn't resist torturing people, couldn't leave them alone. Martin tortured others but Julia turned on herself. Yet she'd called out to him from the net and perhaps only he could set her free.

Free from what? Not from her own nature and heredity. Not from the past that had shaped her and the present that held her down. Not from the guilt of the maimed child. That was her net and it would hold her down forever. She would drink to drown the memory of drinking and what it had perhaps done, she had that urge to overdramatize inherent in her family. She had jealousy and anger and the need for conflict and she wouldn't rest until she had destroyed his memories, driven out his secret joys, drained and possessed and tormented him.

The net was guilt, his task to find a way to release her. That couldn't be done if he entangled his own feet. To release her, he must keep his own freedom. He must destroy the net and cheat the fingers of the man waiting to see him entangled. And this could be done. It would be easy, simple and humane, and it would benefit everyone. There'd be a kill: after a change of foxes.

Dick started back towards Horsington. The wind was in his face now, making his eyes water and his cheeks stiff. He walked mechanically, his thoughts as light and undirected as a blown leaf. The burning kick that had bowled him over in the forest when a bolt had hit him from a bandit's homemade rifle; the abyss of terror, the choking in his lungs and then the wild animal exhilaration when his knife was in his hand; the chant of triumph and laughter of his men and the great blazing bonfire when they burnt the captured weapons; Rose pressing and re-pressing the stiff clean uniform, shining with newness, that he'd worn for the investiture; and the greater moment when he'd led his champion homebred heifer past the royal box, heading the parade; and then a Scottish regiment beating the retreat at sunset under the blue gums and the Last Post greeting the first star, and Rose at his side. Andrew playing like a puppy with the fat old boxer; the puff adder killed in the kitchen; and then, long before, the time his mother had knocked over a lamp and the little wooden house had caught fire and he'd carried Hughie out in his pyjamas and tripped and cut his arm and thought he was going to bleed to death, and his father running out waving a sword salvaged from the cupboard where he'd kept his old uniform. And Hughie in a black rage because Dick wouldn't give him his rook rifle; and helping Hughie to do his sums.

Why had his thoughts strayed back so far? Memories were coming to an end. The only kind of after-death survival he believed in was a survival in living minds: Rose survived so long as he remembered her, no longer, Rose and Hughie and his parents; when the memory died, like the jet-made streak of vapour, they too would be dispersed. But what you did lived after you: the cattle he'd bred, the river dam, the paddocked land, the planted trees—they might survive for a little: and the sons Rose had borne. And mistakes as well as achievements, the omissions and failures. The failures of nerve which were always due to doubt, to a greyness of the soul that spread from old civilized lands where guilt could always be explained away, disloyalty extenuated.

The red tractor had finished discing the field and hitched on a triple roll. Opposite, a field of early corn was already showing green in the drills. At a small farm by the roadside, just where lane and main road joined, a tractor had been drawn up by a saw bench and a pile of logs and miscellaneous timber: rotten fence posts, old planks, a broken gate, odds and ends from hedgerows that would help keep down the coal bill in winter. A man was hitching a belt on to the power drive and as Dick approached he picked up a log, tested it on the iron bench and pushed it towards the circular saw.

The saw bit into the wood, emitting as it did so its characteristic high, rasping whine, rising to a kind of screech as the teeth reached the centre of the log. Dick halted and threw his head back as if he'd been hit in the face and then stood stock-still, stiff all over. The high-pitched whine was like a knife cutting into his body. He felt his arteries parting, his brain falling apart where the knife sliced through him as it was slicing the log. The saw's whine screeched and tore into his head, blinding and deafening his senses. Once the sound got in it couldn't get out and the sound was agony, and agony trapped and confined and screaming to get out of his head.

He shut his eyes because the earth was revolving, and put out his hands, but there was nothing to grip. He was alone, totally alone in the vastness of a universe stretching to infinity and there was no one to help him, no way of getting the sound and the agony out of his head. It was there for all eternity, boring into his brain cells like an auger, stabbing, shrieking like the eternally damned. He cried out for Rose but she wasn't there. He was alone with the panic and the tortured screaming and the screams vibrating and the great auger boring into his head, on fire and icy cold and everything was black. Then once again he saw it happen, he heard the blade whine and saw the sun strike the metal and heard the screams and the shouts and loud, bellowing laughter and he was struggling forward but his legs were helpless and he was like a fly embedded in glue. He saw the blood on the saw and the butchered flesh and his brother's head lying in the sawdust like a doll's, a sawdust doll that had been dropped and broken so that all the stuffing ran out.

He hadn't seen it happen, he was half an hour too late. A gang had surprised his crippled brother and the Indian who helped him and their two servants and tied them up while they looted the place and burnt the house with the dogs inside it, and then they started on their captives. He hadn't seen it happen but the electric motor was still running, the whine was there and the flashing metal and the mangled bits of flesh and the iron bench sticky with blood.

He hadn't seen it happen but his insides had seemed to harden into steel and he'd gone into the forest driven by a power stronger than fear or hunger or exhaustion, charged with a purpose nothing could deflect or deny. Two days later, he and his companions had found them and destroyed them, and that was when he'd got his hole in the shoulder and his bash on the head. But they'd never got the planner of it all, the clever young man who'd dodged them in the forest and issued the orders and deployed the gangs and thought up the refinements, the man at the end of the chain. They never got him but they knew who he was.

They knew who he was: and so did the authorities, they put a price on his head and pronounced him an outcast unfit until his dying day to mix with decent men. And then they pardoned him and called him in to treat with him, and now he was a slimy statesman fawned upon by Cabinet Ministers and wined and dined by businessmen wanting contracts and reporters wanting interviews and delegates to the United Nations wanting votes and diplomats from Iron Curtain countries wanting to destroy the sordid remnants of British influence. A statesman acclaimed in foreign capitals, given V.I.P. treatment at London's most expensive hotels.

And it was Buckle who'd called him back, Buckle who'd talked of bygones being bygones and of fruitful co-operation and the same interests at heart. Buckle might have had advisers but it was he who'd summoned him to London, who'd shaken his hand and talked of partners in

the building of a new future and letting the past bury its
dead.

They couldn't bury Hughie because about all they'd
been able to identify had been his artificial leg. That was
when the change had begun in Rose, as if something had
been torn out of her that could never be replaced. That was
when she had begun to die—it had taken her about two
years. He had not been able to protect her in the end. It
was after Hughie's murderer became a statesman that Dick
had sent his medal back.

Dick found himself cold and sick and shaking on the
ground. One shoelace was undone; he tried to tie it but his
hands were so unsteady that he gave it up. He was icy cold.
The man at the saw bench hadn't noticed him, but a
woman on a bicycle came by. She stared at him, stopped
pedalling and started to brake. "I'm all right," he called out
in a vocie as cracked and dry as a rusty hinge. She looked
uncertain, the cycle wavered, then she thought better of her
impulse and cycled on.

The blood was still pounding in his head but gradually it
quietened down and he got up and walked on. His knees
were weak and he had to summon an effort to put his feet
down steadily and in the right place. He kept his eyes on
the ground as he passed the entrance to the muddy yard.
The man had stopped sawing and was stacking logs. Then
Dick was on the main road, walking on tarmac with traffic
going by, tires screaming on the surface but without
menace. As he walked on, his strength returned.

The wave had gone but it had left behind a hard, polished surface with no cracks or fingerholds. Dick's doubts
and questions, his weakness and procrastination, these had
gone to leave his resolution adamant.

Crimes had been committed and for these there must be
guilt; and for all guilt there must be responsibility. Crimes

couldn't be left floating in the void. Someone had committed them, someone must take responsibility, someone must accept guilt and punishment. There was always a chain: private to commander, helmsman to navigator, tinker to king; you had to work your way back, link by link, to reach the origin. Somewhere you would touch the last link, where responsibility rested and guilt could be redeemed. That might be rough justice but it was justice—not evasion, not prevarication, not sophistry, not betrayal, the worst crime of all.

chapter 34

"THEY won't look at it globally, that's the trouble. Globally—or even nationally, if it comes to that. Their own sectional interests first, last and all the time."

Colonel Watts nodded sympathetically. "The Member has to balance it all up. Mind you, the rural interest isn't what it used to be in this constituency. I have to keep reminding myself we're over eighty per cent urban now."

Peter Buckle leant back in his chair. "I've a good deal of sympathy with these fellows. As a potato grower myself—"

The agent smiled. "Very useful card to play, that. Very."

"I hope I didn't overplay it?"

"Good lord, no. It's true and they know it. Common interests. No, you handled that very nicely if I may say so, very nicely indeed."

"Well, you'd softened them up. It's a good job our chaps aren't like the French farmers. Holy terrors, they are, blocking the roads with tractors and things. I sometimes wonder our blokes don't catch on."

"That wouldn't be quite British, would it? We're a reasonable lot on the whole. . . . D'you mind if I run along now? I've got some fellows waiting to have a word with me about a development site over at Bartonsbury."

Peter glanced at the grandfather clock. On market days the landlord of the Feathers put this room at the agent's disposal, and anyone could look in for a chat. Peter came down himself, whenever he could, to see his constituents, mingle with them in the bar, keep in touch. Now he'd become a Minister these visits weren't nearly as frequent as he'd have liked.

"You run along," he said to his agent. "I'll put in half an hour here on these notes, I don't suppose I'll be disturbed, and then run back to Chaffins. London by five."

"A treadmill—rather you than me. You'll be here next Wednesday?"

Peter shook his head. "There's this constitutional conference. I'll give you a ring over the weekend."

He was glad of the half hour to work on his speech. Normally, he'd have taken the notes back to his own study, but for the moment Chaffins was a place to avoid. Everything there was upside down: Julia in a ghastly state of nerves, these appalling allegations—he supposed they were worse than that, revelations—about Martin, and now even Lavinia turning against him, at this of all times. It didn't bear thinking about. Even when he drove through Larkinglass he couldn't feel at ease. That morning he'd seen Dennis Ryan walking down the village street, wrapped in the muffler he wore simply for effect, to reflect the working-class image—the old image, not the new reality in a sweater and tight trousers behind the wheel of a car.

Ryan had glowered at him like a sullen bull and might well have spat as Peter drove by, it would have been part of the act. Why should he make Peter feel guilty? It wasn't *his* fault about the wretched child. Home life, he thought grimly: that secure, sustaining base from which one conducted one's share of the nation's business. And a Cabinet meeting at six. It was a bit hard.

"Safeguards for democracy," he wrote, and underlined

it. "(1) Bill of rights. (2) Regional Assemblies. (3) Independent Judiciary. (4) Secret Ballot. . . ." He didn't hear the door open but looked up, sensing the presence of an intruder.

"What the hell d'you mean by—" He pushed his chair back with a jerk and half rose, panic all but choking his throat. The man had always been a lunatic and now he looked like one, there was something queer about him, staring eyes, solid eyes, a wild look like a desperate animal.

"Sit down."

Dick spoke quietly, but with such intensity that Peter subsided slowly back into his chair. The intruder had a key in his hand. Without taking his eyes off the man at the desk he put his hand behind his back, fumbled for what seemed an age until he got the key into the lock, and turned it. Then he came forward, threw his raincoat over the chair and leant one hand on the desk. The other hand he put into his pocket, and kept it there.

It was like being penned up with a treacherous bull, but a bull with a warped human intelligence. What did you do? Threats, bluster, force, were worse than useless; he had you at his mercy; you had only one resource, your brain; only one weapon, your tongue. Carefully, as if handling a very fragile piece of glass, Peter pushed forward a packet lying on the desk.

"Cigarette?"

Dick paid no attention. Peter began to talk.

"This accident of Julia's is a bad business, Heron. I quite accept her story that she wasn't in the least to blame. I imagine a good deal will depend on your evidence. Of course, it wouldn't be proper for me to discuss it with you but I believe that if you tell the truth and stick to it however much they try to shake you, and of course they will, she's got a chance."

Dick watched Peter with contempt. Behind the handsome, heavy, swarthy features he saw a soft pulp of cowardice, pretension and conceit. All his life Peter Buckle had been talking and now he was trying to talk his way out of destiny. "It won't work," Dick said.

"You never know with a jury," Peter disagreed, misunderstanding him. "We're briefing Birchall, he's the best money can buy. Of course, it's unfortunate about the child —apart from being such a ghastly tragedy, it's the sort of emotional business that may affect the jury unfavourably. But I know we can count on you. That's what Evan said. You've got rather an admirer in Evan, you know. I think he believes you're a good influence on Julia. He said we could count on you."

Peter ventured to lean back a little, cautiously, as if a sudden movement would release a spring. Dick hadn't taken his eyes off Peter's face and they *were* wild, it wasn't imagination.

"I haven't much time," Dick said. "I've wasted enough already."

Peter went on, afraid that he was beginning to gabble. "Then there's Martin, he's one of your admirers too. Martin—I'll tell you frankly, Heron, it's been a great blow to me. I suppose I've been blind. Even now I can't quite grasp it. What do you think, is it really true? I mean, that he's behaved as badly as Evan . . . That he's been going on like that for years? Not just a bit of indiscretion now and then, something much more serious, a deliberate—well, I suppose one must say it, criminal?"

His voice now was pleading and the odd thing was, his emotion was genuine, he really wanted to get Dick's reassurance, to ask his opinion. But Dick said:

"Before I kill you, Buckle, I want you to know why. Strictly speaking there's no need. The others didn't know, they died and they didn't die like you will, they weren't nearly so lucky. Even in the way you die you'll be lucky— privileged."

Peter gave a kind of laugh, his mouth stiff as a board.

"My dear chap, you're talking like a soap-box—" He broke off quickly, remembering that one shouldn't argue with lunatics. One must humour them: distract them, that was the thing. Dick still had one hand in his pocket.

"Of course, the one you've really made a conquest of is Julia. Well, that's obvious. I must honestly admit, Heron, I was pretty taken aback when I first—well, to be candid, putting yourself in my place, wouldn't you have been? The first I heard of you was when Tompkins told me he'd taken you on as second cowman while Bert was in hospital. That was all I knew. You must admit that when the next thing was you were going round with Julia and she—after all, she engaged to Evan, at least, I thought she was. And without wanting to be pompous about it, I've had a good deal on my plate."

Dick suddenly sat down in the chair and leant across the desk, resting one doubled-up fist on its surface. He spoke conversationally.

"It's all rather hard to explain. Here in England nothing ever really belongs to you, it's more as if you were a sort of trustee. Take Chaffins, for example. I suppose that land was cleared from forest about a thousand years ago. Ever since then, someone's been farming it. Generation after generation, putting something in. So that when you get it, you take over a going concern. You can bring in a few changes but fundamentally you don't alter anything. And then you hand it on very much as it was. That's what I mean, a trustee. You carry on, you look after it, but you don't create anything. So it isn't really yours."

Was it safe to show an interest? Heron was talking strangely but lucidly. Or was it best to go on trying to distract? Cautiously, Peter ventured: "I think I see what you mean."

"But if you start with just a piece of forest, say, and you take it and alter it and make it grow things it's never grown before and carry new kinds of animals, and say you've bred those too—then that's different, you're creating something that wasn't there before. It's yours in a different way. Like marriage almost—one flesh, Eve coming from a rib of Adam's, bone of his bone and flesh of his flesh, all that sort of thing. You have a special feeling for something you create. Perhaps the Saxons had it when they cut down the forest at Chaffins. It must have been a wonderful country in those days, the forest and hills and rivers, nothing else, the silences."

"You know, Heron, you're quite a poet in your way." Peter's voice was almost jaunty, he was gaining time and that was everything. He glanced away for a split second at the clock, and then back to Dick's face.

"I'm not just speaking for myself, most of us feel like this, more or less—even more the women, possibly. They create the homes. And that's different, too. Now Chaffins, that was built about three hundred years ago and I suppose there's no reason why it shouldn't be standing in a thousand years' time. That's more than fifty generations. All you do is take it over and hand it on. Well, of course, there's a difference between Chaffins and a bungalow of slats and shingles, or mud and wattle with a tin roof; but there again, if you've built it with your own hands, perhaps you've even scrounged nails from packing cases to save paying out cash you haven't got, then you've created it, you love it and it's yours. First you imagined it and then you worked for it, finally you built it and it's yours. So naturally, you don't see why you should hand it over to someone else who's never worked for it at all and would wipe it off the map in a couple of years."

"That's a perfectly reasonable point of view." Peter tried to put some warmth and sympathy into his voice, though his throat was dry. "I'm glad you think so well of Chaffins. You're quite right, of course, it's a trust. That's how I've always regarded it. And I always hoped that Martin—he's got splendid taste, you know. If he took it over he'd make it quite superb. He gets that from his mother. I was brought up in a hideous Midland city, lower middle class background without any of that sort of thing. But I can understand what you're driving at. Chaffins means a lot to me."

Dick took no notice of this opening. "That was what Rose thought, too. She didn't say much but she felt it. Well, it was something we shared." Dick opened the fist that lay clenched on the table as if to let something drop, and flexed his fingers. "She saw it all, from the time it was just forest and no one there, just trees and emptiness. All that's gone now. I often wonder if it's a good thing. Instead there's crops and fences and boreholes, paddocks and leys and barns and dips and the pedigree cattle. Now it's their turn, they'll go too. That's another difference, you see. If you hand over Chaffins, it doesn't disappear. In a hundred years the house'll be there and the fields and buildings, and there'll be the pastures, better than ever undoubtedly, and wonderful crops, and everything will be better, not worse. But on my place in five years' time there won't be anything left of what we created. Rose and I. So we might as well not have tried."

"I can't agree there." Peter was tempted from his fortress of non-argument. "That's where I think you go wrong. Setbacks there may be, one can't avoid them, but given proper supervision and the necessary capital—"

"Rose felt it even more than I did. I'm sure of that now. Even though we had the three boys—perhaps because of them, I don't know. She got more secretive as time went on, buttoned up. She didn't like to talk about it, though of course sometimes we did. We had to make the decision, go or stay. That's what got her down, for one thing—the decision, I mean. She couldn't sleep. She kept worrying about the boys. And of course there were other things, gangs raiding farms, robberies with violence, homemade rifles."

"You know, Heron, you can't in fairness blame all this on me. I didn't create the trend of history, the Afro-Asian dynamic, the wind of change, any more than you did. One's got to live with them, that's all. Either you bend or you break. After all—"

"There was the time I was wounded and then there was Hughie. Perhaps it was too much to expect that she'd get over that. She was strong, Rose was, but there was such a softness in her too. She couldn't stand too much horror."

Someone was turning the handle of the door. A pause, the door rattled, Peter opened his mouth but before a sound emerged the black gun was pointing straight at him, steady as a rock, just across the table. He stared at it, fascinated, and slowly closed his mouth. Another rattle followed, then silence. Peter tried to swallow but his throat was dry.

"There's not much longer." Dick didn't vary his tone of voice. "I was telling you about Rose. Or at least about Hughie. Even though he was a cripple and had an artificial leg he did twice as much as most men. He got about amazingly. But there was nothing he could do against a gang."

"It's long past lunch time, Heron." Peter's voice was very faint. "My wife will be wondering what's happened. Hadn't we better go on with this at Chaffins? In here—"

"He was sawing fence posts at the time. I don't think the gang had anything particular against my brother. But they had their orders so they chopped him up all right."

There was a short silence. Peter couldn't take his eyes off the gun. He hadn't grasped what Dick had said, words were bouncing off the surface of his concentration on the gun. Heron *was* mad and his voice was speeding up, there was a sense of time moving, of an approaching climax that could be sensed as sailors feel in their nerves the coming of a typhoon.

"I'm sorry." Peter spoke very quietly, and licked his dry lips. The pit of his stomach felt as if it were falling away.

"I collected the bits."

The broken Crown Derby vase flickered in and out of Peter's mind. Why had he thrown it at Evan? Why should a thought of such futility be the one he was going to die with spinning in his head?

chapter 35

"Do you think I wanted things like that to happen?" Peter's voice sounded as if it were coming through a tunnel from a long way off. "They happen everywhere—bloodshed, violence, revolution—it's a blood-soaked age. Can't you see we were trying to avoid that sort of thing? The sort of thing we had in Cyprus and in Kenya? To remove the frustrations, the bitterness, the anger—make people think constructively?"

"That was three years ago." Dick went on quite calmly, as if thinking aloud. "Our lives grew over it like scar tissue but when things started to get bad again it all flared up underneath the surface, festering in the dark. In Rose's mind. At least I think that's what happened. She didn't say much. If she'd been able to speak more . . ."

He was looking thoughtfully at the gun. Peter risked another glance at the door, a slight movement; immediately the gun was thrust a little closer, black as Satan, staring at him with its wicked open eye. Had the man who tried the door gone away thinking the room was deserted? Or would he ask the landlord why he couldn't get in?

"There were only two things, Heron, we could do."

Peter leant forward a little, with a terrific effort of his will, towards the barrel. "Only two. We could fight those people, go on fighting them, as we tried in Cyprus and the French did in Algeria. And look at the result. Young lives thrown away and bitterness and bloodshed and colossal expense. And how long do you think our people here would have stood for it? Our other alternative, the one we chose, was to come to terms. We had to do that in the end, so we did it before the bloodshed and the bitterness instead of after. To come to terms, hand over peaceably. Wasn't that only common sense? D'you think there was anything else we *could* have done?"

"It was the uncertainty that got her down." Dick spoke thoughtfully. "And worrying about the boys. And then the feeling of futility, of retreat, of everything breaking up and going downhill. We knew we were expendable. Perhaps it couldn't be helped. Perhaps it was inevitable. But *she* needn't have been, she shouldn't have been. Rose was murdered. You can be murdered from a distance just as much as when someone draws a knife across your neck."

For the first time Peter saw a very faint gleam at the end of the tunnel. "You use that word, *inevitable*. You're dead right there. None of us can work things out just as we'd like them, fair to everyone—certain people are going to get hurt whatever you do. Nobody likes it but it's as you said— inevitable. It's a question of the greatest good for the greatest number. One's simply got to accept it, that's all."

"I cut the rope," Dick said. "On a beam in the store."

Peter watched the gun. It was swelling before his eyes into a monstrous growth, a snake's head, an obscene fungus; in another moment it would start to writhe and twist. It filled his eyes, his brain, his whole body.

"Wait a minute, Heron." Peter's lips were parched as sand and he had to force a thick tongue to form the words. The gun didn't move. "Just a minute. Are you sure you've got the right man? You may think I was the one to blame but I wasn't really, I was never the master. I only did what I was told."

Dick's voice was flat and unemotional. "She was twenty-nine."

"If you think all that was done at *my* orders, you flatter me. I'm not that important, that powerful, not by any means. In the end you'll have to settle with my masters. You've met some of them. This chap here who runs the Feathers. Those potato growers who saw me half an hour ago. Then the people you know at Chaffins—Rodney, Jim Tompkins, Walter, Ray, Bert. And their wives. The fellows behind the tractor and the factory bench, in the bar of the Feathers and the Red Lion. They're my masters. They tell me what I'm to do."

Dick said: "In the end, someone's got to be responsible."

"You can shoot me if you like, Heron, but you won't have settled anything. The Hydra-headed monster, remember that? Every time the hero cut off a head—Perseus, wasn't it?—another one grew. World opinion, that's what you're up against, Heron. There's your Hydra-headed monster. That's my master in the long run."

Peter had been gathering confidence as he went on. His own eloquence acted like adrenalin, quickening his blood and bracing his nerves; every minute that he spun things out was like a lifetime gained. And now he thought a crack was opening in the casing of his enemy's mind. The gun was steady still and so was the hand on the gun, but behind the hand was a will and it was the will that was weakening, allowing itself to be suborned.

"Do you really think I could have gone against these masters of mine? That they'd have listened if I had? I'd have been out on my ear and someone else would have taken over and done just the same. Or perhaps not as much, even, for people like you. I've tried to do all I can.

"This is a revolution, Heron, not a church bazaar! Of course it's hard on individuals. Of course it has its personal tragedies. No man on earth can stop these great waves of history from sweeping away good and bad together. They not only can't be stopped, they shouldn't be. It's right, you know it's right, that people should be free!"

Peter was astonished at himself; he hadn't even known that underneath the crust of daily intercourse, routine, there smouldered these residual fires kindled in a youth he could scarcely remember. He was a better man than he'd realized under it all.

"People like you talk about expediency—all right, then, it's expedient, it's doing what you must, giving way to the majority. And what's wrong with that? Who am I, who are you, to say no to them? They don't ask, they take, and why shouldn't they? Aren't they the judges, not you or me?"

Of course he didn't want these questions to be answered but he pressed on, gripping the desk, words tumbling out like a load of gravel released from a grab. "You've got it all wrong, Heron. I've not been carrying out a policy I don't believe in, cynically, jumping on the nationalist band wagon as you think I have. I've been doing what I honestly believe's right, I know's right, right for the people themselves and for my own people, my country, the peace of the world—even right for you and others like you in the end."

He broke off panting and suddenly appalled. Had he really been pouring out all that, shouting almost at this armed maniac? Wouldn't those angry words, barbed with insult, prod Heron's crazed wits over the edge? Dick had moved the hand that held the gun a little closer; the knuckles, smooth and bony, were steady and his voice quiet, matter-of-fact.

"We'd begun another baby, Rose wanted it, four was a

better number and a girl. . . . But then she was sorry, anyway by fits and starts, she was divided, not a whole."

"Go on, then, Heron, shoot me if you like." Peter was still leaning forward, concentrating; he tried to keep his voice down, tried to force his words as through a thick piece of leather into the other's mind. "I'm at your mercy. You'll shoot me and it won't make a ha'porth of difference. Another head will grow before they've even hauled you up and tried you and shut you up for the rest of your life, shut you up until you die."

Dick was looking at the gun in his hand without seeing it. His voice carried a note of surprise.

"There were flies on her tongue."

Peter gave an involuntary twitch, a muscular contraction; Dick wasn't here in this room at the Feathers, other sights were moving like a film across his mad brain. Words had bounced like hailstones off a compacted mind sealed against ideas and human contacts, fossilized.

Desperately Peter thought: Julia—Julia must have touched his feelings, the very word would surely thrust into that clamlike mind. Julia might yet save him, the last throw.

"You haven't only got yourself to think of, Heron. There's Julia now. You know she's in trouble. She needs your help, doesn't she? The fact of the matter is that Julia loves you, whether you want her to or not. She's young— still a kid, too young in many ways. Do you want to hurt her? Is that what your wife would have wanted? *She's* not responsible, whoever else is. But she's the one who'll suffer. . . ."

He'd made a mistake. The mad, solid look had come back into Dick's eyes. For an instant, through the panic that was once more rising, Peter felt a flash of pity for his executioner, a desperate man imprisoned in his haunted dreams, in the illusions that alone sustained him. If the ghost illusions vanished that would be the end of him, no man could stand the hollow, echoing, endless emptiness of the long stair without his ghosts to keep him company. At the core of Dick's bruised mind lay that little germ of knowledge: his companions were ghosts and one day they'd desert him and leave him comfortless. Peter spoke in a whisper.

"Think of Julia, Heron. She loves you. She'll help you, with her you can make a new start, you can . . . The past's over, you're young . . ."

He couldn't stop himself from pleading. Dick must see it now, he must. After a peril that had been so nearly mastered, surely the end wouldn't come now.

"Don't you see what you're throwing away?" Peter almost shouted, though his voice wasn't much higher than a whisper. "She loves you, Dick. I'm glad, we all are. We're going to help you, we're on your side. You've had a raw deal, we're going to make it up to you. I'll buy you a farm, I'll help you make a new start. That's reasonable, isn't it? You'll forget the past. That's right, we've all got to go on living. Julia will . . ."

His voice tailed off; Dick had jumped up and was standing in front of him like some gigantic threatening bird of doom, a pale vulture, all the contempt and hatred concentrated in his unhuman, agate eyes. He began to squeeze the trigger.

"You cringing bastard," he said.

Peter shut his eyes and held down a long scream, beyond thinking or feeling. He sat there for a thousand years, a million, and then the rules, which he knew now for illusions, like the stairway ghosts, began to reappear. He heard a sound and opened his eyes: Dick was still there, the bird of doom, but shrunk in stature to a man's size and the gun was lowered.

"I can't do it," Dick spoke in a tone of amazement.

Peter's breath came out with a rush, as if escaping from a tire.

"You're not worth it, that's why."

He put the gun in his pocket with a slow, dreamlike gesture and his face was stunned with surprise.

"Shooting worms. Crying for your own skin." Peter saw a deep contempt in the eyes—but the mad, solid, agate glint had faded.

"Besides . . ." Dick was looking over Peter's shoulder through the window, which gave on to a dark, paved yard full of empty crates. "Why should I let you off? You can live it out. You've deserved it. There are others. . . ."

He swung round and reached the door, turned the key and went out without another word, without looking back.

In the hospital, the patients had been settled for their afternoon's rest and the nurses had vanished into nooks and crannies of the rambling edifice. There was no one to be seen as Dick walked along the corridor, past the sister's room and into the ward. On each side lay the patients in their spaced, orderly rows, prone or on pillows with a view of the patient opposite.

A shaft of sunlight fell across the shiny plastic tiled floor, barred with shadows thrown by a window frame. Dick halted and looked down at the pattern, at the soft October sunshine reflected on a mottled brown.

From the far end of the long ward, a young nurse was advancing towards him. She had fluffy pale hair and her plump breasts bounded a little as she walked perkily, like a pullet summoned by the hope of corn. Her air of confidence was assumed; she was at the start of her training and still overawed by the impersonality of the machine, the demands of the patients and the sister's authority, and by doubts of her own capacities.

"Visiting hours . . ." she began.

"Can you tell me, please, which is the injured girl, Stella Ryan?"

"She's not allowed any visitors. She's not . . ."

"I'm not a visitor. Though I suppose I seem like one." Dick smiled down at the probationer who couldn't quite suppress a small responding smile; he was handsome.

"Sister wouldn't . . ."

"That's her over there, isn't it?" He walked a few paces to a bed where a clot of white dressings lay against white pillows; all you could see was a waxy nose and chin. The shape under the blankets was tiny. Chrysanthemums, bronze and yellow, glowed from a bedside table. The white clot, the small shape, was totally inert.

"You mustn't disturb her." The probationer spoke nervously. "Poor little mite. She can't talk, you know."

Dick stood looking down at the white dressings, the little mound under the blankets, the waxy flesh between the bandages.

"It's a shame." The probationer had rested one hand on a piece of apparatus used for blood transfusions. "Drunk, they say. If I had my way I'd put them all in prison for life. Too soft with them, they are. If people saw . . ."

"She was pretty."

"You're not supposed to be here, you know. Sister wouldn't half take on . . . Visiting hours are four to six today and Saturdays and Sunday."

"Please, nurse." A patient three beds away was calling out, a wispy-haired old woman. The probationer went across to her. Dick stepped up close to the bedside and leant over the small shape. It was still as an effigy in a church. He pulled out his automatic pistol and put a bullet through the dressings and turned and walked back down the ward.

Silence, a scream, running footsteps, a slow stirring

behind him as if a breeze had started up in a wood. A door opened, a voice called. Without looking back he walked along the corridor and down the stairs.

Julia had loved him and he was glad he was able to do something in return. When you spent a life it was better to get something for it, value for money. And to dispel a load of guilt wasn't a negligible service. After all, perhaps he hadn't wholly failed.

At the bottom of the stairs he halted, put the muzzle in his mouth, pointed it upwards and pulled the trigger.

chapter 36

THE clocks had gone back now and lights were needed in the cowsheds and the dairy towards the end of milking time. Rodney liked the first early nights of winter and tea with curtains drawn, it was snug and cozy. Another thing, if it wasn't for the winter everyone would wear themselves out working late hours, in the garden if there wasn't overtime to do. You didn't pick up so much money in the winter but then you lived on your fat.

It wasn't cold yet, anyway. The wind was none too gentle, quite a nip, but a wet wind, not a hard dry one. Only once or twice, in the early mornings, had there been rime on the grass, making it crunchy, and a brittle skin of ice over the puddles, and that rich, pure, exhilarating smell of frost in the moist earth. Rodney always knew whether there'd been a touch of frost in the night from the smell through the open window while he dressed, strong enough to hit you when you pushed the front door open and went out into a half-light, the sky streaked with yellow and flame-red. Rodney loved the wintry feeling, before it got rough and sodden: clamps full of sweet-smelling silage, corn in the bins, cake in the mixing house, Dutch barns stuffed to the girders with bales. The winter calves had started coming in nicely and his cottage smelt of apples, spread in rows on the floor of the spare room.

Chaffins' Maharajah's Apple Blossom was a fly in the ointment. When she'd calved down she couldn't have looked more promising but now she was falling off and picking at her food. Acetonaemia, he'd thought at first, but she hadn't responded to the glucose and it must be something else. Now there was Snow Queen scouring, one of the best heifers, the drench hadn't put her right and he had an uneasy suspicion it might be Johne's disease. He hadn't had a case for years but it cropped up mysteriously and there was no remedy, and it always took the heifers just as they were coming down to calve. And then there was George. He'd started off all right as many of these lads did, keen and willing, anxious to learn, but now he was deteriorating. Late mornings, a thing Rodney couldn't stomach; slapdash, off at nights on the stroke of five. It was routine they hated, these young fellows. Day after day, they said, the same.

But it wasn't the same. Each day was different: each cow: each milking. It was all surprises, puzzles, disappointments and triumphs, this game. A small world, maybe, but your own, you understood it, and full of infinite variety. The young fellows didn't see it that way. Just cows, they said. Cows to have milk extracted as if they'd been tanks with taps, not living creatures, and then off to bingo or the Horsington cafés, or sit gawping at the television mussing up a girl. That was all it was to them and they'd never make stockmen, that wasn't the way to get on with cows. He'd have to speak to Jim Tompkins about George.

He switched off the in-churn cooler, dismantled it, washed and put away the milking machine, swilled round the dairy and the trough, stumping about in his gumboots and clean white coat. The dairy smelt of disinfectant from the fluid that sterilized the rubber pipes and cups of the machine. The cows, full-bellied after their meals, waited patiently in the muddied yard. George was off, Rodney had said he'd manage on his own though it was too much for one man. But then, when the milking was over, he'd know it was properly done, not a drop left in Gaylord's Wildeyes' near front quarter to bring on mastitis, no shouting at Dream-alone who kicked when she was nervous, the strip cups properly used. George was always "forgetting" to draw the first squirt of milk from each teat into the strip cup and inspect it closely for the least little fleck. By the time George spotted anything, she was stiff with mastitis and her milk full of clots the size of peas.

Rodney hung his overall and cap on a peg and opened the yard gate to release the cows. They plodded in an orderly fashion across more yards and into the paddock, swaying a little like stately ships slightly rocking on a gentle wave. They smelt sweet as musk. How greatly superior, Rodney reflected, in their dignity and patience to human beings—no pushing and hustling, queue-jumping, barging about, or very little; they knew what to do and they got on with the job.

Tea was on the table, it was gone half-past five. Almost at the same time Jim Tompkins arrived with a brace of pheasants for himself and a hare for Rodney. The boss was always generous in sharing out the spoils. Rodney nodded equably.

"Come on in, Jim, the missus'll fetch you a cup. Herrings by the smell of it."

"Thanks, Rod, but I'll have to be getting back. I'm late anyway." Jim Tompkins went in, however—it was always so companionable in the Youngs' kitchen. A bit of a shambles, with the washing strung out on a folding con-traption in front of the Rayburn, kids' things everywhere, old newspapers, empty bottles, muddy shoes lying about.

His own missus would take one look and climb up the wall. She went too far the other way.

He warmed himself in front of the Rayburn. There was a lovely fug inside. Rod's missus came in with a loaf of bread in one hand and a jug of milk in the other and a cigarette, as usual, dangling from her lips. That was the only thing Jim didn't care for, cigarettes all the time and ash falling into everything. It was messy, and sent a lot of Rod's money up in smoke. Her hair flopped round her face and she slopped about all day in down-at-heel slippers—queer, with Rodney always so meticulous and tidy, the feeding buckets scoured and each on its right hook, a clean overall every day; but he didn't seem to mind. She was good-hearted, that was the thing.

"These kids come out with the queerest questions." She plunked down the bread and pushed the kettle on to the hot plate. "Stick a bit more wood in the Rayburn, will you, Jim, there's a dear? D'you know what Mike said just now? When I put in the herrings. 'Why's some got hard roes and the other ones is soft?' he asked me. 'Search me,' I says. 'Just made like that I suppose.' 'Well,' he says, 'I'll tell you, the soft ones is lady herrings and the hard ones is gentlemen.' Can you beat that? Is that right, d'you suppose?"

"He'd better ask his teacher," Jim suggested. "He's a bright one, that boy of yours."

"He's taken to mice—just like his father, pedigrees and all that. Would you believe it, they've got it now with mice, all that breeding stuff, lines and sires and strains and all the rest of it. A.1 next I shouldn't wonder." She laughed. "Doesn't work with people, does it? Look at the boss. Got his faults I know like we all have, but I don't know what he's done to deserve children like he's got. I mean, that Julia getting tight and running down a kid and now this Martin. Did you hear it on the news?"

"Hear what?" Jim inquired.

"Got into trouble with the police."

Jim Tompkins whistled. "No wonder the boss looked down in the mouth. Missed some easy ones, too. He'll take that hard, Martin's always been his favourite, though he's a funny sort of bugger to my mind, Simon's worth ten of him. Best of the bunch by a long chalk, Simon is. What's the trouble, then? Driving case like his sister?"

"Worse than that it sounded—something to do with pictures. Not movies, the kind on walls. Pinching them or fraud or something. Bit of a knock for his old man, giving it out like that on the news and in all the papers. Will he have to resign?"

"Dunno." Jim was rubbing his bottom, enjoying the feel of hot cloth against his skin. "You never know with politics. Wouldn't get mixed up in that for a million dollars. Nothing but a lot of crooks, if you ask me. Tough on his missus."

"It's all this sending them away to boarding schools when they're little if you ask me. Just when they need a mother most they don't get her, they've got some old codfish with a face like a pylon and a bloody great cane. Queer, when you got all that money, spend it getting your kids out of the road. What's Rod up to, must be having a bath and shave the time he's taking." She put her head out of the door and shouted. "Those herrings'll be kippers if you don't come. It's a wonder Buckle didn't call off the shoot today I should think. Put a brave face on it, I suppose."

"He had guests," Jim explained. "Foreigners. Some sultan or other with a bloody great black beard and his head all wrapped up in face towels. He was on the telly— wore a nightgown then but today he just had trousers. Staying at Chaffins with his *entourage*."

"His what?"

"*Entourage*. Pardon my French."

"Did he bang away at all them pheasants?"

"Not half, must have spent a couple of quid at least on

cartridges. Blazed off at anything that flew half a mile away. Made me nervous I can tell you."

"Whatever do you think Rod *is* up to? Shouldn't wonder if he hadn't sneaked back to the dairy. That's all he thinks about, cows. Turn into one if doesn't look out. Now he's fed up with young George. Thought the world of him at first, full of promise George was, but they never keep their promises, not with Rod."

"Expects a lot of them," Tompkins agreed. "George is a good lad, as they go."

"Not good enough to his high and mightiness. Just because Rod thinks the world begins and ends with the Chaffins herd of pedigree Ayrshires everyone else has to think the same. Wasn't there a religion once had a bull for a god? That's what Rod ought to join."

Rodney came in, his face shining from its good scrub, combing his stiff crest of hair with his stubby fingers.

"Thought you'd run up to London to see a show," his wife remarked. "You'll miss Dixon of Dock Green at this rate. I'll make some fresh tea." She took the herrings out of the oven and put them in front of him, emptied the teapot at the sink and put in fresh tea and took it over to the simmering kettle. Rodney admitted:

"I just nipped out to have a look at Marabelle Eighteenth, she'll calve tonight. Last time she played us up a bit."

"So you'll be up all night again."

Rodney addressed himself to Jim Tompkins. "I don't think I'll be able to keep on George."

"You know how hard it is to get single lads these days, Rod. We've no cottage. George is a good worker and in time—"

"He's not interested. You can't do the job else."

"We can't all turn ourselves *into* cows like you," his wife protested.

"Well, cows get into your blood."

"You get those herrings into yours and don't talk so daft."

"It was a shame about Dick," Rodney remarked, tipping the tomato sauce and stirring four lumps into his tea. "I could have made something of him."

"That's all you think about, whether he'd make a good herdsman. Poor fellow, and him only laid to rest today." She was thinking that he wouldn't ever again feel the sharp east wind roughen his skin or the pinch of frost in his toes or the sun on his back, or hear the clink of buckets or a blackbird whistle in the early morning, or kiss a girl or sink a pint or just sit down to a nice juicy herring in a warm kitchen on a winter's evening with the kids messing round, and a good cup of tea, sweet and strong. "It's a shame," she said. Jim Tompkins remarked:

"There was something queer about him, sort of look in the eye. I liked the fellow, mind. Nothing against Dick at all myself. But of course he was touched in the head."

"Must of been," Rodney agreed, munching. "But he didn't show it, not in the dairy."

"Shooting that poor kid, right in the ward, too. Must be off your rocker to do a thing like that."

"He meant it for the best," Vi Young suggested. "Putting her out of her misery, like you would a dog or cat."

"You know, Dennis Ryan was counting on the insurance money," Tompkins said. "Total disablement—if Stella had lived, they'd have got a fortune. Thirty or forty thousand pounds, the lawyers said. It didn't take the Ryans long to order a bedroom suite. I daresay if Dennis'd been given the choice between the money and kid as she was, sound and healthy, he'd have chosen the healthy kid. But she'd got the injuries and that was that. Got to make the best of things, haven't we?"

Vi shook her head. "It's hard to believe anyone could feel that way."

"You should hear the way Dennis carries on, pushing poor old Dick into the flames."

"He did it for Julia," said Rodney. "Good job for her, that was. Drive anyone crackers, thinking about that kid lying there for the rest of her life and you the one responsible."

"Too good for her, Dick was," Vi pronounced, "even if he was an under-cowman and her old man a high-up in the government. Fair flung herself at his head, wouldn't let him be. Well, that's not right."

"He was sweet on her," Tompkins suggested.

"Didn't give him much choice, did she? I reckon he had a wife somewhere of his own."

"Bit of a mystery man," Tompkins agreed. "Mrs. Harris says she'd hear him sometimes walking about upstairs half the night and queer sounds coming from his room. Squeaks and bleeps, she says. Thinks he had a secret wireless transmitter up there sending out messages."

"So now he's a Russian spy!"

Jim Tompkins laughed. "I'm just telling you Mrs. Harris's version. And Ted Harris told me the bloke who looks after the boss's security—you know, Pendlebury, wouldn't mind *his* job—he came nosing round several times and went through Dick's things."

"You think the Russians want to know how we milk cows?" Vi inquired.

"Buckle's in the government, isn't he? Look how quickly Dick found his way inside the house. Through the girl, too, that's the usual method in the spy stories. Queer way for a cowman to go on, wasn't it? Something odd about the whole thing."

"So now he's a Russian spy," Vi repeated. "A *mad* Russian spy."

"Was," Tompkins corrected. "I daresay we shan't ever know the truth. Pity we had to lose a good cowman."